MW01325525

WHITE FIRE

STUART MURRAY

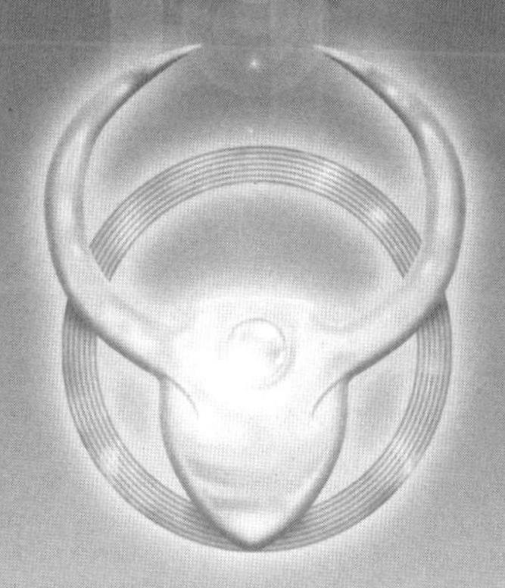

By Arrangement with
The Aberdeen Group, LLC

IMAGES FROM THE PAST
BENNINGTON, VERMONT

WHITE FIRE

STUART MURRAY

This book is a work of fiction. Names, characters, places, and incidents are products of the author's imagination or are used fictitiously. Any resemblance to actual events or persons living or dead is entirely coincidental.

1 2 3 4 5 6 7 8 9 10 XXX 07 06 05 04 03 02 01 00

Library of Congress Cataloging-in-Publication Data

Murray, Stuart, 1948-

White fire / by Stuart Murray.— 1st ed.

p. cm.

ISBN 1-884592-25-2 (cloth)

1. Africa, Southern—History—Mfecane period, 1816-ca. 1840—Fiction. 2. Chaka, Zulu Chief, 1787?-1828—Fiction. 3. Frontier and pioneer life—Fiction. 4. Zulu (African people)—Fiction. 5. Scouts and scouting—Fiction. 6. Amulets—Fiction. I. Title.

PS3563.U788 W48 2000

813'.6—dc21 00-038866

Published by Images from the Past, Inc.,

P.O. Box 137, Bennington, VT 05201

Tordis Ilg Isselhardt, Publisher

Printed in the United States of America

Design and Production: Ron Toelke Associates, Chatham, NY

Printer: Thomson-Shore, Inc., Dexter, MI

Text and Display: New Baskerville, Albertus

For our children:

Aaron, Timothy, Jeremy, and Rachel

Other Images from the Past Books by Stuart Murray

AMERICA'S SONG, THE STORY OF "YANKEE DOODLE"
WASHINGTON'S FAREWELL
RUDYARD KIPLING IN VERMONT:
BIRTHPLACE OF THE JUNGLE BOOKS
THE HONOR OF COMMAND:
BURGOYNE'S SARATOGA CAMPAIGN
NORMAN ROCKWELL AT HOME IN VERMONT

AUTHOR'S NOTE

Magic, faith, sacred amulets, and high courage have ever inspired the folk of southern Africa, just as they inspired this tale of adventurers and warriors, of pioneers, romantics, and rainmakers. Some of the players are conjured from thin air, others named in history, and all are obtained from a writer's day-dreaming. There was no Arendt trek, and Shaka Zulu is not known to have possessed the Amulet of White Fire.

S.M.

CONTENTS

Then from his secret art
the wizard made
a magic mirror,
and looking in that mirror's face
the king beheld
the face of his desire.

Ancient Persian poem

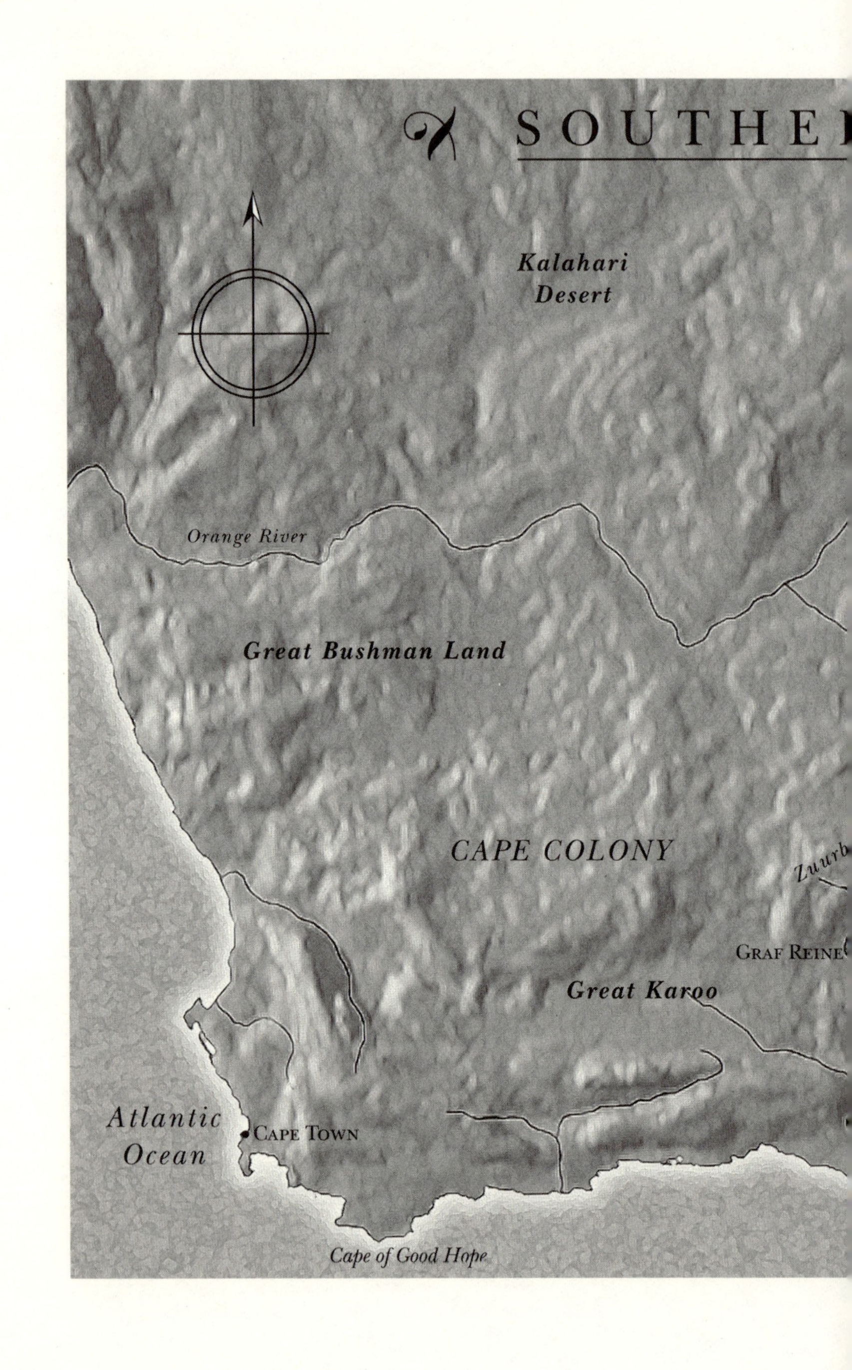
A SOUTHE
Kalahari Desert
Orange River
Great Bushman Land
CAPE COLONY
Zuurb
GRAF REINE
Great Karoo
Atlantic Ocean
CAPE TOWN
Cape of Good Hope

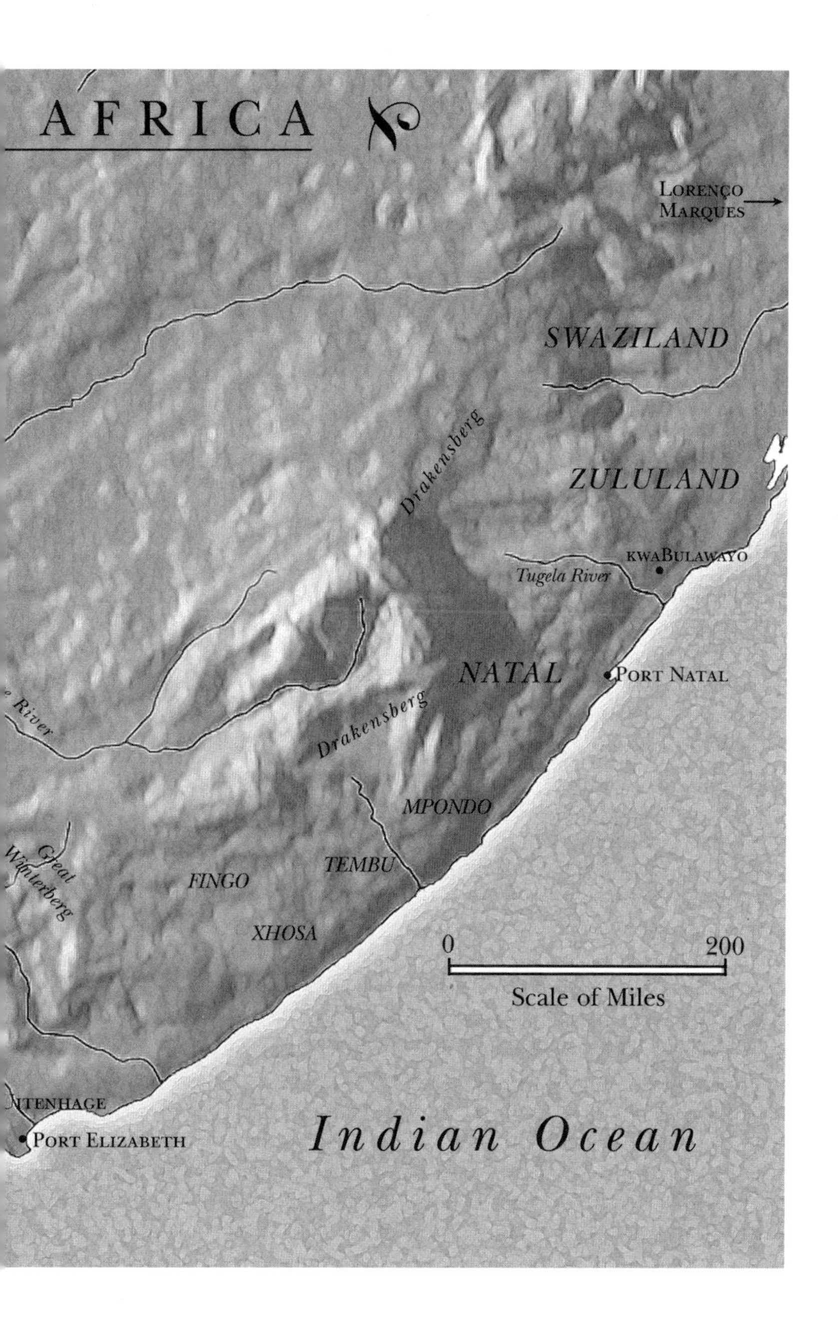

AFRICA
LORENÇO MARQUES
SWAZILAND
Drakensberg
ZULULAND
KWABULAWAYO
Tugela River
NATAL
PORT NATAL
River
Drakensberg
MPONDO
Great Winterberg
TEMBU
FINGO
XHOSA
0
200
Scale of Miles
ITENHAGE
PORT ELIZABETH
Indian Ocean

THE AMULET

Swaziland, September 1822

Spears alone will not save us from Shaka—Mighty Shaka, Black Bull Elephant—merciless Shaka, whose regiments burn every village from the mountains to the great water, killing everyone, everyone . . . even the children."

The Swazi chief sat back in the woven reed chair of honor and closed his eyes. He was a large man and strong, though his hair was turning gray. A leopard skin draped over his massive chest slowly rose and fell with his breathing. As night settled over southeast Africa, firelight and torches illuminated the circle of warriors standing with oxhide shields and spears around the chief and the council of elders who were seated on the ground before him, silent, waiting, worried. Like their chief, the elders wore ceremonial plumes and leopard skin *karosses* for this solemn gathering. Like their chief, they were grim, knowing the village would be "eaten up" if the Zulus attacked, as they had attacked and destroyed hundreds of kraals in their bloodbath, the *Mfecane*, the "crushing" of all who resisted Shaka, their ruthless warrior king.

The Swazi chief spoke again, eyes still closed.

"We will fight when the Zulus come, but spears alone cannot

defeat them." He opened his eyes and leaned toward the elders. "Not spears, but firesticks. We must have firesticks—the firesticks this white thing will sell us."

André Toulouse, an aging French trader sitting by the feet of the chief, and the only pale face at the council fire, was the "white thing," *umlungu* in the Bantu tongue that was spoken by blacks throughout southern Africa and beyond. André had a hundred muskets back at his camp near the Indian Ocean, two days' march to the east. Those firesticks would bring plenty of Swazi ivory now, the best bargain he had made in ten years of fortune-hunting in southern Africa. In those years, André often visited this *kraal,* as villages surrounded by a wall of thornbush were called. He came to exchange trade goods and play concertina for the chief, who honored him with gifts of silver jewelry and the company of beautiful women.

Here in Swaziland, a former French barber could live like a merchant prince; but if Shaka's regiments caught him selling muskets, they would kill him by slow torture.

"Umlungu," the Swazi chief said, with the slightest gesture of a finger, "play your wind box while we consider our fate."

André picked up his old concertina and began a popular tune from the dance halls of Cape Town: "Believe Me, If All Those Endearing Young Charms" was a favorite of the chief. As André swayed from side to side, shaking music from the concertina, he heard a talking drum close by beat out its message. He saw the chief, listening to the drum, slip something from behind the leopard skin kaross, something that gleamed like gold. After a moment, when the talking drum had fallen silent, the chief handed the gold to an elder, who held it and stared long at the chief before passing it to another, who did the same. Thus did the gold move around the circle of elders as André's music went on, each man in turn meeting the chief's gaze.

This, André thought, was exceedingly strange, for no Bantu would dare be so insolent as to look his chief directly in the eyes. At last, the gold was passed to André, who was startled to find a beautiful amulet dangling before him. He had never seen such a treasure. A long-horned bull's head was enclosed in a circle, and set in the bull's forehead was a diamond, glowing as with a light of its own. Heart skipping, André gazed at the amulet and heard himself speaking.

"What have I . . . to do with this talisman, my Lord?"

He could not stop looking at the diamond, for it burned with a white fire as the chief's voice came from a distance.

"Umlungu, if I send warriors to the great water with you, will they bring back firesticks, or will you betray them to the men-stealers, who will enslave them?"

There was no doubt about the answer, but before replying, André tried to hand back the amulet, except that he had a surging, unbearable desire to keep it, and at the same time the chief would not take it.

"Speak, umlungu, while you hold the magic bull's head. Speak, and the white fire of the ancients shall mirror your desires."

The diamond dazzled now with a cold, white glare, almost blinding, and André's heart pounded. He could not look away from that fire. A tingling entered the hand that held it. He wanted to drop it, and he wanted to keep it. The sensation passed along his arm, painful, then shot to the center of his heart, and he jerked, as if struck by a spear.

"I am no slaver!" he cried out. Now he was staring at the Swazi chief, whose eyes held the same white light of the diamond, that glorious and terrifying white, burning fire. "I will send your young men back with firesticks!" He could not breathe. "I intend only . . . to acquire more ivory than . . . the firesticks . . . are worth!"

The chief yanked the amulet away.

Released, André slumped down with a moan, his heart thundering as if it would burst. After a moment, he looked up to find the chief looking at him, the burning white light gone from the Swazi's eyes. Just then the talking drum sounded again, but stopped abruptly. The chief raised the amulet so it dangled, golden red, in the firelight. Now it was only an exquisite ornament, no longer hypnotizing, no longer radiating a light of its own.

"He who beholds the golden bull's head must speak the truth," said the chief. "You, umlungu, can be trusted . . . but some cannot."

There was a sudden commotion, and two warriors entered the circle of shields, casting down what seemed to be a pile of dirty old clothing. Actually, it was a skinny, sour-smelling man, who cowered at the chief's feet. André knew him as Dayega, a would-be witch doctor skilled with the talking drum.

The chief asked: "To whom does your drum call, Dayega?"

"My Lord?" the man squeaked, peering sidelong.

"Your drum said, 'Come, now!' Whom do you call, Dayega?"

With a fawning smile that showed filed, pointed teeth, Dayega crawled close to the chief's leg and whimpered, "My Lord, the drum talks to boys herding thy cattle! Thy blessed royal herd has not been brought back into the kraal. It is dark, dark, and the lion will—"

"Whom do you call?" The chief thrust the bull's head into Dayega's gnarled hands.

Dayega cringed, trembling, his squinting eyes fixed on the golden amulet as he whined like a frightened dog.

"Truth!" the chief demanded. "By the power of Nzambi Ya Mpungu, Ancient of the Ancients, lord of all amulets, speak!"

Dayega collapsed, whimpering, one hand clawing the ground.

"I command you, Dayega, by the white fire of the sacred crystal! Whom do you call?"

"Shaka!" Dayega shrilled insanely, and the elders and warriors gave a start. "Yes! My lord Shaka!" Shriek echoing, eyes glazed, he gaped at the bull's-head amulet in his shaking hands. "Yes! The Zulu host comes to eat you up!"

The Swazis were all on their feet.

"Bullala!" A thousand voices suddenly bellowed from the darkness beyond the kraal wall. "Bullala! Kill! Kill!"

"Shaka!" the Swazi chief shouted.

André was too terrified to stand, legs too weak to hold him. He sat there, powerless, as the night rumbled with the Zulu battle cry: "*uSuthu!* uSuthu!" The kraal gate shuddered from their blows.

A Swazi sprang at Dayega, spear drawn back.

"Would you live?" Dayega screamed, cowering behind the amulet. "Then spare me!" The warrior hesitated. "Spare me, and I will beg Lord Shaka for your lives!" Dayega looked utterly mad now, eyes fixed on the amulet. "I will be his royal witch doctor—his bearer of the sacred bull's head!"

"uSuthu!" the Zulus roared, hurling themselves again at the gate of the Swazi kraal, which splintered, yielding. Swazi men rallied with shields and weapons as women desperately gathered up the children. André shivered with fear. Someone brushed past him. Dayega, a shadow.

"The bull's head?" the chief shouted. "Dayega! Where is Dayega?"

"uSuthu!" The gate shattered and burst open, and howling Zulus plunged into the kraal, spears stabbing. "Bullala! Kill!"

A wall of Zulu shields rammed against Swazi defenders, driving them back and down to die, writhing, screaming, kicking. André staggered as someone reeled heavily against him. It was the chief, who twisted away, yanking a spear from his body, a dying Zulu at his feet. The chief stumbled to his chair, toppling it over, and collapsing.

He managed to speak. "The . . . the bull's head, umlungu? Dayega!"

"Gone!" André answered, crawling to him.

"Ahh. . ." The chief lay on his side, coughing blood. "It will destroy him! Destroy all who are unworthy to carry it—"

André held the chief's head, not daring to look up at the raging battle, expecting to be stabbed at any moment.

"Bullala! Bullala! Bullala!"

The chief gripped André's arm. "Umlungu!" The image of that amulet came to André. "One day, one day . . . you will see again the sacred Stone of White Fire!"

"I?" André's heart thudded.

"Umlungu! Hear me! The Stone of White Fire must never . . . never return to those who would . . . enslave us!"

"Who? Who?"

"The—" Slumping down, the chief murmured: "the Red . . . Brotherhood!"

"What? What is the Red Brotherhood?"

The chief was dead.

After a moment, André stood up, lightheaded, sick inside, holding the concertina to his chest, as if to protect himself from what was coming. Through sweat and fear, he forced himself to look around. He was surrounded by dead and dying. The fighting had swept past, the Zulu horde pushing through the village, killing and killing. Now at the far end of the kraal, their battle roar echoed as they finished the slaughter, finished Shaka's "crushing."

André stood quivering, a helpless white thing so terrified he could not breathe. Then the concertina fell open with a wail, startling him, and he darted into darkness beside a hut. Wheezing for breath, he ran into the deeper shadows along the thornbush wall. He looked for a small gate that was there somewhere. Scampering back and forth, bewildered, the concertina wagging from his hand, he had to find that gate. That gate and a path into the jungle.

"Bullala!"

They were coming back.

"uSuthu!"

He had to find that gate.

DIRK ARENDT

Zululand, September 1828

In the hour before sunset, with the sky still blue, a crescent moon rose over the darkening hills of Zululand to lie on its back. A sign of good luck.

And a lucky moon was welcome to Dirk Arendt as he walked before his horse, leading him up a rocky trail on the way to the Zulu royal kraal—*kwaBulawayo,* "The Place of He Who Kills." Shaka, Lord of the Zulus, was "He Who Kills," and he killed often.

As he went, Dirk read from a battered book held in one hand, his other on the reins. This was the new American novel, *The Last of the Mohicans,* and though he was not perfect in English, Dirk knew the language well enough to follow the story. Failing light made it difficult to read by now, so he reluctantly put the book into a saddlebag, his mind still wandering in the American forests of the old French and Indian War, where there were noble Indians and lovely damsels and the much too-wonderful Natty Bumppo. Dirk was amused by this Hawkeye, whose shot never missed, whose insight as a scout was unfailing, whose overflowing self-confidence would have put to shame the most arrogant Boer frontiersman of southern Africa. . . . Dirk grinned to think of Hawkeye, the perfect scout, and the silliness of his portrayal, but he wanted to keep on reading and would have if the sky were not darkening, the trail becoming ever more difficult.

Dirk Arendt, too, was a scout, now guiding an archaeological expedition that followed a few miles behind. He and his employers were on their way to the distant "Country of Old Stones" to search for the ruins of ancient Monomotapa, a legendary lost city beyond Zululand. To get there they must beg Shaka's permission to pass through his domain. Dirk paused to look back down the trail into a gorge, purple with shadow. The others were not yet in sight. Before long, he would see the expedition come into view. Leading it was Benjamin David, their guarantee of safe passage in Zululand. On a visit here three years ago, Benjamin had saved Shaka's life when the wound from an assassin's blade became infected. A common purgative brought Shaka back from the dead, and now this Benjamin David, the second son of a leading Jewish family in Amsterdam, was revered as the Zulu king's personal *inyanga,* or doctor.

At least, this is what Benjamin had told Dirk last winter when first they met in a Dutch tavern. If not true, they might never leave Zululand.

Dirk led his big gray on up the hillside until he came to a washout, where waves of pebbles and sand covered the trail. The horse balked at the soft footing, reluctant to cross. Zulu hills were not for horses. Dirk pulled on the reins, but the horse whinnied, forelegs stiff and spread.

"Steady, Blueboy!" Dirk's voice rang through the ravine that fell away far below. "Come on!"

Slowly, Blueboy picked his way over the sliding stones. No, this country was not for horses, but somewhere beyond lay vast grasslands, where a horse and man could run. That was a land much like the high veldt of Cape Colony far to the west, where twenty-six years ago Dirk was born of hard-riding Boer stock, proud of their herds and prouder of their independence. He spoke to the nervous Blueboy.

"We'll be out of these damned rocks tomorrow, and I'll give you a run. Race you myself round Shaka's hut!"

Tall and rangy, Dirk wore the slouch hat of the high-veldt borderers, "Bush Boers," as civilized Cape Town Dutch called them, and not intending a compliment. His blond hair straggled over the collar of a flannel shirt, and at his belt were a single-shot pistol and sheath knife. With corduroy trousers tucked into his short boots, Dirk looked the image of a Boer frontiersman, except that he was clean-shaven. For three centuries of settling southern Africa, his people had let their beards flourish according to Old Testament teachings. Though born a Boer, Dirk was different.

For much of the past seven years he had been studying at the university in Leyden, The Netherlands. During those years, he had also seen the capitals of Europe, and it had changed him—now, even on the trail, he shaved each morning. But then he always had been different from his people. For instance, no self-respecting Boer ever walked when he could ride, but Dirk loved to run, and at running he was a champion unbeaten in Africa and Europe. He raced whenever there was a challenge, and had always won. Even now, on his feet he wore soft *veldschoenen,* or *velskoen,* as the Bush Boers called them, good for running.

The big gray stepped clear of the washout and climbed a rocky outcrop. Dirk eased Blueboy onto the ledge, unexpectedly finding himself at the brink of a sheer cliff. From here he could see back down the trail, which wound away into dark ravines, known as dongas, and crowded with clusters of trees in the hollows. Again he spoke to the horse.

"You're a fine mount, Blueboy." He patted the horse's neck, calming him. "Though you're not the fighting stallion a Boer rides on kommando against kaffirs."

But high-strung fighting stallions were no use to expeditions hunting ruins for an English museum. Indeed, archaeological expeditions through Zululand needed dependable mounts like Blueboy, immune to southeast Africa's blowfly sickness that soon killed off horses brought here from the high veldt.

Dirk looked back down the slope. Still no sign of the expedition. Suddenly, his horse whinnied in fright and rose on its hind legs, backing toward the cliff edge.

"Whoa, Blueboy! Whoa!"

Dirk lashed the reins around one arm, pulling hard, fighting Blueboy down while looking for what had spooked him. Eyes rolling, the terrified horse shied toward the brink of the cliff. Dirk could barely hold him. There! A black mamba rose and swayed, about to strike. Dirk kicked at it. The horse reared again, impossible to hold down.

"Whoa, Blueboy!"

The horse screamed and stamped, now right at the edge. The snake's head drew back. Dirk whipped off his hat as a shield, and the mamba struck at it, fell, and rose again. Dirk blocked the next blow, at the same time grappling with Blueboy. The snake darted again, and jerked the hat away. The panicked horse slid back, a hind leg kicking over the brink. Dirk fought with the reins to keep him from falling.

The snake rose, tongue flicking. Blueboy screamed, hooves flashing close to Dirk's head. The mamba swayed. With all his might, Dirk yanked the stumbling Blueboy back from the edge, but slipped, dropping to one knee, eye to eye with the mamba, which struck— But a spear struck first.

Entering the mamba's open mouth, the black iron blade pinned the snake to the ground, where it writhed around the spear shaft, lashing back and forth, back and forth, and then lay still. Shaken, Dirk steadied the horse and turned to see old Sebe, the expedition's Xhosa guide, silhouetted thin and tall against the evening sky. Sebe gave a slow chuckle and spoke in the clicking singsong of his people.

"When you dance with the mamba, my Boer baas, dance more lightly, for you dance with Death . . . who is swift."

Dirk led the trembling Blueboy away from the cliff's edge and answered Sebe in the Xhosa tongue: "It was not I, but the mamba who danced with Death—with you!" He wiped sweat from his eyes, picked up the hat and dusted it against a thigh. "I owe you my life, ancient one."

Grinning, Sebe recovered his throwing spear, cutting off the mamba's head and stuffing it into a beaded medicine pouch. Sebe's hair, cropped close and almost silver, caught a sheen of red from the sunset.

"Now, come and behold, Baas Dirk!" His eyes glittered as he grinned, waving sinewy arms. "Hurry, Master Dirk! Come and behold a place where a warrior can die in glory!"

Sebe let out a cry that was half croak, half howl of joy, and gripped the short stabbing spear with both hands. His twisted rags and bits of white man's clothes fluttered in a confusion of color and shape as he leaped high.

"Aiee! Baas Dirk, come and behold!" Legs and arms flapping, Sebe beckoned ahead on the trail. "Come and behold!"

"Don't spook the Zulus, ancient one." Dirk had learned his first Xhosa from the family servants, and more later as a youth, fighting invading Xhosa hosts. "If the Zulu see you dancing like a demon, they'll flee to the great water!"

"If they do," Sebe cackled, "then I will personally throw them in! Shaka, too!" Rattling both spears in one hand, he crowed: "And I will return to 'The Place of He Who Kills' and rule the Zulu women so that they will call my kraal 'The Place of He Who Loves.'"

Dirk chuckled and hauled at Blueboy's reins, eager to see kwaBulawayo. This was his first trip to Zululand, but he had heard much about the *amaZulu,* the "People of the Heavens," as they styled themselves. He was familiar with such boasts, for his own Boer folk also called themselves a divinely "Chosen People." He was not so certain about such things.

Sebe dropped to a half-crouch and pointed up the trail with his spears. "Come, Baas Dirk, and behold the mightiest kraal of the mightiest lord of all the Zulus. How I hate Shaka, but how I admire his power!"

And Dirk admired Sebe's boldness.

Dirk called, "You delight in danger, here, where the royal Zulu lion devours wandering Xhosas."

Sebe cackled, "I'll twist the lion's tail and outrun him to a tree. Come and watch me!"

The old man bounded away, and Dirk followed, leading his mount. He liked this tireless Xhosa, whom he first had met three weeks ago back at Port Natal, where Sebe served the white traders as interpreter and was a big man with the blacks who herded the post's cattle and worked the crops. Sebe's age was impossible to tell, but he could run and scout a trail like a young warrior. And he could throw a spear with the best of them. This was Sebe's third journey here with Benjamin David. Sebe apparently was the only Xhosa who ever had seen Zululand and survived. Decades of war between Xhosas and Zulus had gone badly for Sebe's folk, and no Xhosa force had ever come close to the royal kraal.

Dirk understood Sebe's excitement at approaching kwaBulawayo. The Boers had fought plenty against blacks, but had never clashed with Zulus. No Zulu had ever crossed the Boers' Cape Colony frontier, three hundred miles to the west, and, until tonight, no Boer had ever seen Zululand. Shaka was known, however, as far away as Cape Town for his bloody, merciless conquest of the vast interior in just ten stormy years.

Sebe was standing at the crest of the escarpment, looking out, and Dirk tied Blueboy to a baobab tree and hurried to join him. What Dirk saw made him gasp.

"In God's name, Sebe! In God's name, that is a royal kraal!"

Across a deep valley, and tilted against the darkening sky, the great circular kraal of King Shaka lay before them. An outer wall of woven thornbush surrounded a vast circle of huts and firelight, and an inner wall enclosed the central kraal, full to bursting with massed, dancing Zulus.

"The whole nation is here tonight!"

"Aiee!" Sebe replied, "Shaka has gathered them all to honor Baas Benjamin, his inyanga."

The central enclosure of the kraal, normally for penning cattle at night, was like a broken colony of ants, swarming with humanity and sparkling with torches and bonfires glowing brighter as night began to fall. Zulus, rank on rank, danced back and forth, and from this distance their voices were like a rush of wind through the mountains, the sound rising and falling as they sang.

Sebe cried out, "Is this not a sight to stir the blood of fighting men as we? Would you not glory to charge against them, with this old Xhosa clinging to your stirrups, and die there in a tale that your children's children would marvel to hear?"

Dirk was not so eager. "I have no children, and I am too young for such a glorious death. And you, tail-twister, are too old for it."

Sebe grinned as he gazed at the kraal. "Now, when I dream, I know where my soul will be. Here, at kwaBulawayo, when all the Zulu regiments are gathered—here as the honored guest of King Shaka and guide of the royal inyanga, Baas Benjamin." He nodded. "Ah, my young Boer master, I do, indeed, want to live to tell our story to my wives and children."

Peering at the kraal, Dirk said, "There must be fifteen thousand warriors there!"

"Fifteen thousand one hundred and twenty-one," Sebe replied, fiddling with his fingers as if counting. "The Zulus do Baas Benjamin the greatest of honors for once having saved the king's life."

Dirk again hoped Benjamin David was as beloved by Shaka as he claimed. He shook off these thoughts, saying, "Go back now, Sebe, and find the others. We'll camp up here and wait for the Zulus to take us down to their king."

"Look there." Sebe motioned at the crescent moon. "It is on its back and full of luck, Baas." Then he pondered, eyes clouding as he knuckled his grizzled chin. "Baas Dirk, listen: My magic tells me that a time of great trial has begun for us."

Dirk was momentarily taken aback when Sebe's gaze seemed to penetrate his very soul. He did not ask what Sebe meant by "a time of great trial," but he knew the old man was considered a witch doctor, one who could foretell and who had the power to make rain.

In spite of his uneasiness, Dirk scoffed, "Doesn't take kaffir magic to know danger lies before us, ancient one. Now, go find the others in case they get lost and miss the Zulu ball."

Sebe's eyelids slowly closed, then he opened them, alert as ever. "Wait here, then, and do not go riding into kwaBulawayo like some fool of a Boer on kommando!"

Then Sebe was gone, leaving Dirk with his thoughts. The distant fires of kwaBulawayo glowed brighter as darkness descended. Dirk looked up at the crescent moon through the spidery baobab branches. How good it was to be once more under the African sky, with its moon and stars brighter than any sky in Europe.

After watering Blueboy with hat and canteen, Dirk settled down against the baobab trunk, chewing some dried antelope meat—*biltong,* the Boers called it. What would his mother and father say about his serving an English expedition seeking old stones? Dirk found himself thinking about the university at Leyden, how hard he had worked, even learning English and how to sail, like a proper gentleman. His father was one of the few Boers who might think it useful for a stockman to know how to handle a boat, for he himself had gone to sea as a young man. When all was said and done, however, Dirk felt he had failed his parents—they who had taught him night after night at the kitchen table, and who had saved every penny for his passage to Europe. He had failed them, having been unceremoniously thrown out of the university.

Dirk recalled the New Year's celebration that Benjamin David's family had given. How could he forget? It was not a pleasant memory: The arrogant highborn cavalry officer who objected to a colonial farmer from Africa dancing with a certain young lady. Unfortunately for the officer, his sword and nose were both broken. Unfortunately for Dirk, the officer was the son of the university chancellor. Only the influence of

Benjamin's family kept Dirk from a year in prison, but he was summarily thrown out of the university.

At that same time, letters from home told that his family was set on trekking out of the colony, heading north over the mountains and into the wilderness. He determined to join them, and the chance to get home to Africa came when Benjamin introduced him to an English archaeologist who was mounting an expedition. So it was that Dirk and the others sailed into a bay on the Indian Ocean, landing at the remote trading post called Port Natal. Now he was hunter and scout for an expedition searching for artifacts that the Englishman, one Thomas Lovell, said were coveted by "prominent, but anonymous gentlemen" who were building the British Empire's greatest museum. Dirk had no interest in old stones or museums. He wanted only to rejoin his family, as he expected to do in a few months. Then he would start life over. If he got out of Zululand alive.

"The royal herds! Baas! The royal herds have come!" Sebe was back, scampering up the trail.

Dirk went to the edge of the escarpment and looked down to see thousands of Zulu cattle passing through the narrow gorge. In the failing light they were a living carpet of red and brown and white, drifting slowly through gullies and across slopes toward kwaBulawayo. Sebe told Dirk the expedition would be here soon. Then he turned back to the cattle.

"Have you ever seen such a sight in all your wanderings, Baas?"

Dirk never had. "There must be twenty thousand down there—"

"Twenty thousand and eight." Sebe again made that quick counting movement of his bony fingers. "See over there, Baas, that herd of pure white cattle, the most beautiful in creation!

Those are the sacred royal cattle of Lord Shaka himself."

Dirk saw them, all white, like ghosts floating through the dongas. He shook his head, marveling.

"My Boer father would give much to gaze upon this Zulu wealth."

Then Sebe surprised him by saying, "There will come a day when Boer and Zulu clash in a war to the death. So my medicine tells me."

Sebe stared at the Zulu kraal. For a moment Dirk did not reply, watching how both Zulu warriors and women danced in close, disciplined ranks, advancing and withdrawing like trained infantry, an entire nation bred to battle.

Then he said, "The Zulus look brave and proud, but Boers, too, are brave and proud, and we have fast horses and good rifles and have never been defeated by blacks."

Sebe's expression was unfathomable as he answered quietly, "Bravery and pride make a fatal potion when mixed with arrogance, Baas."

"Do you think me arrogant?"

Dirk was teasing, but he respected Sebe's judgment.

After a pause, the Xhosa said, "Men who are arrogant have never tasted defeat, Baas."

"I have tasted defeat."

"Even you, my proud Boer Baas?" Sebe's smile was not mocking, but was a smile of understanding and affection. "True defeat? Not just a boy's embarrassment?"

Dirk said, "There are many kinds of defeat, ancient one." He was thinking of his troubles at university, of the brawl and the expulsion from Leyden. . . .

"A man who has never tasted defeat has not learned wisdom," Sebe said. "A man who has not learned wisdom is doomed one day to learn it . . . by defeat."

What would Dirk's family think of this wise old witch doctor, this ageless Xhosa fighting man who could make rain, who could speak Afrikaans and who looked white men in the eye, as equals? Dirk thought again of his people, trekking out of the colony, and he worried about them, journeying in the wild. He longed to be there, to fight alongside them if warrior hordes fell upon them.

Watching the mighty Zulu kraal, Dirk was glad his family and the pioneer trekkers were heading northward, far away from Zululand, and far from Shaka, "He Who Kills."

RACHEL DRENTE

Northeastern Cape Colony

Four hundred miles west of Zululand lay Sweetfountain, a Boer farm rich in water, rich in grass, and rich in herds and flocks that darkened the veldt like shadows of clouds.

For Rachel Drente, Sweetfountain was also rich in memories. It had been home all her twenty years, and now, about to leave it forever, she was not ready to go.

In the soft light of early evening, Rachel knelt, praying, in a graveyard of four wooden crosses.

"One day, Mother and Father, I will see you again in the eyes of my children, if ever I marry, and that day will come in a distant homeland."

The cemetery was on a lonely hill in grasslands that reached over Cape Colony's northeastern border all the way to the far-off mountains. The orange light of the setting sun rippled the grass like a wave swept onward by the breeze. That breeze fluttered the brim of the white *kappie* on Rachel's head, pushing it back to let dark curls fall over her shoulders as she prayed.

"May we who depart for the promised land never again lose loved ones the way we lost you, my dears . . ."

No more dying under the spears of black raiders, as her parents had died last spring. No more dying from foreigners' disease brought to southern Africa by soldiers in the English Army. Two months ago, Rachel's older brother, Johannes, had lost both his little children to fever that struck during a journey to Port Elizabeth on the Indian Ocean. Rachel prayed for his wife, Sannie, who still seemed ill from fever, but was expecting another child in a few months, one who would be born in the back of a *trekwagon* somewhere in the wild.

Heartbroken, and sick of British colonial rule, Johannes and Sannie were abandoning Cape Colony for good. Rachel, who was unmarried and their ward, must go with them. There would be no returning here, for they had sold *Soetfontein,* as the farm was called in the language of the Boers, who were a mix of Dutch, German, and French. Rachel's own mother had been mostly of French blood.

Tomorrow at dawn, Rachel and her family would start a long *trek*—a "haul" by ox-drawn wagon—out of Cape Colony, joining other Boer families who for years had been talking about going north to get away from the British once and for all. These *voortrekkers,* pioneers, believed they would be the first of many to go. Though Rachel could not see them as she knelt at the gravesides on the hill, forty-five families and their servants, livestock, and trekwagons had gathered here at Soetfontein in the last month, preparing to cross the rivers and keep on going, even beyond the Dragon Mountains. Somewhere far from Cape Colony they would find the land of milk and honey, the land promised to them by their god, Jehovah.

From down near the Drente farmyard came the sound of Johannes's fiddle being tuned. Then the concertina of André Toulouse, the blind French merchant, began to chime. There would be feasting and dancing that evening, a celebration for the trek's last night at the last, outermost farm in Cape Colony.

Rachel clasped a small book of poetry, the works of Joost van den Vondel, Holland's Shakespeare, as they called him. She had always found peace here at the graveyard, but now she was saying goodbye forever, and there was no peace in that.

"Lord, I would rather not go away . . . or, I mean I would like to go away, and see the world, all of it, but I confess that the wilderness, with wild beasts and wilder men, makes me afraid."

She opened the book, dog-eared and well-worn, to verse that had become bittersweet since the loss of her parents and Sannie's children. It was titled "Epitaph," and though the first image might seem harsh, she understood it, for she was a farmer's daughter.

Here rests the mortal part, the bait and food for worms,
As a grain of wheat rots in the earth,
So that someday it will rise up in glory,
The body with the soul, by Almighty God.

Vondel said mankind would be raised up by angels' trumpets and led, godlike, toward the eternal kingdom. As for her burdensome life on earth without her parents, Rachel drew hope from the closing lines:

Here, all is transitory, the sound of clock and hours—
Above is eternity, which will overcome it all.

The fiddle played brightly in the farmyard, accompanied by a burst from the concertina, and mortal life seemed not so gloomy in that moment. Hearing shouts and laughter, Rachel said a hurried "Amen" and stood up, tucking the poetry book into a pocket of her apron. Soon, she must dress for the celebration. Also, the Arendt family had driven in today, and she wanted to see them, for they had been close friends of her family. More than that, they had an eldest son, Dirkie. . . .

Rachel felt her heart beat faster. She had not seen Dirk Arendt for an eternity, and anyway he was somewhere far away, in a place full of foreigners. How could the son of a Boer live among Europeans for so many years? Would he ever come back? Well, when he did she would be long gone from here. But, then, perhaps Dirkie would one day follow his family on the trek.

Oh, this was such idle dreaming! What mattered now was that his parents, Willem and Marta Arendt, were to lead the trek, and that was good. Rachel trusted them more than anyone to get the folk safely to the promised land.

She sighed to think of going into the wilderness. Yet she could not stay, having no family left in Cape Colony, no husband, not even a sweetheart. Some said she was now too old for love and marriage! Well, still fit for marriage, maybe, but too old for love.

Likely she never would marry.

She had not met a fellow who attracted her, not since she had been a clumsy child, and then Dirkie Arendt had scarcely noticed her. Anyway, he was probably comfortably married by now, a prosperous European lawyer living with some soft-handed, milk-white lady with a removable beauty mark stuck to her chin.

Rachel turned away from the graves and from those thoughts, admitting to herself that she was, indeed, impatient to ask the Arendts all the latest news about Dirk, for she had not seen them for several months, not since the springtime gathering of the folk at *Nachmaal.* She removed her shoes and set off, running down the grassy slope toward the farmyard, one hand catching up the hem of her brown skirt, the other with the shoes as she ran over the well-worn path.

The kappie slipped all the way down, hanging by its string as her hair fell free. How good the music sounded! For days she had been sad and worried about leaving, but now as she ran, she felt like dancing— There was movement in the deep grass behind. Who was there? A figure leaped at her, shouting, "Bullala!"

Rachel spun away as hands clawed at her waist. Screaming, she whacked the heel of a shoe into the attacker's face.

"Rachel! *Verdommte!*" Gerrit Schuman staggered from the blow, which had knocked off his hat. "Ach, *meisje,* you be too harsh on a man who just wants to surprise you! Verdommte!"

"Oh, Gerrit, you *kerel!*" she exclaimed, calling him a knave, and then put a hand to his cut cheek, concerned. "Oh, I'm sorry. Why did you have to scare me like you were some wild kaffir?"

Rachel was annoyed, but regretted hitting poor Gerrit so hard. Blood trickled down the side of his face, into his golden beard. He grinned, his blue eyes twinkling good-naturedly as if he liked her spirit. She had seen him look at a young horse the same way.

"A wild kaffir?" He chuckled and brushed at the blood, cleaning his fingers on his shirt. "It'd take a regiment of kaffirs to capture the likes of you, girl."

A little older than Rachel, Gerrit was immense of shoulder and tall, his rugged face darkly sunburned. He was the very epitome of the proud young Boer. Rachel gently probed the wound on his cheek, and he touched her fingers. His hands were strong, the nails short and thick. When he smiled, Rachel flushed a little, perhaps still excited from the fright, or perhaps because he took hold of her hand. She did not know what to say or do at that. She liked Gerrit, but not well enough to stand there with her hand in his. She drew away, then lifted her apron to wipe the blood from the cut.

"Gerrit, you've been following me again, just as you used to when we were children, and your family came to visit." She hastily cleaned the blood away.

"Then why don't you follow me instead, meisje?"

"Enough meisjes follow you already."

Gerrit laughed and tried catching her hand, but missed.

"There," she said, standing back and dropping the apron. "You'll live. Come on, let's go back to the farmyard." She smoothed her apron as he bent to pick up his hat.

Gerrit was kindly, but he annoyed her, forever showing off, whether it was marksmanship, horsemanship, physical strength, or courage. Some thought him the best young stockman in the Great Karoo, as this hilly grassland was called. Many a Boer maid flirted with him at Nachmaal—the quarterly gathering of the people, who came from hundreds of miles around for religious services, to feast, and to match their children.

No matter how many girls flapped their eyelashes and flounced their bottoms at Gerrit, he seemed interested only in Rachel. Suddenly, he tugged at the apron to make her come closer, and he laughed again. She protested, yanking backwards so that she almost lost her balance, and her dress flew up in a gust of wind.

"Machtig!" He roared. "Almighty! But you've the legs of a pretty filly, Rachel."

"You rude kerel!" She started off down the slope, a hand on her hip, the other waving the shoes. "Watch out you don't get the other heel!"

"Ach, don't be so skittish." He jammed on his hat and went with her, smiling in that boyish way of his. "*Ja,* meisje, like an unbroke filly you be."

"And you're like an elephant, with your clumsy manners!"

"A bull elephant, at least. Give some praise, meisje, so I know you be not angry with me for just wanting to make you laugh."

"Oh, Gerrit, you—"

The rising melody of fiddle and concertina enchanted her, and she paused to look down at the farmyard, with its low, white-washed buildings and farmhouse, all shaded by the only trees for miles around. Early sunset laid long shadows around the thatched house and outbuildings, shadows that were filled with movement of people and stock. The farm had not been as crowded since the wedding of Johannes and Sannie, when all the neighbors came.

"Gerrit, it seems everyone we know is leaving Cape Colony!"

"They all should go! Every God-fearing farmer should get away from this here Egyptian land of the English pharaoh."

He complained about Boers having no say in colonial politics, about the government at Cape Town declaring which black nations were friends or enemies, even if the truth on the borderlands was otherwise.

"Boers be fined, shamed, even jailed if they cross the border to fight kaffir raiders that Cape Town says are protected under treaty. Even if them raiders've run off stock and massacred families!"

Rachel knew the stories, and that some rebellious Boers had fought the black colonial troops Cape Town had sent to arrest them. For that, men had been hanged by the British as rebels. Colonial administrators would never listen to frontier Boers, and so there would be more anger, more insurrections, and more hangings. She knew why she and her folk were trekking tomorrow, but she wondered what would become of them.

"Lord, what is Thy great purpose for us?" she murmured.

"What be Jehovah's purpose for us, His chosen people?" Gerrit grumbled, then went on, louder. "That purpose'll be revealed in due time, in due time if we be faithful."

In the distance, servant boys were driving the Drente goats and sheep into pens of limestone and thornbush, pens built long ago by her father, who with her mother had carved out this farm from virgin wilderness. Tonight would be the last that a Drente herd or flock would be protected by those walls. Tonight's gathering of trekkers at Sweetfountain would be Rachel's final memory of the farm.

The farmyard was swirling with activity. Dozens of colored and Hottentot servant women were hauling water from the well in the center of the yard. Here and there the husbands of those women were repairing harnesses, replacing horseshoes, doctoring oxen, and packing up tools. No slavery was allowed in Cape Colony, and the Boers had voted against allowing it in the new homeland, but every family had its colored, Hottentot, and black servants who stayed with them for life.

Servants did both menial and skilled labor on the farm, and most of the men knew how to ride and use a rifle. Riflemen would be needed in the promised land of Canaan, for according to the Word there might be hostile Canaanites to fight.

Contemplating the farmyard and the crowd of people around her home, Rachel said to Gerrit: "I hear that in the north the kaffirs are all driven out or killed by the rampaging Zulus, who've laid waste their kraals."

"They say that," Gerrit nodded, tight-lipped. "Kaffir Canaanites or Zulu Canaanites, none'll prevent the exodus of

God's chosen people." He drew a breath that swelled his chest, and he sounded much older as he said, "Righteousness'll give us strength in the wilderness, and Jehovah hisself'll fight for us."

Rachel hoped Gerrit and the others were right, that they were hardy enough to survive in the north. Yet, deep down, she wondered if they were too sure of themselves.

She said, "We are not very many."

He nodded. "But we be strong and able. Look at all them fine wagons, meisje!"

In the pasture beyond the farmyard stood the great trekwagons, almost a hundred of them, each painted a brilliant blue with red wheels, like sailing ships when their white canvas covers were tented, and each was fitted out for the long haul. When locked together in a circle they made a stout defense. Thus had these very lands been won by pioneers who migrated, generation after generation, from the first colony at Cape Town, four hundred miles to the southwest of Sweetfountain.

Gerrit took her hand, saying, "We'll people the promised land, Rachel, we'll multiply, and we'll hold that land till eternity, God willing." He gestured toward the far-off meadows. "See our fine stock!"

Out beyond the trekwagons were cattle, horses, sheep, and goats, all being settled down for the night by boys on horseback, and by shepherds and goatherds with their dogs. Prime livestock by the thousand was resting for the hard journey northward. Already feeling weary to contemplate a journey of which no one knew the end, Rachel sighed.

"This be only the beginning, pretty one," Gerrit said eagerly. "Many more'll go a'trekking one day, and they'll find us waiting up there, in fat country, with fat stock!"

Rachel drew away and said, "Oh, to imagine that we're about

to begin all over again. . . ." Gerrit nodded and grinned, even though she added, "The very thought breaks my heart."

"Come, now! You be too serious for a female. Let me make you laugh, meisje!" He wiggled his fingers awkwardly, but did not touch her. "Laugh a little!"

"I can't laugh now, when I see where we're going."

She was facing north, staring through the smoke from fifty cooking fires, toward distant mountains the color of red mist. Those were the Winterbergs, which marched northeast into the evening sky. Somewhere beyond were the *Drakensberg*—Dragon Mountains—a jagged range more than six hundred miles long.

Rachel turned away and looked to the south and east, where the rising crescent moon lay on its back.

"Ja, out there!" Gerrit declared, gesturing to the north, then following Rachel as she began to walk down the slope. "Out there across the high plains beyond the Drakensberg, there be the land of milk and honey! There we'll find the country the Lord's set aside for us!"

He put a hand lightly on her shoulder as they walked, speaking with sincerity and mounting excitement.

"We'll plow new fields and breed the finest horses and cattle; we'll plant vineyards and orchards, and we'll thrive, with lots and lots of children, eh, meisje?"

Rachel did not respond. She was looking at a group of married Boer women, comfortably plump in their starched kappies and broad white aprons. They stood, sheltered, under a canvas awning slung across the face of the barn. Unlike Rachel, who loved the sun, most Boer *vrouwen*—a term meaning both grown women and wives—kept inside or to the shade, taking pride in milk-white complexions, even wearing lambskin masks when they had to go out in the sun. Rachel had never worn such a mask—some of which covered half the face, others all of it—and she never would.

No doubt the vrouwen were talking about the farewell dance and feast that evening. Seated on the stone corral fence across the yard, their men, bearded and most of them heavily built, smoked pipes and admired Tempest, the Drente stallion, who was being led into the barn for the last time.

Gerrit, walking at Rachel's shoulder, was talking. "No more will verdommte English law forbid us riding out to avenge attacks by kaffirs like those dogs who killed your parents—"

"Please, Gerrit!"

"—and no more will a government we ain't picked tell us what we can and can't do!"

Rachel knew that if Gerrit had his way, he would tell her, too, just what she could and could not do, and she would be under that awning with the married women, behaving herself. He, in turn, would be with the men, boasting about the fertility of horses and wives, and of the potency of stallions and stockmen, and in the evening, every evening for the rest of her life, they would be abed together. She did not want to think of that. She walked on more quickly, the cheerful Gerrit close by her side.

"Ach, God! I never seen such a gloomy maid, or one so beautiful when gloomy. Come on, Rachel, let's have a laugh! Life be too short for such verdommte gloom."

They were almost to the farmyard, passing two colored men working on a wagon that had been jacked up for a final greasing of the axles. Here was a large tent and, under its marquee, Johannes was playing his violin along with André Toulouse, the sightless French merchant with the concertina. André was seated on a low stool, legs spread, Rachel's brother standing beside him, both swaying with the music.

André, whom Rachel affectionately called "uncle," looked even older than his years, eyes blank, his long hair completely white. He was dressed like a Gypsy, in bright colors and puffy-sleeved, old-fashioned shirts that his wife, Emmy, made for him. Johannes wore no hat, and his combed black hair glistened as he played with passion and skill. A dashing fellow of thirty who kept his mustache and beard neatly trimmed, Johannes looked more like an English officer than a Cape Dutch farmer.

Passing the tent, Gerrit winked at Johannes and then gave a loud sound of exasperation. "Come, Rachel, let a good man make you laugh! You be getting no younger. Let me make you laugh afore it be too late for you!"

"Too late, Gerrit?" Rachel whirled on him, her face suddenly close to his. "Too late for what? Too late to get a good man? Am I too old for marrying?"

Startled, Gerrit tried to chuckle, but backed up a little when she wagged her finger at him and said, "Well, then, go make a younger girl laugh with your stupid kaffir ambushes, but remember to duck next time in case she doesn't think it funny, either!"

Rachel left Gerrit there, smiling stiffly.

Johannes whistled to him and began playing a Viennese waltz.

"Hey, Schuman, don't try to catch her until she's good and ready to be caught, or you'll die from loss of blood."

André Toulouse followed the violin's melody with his concertina, grinning as he said with a wheeze, "Gerrit, that's no simple Boer meisje you're romancing there! Rachel has the passion of her French mother, and to win the amour of a *mademoiselle,* you have to charm her! You have to charm her with enchantment like . . . like the fire of electricity!"

Gerrit rubbed away the trickle of blood on his face and asked, "What be an elec—elec—triatic fire, old merchant? Something you want to sell me to take to the promised land? Must be verdommte dear, that there elec— that fire of yours!"

"You'll see it tonight," André said with a cackle, sounding short of breath, as always. "See and feel it, but you can't buy or sell electric fire, no! You must learn to make it!"

Rachel was almost out of earshot, heading for the wagons of Willem and Marta Arendt, but she glanced back at hearing the Frenchman say he would that very evening show everyone "electric fire."

"And, Gerrit," André added, "once you've experienced electricity, you'll be able to romance even hot-blooded Frenchwomen like Rachel, because you'll kiss them just as a Frenchman kisses!" He touched fingertips to his thin lips and declared, "You will be irresistible!"

Folk who heard laughed, Gerrit the loudest, and Rachel stormed away, red with embarrassment. Gerrit was such an oaf at times! Yes, everyone believed he would catch her soon, but she was not so sure. How it bothered her that folk thought she was too old at twenty to be still unmarried! So what if there were many wives of fifteen years here and mothers of sixteen years! So what if Gerrit was such an excellent catch, and all the women and girls said he was a better man than any meisje had the right to hope for! Maybe so, but no teasing kerel would yank her apron like that—not unless she loved him!

And she did not love Gerrit Schuman. Not yet, anyway.

THE ADVENTURERS

Above the far-off music of the Zulu kraal, Dirk Arendt heard another song, this one rising from the shallow donga below and carrying across the hillside on the evening air. It was a high-pitched English hymn that rang and echoed against the rocky slopes in a counterpoint to the deep, melodious voices of the mass singing in Shaka's kraal.

While Sebe continued to gaze at kwaBulawayo, Dirk looked back down the trail and saw the others of the expedition appear, one by one, a line of twelve men and two horses entering the sunlight. First came Benjamin David and Thomas Lovell, wearing broad-brimmed hats and walking beside the horses. They were followed by ten heavy-laden bearers in colorful trade shirts and trousers and carrying bundles on their heads.

Lovell was gamely singing away at "Rock of Ages," his strained tenor joined by the voices of the native bearers, who had no idea of the words, but liked the melody, which was fortifying to their courage now that they were in the heart of Zululand. Lovell was an enthusiastic choirmaster who had taught them the tunes to many Protestant hymns during the long march from base camp, and now the singing of the bearers harmonized with his high voice:

Rock of Ages, cleft for me.

Let me hide myself in Thee.

Dirk waved when they saw him standing at the crest of the trail. There was quite a contrast between Benjamin David and Thomas Lovell: Benjamin was dark and slender, strikingly handsome, with long legs that covered much ground with every step; the paunchy Lovell was ruddy and plodding, not made for tramping through African wilderness.

In his late twenties, Benjamin was dignified in bearing, even with a month-old unkempt beard that crept up his high cheekbones. Confident, always elegant in manner and word, he was a welcome guest at the tables of Europe's best families. Dirk often had seen how his friend was so attractive to older women, who seemed to light up in his presence, becoming almost youthful, sometimes motherly, at other times mistress-like. Benjamin was a gifted artist, too, ever with drawing pad and charcoal, a talent that further won him the adoration of the ladies.

Thomas Lovell was about fifty years of age, really too old for adventuring such as this, but, as he had from the beginning of the expedition, Lovell tenaciously pressed on up the hill without complaint. Struggling close behind Benjamin on the last turn of the trail, sweating from the climb, he dragged at the reins of his reluctant horse. With scarcely a pause in the singing, he wiped his mustache with a silk handkerchief, of which he seemed to have an endless supply.

Contrasting with Benjamin's composure, Lovell wore the haggard look of a man always in a hurry, always late for something. Since meeting him in Holland, Dirk had become used to his persistent nervousness and his impatience to get on with the business of the day, whether it was hiring bearers, buying supplies or gifts for Shaka, or just starting that morning's march.

Devoutly religious, Lovell often quoted the Gospels. He spoke perfect Dutch and was acquainted with many important personages in Holland as well as with political figures in England, where he had some obscure position as a government functionary.

As Dirk tied Blueboy's reins to a tree, he appraised his little company: the wizened Xhosa afraid of nothing; the gentlemanly Jewish trader, inyanga to the Zulu king; the English archaeologist with formidable connections; and the restless, homesick Boer. They and their ten bearers—half of them wiry-haired little Hottentots, nicknamed *totties,* and the others being coloreds, as mixed-race folk were called—were a strange collection of adventurers. Yet, Dirk sensed he could count on all of them, from insolent old Sebe to the determined Thomas Lovell.

Lovell was highly regarded as an archaeologist and could be a fascinating storyteller, entertaining them with legends of southeast Africa's ancient civilizations, once known to King Solomon but now just forgotten ruins. He also had a zealot's fervor to minister to the downtrodden, and had donated scores of Bibles, hymnals, spelling books, and boxes of pencils and writing paper to Cape Town missionaries. He had also brought them supplies of drugs for malaria and plague. All these things had been placed in his care by a religious society eager to spread the Gospel among the natives of southern Africa. In those few weeks when the expedition was being readied for the journey to Port Natal, Lovell also had even started up two choirs.

Dirk respected all that well enough, but he was ever wary of English missionary zealotry, which too often led to public condemnation of Catholics, Moslems, and Cape Boers alike for allegedly following paths of sin and iniquity and taking the natives along with them.

☾ ☾ ☾

Listening to Lovell sing, Dirk was gazing down at the drifting Zulu cattle when he heard Benjamin David's voice close at hand.

"I'll wager that your dear father would prefer you here, witnessing this, old boy, than turning to dust in some library in Leyden." He slapped Dirk on the shoulder and smiled, indicating the Zulu kraal with a nod as he handed a telescope to Dirk. "You must admit I was right to invite you on this expedition."

"Yes, but now you've to see I get home again to tell this tale to my dear father." Through the lens Dirk viewed the kraal, seeing the regiments wheel and parade in precise order that was astonishing. "Shaka means to welcome you with his entire army, Benjamin. And, machtig, what an army!"

Benjamin gave the reins of his horse to a bearer and took the telescope. Like Dirk, he was well over six feet, but slim by comparison. Dressed in dark blue military trousers and a white seaman's shirt, he looked every bit the self-assured adventurer, and his eyes gleamed as he once again looked upon kwaBulawayo.

"Is this all really in my honor?" he murmured to himself.

Dirk spoke: "Never had I imagined such power in any African nation! The kaffirs I've fought were no more than a mob compared to those regiments."

Sebe agreed, saying in halting Dutch, "We Xhosa water grass with blood when we fight Boer, but Zulu run like cheetah, faster than horse—surround enemy, bewitch with strong medicine, devour with fury of hungry lion!"

As the three of them gazed across the valley, there was a spell of silence until Lovell arrived, noisily panting, breathless. Wiping his face as he recovered from the climb, he took the telescope Benjamin offered him and viewed kwaBulawayo.

"Holy God in heaven!" Lovell exclaimed. "They're drilling like King George's own infantry!" Wide-eyed, he turned to Benjamin, a tremble in his voice. "I thought Shaka was just a savage. How possibly can he have such a . . . such a military organization?"

It was Sebe who replied in Dutch: "Shaka make big medicine! Eat up good men, the best; eat up wise chief, eat up great warrior, eat up clever leader! This give Shaka power, very much power—"

"Hold your tongue!" Lovell demanded. "Keep such beastly thoughts to yourself, you rogue!"

As if Lovell had not spoken, Sebe went on, savoring his description of Shaka's "medicine," and saying, "Wise man's blood good for Shaka's mind; warrior's marrow good for Shaka's heart; bowels of clever leader make Shaka cunning—"

"Shut up!" Lovell sputtered, threatening to strike Sebe with the telescope. "You make light of cannibalism. Damnable, godlessness! Shut up, or—"

Benjamin touched Lovell's arm.

"Steady, Thomas."

Benjamin gave Sebe a warning glance, but the Xhosa already had turned away to look over the valley. Dirk saw Sebe smile and tried not to do the same.

Lovell muttered, then stamped off to fume at the bearers as they arrived, one by one. With Lovell complaining about their handling of the packs, they laid the baggage beside the trail, then huddled together, staring in cold dread at the Zulu kraal. Benjamin said they all would wait here until Shaka made it clear what he wanted them to do next. The bearers begged to stay behind while Benjamin made his visit to Shaka. None of them wanted to enter "The Place of He Who Kills," but Benjamin said some would have to carry the bundles of gifts to Shaka.

Sebe suddenly pointed at the kraal.

"They come."

A column of warriors poured out of the kraal gate and onto a winding trail that led to the hilltop where the expedition stood. The Zulus would be upon them shortly. The bearers, resting on their haunches, became very quiet.

"This," said Benjamin, "will be our escort."

Dirk said, "Or our death."

He meant it, his heart pounding, mouth unexpectedly dry. Boers did not trust any force of armed blacks to be peaceable. He had unconsciously taken his rifle from the saddle holster. It felt good in his hands but would be useless if there were trouble. He steeled himself to remain calm.

Lovell took a shaky breath. "Benjamin, my good fellow, I pray to heaven you're right, that these savages will not harm us."

"So do I," Benjamin answered.

"What do you say?" Lovell gasped. "So do you?"

Sebe howled with laughter, bending over and slapping his thighs.

"What's so funny?" Lovell snapped.

Sebe covered his mouth and winked at Dirk, who could not help but grin as Sebe again got on Lovell's nerves. From the start, the Xhosa had taken a disliking to Lovell and now was enjoying seeing the man squirm.

"Baas Benjamin make joke," Sebe said to Lovell. "No worry, Englishman safe with Baas Benjamin, but—no sing! Want to live? Then no sing!"

"What the devil do you mean?" Lovell was trying to maintain composure as he blinked at Sebe. "Explain yourself!"

"Shaka maybe like to have your song . . . maybe like to eat up tongue of English singing man."

Lovell winced, turning to Benjamin, who cast an annoyed look at Sebe.

"English singing tongue good medicine for Shaka voice," Sebe remarked, rubbing his stomach.

"Come now, Sebe," Benjamin said sternly, then turned to Lovell: "Have no fear, Tom. This knave is pulling your leg about Shaka being interested in . . . in, ah . . . ."

Fear showed in Lovell's eyes, and his lips trembled slightly as he turned to watch the Zulus approach. Sebe was laughing, but silently, and holding his sides.

☾ ☾ ☾

The Zulu impi halted two hundred yards from Dirk's party and formed straight, tight ranks twenty men deep and a hundred across. A ray of sunset slanted through clouds of red dust, shining on two thousand spear points, and illuminating a wall of white and black oval oxhide shields. The Zulus began to chant, a deep, whooshing sound, and swayed from side to side, stamping their feet in perfect unison.

Dirk stared, astonished, heart racing, aroused by the Zulu host and by memories: As a small boy he had stood with a rifle that was too heavy behind wagons locked in a circle, a *laager,* watching hordes of roaring Xhosas prepare to attack. Those warriors were wild and brave, their headlong rushes suicidal, disorganized, and their ranks had fallen like scythed wheat under Boer volleys. After their last reckless assault broke and withered against the bulwark of that blazing, smoke-shrouded laager, the veldt was left covered with hundreds of glistening black bodies. The Boers stood behind their wagons, almost unscathed. From time to time, Dirk still dreamed of all those shining bodies in the trampled grass, a dream terrifying and thrilling and horrible all at once.

This force of Zulus was, however, far different from a mass of overconfident Xhosa. A Zulu impi would be a match for Boers defending a laager. They would know how to attack one defensive point and break through the wagons. Zulus would have to be fought in the open from horseback, shooting fast, riding fast, and it would cost many a Boer life to defeat even a comparatively small Zulu force, such as this one that had come to honor and impress Benjamin David and the archaeological expedition.

Benjamin said, "This regiment is the uFazimba, 'The Haze,' Shaka's finest."

Rhythmically, the Zulus began to shake long wooden clubs against their spears, setting up a sound like a plague of giant crickets. Then, one by one, out of the ranks leaped warriors who took turns dancing and jumping high, stabbing at imaginary enemies. With every blow and thrust from the dancer, the Zulu host grunted as one man, and with every bound into the air the dancing warrior howled a war shout.

Benjamin came to Dirk's side, saying, "This is how Zulu war chiefs display their prowess, in a *giya,* a war dance just before they go into battle."

To Dirk, these chieftains were each and every one magnificent and ferocious. Behind the massed impi, reed torches were flaring up and being brought to the front ranks to light the spectacle of the dancers. Above it all, the crescent moon rose higher in the darkening sky, and stars began to twinkle.

Tom Lovell exclaimed: "Look at that black devil! He's a giant!"

A huge warrior, with a feathered cap and wearing the leopard-skin kaross that said he was of royal blood, had just sprung to the fore, and the entire impi roared for him as he flew high into the air.

"Mazibe, their commander, called *induna,* is the greatest fighter Shaka possesses," Benjamin said, staring at the Zulu, who wore a black plume bound at his forehead. "Mazibe is the king's bodyguard, called the 'Shield of Shaka.'"

If there had been a battle, and Dirk had only one shot, this would be the man who would receive it, the one whose fall might take the heart out of the others. Suddenly Mazibe cried out, and the entire impi sent up a thunderous roar that echoed in the hills. Mazibe shouted again and again, and each time they roared in response.

"Lord, protect us," Tom Lovell murmured, and shakily began to recite the Twenty-third psalm, fingers clasped at his lips: ". . . Yea, though I walk through the valley of the shadow of death, I will fear no evil . . ."

Sebe gave a shrill of delight, and Dirk turned to find the old man a little to the rear, on his knees, throwing dice amidst a pile of bones, shells, bits of feathers, metal, dried skins, and that mamba's bloody head. Consulting his medicine. Sebe cackled, shook the stones, and threw them again.

Lovell shouted, "Is he mad to sport at a time like this?" The Zulus bellowed, and Lovell shuddered, chewing his lip as he said to Benjamin, "Forgive me, but I have never been so afraid!"

Benjamin patted Lovell on his shoulder and tried to steady him by saying this reception was a sign of friendship, and was the way Zulus honored their most important guests.

"Why, my dear Thomas, be assured that in an hour we'll be feasting with King Shaka himself, drinking the royal Zulu beer and eating all sorts of exotic sweetmeats."

Without looking up, Sebe gleefully added: "Not to worry, Englishman. Shaka never yet eat sweet English meat . . . but remember, no sing! No sing!"

Lovell shook a pudgy fist at him.

In Xhosa, Dirk said to Sebe, "Spare our companion, ancient one, and tell me why you are so happy with your bones and dice. Will Shaka make you his ambassador to Cape Colony? Or will he lend you a wife?"

"Ah, Baas Dirk, this Xhosa is overjoyed, for the divining charms say I am imbued with unconquerable medicine tonight." He pointed at the sky. "My god tells me I am invincible while the moon lies on its back." He nimbly rose and came forward, passing the huddled bearers, who were shivering in fear as they heard the Zulu shouts roll over the hillside.

Sebe spread his arms and declared, "Under this moon I may open the mouth of the bearded lion and pick his teeth with my dagger! Tonight, Sebe the rainmaker fears nothing, for he cannot be harmed."

Dirk translated for Lovell, who angrily said, "Filthy bones and dried skins for heathen courage!" He winced at the next roar of the Zulus. "Oh, but I'm sore afraid that I'll fail, Benjamin, that I'll not survive to—"

An even mightier shout came from the Zulus, who began to run, quickly forming two great horns, one racing around to the right and the other to the left, streaming across the hillside until the expedition was surrounded by spears and shields and flaming torches.

"That," said Benjamin, quietly, "is the principal battle tactic of Shaka's Zulus: The two horns envelope and strike from behind, while the 'chest' of the impi charges straight ahead. No native force has ever withstood it."

Dirk would remember this Zulu tactic if he got out of here alive. He had put his rifle back in its saddle holster, but now itched to yank it out again.

Lovell fought down panic. "I had not expected this!" He cringed as the Zulus bellowed. "I see now that I may die here, after all I have done, though I have come so far on my mission."

"My dear sir," Benjamin interrupted. "You need not worry so."

"Wait!" Lovell raised both hands, which quaked until he clenched and lowered them. "Hear me out! Hear me out!" With great force of will, he steadied himself. "It is not my death alone that I fear. But this mission must not be allowed to fail!"

He swallowed hard.

"The time has come to reveal the true object of our expedition, for if I should fall, one of you must carry out my task—must recover that which has been lost for a thousand years. We are so close! Do what I ask, and there will be a great reward, a reward beyond any of your dreams."

Sebe moved nearer to listen. Dirk and Benjamin, too, were intent on Lovell's words, which came only with great effort. All the while the Zulus sang and shouted, rattling spears and clubs.

Benjamin asked, "What mission? Are we not seeking the legendary cities of Zimbabwe and Monomotapa? Is there something more important, more valuable?"

"Yes . . . far more valuable!" Lovell wiped his face with a handkerchief, and when he began again, the Zulu singing almost drowned him out. "A priceless golden amulet of great antiquity has come into the hands of Shaka, a precious treasure of which he does not understand the true worth."

Dirk listened closely, but to him old amulets or old ruins were about the same. He would help guide expeditions to find them if it paid well enough and got him home; nothing more about such things excited him.

Composing himself, Lovell said, "This amulet was a treasure of ancient Persian kings, then possessed by the Greek Tyrants, then Roman Caesars, and lastly by the rightful rulers of Byzantium, from whom it was stolen, taken into Africa a thousand years ago, and lost to history.

"Until now." Atremble, he turned to face the royal kraal, a blazing ring of bonfires in the velvet darkness of the valley. "The rightful owners have sought it ever since, and at last have traced it to Shaka's hovel." He gave a little laugh, saying, "Strangely enough, it is set with a wondrous diamond that originally came from southern Africa, not so far from here."

Surprised, Dirk said, "I've never heard tell of diamond fields in this country! Why, if diamonds were found here, it would be invaded by all the European powers, there'd be war—"

"That is another matter," Lovell said, raising a hand. "It is not my duty to seek treasure in the earth, but to recover the amulet, a token of earthly power—this golden bull's-head with a stone of white fire, which must be brought back to my masters."

As if this speech had imparted courage, Lovell stared unblinkingly beyond the dancing Zulus toward Shaka's kraal.

"It is there."

There was a pause until Benjamin spoke.

"But, Tom, how shall we acquire this amulet? Shaka must know its worth. He's no fool. I have gifts and trade goods, but we'll need a fortune in merchandise to persuade him to part with something which you say is so wondrous."

"No, Shaka does not know its worth." Lovell shook his head, still staring at the Zulu kraal. "Few know its true worth, but he surely values it greatly, for he will have discovered some of its more . . . interesting qualities."

Dirk asked, "One golden trinket with one diamond? If it's so precious, then those who send you here with orders to take it from Shaka must be fools."

"Fools?" Lovell turned on him with a look of scorn. "You insult the greatest men of our age. Our brotherhood has sought this stolen amulet for centuries! See, even after centuries of treachery, it has been found by us, found even though secreted in the unknown wilderness of black Africa."

"Then let your brothers come down here themselves with an army and cannon and demand this amulet from Shaka," Dirk scoffed. "They're endangering your life, and mine, too, these so-called great men, if they expect you to wheedle a favored trinket from a jealous Zulu king."

"Great men, I say!" Lovell was quivering. "You cannot imagine who they are, you blinded by your Afrikaner ignorance!"

"I know about African kings!" Dirk's anger was mounting. "And your so-called brothers are putting you in mortal danger with their missions! These great men, whoever they are."

"The likes of you will never understand who they are—"

"But, Tom!" Benjamin broke in. "How shall this amulet be got from Shaka?"

Lovell seemed to catch himself, eyes becoming clearer. He shook his head slowly, then spoke to Dirk.

"Forgive my outburst, Mister Arendt, I do not mean to offend you. Let me simply say that we . . . we are founding the greatest museum of antiquity, and untold sums are being spent to acquire the rarest of treasures; believe me, my man, if I should fall here, and you survive to return this bull's-head amulet to its rightful owners, to my associates, then you'll be the richest Boer in all southern Africa!"

The Zulus began singing a beautiful, surging melody, a song honoring their guests.

"Benjamin knows the address of my office in London," Lovell said hurriedly, taking out a pencil and a sheet of paper from his pockets. "I'll write it down for you, Mister Arendt."

Benjamin said, "If this amulet is here in Zululand, Tom, I believe Shaka would not conceal it from me, his inyanga."

"Precisely!" Lovell retorted. "That's why we came to you, for we heard of your success with Shaka, and how he trusts you. You see, this amulet must never be taken by force—this is a sacred rule! It must be given to us, willingly, by its bearer."

Dirk asked, "Why so?"

"Ah," said Lovell, touching the side of his nose almost coyly. "That condition is part of the . . . the charm, shall we say? So must it be: The amulet may not be taken by force, and thus have I come here with Benjamin David, Shaka's revered inyanga, the man to whom the king owes his very life." Lovell's eyes narrowed as he stared at Benjamin, his voice turning soft. "By custom, we know that Shaka cannot refuse if you, Benjamin David, the inyanga to whom he owes his life, would ask him for the amulet."

Dirk saw what might be the flicker of madness in Lovell's eyes. Benjamin made no reply. He was somber, gazing at the Zulu host.

Then Lovell addressed all of them, sweat beading on his face as he declared, "I say again, if I should fall, and any of you succeed in recovering the amulet, we will make you rich! You, too, Mister Arendt! Rich beyond your dreams!"

Lovell clapped Dirk on the shoulder, as if they were friends, and stuffed the paper with his London address into Dirk's shirt pocket. Turning to watch the swaying Zulus and listening to them sing, Dirk would not let himself dream about riches to be won from recovering lost amulets for eccentric Englishmen. At this point, it would be enough to survive the expedition, be duly paid off, and return home to Cape Colony and his family.

Bah! he almost said aloud. *Museums of antiquity. The greatest men of the age. Bull's-head amulets.*

Abruptly, all thought of ancient amulets left Dirk, as the Zulu induna called Mazibe howled and sprang forward, racing alone up the slope toward the expedition. The shouts of the admiring Zulu host engulfed the hillside.

"Look how he can fly!" Dirk exclaimed.

Benjamin said, "Think you could outrun him?"

"I would like to try," Dirk said, unable to take his eyes from the induna.

☾ ☾ ☾

After one final great bound to reach them, Mazibe laid aside shield and weapons, clasping his hands at his chest, and bowed to Benjamin. He was a head taller than Dirk, and had penetrating eyes that gleamed in the dimness as a smile came over his handsome face.

"It is with a glad heart that my lord, King Shaka, the Great Elephant, Destroyer of His Enemies, welcomes back his beloved inyanga, for he has long awaited you and the gift you promised to bring to him."

Benjamin returned the greeting in appropriately flowery Bantu, praising Shaka, "Bull of the People," "Inexplicable Sun of the Nation."

"We bring the goodwill of the English King George, who sends his beneficent wishes to his cousin, King Shaka."

King George knew nothing of Benjamin David's expedition, but Shaka believed they were distant relations, so Benjamin passed on the best of royal regards. The two men then exchanged warm personal greetings, shaking hands, and Benjamin introduced Lovell, Dirk, and Sebe, describing them as peaceful travelers who wished to journey to the land of old stones.

Mazibe looked them over. He first regarded Dirk, and their eyes met and held momentarily. Next was Sebe, who grinned almost impudently and received a half smile in return. When the Zulu induna turned to Lovell, the Englishman seemed unable to look directly at him, instead wiping awkwardly at sweat on his face as Mazibe stared long and hard. After a moment, the induna turned and called out to his regiment, which had reduced its chants to a low growling noise. In reply the Zulus shouted and rushed forward, closely surrounding the expedition with a wall of humanity. The whites were told to leave their horses and rifles behind because they were "instruments of war." Two grateful servants were to stay with the horses, and the rest of the expedition joined the Zulus on the march down to the kraal.

Dirk walked beside Mazibe at the front of the column as the Zulus sang and rattled clubs against shields. In the light of the torches, Dirk could see Lovell and Benjamin close behind, followed by a grinning Sebe, and then came the frightened bearers carrying Benjamin's packages for Shaka. Mazibe gave a command, and everyone began to trot through the darkness, following torches held by men out in front, the Zulus chanting as they ran.

Dirk found himself afloat in rhythmic sound that quickened his blood. He was running beside Mazibe, who gave him a look, then picked up the pace, passing the men carrying the torches. Not losing a stride on the induna, Dirk kept at his side, and in that moment knew with mounting excitement that he must find a way to race this Zulu champion.

Perhaps even right now.

THE TREKKERS

Sitting on a folding chair by the wagons of Marta and Willem Arendt, Rachel stared at the flames of the cooking fire and wondered about the blind Frenchman's strange talk. Ever since André Toulouse first came to the Great Karoo six years ago to marry Emmy Mohler, the wealthy widow, that chatterbox of a man had always had something outlandish about him.

André was forever making predictions about rain and locusts and unexpected visitors. The most disturbing thing was that he was inevitably right. No one understood André, but he was tolerated, partly because he was a dependable trader, a tireless *smous,* who journeyed with ox cart and servants through the bush from farm to farm. André brought the essentials to distant families, trading them black powder and needles and thread for hides and honey, giraffe-skin whips and ivory, and sometimes he even took money, if the Boers had nothing better to offer. Mostly, André was accepted by the Boers because his wife, whom everyone called "Tante" Emmy, was such a wise woman and the best doctor of man or beast for five hundred miles around.

Marta Arendt, sitting at the plank table across from Rachel, also knew a thing or two about wisdom and doctoring, and like Tante Emmy was admired by everyone.

Rachel leaned over to Marta and asked, "Can you tell me, *Mevrouw* Arendt, anything about the fire of el . . . ec . . . ectric . . . itus?"

"The fire of what, dear?" Marta did not look up from a pile of papers she had been rummaging through while Rachel sipped coffee from an old blue Delft cup. Marta's fair, graying hair was tied back in a bun and held with a cheerful pink ribbon, making her look much younger than her fifty-five years. She was a small woman, not portly like the ideal Boer vrouw, but trim and neat, wearing silver spectacles that kept sliding down her nose. She had on a khaki dress with a big blue collar that folded over, and the sleeves were not buttoned to her wrists, as was proper, but were rolled up, showing bare arms in a way most Boer wives thought extremely immodest.

Rachel had to ask, "Have you heard of a fire that can make a Boer *jonge* kiss like a Frenchman? Called elec . . . trus—"

"Elec . . . what?" Marta was only half listening as she fumbled with the pile of papers.

"Some magic thing the blind French merchant said he'd show us tonight."

"Machtig, Rachel!" Marta chuckled, pulling out a yellowed sheet. "Magic! That man is half mad from getting lost in the jungle! How could a plain Boer boy kiss like any Frenchman?" She shook the paper. "Look, now. Here's the letter from my Dirkie that I want to read you."

Pushing aside her own coffee cup, Marta drew Rachel close to listen. Willem Arendt came to stand at his wife's shoulder as she prepared to read. He was a robust, fine-looking man, his black hair starting to gray, and with a long beard that covered his powerful chest. He took off his hat and puffed at a stone pipe as he listened to Dirkie's letter describe great cities, paved roads, ancient buildings, and comical foreigners—*uitlanders.*

Rachel interrupted: "How I'd love to see all those things, to see a whole city of such people, to journey over the great water on ships."

Marta pressed the spectacles farther back on her nose as she read how Dirkie had tasted the wine of Paris, the cuisine of Florence and Rome, but ". . . none as good as the pastries of home, and no wine better than the one Father bottled back in 'sixteen. . . ."

To Rachel, the Arendts were nothing like other people she knew. Marta had been born in Holland, and Willem met her when he was a seaman, the only Boer Rachel had ever known to spend time as a sailor. They had settled down twenty-five years ago to farm and make wine in Bredasdorp, which lay far to the south, near the coast. Both could read, and Marta had taught school for years. Willem, still physically powerful at sixty, had been an elected district official, respected by his own kind, but too often at odds with the royal governor in Cape Town and in opposition to the British colonial office's policies. Now, like others of his temperament, Willem was about to trek far from the borders of the colony.

Marta gripped Rachel's hand. "Listen to this, child!" She went on with the letter: "One day soon I will return to Africa, Mother and Father, for I long for home." There was a tear in Marta's eye as she read in a trembling voice: "Europe is strange and wonderful, and sometimes more dangerous than lion country, but I weary of it. I need to breathe the sweet air of Africa and to ride free across the veldt again."

Marta bit her lip. "My son's coming home! Isn't that wonderful?"

Rachel's heart skipped to think of Dirkie, the eldest of five

Arendt sons. She still remembered him from those Nachmaal gatherings years ago, a tall, rambunctious boy who often teased her. It was not the rough teasing of Gerrit Schuman, but was funny, light-hearted, and clever, though it still made her furious. No wonder Dirkie had teased her, for she had followed him everywhere and made herself a pest. He was six years older than she, and the cleverest jonge she had ever met. Dirk also had been the best runner anywhere, but what she remembered most was how handsome he was. He had seldom noticed her, of course, except to tease.

Rachel tried to imagine how he looked now, this Dirkie Arendt, this Boer jonge who had seen so much of the world.

She asked, "Has he heard you're trekking?"

"We know not," Willem shrugged. "The letter from him arrived just a month ago, the day we left to come up here." He knocked out the pipe against the wagon wheel, saying, "We've written to Holland to tell him, and left word for him back in Bredasdorp when he returns, but we don't know if he received our letters, for he was taking the grand tour of the Continent, as they say every young gentleman of breeding must take."

"Young gentleman," Marta said with a smile. "Young gentlemen will not tramp away with trekkers into the empty African wilderness, Willem."

Rachel touched Marta's hand. "He will come after you, Mevrouw, if only to taste your pastry again."

"Ach, I wish Dirkie knew you as you are now, Rachel," Marta smiled, "for I believe he would trek ten thousand miles to be with you."

That made Rachel blush, and she sat back in her chair, saying, "I think he'd find me too old, your Dirkie."

Willem laughed, saying, "My son should've married and built

a family and a herd for himself by now, not go all over Europe like a popinjay gentleman! Ach, meisje, you would like him, and he you, because you're one Boer woman who would understand him."

"I? Understand him? A man who has studied law in Holland, who walks through great cities as I cross meadows? Why, your Dirkie has sailed on the great water, and—" She laughed to say what she was thinking. "—and how has he never fallen off the edge of the earth with all his traveling?"

Marta squeezed Rachel's hand. "If the earth really were flat, my sailor husband, too, would have fallen off long ago."

"I don't understand such things, though I've read some geography," Rachel said, and thought a moment before going on. "Maybe it's not flat as the Boers claim, but it doesn't make any more sense that the earth is a ball!"

From out of the twilight there came the clanging of the bell that told the evening's festivities were at hand. Rachel could feel the excitement in the air as people all around the camp began to gather for the celebration of this pilgrimage into the wilderness. Voices called to Willem and Marta, saying it was time to open with a prayer, which was Willem's duty as trek leader. The Arendts, who had sold out everything at Bredasdorp and were instrumental in organizing the trek, were the ones to whom the people would look in the uncertain days of journeying ahead. Then, one day these pioneers would settle down and establish a new country across the mountains, a country of free men far beyond the jurisdiction of the British government.

Or die trying.

"Go now, Rachel," Willem said heartily, "and get ready for the feast; it soon will be time to dance, and a meisje should be at her best when the likes of Gerrit Schuman pursue her."

Rachel almost said Gerrit Schuman could not compare to Dirkie Arendt; but truth was that Gerrit was here, and Dirkie was somewhere sailing along the edge of the earth. Yet, as she got up to go, she could not help saying, "I do wish your Dirkie were here to dance with me."

"Ja, dearest," said Marta. "And so do I."

☾ ☾ ☾

Sweetfountain's farmyard was bright with a bonfire, cooking fires, and standing torches. In the center of the yard an ox roasted on the spit, and plank tables were laden with overflowing platters of food and jugs of drink brought in by the folk, who generously contributed to the occasion from their precious stores.

Everyone sat on makeshift benches at long tables, Rachel and her brother, Johannes, with his wife, Sannie, between. For all that she was weak from recent illness, Sannie looked beautiful, wearing the smallest of kappies so that her blond hair showed, framing her serene, lovely face. At Rachel's feet was Jaeger, the family's big Boerhound, a muscular breed of yellow dog developed over two centuries to fight off lions. Gerrit Schuman was as near as he could get to Rachel, sitting just across the table, bantering with other young men who also had an eye on her but dared not risk his wrath.

This last night in Cape Colony would be a celebration for the trekker children to remember when they were out on the high veldt, surrounded by danger from man and beast. They ate until they could eat no more, devouring sweet potatoes with the roast, sharing a barrel of smoked fish brought up from Port Elizabeth, tasting every baker's fresh breads and biscuits, and pouring honey on thin pancakes made from maize or "mealies," as the Boers called it.

There were tarts with fresh cream, dried peaches from Uitenhage, and raisins from the Arendt vineyard at Bredasdorp. Tea and coffee were in abundance, as though the day would never come when both would run out. No one wanted to think of that tonight, however, and many hearty toasts were offered with Arendt wine and with twenty kinds of hard cider from a dozen Boer orchards, and smooth plum brandy made by Sannie and Johannes from their last harvest here at Sweetfountain.

Rachel felt pretty in a black satin kappie and a satin gown lent to her by Sannie, who was too big with child to wear it. The dress was the color of burgundy, and it looked like a dark flame in the firelight. The collar was close at her throat, with a lace frill, and two buff-hued petticoats under flounces spun and lifted when she turned.

After the meal, Rachel told Sannie, "I can't wait to dance, can you?"

Johannes leaned over and said with forced cheerfulness, "My dancing-mad vrouw had better take it easy tonight; she's not so well, though she's still the most beautiful girl here."

Sannie touched his hand. "If you opened your eyes, dearest, you'd see that your sister's the prettiest of all, as any of these young men would tell you."

Gerrit was listening, and he grinned, nodding vigorously, making Rachel smile.

Sannie turned to her and said quietly, so Johannes could not hear, "You dance for both of us, Sis; it's true, I really don't feel well."

Disguising her own worry, Rachel said, "But you can play the flute for us?"

Sannie nodded, seeming cheerful, though she was paler than usual, even in the light of torches. Johannes would watch her closely, as would Tante Emmy Toulouse, who sat at the end of the table in her large chair, for she was too enormously fat to fit on the bench. Even now, as Tante Emmy held forth on the glory of her prize peacocks and fat-tailed sheep, her keen black eyes were observing Sannie, for whom she would be midwife when the baby came.

At the corner of the table beside Emmy was her husband, André, drinking coffee with gin, contentedly listening to the conversations around him, his blind eyes almost merry, Rachel thought. She wondered again about the fire that he said made Boers kiss like Frenchmen.

Willem Arendt rose to read from the Good Book—the Old Testament, for the New Testament was not of interest to Boers. The entire trek left the tables and gathered close, men holding hats, women and children in an inner circle. Outside the circles of whites were the colored and black servants and their families.

As was the custom of Boers who sought a sign with which to know God's will, Willem opened the Bible at random and, without looking, placed his finger on a page. There, he began to read, there where God had guided his touch. Thus was divine wisdom revealed for the faithful to understand and to follow.

Willem's deep voice carried over the trekkers as he read a passage from Deuteronomy, telling of Moses directing his people to follow the Ten Commandments. The passage closed with, "Hear therefore, O Israel, and observe to do it; that it may be well with thee, and that ye may increase mightily, as the Lord God of thy fathers hath promised thee, in the land that floweth with milk and honey."

What more inspiring instruction than this, as the Boers

prepared to depart for the unknown? Obey the Ten Commandments and increase mightily in the promised land. There followed a moment of silence, and then Willem nodded for Johannes to play a hymn. In the dark of the soft African night, as the strains of the violin lifted, the pioneers stood quietly with heads bowed. These Boers did not sing their hymns. Rather, they silently pondered some inner question, or prayed for revelation, for a practical understanding of what had just been read to them. Rachel was thinking of having to leave her home tomorrow. She still had her own bed for this last night, because the family who had bought the Drente farm would not be moving here for another month.

Strange, but now that she had said goodbye to the graveyard on the hill, it felt as if she had already left Sweetfountain.

After prayers, André's concertina chimed and Johannes's violin began again, this time with dance music. The musicians mounted the back of a trekwagon, and among them with his clarinet was Klaas, the Drentes' old colored servant, whose music Rachel had known all her life. There, too, was Joop, the robust Hottentot servant of the Arendts, tapping gaily on a tambourine and singing. Sannie played her flute as she sat on the end of the wagon. It did Rachel's heart good to see that.

Soon, everyone was laughing and dancing, wine and cider flowing, children weaving in and out of their elders' feet, old women clapping as their fat bellies rocked with merriment. The blacks and coloreds danced together in their own circles and quadrilles, next to their white masters. Firelight and torchlight flickered and blazed in time with the music, and Rachel danced without pause, all the eligible young men striving for a turn at her side. Jaeger, the Boerhound, was suspicious of all of them, sometimes trying to get between Rachel and her partner as they danced. Jaeger whined whenever she shooed him away, and he returned to her side every time there was a new burst of laughter or excitement among the dancers.

How the satin gown did fly when Rachel spun! No other young woman was dressed as splendidly, and no other danced as often with Gerrit Schuman, though many wanted to, especially pretty, blond Anneke Graven, the daughter of the blacksmith. Anneke seemed most able to get Gerrit's attention, and he danced with her more than once, but not as often as he did with Rachel.

Then there came a moment when Gerrit suddenly swung Rachel out of a dancing line, his strength overpowering her.

"Come, meisje, I want to talk to you, alone."

Rachel did not resist, wondering what he had to say. Though she was leaving Sweetfountain, she felt happy tonight and did not mind being courted a little, if that was what he was up to. The wine was strong, the cider stronger, and Rachel was warm inside and out. They moved away from the dancing people and the torchlight, into the lingering twilight of the southern African springtime. As she walked, Rachel watched how the long grass swished, rippling like water against her satin dress. She and Gerrit did not talk, but went around the feast, passing and joking with young lovers huddled here and there in the grass. Soon the folk at the wagons were singing the favorite songs, the sound warm and sentimental. Gerrit put his arm about Rachel's waist, and she let him, feeling just a little intoxicated by it all.

He asked, "What be you thinking?"

"Oh, I was watching how the grass brushes against my gown and wondering if water looks like that when a boat sails on the sea. Ever been in a boat or seen the sea, Gerrit?"

"No, 'course not, I be a farmer. But I seen never-ending grass, and I hear the high veldt can look just like the sea, and here we be on the edge of it."

She liked that. "Gerrit, do you think the earth is flat?"

"What?" He stopped and they faced each other. "'Course it be. Why ask such a thing? By God, Rachel, you be a different creature! So full of questions, and some you should know the answers to. Be the earth flat! I swear, sometimes you sound like an Englishman!"

Rachel resumed strolling, and he followed. She did not take it wrong, what he had said, for she understood him. If only he understood her better.

Then he was saying, "And you even read books, hour after hour when you could be making something useful, or . . . or maybe finding yourself a good man! If nobody told you, there be no good men to be found in them pages of books . . ."

He went on like this, good-humoredly, and Rachel did not mind. The world was beautiful here on the edge of a sea of grass, safe with big, kind-hearted Gerrit Schuman. She enjoyed his company tonight, seeing the dark, starry blue of early evening behind him as he smiled down at her. The singing, and the touch of distant firelight in Gerrit's eyes, the soft night and the thought of sailing on the ocean gave Rachel a rush of good feeling. She sensed that Gerrit might kiss her just then, and she just might let him.

"Rachel," he said softly.

"Yes?"

He put a hand lightly to her waist, and she would take hold of it in a moment.

He said, "I want to give you something."

A kiss? She had never been kissed before by a man who loved

her. Well, if ever there was a moment, this was it, with the old songs, the crescent moon, and the stars and a warm breeze springing up . . .

"Give me what?"

"It's something I know you want very much."

"Do you know me so well?"

"Better than you think." He grinned. "I know what you like, meisje, and it be this!" There before her was the small book of poetry by Vondel, Gerrit holding it up proudly.

"My book!" She reached for it, but he drew it back a little. "How did you get my book?"

"You dropped it at the graveyard, and I thought I could make a horse trade with you for it."

"What trade?" She did not mind his teasing, but it would have been better if he just had kissed her. The singing had stopped now and someone was speaking loudly to the people. It sounded like the hoarse voice of André Toulouse.

Gerrit said, "I'll give back your book for a kiss!" His eyes glittered; he was pleased with himself for what he thought was a witty approach to courting.

Rachel, however, had cooled. She was uneasy because she had written quite a bit in the back of the book, a sort of diary of her feelings, and she had made intimate notes beside poems that meant especially much to her.

In a tone that was more demanding than she meant, she said, "Did you read anything of mine in there?"

Gerrit's gaze went blank and he shrugged. "You know I can't read."

"Of course." Why had he not simply kissed her when the moment was right? He was smiling again, but a little unsure of himself. Rachel cleared her throat. "A kiss for the book?"

"A kiss for the book." He offered it to her.

"Very well, a kiss for the book." She took the volume and touched it lightly to his lips. "Here, a kiss for the book."

"Hey!" he exclaimed as she darted away, laughing, running around the celebration. She did not know why or where she would go, and when at last he caught her, she was breathless, but the romance had gone out of her. Gerrit whirled her into his arms, and she smelled his tobacco and gin and soap, and knew he would have his kiss now. But before Gerrit could kiss her, big Jaeger appeared, whining loudly, and shoving himself between them so that Rachel had to laugh. Gerrit was exasperated, trying to no avail to order the dog away. Then came a loud commotion in the center of the farmyard, and they turned to look.

Everyone was talking at once, crowding around André Toulouse, who was sitting at a table, one hand cranking away at what seemed to be a large glass ball turning within a framework. His other hand pressed some sort of pad to the ball, and there was a wire leading from the pad to a tall glass jar coated in silver foil.

Rachel exclaimed: "Look, Gerrit! I think Uncle André will show us the electri . . . trikaty fire!" She pulled him toward the edge of the people. "Come on!"

"Wait, meisje!"

She did not.

☾ ☾ ☾

Beside André was Tante Emmy, looking proud, and perched majestically on her shoulder was an old green parrot with an orange crest, chattering and swearing in French and Dutch. Wortelkop was its name, "Carrot-top"; it could not fly, and barely managed to flap its wings from time to time.

Johannes Drente was earnestly examining André's glass jar, its top plugged by a cork that had a nail stuck in it. The wire from the pad that André held against the rotating ball was attached to the nail in the cork.

"Ach!" Gerrit scoffed, trying to pull Rachel away. "A damned carnival trick. Come on! Kiss me!"

Suddenly, there was a loud crackle as a blue flame leaped from Johannes's hand, and he sprang back, shaking his fingers. Everyone whooped, dogs barking in fright, some servants diving for cover.

"Machtig!" Johannes shouted. "I'm burned and stabbed and shot all at once!"

Curious, Rachel drew closer to the crowd, and Gerrit followed, more interested himself now.

André laughed and kept cranking at the ball as he declared, "You have touched the blue fire of electricity, the flame of the cosmos, the glory of the stars, and the very force of life itself, my friend!"

"That's sacrilegious to say!" grunted Ton Graven, the blacksmith and the widowed father of pretty Anneke; the squat Ton stuck out his chest so that his massive beard was like a thornbush: "The force of life is from God's hand alone, Frenchman!"

"Of course," André agreed, smiling in the direction of the chuckling Tante Emmy, as if he could see her lolling on the big chair. "But with the magic of my friction machine, we mortals may touch that godly, cosmic force, the fire of life itself, the fire that so surprised my friend Johannes! Touch the bottle again, jonge!"

Johannes did, and once more a bright blue spark appeared, this time knocking him backwards. The people were amazed, babbling among themselves. Johannes was half smiling with delight, and half astonished by what had happened.

"Just like a Lucifer!" he declared.

It had not been long since the folk had discovered safety matches, recently imported from Europe—in fact brought in by André Toulouse. Many Boers did not like to use them because they were called, irreverently, "Lucifers." This blue light of electricity reminded some of them of those devilish matches.

"Electricity is the power of the future," said the blind Frenchman, staring unseeing at the sky. "I have seen in my dreams that electricity under harness will work wonders, will give light and motion and sound and will make great distances as nothing, great weights weightless, and images will be cast from mirror to mirror as if by magic!"

People were glancing in question at one another, not knowing what to think as André went on: ". . . and, my worthy Boer friends, there shall come a day when folk like you will be borne aloft into the sky on airships!"

Ton Graven laughed loudly, turning to the others for agreement, but most were attentive to André, who raised a bony hand and called out to them.

"Now, come one and all! You may feel the thrill of electricity, the cosmic life force distilled and stored in this jar, just the way Myneer Graven distills his powerful gin—now, join hands . . . go on, all of you, join hands, as many as there are, make a great chain together and hold on tightly!"

Some curious, some afraid, many did join hands—but not Sannie, who was told by Tante Emmy to stay back, saying the electricity was "too powerful for the baby in your womb." Finally, seventy people were linked, Boer and servant, young and old, white, black, and colored. The last one in line was Gerrit

Schuman, and second to last was Rachel. By now, Gerrit was not paying much attention, enjoying instead the antics of Tante Emmy's parrot. Wortelkop had clumsily fluttered onto his shoulder and was hurling curses that made Gerrit laugh as he leaned against the iron rim of a wagon wheel.

André cranked hard at the glass ball of the friction machine, and he hummed the song that had become his favorite at significant times like these: "Believe Me, If All Those Endearing Young Charms."

"Is everyone ready?" he called out. "All right, then hold hands tightly! You, Johannes, take good hold of that wire."

Johannes was not so sure anymore, but everyone clamored at him to do so, and he bravely grabbed hold. There was a sudden thrill, as if every muscle in Rachel's arms had been jerked tight. Right beside her, where Gerrit stood, there was a great blue spark that knocked him over, and Wortelkop shrieked like a demon, somehow managing to flap up to the top of a thornbush tree.

The whole chain of people staggered from the electric shock that had thrilled through them, some laughing, some frightened, others stunned with surprise. Above the noise of confusion, Tante Emmy was howling over and over.

"Wortelkop can fly! My dear one can fly!"

"Electric fire!" André chortled with glee. "The glory of the stars, shooting through the bones of southern Africa farmers! Hallelujah to the wonders of science!"

"Let's do it again!" Ton Graven yelled, and many people grabbed hands, while others scurried out of the way.

Not sure whether to giggle or worry, Rachel helped the startled Gerrit to his feet and straightened his hat. She giggled. There was a singed spot on his shoulder where he had been leaning against the wagon wheel, the same shoulder where poor Wortelkop had perched.

"What happened?" Gerrit asked, shaken.

"That," Rachel said, laughing now, "is how the French feel when they kiss."

Gerrit thought a moment, then grinned and pulled Rachel roughly around behind the wagon. "You be half French, meisje. Let's see about that!"

He kissed her hard, and she gasped for air. It was her first kiss like this, the first from a young man who wanted her. She backed against the wagon wheel and pulled away to catch her breath.

Gerrit's eyes were shining, and he laughed, saying, "Machtig! But that were a kiss of French fire! And has a Boer's kiss its own fire, Rachel Drente?"

She held him off a little, trying to catch her breath, and thinking of what to say that would not hurt his feelings. His kiss had been . . . interesting, breathtaking, but there was surely no electric fire there, no fire at all. Before she could answer, there was another commotion, and Tante Emmy was calling loudly for her.

"It be Sannie!" Gerrit said.

Sannie had collapsed, and Johannes was carrying her to the house. Close behind waddled Tante Emmy, clapping her hands and calling to her servants for help.

Frightened, Rachel rushed to follow, asking Emmy, "Is it the baby? Can it be her time so soon?"

Emmy shook her head. "It's the fever, but it may make her give birth before her time, and in my heart I fear for the baby. Say nothing about that to your brother yet, for he has worry enough about his woman."

They hurried inside, and Rachel paused briefly to lean her forehead against a wall and close her eyes.

"Dear God have mercy," she prayed. "Dear God, we've lost so much, and now, when we're ready for Thy promised land, please don't let us lose sweet Sannie, too."

SHAKA AND THE OIL OF YOUTH

At five hundred yards from the Zulu kraal, Mazibe gave a shout that rose above the impi's chants, and the vanguard of the regiment sprang forward as one man, running for the gates.

Dirk stayed with them, excited, feeling strong. He was three strides behind Mazibe, who was increasing speed. Dirk never let anyone run in front of him, not even a Zulu prince. He drove onward fast, gaining on Mazibe, who was shouting praise to Shaka as he sprinted ahead. Dirk surged now, determined to pass him. The gate was coming up rapidly, opening to a long corridor through massed people, and there, Dirk caught the Zulu, who looked surprised. Dirk tried to break ahead. Mazibe did not let him. Stride for stride, they blurred through the kraal gate and down a long corridor lined with torchbearers. Seeing their great induna challenged, the Zulus hushed, so that the feet of the runners could be heard pounding the packed earth of the central kraal.

Dirk stayed at Mazibe's shoulder, with no idea where the race would end. Suddenly, Mazibe was gone, and looming in front of Dirk was an enormous obstacle, ablaze with torches and surrounded by startled Zulus, who held their ground until the last moment and then scattered as Dirk tried to stop short. Too late. He was heading for the very throne of Shaka, a chair of woven reeds and white cattle hides, the king himself in it.

There was only one way to stop. Dirk slid onto his side, skidding across the ground, plowing the last few yards until his feet were just inches from a set of large, bare toes. He looked up at Shaka, who was scowling down, and knew he had blundered. Perhaps fatally.

Lungs heaving, Dirk looked away from those eyes, a cold chill running up his spine. He had violated the royal dignity, and had done it before the entire Zulu nation. Mazibe was nearby, on his knees, forehead touching the ground in obeisance to Shaka. Dirk quickly took the same position, and he knew enough to wait until told to rise.

A vast silence enfolded all those thousands of Zulus, a silence of anticipation, as if everyone was waiting to see how Dirk would be punished for his transgression. For a long time the loudest sounds were the crackle of bonfires and the heavy breathing of Dirk and the king. Then came repressed but painful coughing from someone in the crowd. Next, Dirk heard the patter of feet and the bumping of shield and spear as Mazibe's warriors entered silently into the king's presence to take their places near the front of the people.

Dirk dared not move, not even swallow. His heart pounded as he tried to recover his wind, knowing he must not look up at the king, lest he be considered insolent. He had caused trouble enough. If only Benjamin David would arrive to smooth things over, if that were possible.

With each passing moment, dread grew in him. Yet, what a run that had been! For an instant, cold fear was replaced with excitement.

There came a slight "Hu!" from Shaka, as if clearing his throat, and the silence was shattered by the rolling boom of a voice close by Dirk: "Lord Shaka, Mighty Bull Elephant of the People, is angry!"

It was Mazibe, still kneeling with forehead to the ground as he bellowed, "Mazibe, induna of the uFazimba, what should we do with an insolent white thing who exhibits such abominable disrespect in the royal kraal?"

The induna was for the moment speaking the mind of his king, as was the Bantu custom at such occasions. A king never spoke first, and whenever possible his emotions of anger or fear were not expressed in public—lest his personal magic be discovered and he become vulnerable to the magic of enemies in a time of unguarded weakness. It was a sign of Shaka's profound trust in Mazibe that the induna would speak for the king.

It was also for Mazibe to make reply to the question he had placed on behalf of Shaka, and while he took a moment to ponder, the kraal again fell under an expectant silence, which soon was harshly broken by that sharp coughing.

Looking up at the king's chest, Mazibe addressed Shaka: "O, Great Lion of the People of Heaven, this white thing has come to honor thee from the distant land of horses; he is a loyal companion of inyanga Benjamin, and is the greatest runner of all white things."

Surprised to hear this, Dirk could not help but look in question at Mazibe, who ignored him. Dirk tried keeping his head to the ground while stealing a glance at Shaka. Seeing those glittering, half-closed eyes, Dirk felt stabbed by ice. Gripping the arms of his throne, as if about to spring, Shaka emanated power, unforgiving and terrible. The king of the Zulus was an immense figure, almost too large for his huge throne of white cattle hides. The hides and Shaka's leopard-skin kaross were cast with red from the light of the torches, as were strips of golden fur that formed his kilt and collar. Encircling Shaka's knees and elbows were fringes of white cow tail, and quivering from his headband was the long, blue feather of the lory bird. Though he was only about thirty-five, Shaka's hair was gray, nearly white; and for all his grandeur, the king's face was soft, youthful, except for those intense, bloodshot eyes.

Mazibe said, "Lord Shaka knows well the land of horses, and that their runners are strong—"

That loud wheezing cough suddenly came again. Shaka's cold glance flickered toward the sound. He gave an almost imperceptible movement of a finger, and from behind the throne slipped a skinny youth with overly large eyes and a shaven head. This man drew a knife from his red cloak and stepped toward the crowd, the people gasping in unison and moving away from his approach. In the next moment, a frail old creature was standing alone, hands to his mouth, gaping helplessly and coughing. He backed away as accomplices of the youth with the knife appeared, surrounding him.

The blade flashed. There was a muffled cry.

The Zulus quickly closed in once more. Shaka gave that same "Hu!" and Mazibe went on.

"For thy pleasure, my Lord, I permitted this umlungu to run with me into thy royal presence because I hoped it would please thee to see his strength tested."

Chin on heaving chest, Shaka appeared to be thinking about this. Mazibe was taking full blame for their rowdy entrance, blame that might be met with severe punishment. All the while, the last of Mazibe's regiment was filing quietly into the kraal, forming up in front of the Zulu multitude. Dirk hoped

Benjamin was coming in with them, and soon would be reunited with the king. Now Dirk realized uneasily that Shaka was peering steadily at him.

The king's face was inscrutable, his dark gaze unnerving. Dirk did his best to stare at the ground, but noticed the boy executioner reappear at Shaka's shoulder, looking contented and licking his thin lips as he smiled ever so slightly at Dirk. He was a sly creature, one who did not have the *isiCoco,* the warrior's head ring, which was a token of honored manhood worn by all married Zulu fighting men. The knife he had just used was not visible.

There came a quick and awkward movement from the shadows behind the king as another figure appeared, issuing a long hiss as it pounced to Shaka's side. Dirk was repelled to see a bent and twisted thing, wearing dirty feathers that were thrust every which way into scraggly braids. This creature began pressing against the throne, stroking the cowhides as if longing to touch the king, who sat as impassively as ever. Obviously a witch doctor, he was draped with beads and horns and skins of snakes and as nervous as a snared bird, watchful and frowning, alert for danger. He had a wrinkled face, skin drawn tighter than parchment, the eyes small and sharp, teeth filed to points. As magnificent as was Shaka, so was this creature repulsive, and yet he had to be of some importance to be flitting so freely about Shaka's throne.

Unexpectedly, this toad gave a cackle and bounded at Dirk, who recoiled, and rose to his knees, hand on his knife hilt. The witch doctor stopped face to face with him, staring just above him with a blank, unseeing expression. Stinking foully of dead things and filth, he hissed again and sniffed loudly several times. Then he scrambled around behind Dirk and sniffed again. Dirk held his ground, wary of being stricken from the back, where there was more sniffing and snorting, smacking of lips, and the rattle of bones and beads clicking together.

Shaka was watching closely. Mazibe, too, was intent on every move of this disgusting creature.

Suddenly leaping around in front of Dirk, the witch doctor shrilled, "If there are sorcerers, Dayega will smell them out! Beware! Beware! Sorcerers, beware! Dayega will smell them out! Will smell them out! And they will perish! Perish, impaled and fed alive to Dayega's friends, the crows!"

In the next moment, he was bounding with a shriek into the massed Zulus, who cringed as he passed. Recovering, Dirk paid attention to Shaka, who seemed calmer now. The king looked at Mazibe and spoke solemnly in a deep voice.

"The induna of the uFazimba, as ever, seeks to please his king." He almost smiled, then said, "It was a good run, loyal Mazibe, but you were too polite. You let this white thing stay with you, and Shaka has never seen that happen before."

Mazibe clasped his hands and bowed, answering with a slight smile: "This white thing is thy guest, my Lord. I treated him with kindness."

Dirk would like to see just how kindly Mazibe would treat him in a real race. Win or lose, he wanted more than ever to challenge this induna, and before he left Zululand he would find a way to do it.

Abruptly, Shaka sprang from the throne and pointed at Mazibe's reforming impi, shrieking, "Disloyal wretches!"

He strode a few paces toward Mazibe's startled warriors.

"Does the cherished uFazimba return to the presence of their king without saluting?" The entire regiment stopped moving as Shaka roared at them: "Would you shame your king, we who have loved you, we who have lavished care and fortune upon the uFazimba as upon no other impi? Do you dare bring honored guests into the royal kraal without ceremony, as if the king's very residence were a cowherd's hut?"

Shaka's face was contorted, spittle flying as he screamed, "The king has trusted you above all, uFazimba, but now, do you betray our trust as too many traitors have before? Traitors! Are you, too, traitors to your king, you spoiled and ungrateful wretches?"

Such wild behavior was unbecoming for a Bantu king, Dirk thought, but Shaka howled on against the dismayed impi and seemed on the edge of madness. The young executioner again was close by, eyes alight. Except for him, every other Zulu in the kraal was aghast as this proud regiment was scorched by Shaka's hysterical wrath. Older uFazimba men stiffened. Junior warriors wavered, confused, glancing nervously at one another.

Benjamin had told Dirk that more than one impi had been slain to the last man when the king felt betrayed by them. All Zululand had suffered since the death last year of Shaka's beloved mother, the iron-willed Nandi, who had shaped and nurtured him and guided him to power. Benjamin had said the king was horrified by fear of his death—driven almost mad by the thought that he would be murdered. A number of local chiefs and even important indunas had been executed, accused of plotting assassination. Indeed, there had been a few unsuccessful attempts to murder Shaka, but many complete innocents had been falsely accused and killed on his orders because of his irrational fears.

Shaka gave a slow, empty smile as he asked, "How shall we punish such disrespect, uFazimba?"

Though the warriors had recovered from their initial surprise and now showed no sign of fear, the women and close relations of the impi began to shuffle anxiously, whispering, like a breeze passing through the kraal. Shaka glared all about him, casting suspicious glances here and there, as if seeking, seeking. He trembled, massive fists clenched, mouth working, flecks of foam on his lips. The terror in the kraal was overpowering.

Then Mazibe spoke loudly, smoothly: "Thy devoted impi, O beloved Shaka, wished not to disturb thy profound thoughts, thy sacred contemplation, and thy blessed silence, which lay sublimely upon thy royal kraal when first we came into thy glorious presence."

Mazibe clasped his hands and bowed low. Dirk noticed Shaka's face fall, as if the king were bewildered.

Mazibe proceeded in his beautiful voice: "If we have displeased thee, my Lord, then it is I, thy loyal induna and thy shield, who must beg forgiveness for poor judgment; if there must be punishment, pray, let it be the Shield of Shaka alone who is chastised, for it is my guilt, my error, O Lord."

Shaka looked quickly from Mazibe to the warriors and back again. Unsure, hands opening and closing, he wavered as two thousand lives hung in the balance.

Mazibe raised a fist in salute and called out, "Say the word, my Lord, and thy loyal uFazimba impi shall sing in praise of thee and worship the memory of thine ancestors until the stars shake and the heavens shudder with tales of thy mighty deeds!"

Shaka appeared too distressed to reply. Again silence enveloped the kraal. Then, with a stamp of his foot, Shaka gave a grunt of frustration and sat down heavily on the throne, sulking. The executioner in the red cloak stepped out of sight once more.

Shaka again gave a curt "Hu!"

Mazibe bellowed to the kraal, "Bring forth the honored

inyanga Benjamin! Let him soothe our aching heart with gifts!"

Shaka beamed, leaning forward on his throne. Mazibe stood and motioned for Dirk to rise and step back. Dirk sensed that the king had been foiled by the bold Mazibe, and that Shaka seemed unable or unwilling to punish the induna, who looked so composed, head bowed, hands clasped. Mazibe was obedient, but clearly had some powerful influence over the king.

Just then the uFazimba ranks parted. Through the breach strode Benjamin David, followed by Tom Lovell and then Sebe. Benjamin knelt and touched his forehead to the ground, Lovell awkwardly following. Dirk saw profound terror in the man, but Lovell was fighting down his dread, and that was to his credit.

Sebe's appearance took Dirk by surprise, for the Xhosa was wearing a lion's claw in the center of his forehead, held by a thong. Some personal magic. Sebe, too, bowed deeply in homage to the Zulu king, but Dirk thought he appeared full of juice, too sure of himself. When Sebe came to stand beside him, Dirk meant to keep a close eye on the Xhosa. Crawling on hands and knees behind Benjamin came the bearers, all of them shaking with fright, clutching blankets filled with gifts for Shaka.

To Dirk's amazement, Shaka actually laughed aloud and opened his arms wide, as if to receive Benjamin. Of course Benjamin could not touch Shaka, but he straightened up and ceremoniously opened his own arms, exchanging flowery greetings and passing along the warm regards of cousin George in Windsor Castle.

It was bizarre to see Shaka suddenly so joyful, when he had just been ablaze with a killing fury. Truly, the Zulu king had high regard for Benjamin David. He even spoke directly to Benjamin, a remarkable honor.

"Too long have we awaited your return to kwaBulawayo, inyanga!" he declared, "Too long have our impis searched the borderlands for some sign of you. When you left, you promised to return soon, but it was not soon. Now that you are again with us, the king can rest peacefully once more."

In response, Mazibe led a mighty cheer from the multitude, hailing the happiness of their king: *"Bayete! Bayete!"*

Benjamin broke into a grin as boyish as it was pleased. The uFazimba began a stamping dance, four thousand feet moving as one, their oiled bodies gleaming in the firelight. Shaka contentedly sat back, legs splayed, utterly relaxed, watching Benjamin beckon for the bearers to drag forth the blankets and uncover the gifts for the king.

Shaka stood up to walk beside the colorful blankets and cheerfully inspect the many things that lay upon them. He laughed with delight. Overjoyed, the thousands and thousands in the kraal sent up their own songs that mingled and blended and thundered against the uFazimba chorus. Drums broke into fast rhythms, other dancing began, and the royal kraal resounded with happiness.

☾ ☾ ☾

The only unpleasantness in that genial scene was the sudden reappearance of the scuffling, jerky little witch doctor called Dayega, who sniffed at Sebe and moved along to annoy Lovell and the frightened bearers.

Sebe leaned over to Dirk and whispered, "Zulus fear that malignant sorcerers will come here disguised as strangers, and this ugly one must smell them out, if he can. When sorcerers are smelled out, they die by torture."

Dirk knew that if Dayega accused even one of Benjamin's people of being a sorcerer, and Shaka believed him, it would go badly for them all.

With a sound of disgust, Sebe said, "Many an innocent induna with too much cattle has been accused of sorcery by the evil Dayega and executed. Shaka gets the dead man's cattle, and Dayega earns Shaka's gratitude. Have a care for this stinging adder, Baas."

The stamping of feet and the singing drowned out Dayega's voice as he did his own dance, hopping back and forth, eyeing Dirk with that blank yet malevolent stare, nostrils flaring, as if sniffing something.

On his knees, Benjamin explained each gift to Shaka: Mirrors and jewelry, fine silk cloth, ceremonial swords, and delicate lace; here were the best English shirts with ruffles, and combs of all sizes, beaver hats for occasions of ceremony, "just like your cousin, King George, wears, and here are harmonicas to delight the children. . . ."

Shaka was pleased. There was snuff and sweet condiments, even some of those newfangled tin cans, called "preservers," containing oysters from New York City. Shaka picked up a magnifying glass and looked through it, turning to stare right at the fish-eyed executioner, who was close behind. Both men jumped back, startled by what they saw through the glass. Sebe chortled aloud, and it seemed he attracted Shaka's attention, though the king did not look at him.

Shaka grunted and threw the glass down. Dirk gave Sebe a look of warning, but the Xhosa only winked and covered his mouth. Benjamin was speaking again, walking alongside Shaka, and pointing out more gifts.

"And for thy sisters—" Shaka had no wives, but twelve hundred "sisters" in his *isiGodlo,* or harem, and none dared become pregnant if they wanted to survive, for he was said to be impotent. "—we have needles and thread, ribbons and beads and cloth of every color and description, stockings and handkerchiefs, pots and kettles, and here are enough tin whistles to supply them all."

As Shaka strode past, admiring the goods, Benjamin took the opportunity to pause beside Dirk and say, "Keep away from that witch doctor, because he hates me, thinks I challenge him for the king's affection. And make sure Sebe does nothing rash, for the old goat believes he's protected by magic tonight."

Dirk watched Dayega shuffling on his knees, coyly playing up to Shaka, begging permission to choose a tin whistle. At a nod from Shaka, Dayega shrieked with joy and bounded across the clearing, blowing harshly on the shrill whistle.

Dirk said to Benjamin, "If that witch doctor touches me I'll be hard put not to throw him over the wall, but I can't predict what Sebe might do."

"If Sebe acts the fool, Shaka will cook him," Benjamin replied. "But, as you can see, I've got our Zulu nabob quite happy now."

Lovell was beside them, and he whispered, "When can you ask Shaka about the bull's-head amulet, Benjamin? You saved his life, and you've given him all those presents whenever you came here. He owes it to you."

"Hush about the amulet!" Benjamin replied. "We'd best take care how we inquire about—"

Dayega was close by, scrabbling on the ground, his breath pushing little squeaks through the tin whistle, which stuck out of his mouth. The creature sniffed rudely about the legs of Lovell, who whined in revulsion, making as if to kick at him.

Dirk got between Dayega and Lovell and stepped discreetly on the witch doctor's toes, causing him to scramble back with a yelp.

Benjamin spoke to Dirk.

"Watch out for this lap dog of the king, but let him play his act. He's harmless because he won't dare accuse us of being sorcerers, for that wouldn't go down well with Shaka, not as long as he adores our gifts."

Dayega had crawled a little distance away, playing the whistle, malignant eyes on Lovell, who well knew it.

Benjamin said, "Shaka will do much for our gifts, even if he has to contradict a witch doctor's smelling-out." Then he cheerfully rejoined the king.

Dirk nudged Lovell, saying with an encouraging wink, "Don't worry about this scabby little rascal, Tom; he won't come near you again, I'll see to that."

"I'll be all right." Lovell swallowed. "I'll be all right."

Dirk thought the poor fellow might faint, and for a moment was prepared to catch him. Then Shaka gave a long, slow chuckle, and a hush passed through the Zulus as they became still to hear their king. Except for his rolling laugh, the kraal was completely silent.

Shaka said gaily, "These are truly gifts of love, inyanga, gifts to uplift our heart! Truly, you deserve to eat of our *amaSi!*"

Milk curds, or amaSi, were given only to a Zulu's very closest and most trusted friends. Benjamin, too, was beaming. Lovell hung on every word as Dirk whispered the translation. Dirk saw that Sebe, crouching beside him, had his eyes almost shut, as if he were thinking hard while listening to Shaka.

"And because we honor you, inyanga, for saving our life, we grant you, in return, your companion's life." That got Dirk's attention. "We will not execute this white thing from the land of horses for his insult to us, for we know he is ignorant of the ways of the People of Heaven. He is forgiven. His life, inyanga, now belongs to you."

As Benjamin bowed, Dirk's insides turned over.

Quietly, Shaka said, "Mark well, inyanga, that we no longer owe you anything."

Shaka had found a way to repay his debt to Benjamin; no African king wanted to remain obligated to anyone, for it compromised his pride and royal magic. They were even, Shaka and Benjamin, and that weakened Benjamin's position with the king, who surely wanted it that way. Then Shaka raised his muscular arms and called out so all could hear him.

"And now, faithful inyanga, we are prepared for the most wonderful gift, which you promised to bring us, the gift for which we have waited so anxiously these many moons! We are ready and are overjoyed to receive it!"

Benjamin no longer beamed. He smiled uncertainly and cleared his throat. Lightly wiping his lips, he glanced at Sebe, who had been here with him last time and might know what Shaka meant. It was apparent from the Xhosa's expression that he did not know either.

"For the glory of the amaZulu, the people of heaven!" Shaka exclaimed. "The founder of their nation, their king and creator, will be anointed with the blessed oil of youth!" Led by Mazibe, the people shouted in salute, and Shaka cried out, "Anoint us now, honored inyanga, as you promised to do!"

The Zulus roared, "Bayete!"

Shaka was impassioned, arms raised, awaiting the oil of youth. Benjamin bowed, said something complimentary and excused himself, leaving Shaka with arms uplifted. Benjamin came to his friends.

Sebe stood up as Benjamin asked, "What does he mean? What oil of youth?"

Sebe was thinking hard.

"What in God's name, Benjamin!" Lovell gasped. "You don't know what he wants?"

Shaka boomed out a giddy laugh: "The oil of youth will rejuvenate the Bull of the Nation, invigorate the Black Elephant of the amaZulu." Mazibe raised another cheer, and Shaka laughed once more, shouting, "When last you departed, inyanga, we sent scores of runners seeking far and wide through all the known world for the wondrous rejuvenator of which you had told us."

Benjamin looked worried now as he fumbled through his kit bags and then through those of Sebe and Lovell, if only to buy time while he tried to comprehend what exactly the king meant.

Shaka went on happily: "But no runner was successful in the quest, and all paid for failure with their lives! Now you have returned at last to us with the oil of youth, inyanga, and in honor of this glorious moment, we have called all our children to kwaBulawayo, every Zulu from far and wide, with all our sacred cattle, to witness the great moment of anointment!"

Benjamin bowed again to Shaka, smiling broadly, then turned back to his friends, as if consulting them about the ceremony. His lips were white, and he spoke hoarsely: "I . . . I just don't understand—"

Dirk was prepared for whatever might happen. He wished his horse were here, and his rifle. Then, at least, he would go down fighting, like a Boer.

Lovell whispered, "Hurry, Benjamin, please! Do something quickly!"

"Inyanga!" Shaka called out. "We are ready."

"Benjamin!" Lovell pleaded. "Quickly! For God's sake!"

Dayega crept close, observing, prying, sensing something amiss with the whites, though he could not understand their tongue. The tin whistle wheezed with his breathing, and he worked himself closer until Dirk stepped into his path. Dayega rose and bounded around them, sniffing, cackling, wheezing, and whistling.

"Inyanga!" Shaka called.

"Yes, O King." Benjamin motioned with a hand, as if about to make that fabled oil of youth somehow materialize. Dayega was chanting and whistling, hopping faster and faster around them now.

Shaka laughed and cried out to his people, "Behold! The oil of youth, the magic potion that renews vigor, that cheats death, that darkens the graying hair!"

"What?" With a look of dismay and surprise, Benjamin sprang around to face Shaka. "Macassar oil!" Benjamin blurted out in Dutch, which Shaka could not comprehend.

"He means hair tonic—hair dye!" Benjamin declared to his friends. "Dear God! I promised him Rowland's Macassar oil to color his gray hair! But I'd no idea it meant so much to him, or that he'd consider it a tonic of youth. I forgot about it!"

"Rowland's?" Lovell gushed. "Why, I've got six bottles of it back at Port Natal! Oh, if only I'd known—"

Benjamin quickly raised his hands to address Shaka: "O king, I will bestow the oil of youth which I have promised, but it . . . it is not with me now."

Shaka frowned, a storm overtaking him.

Benjamin attempted a smile. "We do have the oil of youth, my Lord, it's just not in our possession at this very moment. I can explain—"

Shaka snarled.

"Not here? The oil of youth for which we have longed so, for which we have waited, day after day, while we have aged day after day and have contested death's tightening grip! You solemnly promised!"

"My dear King—"

Shaka picked up a ceremonial sword and scabbard and snapped them over his knee. "You, inyanga, who have been protected by the royal hand, who have dined upon royal milk, you would break such a promise!"

"No, Shaka! I do have the oil, but—"

Shaka hurled the broken sword and scabbard at Benjamin's feet.

"Have you, too, betrayed us, inyanga?"

Dayega was again at the startled Lovell's legs, nipping at the Englishman's trousers. Lovell moaned. Furious, Dirk caught Dayega by the scruff of the neck and pitched him to the ground in a clatter of bony limbs and a cloud of dust.

"Sorcerer!" the witch doctor shrieked and sprang up, pointing at the terrified Lovell. "Sorcerer! Dayega has smelled him out! Sorcerer! A sorcerer in disguise come to cast a fatal spell upon the Lord Shaka!"

Lovell frantically asked what the man was saying, but Dirk did not reply, lest the fellow collapse. Shaka was startled. Mazibe came to his side, looking worried. Dayega bounced around, screaming that he had smelled out a sorcerer "who must be expelled, must be killed!"

Shaka's eyes were wide as he glared at the uncomprehending Lovell, who cast about, not knowing what was happening. Benjamin was in shock. It was all happening too fast. The situation was beyond him now. Suddenly, there came a high-pitched howl of derision that shut up the squealing Dayega.

It was Sebe, who slapped his thighs, bent over, and held his sides as he hooted. Then he pointed at Dayega, who stopped his capering. Sebe laughed good-humoredly, every eye in the kraal upon him. Straightening up, he stepped forward and bowed elegantly to Shaka.

"O mighty Lord, Mountain of Africa," Sebe declared loudly. "Permit it to be announced that this worthless carrion-eater is a fraud!" Pointing at Dayega, he threw his head back and howled derisively again, and the witch doctor scrambled to the king's feet, hissing in anger.

Shaka looked at Mazibe, but the induna made no reply, seeming only intent on what Sebe would do or say next.

Dayega shrieked, fingers working like claws: "I have smelled a sorcerer, my Lord, and now must thee slay—"

Sebe roared and sprang into the air, bounding like a bird of prey toward the witch doctor, throwing up his arms and flapping them as he came down. Shaka did not flinch, but Dayega took shelter behind the king's legs.

"Liar!" Sebe shouted at Dayega. "Fraud! You are no smeller of sorcerers! Were you a smeller-out, you would not have passed Sebe by, for he is a sorcerer of magnificent proportions! Sebe-rainmaker, Sebe-diviner, Sebe-changeling, he who discerns secrets, invisible hunter and destroyer of crocodiles! Be gone you fraud, lest Sebe vanish and appear again in your belly, as Sebe-mamba who would feed on your heart were it not so foully black and poisoned!"

Dayega scampered to the other side of Shaka and shrilled, "Slay him, my Lord! Slay him lest he threaten the sacred bull's head!"

"Aha!" Sebe bellowed and stepped back, again bowing low in careful deference to Shaka. Then he spoke to the king, just loud enough for Dirk and the others to hear him: "Yes, O Shaka, the bull's head set with the crystal stone of white fire is known to Sebe-diviner!"

Shaka gave a start, and glared at Sebe, who bowed again and said placidly, "O Shaka, thy sacred possession is known to Sebe, greatest sorcerer of the Xhosa, who cares nothing for such secrets, for they are the affairs of kings only, affairs too lofty for mere sorcerers."

Sebe paused, hands to his temples, waiting.

Shaka stirred. "Hu!"

Sebe spoke in cheery tone of delight and surprise: "Behold, my magic has brought me a vision—a vision that would be revealed to the king!"

He paused.

"Hu!"

In the next moment, Sebe was dancing, arms spread as if in flight, and he loudly sang his tale so all could hear it: "One windy night when the moon lay on her back, an eagle flew across the heavens and was blown by good fortune over Zululand, and as the eagle soared he saw to his horror a traitorous crocodile slithering into the king's kraal, to feed and warm itself at the king's fire!"

The people gasped, and Shaka listened intently.

"The crocodile lurked by the king's fire, disguised as a loyal subject, but the wise eagle saw with keen eye that the crocodile would prove false . . . to Lord Shaka!"

Sebe soared about the clearing.

"This crocodile is a threat! In the royal kraal is a threat, a danger from one who has eaten the king's amaSi. In the king's own kraal, one would betray the royal trust, and . . . and. . . ."

Sebe stopped, as if unable to go on. He faced Shaka and lowered his eyes, which were filled with sorrow. Tears actually appeared on Sebe's wrinkled cheeks.

"Speak on!" Shaka demanded.

"That traitor crocodile crawls at the king's praiseworthy feet; that betrayer is the crocodile who huddles now behind thy shining garment!" Then Sebe half-whispered, "And he would take thy bull's-head amulet from thee!"

Dayega hissed in protest, but seemed dazed, as if overpowered by Sebe's tremendous force of will. Dirk noticed for the first time an imposing figure at the forefront of the crowd. He was a tall, bearded man who also wore the leopard skin of royalty. He seemed to hang on Sebe's words.

"Dayega the fraud, the liar! The traitor crocodile! Sebe has seen it, for it was he who soared, when the moon was on her back, soared as an eagle above kwaBulawayo!"

The people were agitated, jabbering and confused. Dirk guessed that Dayega was not loved, for he had caused much sorrow and bloodshed. Still, Dirk was as confused as anyone. Had his friend gone mad? To call a witch doctor a crocodile was to accuse him of being an fake. Of course, to hear Sebe openly, boldly, admit to being a sorcerer himself was astonishing to the Zulus, who were used to executing accused sorcerers, dragging them away kicking and screaming as they denied everything to their last breath. Would Shaka have this uncloaked sorcerer slain? Dirk wanted to do something, but he, too, was entranced by Sebe's performance, which was not yet over.

"Dayega has no witchcraft!" Sebe bellowed to the people. "He is a crocodile!"

With that, Sebe fell to his knees before Shaka, forehead to the ground, unmoving. The Zulu throng roared, and even Shaka appeared concerned by their sudden surge forward against the restraining ranks of the uFazimba. The tall man in the leopard skins withdrew again into the mob, as if he had heard enough.

Dayega sprang up to protest, but Shaka cuffed him down, shouting for quiet.

"Sorcerers and treachery in our kraal!" the king cried out. "Eagles and crocodiles!" He shook a fist. "Silence! Shaka must have silence to think . . . to think deeply!"

The Zulus hushed, but they were restive. Shaka glanced at Mazibe, who attended him closely. The induna put a hand inside his own kaross, as if touching something hidden there. Shaka and he were speaking quietly, as all the while, Dayega whimpered at the king's feet. Shaka took something from Mazibe and turned to look at Dayega, who shuddered and began to slide away backwards. Shaka stared at him. It was a penetrating gaze that made the witch doctor tremble, then whine softly, and at last slowly lie down on his side and become silent.

With a deep sigh, Shaka turned and looked at Sebe, who respectfully kept his forehead close to the ground. Even Benjamin dared not interfere. Lovell was breathless behind his handkerchief. Shaka seemed uncertain, beginning to shake. Dirk could think of only one way to forestall the storm he feared was about to break upon them all.

It was a gamble.

"O mighty Lord, whose wounds emit smoke and flame!" he shouted, then dropped to his knees, arms outstretched. "I beg leave to reveal inyanga Benjamin's plan for a glorious celebration of the oil of youth, an anointment, a great festivity never before seen in Zululand, a spectacle to honor the great Shaka's triumph over . . . gray hair!"

Even Sebe was speechless now.

Shaka cocked his head, again eyeing Mazibe, who nodded ever so slightly. The king stepped toward Dirk, and something gleamed in the hand he held against his chest.

"There have been many gifts and surprises for us this night," Shaka said resolutely and gestured at the kneeling Sebe. "Even a visit from a benevolent sorcerer."

The casual movement of Shaka's hand revealed a golden amulet, and Dirk caught his breath to see it shine, giving off a white sparkle from the crystal stone. He restrained himself from gaping, but heard Lovell gulp and exclaim to Benjamin.

"The amulet!"

Shaka gave all his attention to Dirk.

"Speak about the oil of youth!" Shaka thrust forth the amulet so that it dangled, glimmering, before Dirk's eyes. "Speak, by the power of Nzambi Ya Mpungu, Ancient of the Ancients! Look upon the face of your desire! Look, and speak the truth!"

Dirk stared, transfixed, at the shining crystal between the horns of the golden bull, the crystal glowing white, becoming brighter than the torchlight in the kraal, whiter and more dazzling, until it was almost blinding. The voice of the Zulu king echoed over and over.

"Look upon the face of your desire! The face of your desire . . . of your desire!"

Dirk felt to be dreaming or intoxicated, but he was clear-headed, though overpowered by that glorious white fire. He wanted to reach out and touch it, but could not move. He heard, ". . . the face of desire . . ."

A jolt shook Dirk, forcing him to blurt out, "O terrible Shaka, who kills for joy, this white person challenges thy greatest runner!"

Dirk was breathless, speaking against his will, yet saying what he truly wished to say, even using the respectful term umuntu, "person," not the derogatory "white thing," as the Zulus called him.

"I challenge the Zulu champion to a test of speed and endurance, each of us to carry the hair tonic back to Zululand from our camp by the sea! Whoever triumphs will be supreme champion of both Zulus and Boers." He could not help adding, "And by God I would run until my heart burst to defeat thy induna, Mazibe of the uFazimba!"

Dirk staggered then, as if struck, and fell to his knees. He could barely breathe. He could not see.

There was a face, the face of desire, the face of a woman. He called out to her, but she did not answer. Who was she? He knew her, but from where? She was a Boer daughter, dark-haired, strong and beautiful, and she knew him. She loved him.

☾ ☾ ☾

The glaring white fire had withdrawn.

Dirk was still on his knees. Shaka was above him. The king's face showed calm interest. A spell had broken. Behind Shaka, Mazibe was smiling.

Enclosing the amulet in his hand once more, Shaka asked over his shoulder, "How say you, induna? Is this white thing a worthy challenge?"

Mazibe bowed and clasped his hands. "Thy will is my will, O Lord." He looked at Dirk as he said to Shaka, "It would be my honor to bear the oil of youth back from the sea to my king, and a worthy challenge to defeat this white champion."

Dirk's heart leaped. Shaka laughed and turned to Mazibe, pressing the amulet back inside the induna's kaross.

"So be it!" Shaka called out, and raised his arms for the throng to cheer, which they obediently did; then, grinning amiably, he turned to the astounded Benjamin David, whose mouth hung open. "Once again, inyanga, you have found a way to please us. *Boyala* for the guests!"

As gourds of boyala—beer—were brought forth, Shaka cheerfully went to look through the presents, chatting with Mazibe, who occasionally glanced at Dirk, sizing him up. The Zulu masses again began to sing for happiness, and the uFazimba closed ranks, once more to dance in place.

Dirk saw Benjamin slump a little against Lovell, each holding up the other. The Englishman's lips were parched, face and clothing soaked. He trembled as he drank some beer. Benjamin was pale as he sat staring into the gourd, held in both quivering hands. Dirk accepted boyala, drank deeply, and sighed. That burning white light from the amulet had left him confused as well as dazzled, for he was not given to believing in magic. Yet some mighty power had touched him, that he knew. Just then he felt something flutter inside, as if his heart had taken a blow. His thoughts whirled, and he wondered what that bull's-head talisman was all about. Why was it so important to Lovell? What did it do for Shaka?

Dirk had the most inexplicable urge to see it again, to touch it, to hold it, if just for a moment. The image of the golden bull and the shining crystal shimmered before him, until it was replaced by the face of that lovely woman, so familiar. He was distracted by Sebe, still kneeling nearby, closely observing him. Dirk winked. Then there came a flurry of movement to one side, and the bedraggled, defeated Dayega was being helped away by the bearded man in the leopard skin. Dirk asked Benjamin who that was.

"Prince Dingaane," Benjamin answered, slowly recovering. "Shaka's half-brother and next in line for the throne; if there are traitors drinking the royal milk, he could be one. I don't think he'll be allowed to live much longer, and he must know it, too."

Then Sebe was with them, as cool and relaxed as ever, quaffing boyala, draining the gourd. When it was clear they were dismissed, they moved off together to pass through the ring of torches.

"You saved Tom Lovell's life," Benjamin said, affectionately patting Sebe on the shoulder. "But had you failed, it would have cost your own."

"Impossible to fail, Baas Benjamin," Sebe replied, giving an easy laugh as he went toward the expedition's extra packs, which had been laid in the darkness, away from the mass of singing Zulus. "Tonight Sebe is invulnerable, so says my god; invulnerable. And now, I fetch my pipe, for an old sorcerer deserves a smoke."

He chuckled and passed beyond the light of the torch ring, the others following. Then, from the darkness there came a grunt and the sound of Sebe stumbling. Dirk and Benjamin hurried to his side, kneeling down.

"He tripped and hit his head," Benjamin said. "Our sorcerer's out cold."

THE TREK DEPARTS

At break of dawn, Rachel pushed open the top half of the kitchen door and let in the morning light. Closing her eyes and breathing deeply, she felt exhausted, having been awake all night tending the delirious Sannie, who had come down with another attack of fever. Mercifully, Sannie was asleep now, the fever broken, but the relapse had been severe.

The Drente farmyard was strangely quiet this morning, even lonely now that the animals had been taken away for the trek. The Drente cattle and extra horses had been on the move northward for days, driven to water holes at the northern reaches of the farm. Selected chickens, geese, ducks, turkeys, and peacocks had been crated and loaded onto a trekwagon for the journey, the rest sold off or slaughtered to be preserved for food. Goats and sheep had been counted, marked with Drente ear crops, and taken out to pasture to be driven into the main trekker flocks. Even the cats were gone this morning, as if they knew that things were changing, since the milk cow was not standing in the barn.

Rachel gave a low whistle to Tempest out in the kraal, and he snorted, pricking up his ears, his handsome head looking back over the stone wall. This was the time of day when Rachel loved to ride Tempest across the veldt, wet with dew, until she and the chestnut stallion were soaked and steaming as they galloped home for breakfast. Jaeger appeared in the farmyard, padding up to the door and standing on his hind legs to have his floppy ears rubbed. He was golden brown, with short hair and a contrary ridge growing down his back, giving his breed the name "ridgeback."

"So, dog, one day in the wild we may see if you were truly bred to fight lions, like a real Boerhound." Rachel let him lick her cheek, then faced the orange rising of the sun.

Distracted by the caw of a crow on the orchard wall, she let her eyes rove around the silent farmyard, usually so bustling and noisy at this time of day. The stable hands and herd boys were weary from dancing late into the night, and anyway what work was there to do on a farm that was being left behind in a few hours? Johannes should have been out on the veldt with the cattle, but he was still at Sannie's bedside, along with Tante Emmy, who had been a godsend that night, mixing potions and medicines and likely saving Sannie's life.

Rachel turned and leaned against the door, looking around at the nearly empty kitchen as if seeing it for the first time. The farmhouse was thirty-five years old, built by Rachel's father to last. It was one level and solid, of thick timber and plastered fieldstone, its windows shuttered to withstand a native raid or a fierce rainstorm. Yet when those windows were open, as they were now, the house filled with sunlight, especially on spring mornings like this, when the sun was low.

Every room had fine, wooden puncheon floors, not the packed earth coated with beeswax that was good enough for so many Boers; and the walls were whitewashed inside and out.

The ceiling beams were bare now, the drying herbs and pots taken down and crated. The bookcase, too, was bare, the kitchen cupboards Johannes had built now empty. Rachel had left the light blue curtains in the kitchen windows, so the new owners might feel at home, or at least would remember that someone had loved this place before them. She thought to pick some wildflowers and put them in a vase, as her mother always did . . . but there was no point to that when they were leaving as soon as Sannie could be lifted into a wagon.

For the first time in her life Rachel imagined this land before the farm, when her parents had found it open, deep in grass, without the orchard and its wall, without the oaks near the barn that once had been saplings, without the garden in low ground down by the spring, and without horses in a walled kraal. How could that time before ever have been? Would the new homeland one day really be like that for her, untouched, unproductive, empty, save for wilderness and the need for backbreaking work?

Tante Emmy came into the kitchen from Sannie's room and sat down heavily at the long table. Spreading her fat legs and leaning back, Emmy wiped her face with the sleeve of her best green dress, worn especially for the feast and not changed since last night. It was wrinkled now, and she looked utterly spent. Rachel, who had put on pantaloons for riding, wanted to sit a while with Emmy before going out. Rachel set down two beakers and fetched coffee from the large pot that, in a Boer house, was never empty.

"How is it with Sannie?" she asked.

Tante Emmy slurped, then poured more cream into the beaker.

"Not good, child. She needs rest, much rest, and the babe she carries needs to be protected, not taken out onto the veldt in a bouncing trekwagon."

Rachel saw the glint of a tear in Emmy's dark eyes.

"Verdommte trek!" Emmy cursed. "Verdommte uitlanders! They drive us to the ends of the earth with their laws and their meddling!"

"But we go to the promised land, Tante."

Even though she was not so keen on going, Rachel had thought of the trek as a glorious deliverance of God's chosen people from the Egyptian bondage of English law. Theoretically, at least.

Emmy looked at Rachel and shook her head. "Is there a more bountiful land than this? A finer farmhouse than this? Whatever land we find will be unclothed, raw, and in need of hard labor. How many years in the promised land will it take to build a house like this, to grow pear trees like those?"

She drank coffee and wiped away a tear with the sleeve of her dress.

"Ach, my man wants to trek just because he's always been on the move, and the old fool thinks these Boers will find gold and diamonds under the rivers one day. Verdommte! Rachel, tell me what a Boer would do with gold and diamonds? All a Boer wants is the good life, healthy children, a fat, pretty woman, and the veldt covered with his herds begetting more herds! Will this trek truly bring them that good life?"

Rachel knew all the right answers for trekking now, about liberty and the *lekker leven,* "the good life," the awaiting land of plenty and the guiding hand of God. Yet she felt much as Tante Emmy did just then and could not help but slurp at her own coffee and sniff. She tried not to cry, for she heard Johannes coming from the bedroom.

Wearily, he sat down to a beaker Rachel poured for him. He was as rumpled and haggard as Emmy, and still wearing his best clothes from last night. Rachel had never seen her brother so troubled, his eyes hollow and distant as he patted Emmy's hand. Then, choosing each word slowly, he continued what must have been a previous discussion with her:

"Ja, Tante, you're right. Now I've thought about it. We'll stay behind until Sannie is strong enough to travel."

Rachel was startled, for she had not considered this. She looked from one to the other as Emmy nodded sagely, not displaying her satisfaction, though she hummed to herself and took another cup of coffee. Apparently she had been laboring hard to persuade Johannes not to go yet.

Rachel asked her brother, "You mean we'll stay here? How long do you think?"

Johannes drew a breath and sat back in the chair, rubbing his eyes. "Tante Emmy thinks it may be two weeks before Sannie's well enough to travel, maybe three—"

"A month," Emmy interrupted. "She's so weak."

"Very well," Johannes said, "but if we push ourselves, we can catch up to the trek in three weeks."

Rachel did not know what to think. It was troubling to contemplate the idea of their family going out there alone, with only Johannes and old Klaas and the herd boys to protect them. But she realized they would risk Sannie's life and that of the baby by going now. Rachel prayed silently that they would catch up to the trek without meeting danger.

One family on a lonely *trekpad* could suffer from lions or half-caste outlaw bandits or from roving bands of wild natives. Crossing the sandy drifts of dry riverbeds would be tedious work for one family with three laden wagons. Storms would leave them desperately struggling to protect their stock, forced to spend days collecting their animals after they had been stampeded by lighting. Rachel had heard all about such things.

Johannes must have known her concern, for he took her hand and said not to worry. "We'll catch up before long, Sis."

Rachel tried to smile. "Perhaps it's just that I've become used to all these trekkers being here, and I'll miss them when they go."

There was silence until Johannes said he had to see to Sannie. Just before he left the room, Emmy grabbed his arm.

"You won't be alone," she said and looked from him to Rachel and back. "My man and I will stay with you."

Johannes gave Emmy a rough kiss on the cheek, and her sides shook as she laughed. Rachel was delighted, for although old André was blind, Emmy's servants would be a great help. Further, Rachel loved and trusted Emmy, who was so capable and knowledgeable.

"Oh, Tante Emmy, you're precious!" She kissed Emmy and made her laugh once more.

"All right! All right! Machtig, you'd think I was Sinte Klaas himself come to bless you! Go to your wife, Johannes; and you, girl, go and say goodbye to your friends before they pull away."

Johannes said to Rachel, "Sis, I know you'll be sorry to part with Gerrit."

"What?" That startled her, for she really had not thought about Gerrit Schuman one way or the other. "Why do you say that?"

Johannes winked at Emmy, who was watching Rachel closely.

"We all saw you slip away with Gerrit last night, and—"

"Stop!" Rachel sputtered as she tried to find the right words of protest. "We just went for a stroll, a look at the grass, and to talk—you know, about how it seems like the sea sometimes."

Johannes smiled. "A look at the grass, eh? From the ground up, I'll wager."

"Before God!" Rachel did not like to hear this, and she was more resentful than embarrassed. "You're as much a kerel as Gerrit, you are! And what business is it of yours, anyway?"

Johannes moved toward Sannie's room and said over his shoulder, "Until you marry Gerrit and belong to him, you're certainly my business, Sis. But don't be so touchy, for I was only teasing."

"Who says I'll marry Gerrit? Belong to him! Bah! Will you arrange it as they did in the old days?" She was now plainly angry. "I thought you were a free-thinking man!"

"Shall I arrange the marriage, then?" Johannes had humor in his eyes. "Won't he ask you himself? Maybe Tante Emmy can give you some hints on how to make a man propose even if he's too shy."

Emmy interrupted with a wave of her fat hand. "Hold on, Johannes, go easy on the child."

"She's no child."

"No!" Rachel almost shouted. "I'm no child, and I need no one to arrange a marriage for me! Perhaps I won't ever marry, and you'll have to watch over me until I shrivel up and die at your kitchen fire in the promised land."

Johannes smiled. "Say the word, Sis, and I'll tell Gerrit how to win your hand if he hasn't won it yet."

Emmy waved at him again. "Go to Sannie, Johannes, and let nature take its course with Rachel and her beau."

"Gerrit Schuman's not my beau!" Rachel was exasperated now, though she knew both Emmy and Johannes really only meant the best for her. "And if I want him to propose, I'll make it happen my own way!"

Johannes suddenly was serious, and he said, "Rachel, if you want to go off with him now, it's all right with me—"

"Before God, you're a pig-headed Boer, Johannes!" She shook her head and drew a long breath in helplessness. "I'm staying with you and Sannie, and that's that."

Johannes grinned, saying, "That's good, for now." He went to look in on Sannie.

Rachel and Tante Emmy faced each other, and Emmy said, "For the moment, it is good that you stay with your brother and Sannie, child, but you have to think of the future, too."

Rachel kissed Emmy's cheeks, saying, "I'm off to bid farewell to everyone."

She ran out the door, Jaeger bounding alongside, and sprang over the kraal gate. In a moment, she had saddled Tempest and was galloping out of the farmyard, past Tante Emmy's servants. They had just driven their wagons up to the barn and were making preparations to camp. Emmy must have planned all this hours ago, determined to persuade Johannes to stay for Sannie's sake. Klaas, the Drentes' old servant, was joking with big Jacob, the good-looking young colored blacksmith who worked for André and Tante Emmy. Nearby was the pretty, coquettish Millie, a mixed-blood serving girl of the Drentes'. Rachel could see her flirting with Jacob, who like her was as yet unmarried.

André Toulouse, white-haired and cheerful, sat on a wagon seat. Wortelkop was complaining, hopping on his shoulder, the parrot's tail feathers singed from last night's electric fire.

"Good morning, Uncle André!" Rachel called out.

"Bon jour, chérie!" André yelled, as if he could see her as she trotted past with Jaeger running alongside. "Come back soon and have coffee with me!"

Leaning forward, face against the stallion's neck, Rachel let her hair fly in the wind, very un-vrouw-like. She would find the Arendts at the head of the trek and tell them that her family was not leaving yet. She realized how much she would miss the company of Marta Arendt.

☾ ☾ ☾

The lumbering trekwagons were in a long file, and far beyond them the enormous herds were known by their dust clouding the grasslands. The trek oxen had been inspanned—hitched up—since before dawn, teamed eight pair to a wagon, usually matched in color, to the pride of their owners. Ox spans were the greatest treasures of these Boers, after their children.

Rachel galloped past the brightly painted wagons pulling into line, one after the other, heading for an opening in the distant mountains, crossing grassland that never had known a wagon road. To the crack of long whips and the teamster's shouts to the oxen by name, the voortrekkers slowly moved away from Sweetfountain, heading toward the sunny northern horizon.

"It's really happening, Tempest!" Rachel said, excited. "They're going off to find the promised land!"

She raced past wagon after wagon, waving and blowing kisses in farewell, yelling that her family would catch up soon, and that Sannie would be fine.

"Tot ziens!" they cried back and forth. "Until we see each other again!"

She caught up with the swaying wagons of the Arendts and saw Marta sitting on the bed inside the first one, the tent sides rolled up to let in air and light. The entire inside of the trek-wagon was a bed, covered with wildcat skin blankets. Marta waved, then gave a hand as Rachel sprang lightly down from the horse and into the wagon.

"We have to wait for Sannie to get better," Rachel explained, saying Tante Emmy and André would stay with them, and Marta tried to mask her worry.

"Ach, Rachel, we would also remain behind with you, but the folk look to us now, and we must lead them." Marta kissed her hard on the cheeks. "God be with you!"

The servants in the drivers' seats of the four Arendt wagons were singing in unison and cracking their long whips over the oxen. Off to the right rode the four Arendt sons, all in their teens and unmarried.

Marta saw Rachel observing them, and said, "See how they admire you, child! They think you are the most beautiful woman in creation."

Rachel could not help but laugh, but did notice the good-looking boys watching her.

"They're too young for me," she said. "But one day they'll be stalwart men in the promised land, the stock of a new race of free people. The girls who get them will be lucky."

Willem Arendt appeared on horseback, saying he had a rope to toss over Tempest's neck for Rachel to remount him. She said that was not needed, for her stallion came when she whistled. Willem asked to breed his mares with Tempest when Rachel's family caught up.

"Speaking of matching good stock," Marta said to Rachel, with a wink. "It may be mad of me even to hope this, but if my

Dirkie should appear out of somewhere, tell him I insist he stay with your party, to protect you until you can rejoin us."

Rachel promised, gave her a farewell kiss, and called Tempest alongside. She leaped nimbly aboard, aware that the Arendt males were grinning at one another to see this.

"Tot ziens!" they all cried out as Rachel rode off and turned on a little *kopje* to wave, her stallion stamping to run some more.

Rachel no longer fought back tears, for no one would see her now. She let them flow, leaned forward, put her arms around Tempest's neck and held tight, sobbing helplessly. After a while, she set out for the farmhouse, turning back several times to wave at passing wagons, hearing the people singing. She watched the last wagons slowly become smaller and smaller, dwindling into the rippling waves of grass. By the time she reached the entrance to the farmyard, the trekkers had all pulled out, leaving clouds of dust and acres of crushed grass in their wake. Then she saw two wagons that were not inspanned, their oxen being led back to pasture by servants. These were the wagons of Gerrit Schuman, and he was at that moment riding toward her on his big bay.

"So, meisje, I have heard it all," Gerrit declared as his stallion pranced about Rachel and Tempest, both mounts flaring their nostrils, stamping, and ready to fight. "You will not be alone on the trekpad, for I will remain with you, so don't look so worried!"

He laughed and tipped his hat, then made his stallion rear, and rode off to tell Johannes. Rachel was glad Gerrit was staying behind. He was one of the most capable of defending them. Still, she wished that someone else would appear just then, though she did not know why. Like Marta Arendt, Rachel thought she was mad to even imagine it, but she wished Dirkie would join them in their wandering through the wilderness, searching for the promised land.

It was strange, but last night she could not stop thinking about Dirk Arendt, and even when Sannie finally had settled down, Rachel had hardly slept. What was even stranger, she really did not know what Dirkie looked like anymore.

LOVELL'S DESIRE

The Zulu army was gone, all of them, impi after impi parading past Shaka as they marched out of kwaBulawayo, beating thunder from clubs against shields, running northward to wage sudden, bloody war. On an impulse, Shaka had ordered them to fall upon some unsuspecting people chosen for destruction.

Dirk sat on a folded blanket by a cow dung fire burning outside the low door of the beehive grass hut where he and the others had stayed that night. Lovell and Benjamin were inside, arguing about Shaka's remarkable amulet. Dirk was sick and tired of Lovell, begging them to find a way to get it. He stood up and yawned, stretching, feeling hungry and weary, for he had slept but little.

In the cool morning sunshine, it seemed as if last night's dangers, the blazing torches, the dancing and loud singing, were all a dream, just like the fire of the amulet and the face of the woman. All night the images of white fire and that woman's face had lingered at the edge of his wakefulness, at the borderlands of sleep, and he had been unable to rest. The great circular kraal of kwaBulawayo was hushed, hauntingly empty of men, with only a few older boys standing guard, and some glum women stirring pots on cooking fires that sent blue smoke over the surrounding green hillsides. The many thousands of women and children and old men who had come in from outlying kraals were already making their way home, where they would stay until Shaka summoned them once more for his ceremonial anointment with Benjamin David's "oil of youth." At the moment, Shaka and the small bodyguard he had retained were nowhere in sight.

Nearby, Sebe crouched with the expedition's bearers, smoking *dagga*, hemp, and talking languidly. The bearers had made a small hole in the ground and filled it with dagga, which had been lit and then covered with earth. Murmuring contentedly, glad the Zulu army was gone, the smokers inhaled through hollow reeds or buffalo horn that had been worked into the smoldering hemp. They were forgetful of time and place, and even the nasty lump on Sebe's forehead seemed not to trouble him now.

Over Dirk's cook fire stood a pot of coffee, which the bearers had made for the whites, while they themselves were drinking boyala from woven-reed cups. Dirk poured coffee into his tin mug and decided against having the bearers make breakfast yet. It had been terrifying for them last night, and now they needed to find some peace of mind in their smoke and beer. Who knew what Shaka had in store?

Sebe approached, his eyes bleary, the lump on his head smeared with green clay. Dirk moved over on the blanket, and the Xhosa crouched beside him, neither man speaking until Dirk was on his second cup of black coffee.

In Xhosa, Sebe said, "The English fool will try to get Shaka's amulet, even if it kills us all."

Dirk knew this was true, but did not know what to say. Sebe drank beer and stared at the orange and blue flames before he went on: "The Englishman promises riches if we bring the amulet back, but it's not my bag to deprive Zulu kings of their favorite playthings."

"It's not my bag, either, old man," Dirk said.

He liked that phrase, "not my bag," which had come from a mistranslation of the Dutch expression, *"eene groote zaak,"* meaning an important matter or business. The native translator had thought the Dutch words were *"een groot zak,"* which means "a large bag," and the natives began to use this expression amongst themselves—"bag" instead of "business"—and now any important matter was called "a large bag," and someone's personal business or particular interest was his "bag."

After a moment, Sebe shook his head and said, "Every amulet has its magic, but my gods tell me this bull's head with its white fire stone has more magic than most." He thought a moment, then went on, "Such powerful amulets are not possessed by men, but they possess men, especially men who would use them wrongly."

Dirk did not try to press Sebe for an explanation. He had seen too much of native charms and wisdom not to take them seriously. Also, he remembered his own experience last night when Shaka had held the bull's-head amulet before him. Even now, he would like to touch it. He had the good sense, however, not to trouble his mind with finding a way to acquire it from Shaka. He wondered why Shaka did not wear the amulet himself, but instead had Mazibe carry it.

Just then Benjamin crawled from the hut and came for coffee. He looked worn and in need of sleep. Sitting down next to Dirk, he took out some drawing paper and a pencil and began to sketch idly, as he often liked to do. In a few moments, he had captured the outline of the bearers huddled over their dagga.

Benjamin sighed.

"Tom Lovell is ill with fever, or perhaps he's obsessed with this damned amulet, I don't know, but I'm worried about him." He poured more coffee and glanced back at the hut where Lovell remained. "He insists I make an offer to Shaka, but he doesn't understand the risk."

Dirk was glad Benjamin, at least, realized the seriousness of this situation. Then Lovell scrambled out of the hut and joined them, without offering a greeting. He sat gloomily, hands tight over his knees, and stared at the fire, rocking back and forth. Dirk offered coffee, but Lovell made no reply until a moment later, when he grasped Dirk by the sleeve.

"You're a sensible man, Mister Arendt," he croaked. "You know how to deal with an ignorant cannibal like Shaka, although our Zulu expert Benjamin David doesn't seem to have the stomach for it."

Dirk did not want to hear this and shook off Lovell's hand, saying, "This bauble is Shaka's treasure; you saw that last night."

Benjamin kept on sketching. Sebe stared at the fire.

"Treasure?" Lovell said, as if incredulous. "I'll shower him with the kind of treasure he understands! I'll not just bring blankets full of trinkets, but wagon loads, shiploads! He'll be the richest kaffir in Africa, yes, in all the British Empire!"

Sebe said, "Already is."

Lovell gave a snort of annoyance. "I've paid you all dearly, perhaps more than you're worth, because now when it matters most you fail me—"

Benjamin cut in: "What is so damned important about this amulet, Tom, that you'll risk our lives for it?"

Lovell gestured vaguely: "I've told you . . . for the museum. Great museum. The amulet's a valuable antiquity, yes, a token of . . . of past civilization, and the acquisition of it is . . . is the fervent desire of certain men of very high rank."

Dirk said, "You're not telling all the truth." As never before, a feeling in his bones troubled him about Lovell. "You're asking us to risk our lives for some *token of antiquity?* Believe me, if you push Shaka, we'll all die slowly and painfully."

Lovell was expressionless as he said, "For a higher cause."

"Higher cause!" Dirk scoffed. "Are we to be martyrs for the idle fancy of a few wealthy Englishmen?"

He tossed his coffee dregs against the hot stones of the fire, steam and fragrance rising.

"Not idle fancy at all, my man." Lovell looked so harmless, yet his obstinacy proved he had great force of will. "I cannot . . . I am not permitted to tell you all I know, gentlemen; but you must believe me when I say that my mission is for the good of your precious Africa, yes, but more than that . . . it is for the good, the greater good, of all mankind, body and soul!" He leaned toward Dirk. "And soul!"

Dirk and Benjamin exchanged glances. Dirk did not know what to think of any of this. It was strange that the memory of the amulet last night was still so vivid, so disturbing. Lovell's fanaticism seemed to evoke that image all the more, and that, in turn, troubled Dirk all the more.

Lovell pressed on: "Let us say that, for their own reasons, my associates have need, profound need, yes, of this amulet, and mark well that they are great gentlemen whose brilliant minds rise far beyond ours, yes, far beyond, and we have no right—*it is not our place*—to question them. I assure you, as a man of honor, as an Englishman, that my mission is a mission for humanity. A great mission, yes, in time, a great mission for the likes of even you, Sebe, and your own benighted folk."

Sebe said nothing.

A silence hung over them. Benjamin changed drawing paper and sat staring at the blank page. Sebe took up the sheet with the picture of him and the bearers on it, and chuckled admiringly.

☾☾☾

A little later, Mazibe arrived alone, and they rose to greet him. The induna, too, looked tired as he politely bowed, clasping his hands. The whites and Sebe did the same, except for Lovell, who backed away to sit by himself, moodily eyeing the Zulu from a distance. Mazibe sat down, accepting coffee.

"This is a drink I have come to appreciate, thanks to inyanga Benjamin's earlier stays in Zululand." He raised the cup and gestured at Sebe. "And there is a Xhosa I have come to appreciate—destroyer of crocodiles!"

They laughed, and when Mazibe said the humiliated witch doctor Dayega had vanished from the kraal last night, Sebe seemed simultaneously proud and uncharacteristically modest.

Benjamin seemed to be sketching Mazibe as he asked, "Why are you not with your regiment, induna, making war?"

Mazibe's expression changed, becoming downcast as he said, "I wish the uFazimba and all the impis were at home, resting, for they have been on many, many hard campaigns, moon after moon."

He said Shaka had sent them out today just a matter of days after they had returned from their last prolonged war-making. The men were unhappy, suffering great deprivation because of Shaka's driving them so relentlessly these past few months. Also, the king no longer went to fight alongside his men, though it had been his unmatched strength and courage in battle that had built the Zulu empire.

"We miss Shaka leading us like a raging lion," Mazibe went on. "Things are no longer the same with the amaZulu, for much has changed since Nandi, the Great Female Elephant and mother of our king, died a year ago." He shook his head. "It is not the same. It is a time of blood and sorrow and loss among the amaZulu."

He paused, and there were tears in his eyes as he said, "Lord Shaka has changed, inyanga Benjamin, and we must all have a care what we say to him and what we do. He has made many enemies, many husbands whose wives he has slain—three hundred women because they owned cats that the witch doctor said were casting spells on Shaka; a hundred pregnant women whose bellies were slit open because Shaka wanted to understand the meaning of life. . . ." Mazibe's voice broke, and he covered his face with his hands.

Dirk was shaken as he listened to the unexpected outpouring of this great warrior's misery. As if he had held it in for too long, Mazibe told of months of forced mourning among the Zulus after Shaka's mother died. Thousands of Zulus, entire kraals including the children, had been slain by Shaka's orders because he thought they did not weep long enough or sincerely enough.

Mazibe said, "Zululand was created by Shaka the warrior king, but today he who was so fearless in battle now dreads dying of old age, and that is why he hungers so desperately after the oil of youth, inyanga. That is why I am here now and not away with my impi, for the king desires that the race between the white man and me for the oil of youth commence tomorrow."

Dirk was troubled to hear this, for he was still weary from the long journey here. Yet, he was willing to go back to Port Natal immediately, so the terms of the race were established: The two of them would run together to Port Natal, and there would fetch Tom Lovell's six bottles of Macassar oil, three for each man. It would be then that the actual competition would begin, over the one hundred and twenty-five miles, a journey that would end at the gates of kwaBulawayo. As plans were made, Dirk burned inside to ask why Shaka had Mazibe carry the bull's-head amulet. At last, he carefully probed.

"Why do you carry the amulet and not Shaka?"

Mazibe looked searchingly at Dirk before replying: "The bull's head is a great burden for a simple man like me, umuntu. Its powers and secrets mean much to Shaka, and from it he receives guidance, but he cannot, will not, wear it, although he has attempted to." His voice dropped almost to a whisper. "Shaka values the amulet above all other treasures, but it torments him, plagues his dreams—reveals the innocent blood that is on his hands."

Mazibe's voice was strong again when he said, "Therefore, I, Shield of Shaka, wear the amulet, and I do so willingly, for the sake of the nation, because it is my lord's desire."

How exhausted the induna seemed just then. It was as if his very soul begged for relief from its task. The moment of weariness passed, however, and he sat erect once more.

Benjamin asked, "May we see the amulet, induna?"

Mazibe gave a spasmodic movement, his hand coming to his breast at the spot where the amulet hung, hidden by the kaross. He appeared apprehensive, eyes going from Benjamin to Dirk to Sebe. Then he collected himself and glanced over his shoulder in the direction of the king's lodge, which was some distance away.

With a sharp intake of breath, Mazibe pulled out the bull's-head amulet so that it dangled before them. Sebe whispered, "Aha."

Dirk looked closely at it and thought the bull's head looked far less impressive in daylight than it had in the glare of torches last night. Though it was indeed a beautiful piece, and no doubt valuable, he was annoyed, and even troubled, when he felt his pulse quicken as he looked at it. Why was this amulet the quest of Thomas Lovell and his European associates? Dirk longed to ask Mazibe about the supposed powers of the bull's head, but he sensed it was not right to pry.

Inexplicably edgy, Dirk was about to ask such a question anyway, when he was interrupted by a loud gasp. It was Lovell, who was close by, gaping at the amulet over Benjamin's shoulder, eyes popping from his head. Mazibe concealed the amulet again. Dirk watched it vanish, disappointed it was gone.

Lovell was reaching out, hand trembling, fingers clutching at air: "What will he take for it? Tell him what I'm saying, someone! Ask him! Please, what will he take for it? We can all get away! We have guns. The Zulu army is gone—"

Though he did not understand Lovell's Dutch, Mazibe was on his feet, towering over the red-faced Englishman, who opened and closed his hands in supplication.

Benjamin abruptly said, "Induna, our companion is ill; he has fever. Forgive his impoliteness."

Mazibe nodded. "I know that fever, inyanga. It is the fever of those who desire the amulet but are not strong enough. It is the fever of covetous desire, and it is always fatal."

He looked at Dirk. "Our run begins tomorrow, umuntu, when Shaka calls us. Attend King Shaka when he beckons you with the call of the drum." He touched the amulet behind his kaross and looked closely at Lovell, who was indeed feverish and flushed. "Get him out of this land before he is killed."

With that, Mazibe strode away.

Bewildered, Lovell cast about as if his senses were leaving him.

"He spoke of me! What did he say? What did he say?"

Sebe spat and answered, "That Shaka has heard you have a fine singing voice." Then the Xhosa rejoined the bearers with their dagga.

Lovell sat down heavily by the fire, running fingers through his hair again and again. Benjamin suggested he rest a while. Abruptly, Lovell sat up, saying he had forgotten it was Sunday. He dug out his small Bible and for some time sat silently reading, meditating, sometimes praying, while the others busied themselves with their own affairs.

Benjamin was respectfully quiet and found a shirt button that needed mending. Dirk had some religion, though he was nothing like the dogmatic Boers with whom he had grown up. He had a set of beliefs, and of course celebrated the Calvinist holy days when he was at home, just like everyone else. Here, however, as Lovell observed the Sabbath, Dirk was not inspired to pray with him. Instead, he fetched out the *Last of the Mohicans* to pass the time.

☾ ☾ ☾

Shortly, Lovell called out to him, and Dirk was amazed to see the man self-possessed once more. Lovell had laid aside the

Bible and straightened his clothing. With fingers primly interlocked, he peered at Dirk and spoke blithely.

"Mister Arendt, this Zulu and you will be alone for several days during the course of this race. You will have your firearms and could take the first opportunity to force him to turn over the amulet, could you not?"

Dirk's anger rose. "Enough of this! I want nothing more to do with it!" He turned away, saying, "The only way I could get that amulet would be cold-blooded murder."

Lovell made no reply, but Dirk was taken aback by his almost radiant, tranquil expression.

"Find the savage's price, then," Lovell said. "But get the amulet however you can, and go to England, where you will become wealthy beyond your dreams. I have well-placed friends from here to London who will aid you, Mister Arendt, officers at British bases, agents in our colonial office, some missionaries; we who are left behind here when you depart will find our way to safety however we must."

Dirk and Benjamin stared at Lovell, who seemed so utterly determined. Benjamin got to his feet and slapped the sketch pad on his thigh, now furious.

"By damn, Tom!" he said, exasperated. "By damn, sir! You'll not betray Mazibe, not if I can help it!"

"And I'm no murderer," Dirk added, "whatever the cause."

Lovell grunted. "Apparently you've never had a cause worthy of the deed, Mister Arendt."

Benjamin was astounded. "Have you such a cause, Tom?"

Lovell stuck out his jaw. "When the course of civilization is at stake—the purpose of the Lord's work to save humanity from its own folly—then even a man such as I, one who has never known violence, yes, even I would stop at nothing, nothing, to build an eternal empire of peace on earth!"

Dirk was not sure whether to loathe or pity this man. Benjamin sat down heavily, head in his hands.

Lovell peered at Dirk, appraising him, then said, "Very well, sir." He got up and went toward the hut, calling back over his shoulder, "By the way, Mister Arendt, my sloop's master in Port Natal knows where the bottles of Macassar oil are kept; I'll send a letter with you authorizing him to assist you."

Lovell disappeared into the opening of the hut. Dirk and Benjamin were both quiet, Benjamin sketching. Dirk's thoughts wandered from the coming race with Mazibe to the amulet and back. After a while, Benjamin passed him the sheet of paper. It was a sketch of the bull's-head amulet, with the diamond shining brightly.

Benjamin smiled. "Something to remember last night by."

"Yes," Dirk said, "you've captured it well, save for the diamond's glow, which was incredibly brilliant, as if coming from inside the stone."

"Here, give it back and I'll fix it up."

Benjamin made the diamond in the drawing gleam a bit more, but it was still not enough, said Dirk.

"The light I saw was white, glaringly bright, in a way that seemed to blind me, but somehow it didn't blind me, instead illuminating things, making things clear."

"Things?"

"Well. . . ." He could not express what he meant. "You didn't see that bright light, as if the diamond had a glow, a radiance of its own?"

Benjamin shrugged. "An excellent stone, I'll warrant, but no diamond gives off light of its own, my friend."

Lovell was standing there. "You saw the white fire?"

"What do you say?"

"The white fire. You experienced it?"

Lovell's wide-eyed, haunted expression chilled Dirk, who stood up and paced, saying gruffly, "I don't know what I saw. Just a bright trick of light, that's all."

Lovell's arms hung limply, one hand holding the letter he had written, folded, and sealed with wax. Taking a step toward Dirk, he pressed, "Did you see the white fire? A light from within the stone, like the glare of a mirror glass in the sun?"

"Did you see it, too?" Dirk asked.

"Would to God that I could," Lovell murmured.

Dirk was agitated. Lovell had given a good description of the diamond's light, but Dirk wanted no more talk of it. He was relieved when Lovell handed over the letter and went back into the hut. On the envelope, which bore Lovell's wax seal, was written, "Strictly Private for Captain Homan, Sloop Red Witch." Dirk put the letter into his shirt's inside pocket and sat down beside Benjamin.

"I don't like this turn of things," he said, "but I'll be damned if I understand any of it."

Benjamin rested his chin in one hand, and after some thought said, "Perhaps we should call off this race and go down to Port Natal together, put Lovell safely on a ship to Cape Town, then fetch back the damned hair tonic for the king!"

"Call off the race, when Shaka's expecting a great festivity in his honor?" Dirk really was not thinking of the danger now, only of competing against Mazibe, the greatest challenge he had ever faced. "Shaka won't let you get away from here without the oil being in his hands."

"I'll think of another way to please Shaka. We'll call off the race—"

"Never! That would be admitting defeat!" Dirk was worked up. "This chance for me to beat the Zulu champion won't come again, Benjamin. I won't let it pass."

Benjamin took the sketch of the amulet and looked at it, saying, "There's something more to Lovell's obsession with this talisman than meets the eye, and it worries me." He rubbed his forehead. "This affair isn't our business."

"But beating Mazibe is my business—running is my bag, as Sebe says. And it'll be the race of my life!"

TO PORT NATAL

Running shoulder to shoulder at a steady pace, Dirk and Mazibe would cover the hundred and twenty-five miles southward to Port Natal in six or seven days. They were conserving their strength for the return race, which would begin as soon as they acquired the bottles of Macassar oil from Tom Lovell's man at the settlement.

Following the two runners was an escort of twenty grown boys, immensely proud at their good fortune to have been chosen by Shaka for this honor because the Zulu warriors were all away on the campaign. Even though the runners did not yet push themselves to the limit, their young escort soon fell far behind, unable to keep up.

Dirk was outfitted with little more than a rifle and hat: a cartridge pouch was slung across his back; a rolled blanket tied with a length of rope hung over his chest; a canteen for water and another with peach brandy were at his belt. He wore his soft veldschoenen, good for running. In his belt were a pistol and knife, and a pouch full of dried antelope meat, cut in strips, was suspended by a cord over his shoulder. This meat was emergency food, but for the most part they could count on eating well at the kraals they passed, where they would be honored guests.

At night, Dirk and Mazibe would sleep in these small kraals, which stood every few miles along the trail to Port Natal. Kraals were often next to streams that had to be crossed by dugout, as did a few larger rivers. This part of Zululand was fairly safe from crocodiles and lions, but farther south, the country was less populated and would be wilder.

Mazibe had little more than a leather loincloth, a purple sleeping cloak bundled on his back, one stabbing *assegai* and his long-handled club called a *knobkerrie.* The amulet was carried in a small leather pouch tied to a thong around his waist. Mazibe went barefoot in the hardy tradition of the Zulus.

From the start of the empire-building, Shaka had forced his soldiers to harden feet and wills by discarding their sandals and running in place on thorns scattered on the ground. Men who collapsed in agony, who complained, or even ran too slowly, were killed on the spot. Callused feet and a will of steel combined with fierce physical conditioning so that the best impis could run fifty miles a day and still fight a pitched battle. A European soldier had a good day if he marched ten miles over roads.

On the journey, Dirk recalled the departure from kwaBulawayo, when the king had stood before him, towering above everyone, showing Dirk kindness he had never expected.

"Although you will lose this race, umuntu," Shaka had said, "you will always be welcome in Zululand as a bearer of the oil of youth to the king."

With that, Shaka had brought forth a beautifully woven reed bowl of amaSi and shared it with Dirk and Mazibe, who drank from the bowl. Surely no greater honor could have been shown to Dirk, and he still felt moved to think about it. Dirk had no love for Shaka, but knew he was one of the most remarkable of men.

The rest of the parting ceremony had been brief, with little of the usual Zulu pageantry: There had been no herdsmen conducting trained cattle that could dance on command, cattle adorned with ribbons and bizarrely shaped horns. No impis had been available to parade by the thousands before the king and his guests. There had been only the women with their little children, the old men and a handful of boys who guarded the royal kraal until the army returned.

Dirk could not help remembering the loathsome executioner, Ineto, "The King's Knife," who had lurked behind Shaka's throne. Beside Ineto had been the king's half-brother, Dingaane, who had kept his eyes partly closed as Shaka spoke, his face expressionless. Dingaane had claimed to be too ill to take part in the Zulu campaign that called the impis away, and he had remained behind with Shaka.

Indeed, the farewell of the two runners was a moment Dirk would never forget: the sour taste of royal milk curds, the ringing voice of the king, who was wrapped in a robe of purple trade cloth presented by Benjamin, and the cheers of the Zulu women and old men who sent the runners off to fetch the oil of youth.

It was the image of King Shaka that Dirk remembered most. Shaka, a king so terrible and so mighty, who had honored Dirk Arendt as he never could be honored again.

Sebe had said it best the first time they had looked upon the royal Zulu kraal, "Now, when you dream of glory, your soul will be at kwaBulawayo, esteemed by Shaka, king of all the Zulus!"

Sebe had smeared some smelly concoction on Dirk's chest "to protect the Boer baas from black magic," and Dirk had let him do so because the old rascal had made such a fuss about the need for it. Benjamin had tried to be encouraging, though worry showed through his bold facade. Only Lovell had been dour at the send-off, saying nothing. At least the Englishman had not mentioned the amulet again. Later, as Dirk lay at night in a grass hut, looking up through the smoke hole that showed a star or two, he found he had taken Lovell's letter from the inside pocket of his shirt. Just holding it made him restless, uneasy. The wax seal tempted him to break it open and read the contents, but that would have been dishonorable, so he put the letter away.

Dirk decided that once they got to Port Natal, he would not let the induna out of his sight.

☾ ☾ ☾

On the afternoon of the third day, Dirk and Mazibe topped a rise on the trail and paused to look back over the pale green hills covered with grass and a few trees. Spring was quickening, and wilted leaves and grasses were regaining life.

"Look," Mazibe said, smiling and pointing at the escort of boys, who were strung out along the trail, unhappily dragging spears, clubs, and shields as they tried to keep running. "My eldest son is amongst them; see there, the first one."

Dirk could mark the resemblance. The boy was tall, as yet still lanky, but superior in build to the others. He was obviously exhausted, his feet barely coming off the ground. Unlike the rest of the boys, he held his shield in proper vertical position at his left shoulder, knobkerrie and assegais pointing upwards in his right fist. By now they must be very heavy.

"He's strong," Dirk remarked. "In another year or two he'll outrun us."

"His name is Senzana, and he is more like his mother than like me." Mazibe laughed, his head tilting back as he said, "She is one who can run! Aiee! She made me chase her through the forest before I could give her the boy, and I think at last she let me catch her."

Just then, Senzana spotted them looking down, and he gave a shout to the others, waving a spear as they struggled to reform into two files. Despite their pain, the boys stoically increased their pace, shields and weapons held properly, heads up.

Mazibe cupped his hands and whooped encouragement to them. They chanted in response, shaking their weapons, causing him to laugh.

"Come on, induna," Dirk said. "Let's give them a lesson."

They saluted the boys with a fist held high, and then set off fast down the long southeasterly slope into land that was thickly wooded. Soon, the boys would be left miles behind and, as had happened the day before, would not reach the night's stopping place until hours after the two men arrived. Still, the boys would not give up.

☾ ☾ ☾

At night, lying on a woven grass mat and wrapped in his blanket, Dirk listened to Mazibe play the native instrument known to whites as a "thumb piano." It sounded like a harp. It was small, made of wood, the music coming from a row of thin metal strips that were plucked downward with the thumb. Dirk came to know some Zulu tunes as Mazibe sang them for him, and learned their stories of romance and cattle and war. Though Mazibe traveled light, he would not be without his thumb piano and kept it in a pouch at his side.

Usually, they talked far into the night about Dirk's travels, about the rise of the Zulus in the short lifetime of Shaka, and about the Boers with their rifles and horses.

Dirk's respect for the Zulus was increasing, and he hoped his own people would never have to go to war against them. Well, southern Africa was a big place, and the talk he had heard of Boers wanting to journey northward and settle new country meant the two warlike peoples need not clash, for Zululand was due east from Cape Colony.

☾ ☾ ☾

The weather turned cool, with a steady breeze that smelled damp, of sea and salt marshes, for they were drawing nearer to the coast. Good weather for running, Dirk told Mazibe, who replied that Shaka had used his magic to give them only dry days for the race, even though it was rainy season.

"And what if it should rain before we return to kwaBulawayo?" Dirk asked casually as they trotted along in the shade of mangrove trees that draped the path. "What would that say about Shaka's magic?"

Mazibe gave a sidelong look of disapproval before he answered: "If it should rain, umuntu, it would mean that my lord Shaka is dead."

They ran on, saying little.

That night, the escort arrived later than usual at the kraal where the runners stopped. The boys were so tired that they scarcely spoke when they came in. They slumped to the ground and fell asleep where they lay, too weary even to eat. At dawn, Dirk and Mazibe were off again, and the boys struggled in silence to rise, snatch a bite of food, and follow.

The young escort arrived at the next kraal long after nightfall, utterly exhausted and frightened from their ordeal, having hurried through blackness to reach safety. Twice they had been stalked by hunting lions, and once they had to stop because the trail was thick with snakes in some sort of bizarre migration—or so they had imagined in the eerie darkness.

Out of earshot from the boys, Dirk asked Mazibe about the snakes.

"Spirits of the dead-who-walk can take many forms at such an hour," Mazibe said, and that closed the matter.

The following night, the escort did not arrive at all at the camp Dirk and Mazibe made, apparently having taken shelter somewhere back on the trail. This stretch had no kraals for the last forty miles to Port Natal.

That night Mazibe cooked meat on a stick over the campfire and said, "It is better that the young ones have stopped somewhere and built a big fire, for it is too dangerous in this country to be on the road after dark—" His voice fell to a whisper. "—when the boy with the beard prowls."

Dirk knew Mazibe referred obliquely to the male lion, and that in lion country it was bad luck when on the road to mention the lion by name, *tao,* for that could make him appear. Even the bravest of warriors spoke in a whisper when referring to tao, so as not to arouse the beast.

"This country is not nice," Mazibe continued, that expression meaning there were many lions. "In these parts, those who herd the cattle must be men, and not children, for the boy with the beard is very savage here."

Dirk and Mazibe slept high up in a tree that night. About midnight, Dirk awoke, hearing a lioness growling below, and for the rest of the night he remained half-awake, listening, the loaded rifle across his knees. More than once he would have dozed off and fallen out of the tree had he not been secured by the piece of rope he had brought along.

☾☾☾

Mazibe had no difficulty with the twenty or so miles, day after day, that he and Dirk covered on the way to Port Natal. Dirk was not in such splendid condition as the Zulu, though, and he felt sore, stiff, and weary. By the last day, however, he was growing stronger.

It was then that they agreed to match their speed and stamina. They learned that Dirk was quicker in short bursts, but Mazibe was better in distances. By the time they came up a long rise that brought them in sight of the Indian Ocean, they had twice raced hard for five miles, and Mazibe had left Dirk hundreds of yards behind each time.

Still, a race back to kwaBulawayo would not be decided by five-mile dashes. To win, Dirk must run as never before, but he must also run intelligently. He resolved to run after dark and before dawn to make up the lost miles Mazibe would gain during the day. There would be a full moon during their journey back to Shaka, and that would help. But there would also be lions.

Late that afternoon, they paused on a wind-swept ridge, looking down on the vast, circular bay of Port Natal, which was landlocked because of a sandbar that lay across the harbor mouth. In the distance, a high forested bluff overlooked the southern edge of the bay and the bar; from the base of this bluff a long white beach edged the water for miles, leading all the way to the foot of the ridge where Dirk and Mazibe stood.

"It's beautiful!" Dirk declared, breathing deeply of sea air and gesturing at the ocean. "Beyond that great water are many places with more souls than a hundred kwaBulawayos, people of all colors and sizes, with stone houses and ruled by powerful kings with thousands of indunas and enormous firesticks and boxes full of jewelry even more beautiful than the bull's-head amulet!"

This was the first time during the journey from Zululand that Dirk had even thought about the amulet in its leather pouch at Mazibe's waist. He observed Mazibe marveling at the expanse of horizon and blue water, all the while with his right hand on the leather bag with the amulet. It occurred to Dirk that touching the bag somehow helped Mazibe judge whether this description of faraway places could possibly be true.

Below the ridge, clustered near the shore where a stream let into the bay, were two dozen grass and wooden huts beside a few thornbush kraals with cattle in them. This was the trading post. A couple of smallboats were beached nearby. Tom Lovell's little sloop, the *Red Witch,* was anchored outside the sandbar, drawing too much water to get into the bay. Port Natal was the toehold for a handful of British merchants who had dreams of greater things, such as acquiring loads of Zulu ivory.

The hovels near the beach and the overgrown vegetable gardens were not much to look at, but Dirk unexpectedly had a vision that one day there would be a great city here. It was a startling idea, and it seemed to come from nowhere. He was completely taken aback to hear what Mazibe said next.

"I see many houses and great canoes on the water here one day, and dwellings of stone . . . many, many white things." He paused, hand to his face. "I do not understand what my closed eyes see, umuntu, but it makes me long for my own kraal."

In fact, Mazibe's eyes were wide open, as he faced the windswept bay. Grimacing, still touching the pouch with the amulet, he went on: "Ahh, umuntu, the burden of the bull's head is great, for it is not my wish to see these things, and yet they come upon me like demons, those strange images of great shining birds like silver vultures, and stone upon stone upon stone rising to the sky."

The induna groaned, as if fighting off some distress. He walked in a circle, hands covering his ears, muttering to himself and seemingly in pain. Dirk did not want to interfere, but he was concerned.

At last Mazibe stopped pacing and turned to Dirk, saying, "It has passed."

"What happened?" It was a rude question to ask of a proud Zulu induna who had shown such vulnerability, but by now Dirk felt Mazibe was a friend, and would not object to the asking.

"As always, the visions have passed." Mazibe forced a smile and sighed. "But they will come again as ever they have, so long as I carry the bull's head."

He put his hands to his head. "It is clear to me that I have borne the sacred amulet too long." He spoke as if to himself. "When I return to Shaka, I will ask that he relieve me of it, no matter what the consequences for me."

In the next moment, Mazibe sprang into the air, shaking his assegai.

"It is done!" he cried out. "It is done!"

He whirled and shouted to the sea: "At last!" Turning to Dirk, who saw his joy, he exclaimed, "Once, I desired to carry the bull's head, for the wisdom it imparted. But then there came a time when I dreaded its power and terrible weight, yet I still wished to carry it because I was proud of my warrior's strength."

Eyes fierce, he spoke from the bottom of his heart.

"Now, I know I am not strong enough. I no longer desire to be the amulet bearer. Now, the burden is lifted from me. Yes! Lifted! At last, it is done!"

He shouted and leaped high again, like a young boy, and Dirk could not help laughing with him, though he did not understand what the induna was talking about.

Then Mazibe changed, chest heaving as he calmed himself, and he pointed his spear toward the English sloop bobbing at anchor.

"That bird from the sea, umuntu—I would like once to fly on such a thing before my life ends."

Dirk said that could be arranged. "Tom Lovell owns it, and the ship's master will be obliging, I'm sure. Captain Homan can say he brought aboard the first Zulu ever to sail the ocean blue."

Mazibe chuckled in that infectious way of his.

"When I return to Shaka, I will be honored as bearer of the oil of youth, will be released from the burden of the amulet, and will be the first amaZulu to have flown upon the great water! Hah!"

He leaped ahead, running down the trail.

Dirk caught up and said, "You mean you'll be the *second* bearer of the oil to Shaka."

Mazibe shouted and took off, sprinting, Dirk on his heels. It was on this happy dash that the Boer knew he could never outrun the Zulu. But he would try.

GERRIT'S HOPE

Rachel realized, quite as a shock, that there would be no window glass in the promised land.

The thought struck her as she and Sannie sat in the parlor a few hours after Sabbath prayers. Sannie, looking much stronger, was on a cot embroidering a shirt for the baby she carried. Rachel was at the table finishing a pretty needlepoint stretched on a framework: It was a French hunting scene alive with scarlet riders and white horses pursuing a golden stag, which was fleeing toward mountains.

With some anxiety, Rachel remarked to Sannie that in the northern wilderness there would be no way to get window glass for the house they would build. Sannie brushed back a wisp of blond hair as she considered that.

"We didn't think about glass," she said, looking at the room's only window, which was a large one made up of several lights.

Sannie's legs were warmly covered with a gray blanket, a scarf about her slender neck, and the late afternoon sunlight imparted color to her wan face. Rachel was dressed in pantaloons and a flannel shirt, her long brown hair hanging loose about her shoulders. She had changed from a prim black gown worn for prayer time, when Johannes, as the eldest religious white man in the group still at Sweetfountain, led them for two hours in reading from the Good Book.

Though André Toulouse was the oldest white man there, he was not religious, claiming to believe "only in the Ten Commandments, and the rest is all so much speculation created by the Supreme Being to make small minds think once in a while and argue about it all." At least, that's what André said in public. Rachel thought he had a spiritual side, though he did not spout Scripture or constantly refer to God the way so many folk did in everyday conversation.

Rachel savored this peaceful time on Sundays when she could enjoy her needlework. The Drentes would make supper in an hour, and at dark everyone would be off to bed, for candles were scarce and lamp oil a luxury.

Sannie said, "Your father fetched that window all the way from Cape Town in 'fifteen, and he planned this room around it; then a Hebrew smous came by with a few more windows in 'eighteen, and those are now in the kitchen. Windows cost a lot everywhere in southern Africa, but who'll come to sell them to us when we're so far beyond the borderlands?"

Rachel let the needle and thread fall to her lap. What would they do in the north when they built a new house, so far from Cape Town, so far from anyone who sold glass panes, even too distant for the traveling merchant traders in the first years? Oiled paper was a possibility, but it was not the same as lovely, clear glass. She wished they had arranged with the new owners of the house to bring their own windows here, and that her father's windows could have been taken out and carried on the trek. Even in the promised land, a house would be dark and dreary without windows, and holes in the walls with only shutters let in flies and mosquitoes.

Rachel raised her needle again, but the disappointment of knowing that she would not have windows for years to come in the promised land stayed with her. It made her almost sad.

When there came a knock and Gerrit Schuman entered, hat in hand, she had to shake the heaviness from her heart to greet him.

Gerrit was still in his Sunday clothes: coat and trousers of pin-striped velveteen, a starched white shirt, and a black waistcoat with a silver watch chain in the pocket. He looked dapper, even his shoes polished, as if he had not been wearing them all day long. As Gerrit bowed to Sannie, Rachel noticed the back of his legs were covered with dust, where he had wiped off his shoe tops before entering the house.

After a few polite words, he asked what Rachel was making, and she cheered up at his interest, showing him the colorful needlepoint.

"What be it for?" He cocked his head from side to side as if to see it better. "Be it a riding blanket?"

"What is it for?" She held it out to admire it herself, annoyed that this practical farmer would ask such a typically practical question. "No, not a riding blanket. It's to look at."

"Just look at?"

"Yes, to enjoy—for its beauty. What else?"

"Beauty?" He thought about that. "You really make all them little stitches there just to look at? A waste of time and work, I be thinking."

"Spoken like a true Boer," Rachel declared, huffily putting the needlepoint down on her sewing basket. "To you, beauty's in the fat-tailed sheep or the newborn calf, in a horse's gait or a rifle's stock, all beautiful because they're useful!"

Gerrit grinned.

With a laugh, Sannie said, "And beauty's in the waddling behind of a fat wife!" She, like Rachel, was slim, while most Boer vrouwen were proud of being heavy and "substantial."

"Ja!" Gerrit nodded. "Especially a beautiful pregnant fat wife! And pregnant cows and pregnant ewes and goats and mares—"

Rachel sprang from her seat, flitting her hands to drive him out of the room.

"Away with you, Gerrit Schuman, insensitive wretch! You'll be very happy out there on the high veldt with your pregnant cattle and multiplying horses, as long as a fat wife is at home brewing coffee and dropping you a newborn stockman every nine months!"

Gerrit laughed loudly and held Rachel back. "Ach, Sannie, tell this skinny wench that even I got more in my mind than cattle and horses—"

"Be off!" Rachel demanded, half in jest, but annoyed with his attitude, one she had seen enough of in her lifetime. "Why, have you never thought that in the promised land we won't have any window glass? Not a sliver! We women'll be stuck in black holes of kitchens for the rest of our lives, unless the smous finds us, and then he'll sell us windows that will cost our very souls! Do you care?"

Gerrit grabbed her wrists and said with sudden excitement, "Come, I want to show you something!"

He was smiling broadly, and Rachel cast a glance at Sannie, who was enjoying it all.

"Ride with me, meisje, and I'll show you something special!"

Rachel was interested. She had been cooped up in the house tending Sannie and would be glad for a ride with Gerrit. She even would have been glad to start out on the trek just then, because she was already tired of being half packed-up, unable to find the spoons she needed or the pots or the clothes she wanted. Most things were in boxes or stowed away in bags in one of the three Drente trekwagons that stood waiting in the farmyard.

Rachel followed Gerrit to the barn, where they saddled up and set off toward his wagons. Tempest was frisky and eager to go. Just outside the farmyard Emmy and André Toulouse had their camp, the servants cooking dinner as the two riders passed at a trot. The air was cool, a steady breeze blowing southward from the mountains. The evening would be clear and chilly. It appealed to Rachel to think that Gerrit had some surprise to show.

☾ ☾ ☾

They soon reached his wagons and greeted the colored servants, who were preparing Gerrit's meal. A table, made by pegging some planks onto four posts sunk into the ground, was set with one stool for him. The servants ate separately at their own table. The colored husband and wife who served him were very capable, and they considered him a fair, if demanding, baas. It was unusual for single men of Gerrit's age to trek, and most his age had been married for years, some already with a second wife, for Boer women had hard lives and often died young. It was said he had been too busy as a stockman to find a wife, but others said he was waiting for Rachel Drente to be ready for him.

As she dismounted and passed the reins to the servants' little boy, Rachel asked Gerrit, "Why do you really want to trek? You could marry any of the girls for a hundred miles around, and you could live well on the land your father has given you."

As he thought about an answer, Gerrit drew out his pipe and filled it with tobacco from his shirt pocket. He found a "Lucifer" to light it.

"I left home 'cause the best land went to my two elder brothers." He struck the match on his shoe sole and soon puffed clouds of smoke that mingled with his beard and wreathed his broad-brimmed hat. "I'm a man as don't like close neighbors, and that means I don't want to see a neighbor's smoke if I ride half a day from my house."

Gerrit said his father's farm had been cut into three pieces, with his own share being too small to suit him.

"A good stockman needs seven thousand *morgens* of land to live decently so his herds and flocks can increase and never run out of grass."

He went to the back of a wagon and beckoned for Rachel to join him.

"Be it too much to ask that I can ride all day and still stay on my own land? Our elders and their elders had it so."

As he spoke, he was pulling a large, thin crate from the wagon. Rachel helped him lift it to the ground.

He said, "But there be more reason to trek." He stared at the western sky, his weathered face lit by the sunset, his voice turning harsh. "I trek 'cause God tells me to. I trek 'cause the heathen English've tormented us too long, hanged our patriots, made the blacks and coloreds equal to us in the eyes of their unholy law, and made little 'totties into soldiers who come to arrest us when we dare wipe the English dog's shit from our shoes."

Gerrit spoke slowly, restraining his anger as he spoke, all the while prying open the end of the crate with a crowbar.

"Ach, even their missionaries slander us and turn their blood-soaked empire against us, calling us kaffir murderers and immoral cattle thieves. Hypocritical bastards, those empire-builders; they be guilty of more sin against the lower races than we'll ever be."

"Let it go, Gerrit, we're leaving all that."

He would not.

"To us, the kaffirs and coloreds be children to civilize by strict discipline. To the empire-building Englishman, they be just so many beasts of burden, to work for nothing and be discarded in the rubbish heap when worn out."

He finished removing the wood that sealed the end of the crate, then turned to Rachel, composing himself as he spoke in a voice that softened: "You said I can have any woman I want, but till now I've not had the gumption to ask the woman I do want."

Rachel almost took a step backward, but instead smiled and felt herself flush.

"What's in the crate?" she quickly asked.

"Maybe this here stockman ain't so dull-witted as you think, Rachel." He set his pipe down on the back of the wagon.

"Don't say that, Gerrit."

She asked again what was in the crate, and was surprised when he stepped forward and took her hand. He became intense, but his voice was gentle.

"I want you to marry me, Rachel Drente, and to fill the promised land with my children, who'll be as beautiful as you."

Rachel forced a smile, but it did not feel right. She tried to speak, but words would not come. There was nothing in her head but confusion just then, and her heart did not want to hurt him by saying: *No, Gerrit, it cannot be you, but I thank you.*

She said only, ". . . cannot . . . but I thank you."

Rachel did not know what to do with her free hand, so it went behind her back. Gerrit looked closely at her, his eyes dimming, but his hand kept hold of hers as he nodded slowly.

"Take time to think about it." He seemed not to be surprised at her response, and began pulling something out of the crate.

"Gerrit," she began, touching his arm as he paused to look at her. "Gerrit, my dear friend, it's just that I'm not ready . . . for marriage, and I don't know why not, or what it all means."

"I know you be different from other women, Rachel, and that you got some dreamy ideas about life." He patted her hand like an understanding elder brother and looked her over. "Girl, you really should wear women's clothes, as the Good Book says you must. And put some meat on your bones to make people take you more serious; but then—" He smiled so warmly that Rachel smiled back, thinking how much she really liked Gerrit Schuman. "—even if you want to act like a man sometimes, I know the real woman you keep inside."

He gave his attention to the crate.

"Consider my proposal with a devout heart, Rachel, and in time, you'll understand that God means for us to be together in the new homeland."

With that, he drew out of the crate the most beautiful leaded window Rachel had ever seen.

"Oh, my!" she exclaimed. "It's glorious!"

"Sent to Cape Town for it, and it come out just in time, thanks be to God." Grinning, he held the window up so Rachel could touch the leading and see her reflection in the beveled panes. "A window for the promised land, meisje, fine enough for a church, but it'd be finer if I could see your face looking through it at the end of the day."

"Dear Gerrit," she murmured. "You're sweet." She kissed him on the cheek, causing the blood to rush to his face.

"Rachel!" He reached for her, but the window slipped, and he had to catch it.

They laughed, the window held between them.

He said, "Rachel, you'll learn to care for me in time, and till then I care enough for us both."

"Please, Gerrit, don't ask me this . . . I simply can't."

She truly did not know why she turned him down, but inwardly she was in turmoil.

"I bought this here window for you, Rachel, so you see, I know something about what you like." He looked so shy now, unlike the arrogant and headstrong jonge she had known all her life. "Rachel, I'll trek with you for many a long day, and in time you'll come to know me, too."

That made her catch a sob, and she said quickly, "I have to return for the evening meal." She felt awkward and stupid and hard-hearted, but she had to be honest with him. "I do love . . . your window . . . I mean—Oh, Gerrit, you kerel, you're a dear friend, but I'm not—"

"Meisje, we can't let too much time pass." He sighed. "You be as old as I."

"Don't start that talk again!" She turned to whistle for Tempest.

"In the promised land there'll be less eligible men than windows, girl!"

"Stop it now, Gerrit." She mounted.

"Don't waste yourself for some foolish dream, Rachel!" He grabbed at the bridle. "It be right! The hand of God brought us together and kept us here while our people went on ahead. It be the hand of God, and we can't deny it!"

"The hand of God? Gerrit, there's not even a man of God to marry us. The Dutch church is set against the people trekking, and no dominee would come into the wilderness to give trekkers a church service, let alone marry anybody."

Tempest wanted to rear, but Gerrit held him down.

"It'd be a righteous joining, Rachel. And when we be rooted in the promised land the church'll follow, and we can be legally bound by the first dominee who visits."

"In ten years?"

"What matter? In our hearts we'll be married afore God, and that's what counts! Afore God."

"Please, Gerrit!" She pulled Tempest away, sorrow coming over her. "Forgive me."

"Entreat me not to leave thee, or to return from following after thee: for whither thou goest, I will go; and where thou lodgest I will lodge. . . ."

She turned Tempest's head and spurred him into a gallop, but Gerrit's voice followed.

"Where thou diest, will I die, and there will I be buried. . . ."

She rode toward the farm as Gerrit's voice pursued her over the pounding of Tempest's hooves. She did not want to hear that passage of Scripture, so well known to her, but the words echoed. Was it truly the hand of God she was against?

Riding gave her time to wipe away the tears, and to think. Not that thinking did any good, for she could not find an answer and did not want to accept the obvious one. There would be few eligible men in the new homeland. Survival would be only for the strong and united.

Yet, Rachel was not going on the trek to find a man. Actually, she had no good reason for trekking. There just seemed to be no choice.

FEEDING SHARKS

If not for the glory of the windswept bay and the purple-hued clouds above the ocean, the squalid shacks of the white traders and their native retainers at Port Natal would have been completely depressing.

Dirk and Mazibe strode through the settlement, past stinking cattle kraals that were managed by sleepy black herdsmen, and past huts piled high with trash. Pigs rooted in front yards, and scrawny chickens scurried here and there, even inside the shelters. Dirk was amazed that so-called civilized Europeans would accept such a grubby way of life. He had never seen the poorest native kraal so foul. When first landing here some weeks ago, he had noted how these lowborn Britishers and Irish did not give a damn about tomorrow, lording it over their dingy households and purchased native wives.

As the newcomers walked, they were surrounded by clutches of mixed-blood children running wild about the place. The whites at Port Natal were short-sighted adventurers, not tillers of soil or harvesters, and they were dependent on trade and sleight of hand for a living. Unfortunately for them, there was little trade, their merchant company virtually bankrupt, and no ships expected any time soon. The village was off the trade routes, unlikely to be visited by passing vessels, so there were few supplies from civilization or tools for construction of decent housing. Yet most of the couple of dozen white inhabitants seemed not to care—rum and women being all they needed. They sat it out, like castaways, fattening on native beer.

A half-finished fort of timber and earthworks had been thrown up near the bay, and over it fluttered a tattered and faded Union Jack. Nearby, some white men were building a sloop at a primitive boatworks, apparently hoping to get it to sea and return to Cape Town, eight hundred miles southwestward. That would be a dangerous journey through waters that were often stormy.

Captain Gabriel Homan, master of the *Red Witch,* was like most other whites at Port Natal, being found in his disheveled hut, idle, and smelling of rum. Long graying hair fell over his eyes as Homan squinted at Lovell's letter. He was a big man, wearing a dirty linen shirt and black sailor's trousers that were half unbuttoned. He read the letter as he stood outside the door of the hut where, by the sound of voices, there were native women and at least one crewman, who was singing hoarsely and calling for more rum. What would the prim Lovell think to see his vessel's commander now?

Dirk had never liked Homan or his three hard-case crewmen. Feeling uneasy, Dirk wanted to get out of Port Natal and have nothing more to do with this rogue, though it was more than the sight of a few low-life characters that was troubling. Some instinct, a sense of danger, gnawed at Dirk.

"Get us the Macassar oil, and we'll be on our way," he said.

Homan eyed Mazibe.

"Whopper of a kaffir, ain't he? He know how to use that pig sticker of his? No doubt."

He laughed roughly and coughed up phlegm, spitting, then wiping his unshaven jaw before continuing.

"This says the Zulu gets three bottles and you three." Homan tugged at his suspenders. "Oil's on the boat, in Mister Lovell's gear, so we'll fetch it tomorrow."

Dirk turned to Mazibe. "We will sleep soon, and this white thing will get us the oil from the sea bird."

Mazibe gazed at the sloop, a light in his eyes. "Ask the white thing if it will take us onto the sea bird."

When Dirk translated, Homan laughed, slapping Mazibe on the shoulder.

"Right you are, matey! We'll give you a taste of salt and tar, we will!" He glanced at the letter as if to be sure of what he had read, then added, almost to himself, "Yes, wonderful notion, my black princeling."

Homan tucked the letter into his greasy shirt and told Dirk to bed down in a hut near the boatyard, saying they would be brought food and drink and would get the Macassar oil from the sloop first thing in the morning. Dirk was glad for the chance to rest, and went with Mazibe to the hut. Some good boyala and native cooking would suit him fine.

Soon, two young Malay women came into the hut, bringing goat cheese, whitefish, hard bread, and a small jug of Cape Colony cider, all courtesy of Captain Homan. The women offered to stay the night, but Dirk sent them on their way, for there was much sickness among these semi-castaways at Port Natal, and he wanted none of it.

They ate ravenously and drank a little cider, but a clumsy move that was the result of weariness caused Dirk to kick over the jug, and most of the drink spilled onto the floor. Mazibe soon fell asleep, and it was not long before Dirk found himself fading fast. Too fast. He was unable to stay awake, though he tried.

His last conscious thought was that they had been drugged.

☾ ☾ ☾

It was almost dark when Dirk came to. He sat up, startled, but groggy. The jug lay on its side, empty. Had they finished the cider instead of spilling it, Dirk would still have been unconscious.

With shock, he realized the induna was gone.

Rushing from the hut and calling out for Mazibe, Dirk hurried through the settlement, asking the Zulu's whereabouts. One of the white carpenters finishing for the day at the boatyard pointed out a jollyboat, its sail catching the last rays of sunset as it bobbed toward the *Red Witch,* about two miles off, beyond the sandbar.

"Cap'n Homan took yer kaffir out a while ago," said the fellow, packing tools into a canvas bag. "Homan and his lads was jabbering away about feeding sharks, though I don't reckon the black bugger knew a word they was saying, he looked so woozy, full-like, drunk as a lord, if a kaffir could be a lord—"

Dirk ran along the beach to a smallboat pulled up on shore. He heaved it into the water and raised the sail. There was a smart land breeze, and he soon had the boat headed for the *Red Witch.* Fear worked at his mind. The boat could not be driven fast enough by the breeze. Too late, he cursed for bringing along only a knife. The first of the moon appeared, white and stark, above the horizon, illuminating the sea with its glare. By the time Dirk's boat slipped over the shallows at the sandbar, the moon was in the sky, the sea glimmering with silver. The breeze was soft, and Dirk would have enjoyed the night if this were one of his outings sailing on the Rijn in Holland.

Something bumped the side of the boat and slid through the water. In the glistening moonlight he saw the fin of a shark, then another, and a third. In a moment, he was surrounded by sharks, and like him they were heading for the *Red Witch.* Cold with dread, he turned the tiller toward the high stern of the sloop, which was in shadow. Three or four lanterns were on the vessel, all forward, near the prow. Now Dirk saw movement on deck—awkward movement, as if men were fighting, and there came shouts of anger.

Dirk dropped the sail so it would not reflect moonlight and rowed hard, slipping under the stern. He tied the boat to the ship's climbing net and drew close alongside, and as he began to clamber up there was a sudden rush of foam. A shark rose, glistening, teeth white. Dirk sprang higher and hung there on the netting. There came a splash from forward. Horror gripped him to think Mazibe had been thrown overboard.

Sharks knifed through the water, thrashing and churning in foam below the prow. Men on board howled with laughter, Homan's voice the loudest.

"Aye, lads, they're getting impatient! Feed the sharks! Feed the sharks!" He howled again. "Here, my lovelies! A nibble of salt beef to whet yer appetites!"

There was another splash as a chunk of meat hit the water.

"Time for their main course! Heave ho, lads! Get the kaffir overboard!"

Dirk shouted, "Homan!" and sprang over the railing, drawing his knife. Three sailors and the captain were there, about to bundle a fishing net over the ship's railing. In that net was

Mazibe, struggling helplessly, lying on his side, the net tottering.

"Get the Dutchman!" Homan yelled.

Two sailors made for Dirk, who darted onto a hatch cover and bounded over them. He tumbled as he landed, coming up feet first, pounding squarely into the chest of the third seaman, who crashed backward and over the rail with a scream. Homan gave Mazibe a shove, and the net and Zulu went down.

"No!" Dirk bellowed and lunged across the rail, grabbing for the net as it fell. "Mazibe!"

The net swung heavily in Dirk's grip. Below, the sharks were striking at the sailor.

"Watch your back!" Mazibe yelled.

Homan was there. Dirk lashed out with the sole of one foot, catching the captain hard in the face, stunning him, and he fell to his knees.

"Get me out!" Mazibe shouted, and pushed his fingers through the netting, clawing for a handhold on the side of the ship.

Dirk tried to heave him up, but the other two seamen were there, one grabbing for his legs, the second leaning over the rail, trying to break his hold on the net. With his free hand, Dirk stabbed at the second man, who fell back with a gasp, blood spurting from his throat. Dirk was lifted off the deck and pushed headlong over the side. He went with the force, but at the last moment locked his legs around the sailor's body, squeezing so that the man was caught.

Now Dirk was half over the railing, one hand clutching the swinging net, the other hand with the knife. If the sailor wanted Dirk in the sea, he too would have to go, and he was terrified, trying to shake Dirk loose, thudding him against the railing.

Then came a shout from Homan, who was recovering.

Mazibe called, "The knife!" and his fingers came through the net.

Dirk thrust the handle at him. The sharks were going mad. Homan was prying Dirk's legs apart. He could not last. His legs were yanked free, and he started to fall.

The net was empty.

Dirk grabbed for the railing. A man wailed and flew over the side to scream his life away in the foaming water. Dirk scrambled back onto the deck to find Homan lying in a heap, his throat cut. Above the captain stood Mazibe, chest heaving, the bloody knife in his hand. Dirk closed his eyes momentarily, then went to the Zulu, who was unhurt. Mazibe looked down at Homan with an expression of disgust.

"What were these white things saying to me, umuntu?" Mazibe tried to pronounce the English words he had heard, until Dirk said in Bantu, "Feed the sharks."

Exhausted, Dirk knelt and removed Lovell's letter from Homan's bloody shirt. He went to the yellow light of a lantern and read the instructions to give Dirk the Macassar oil. Then the letter said:

> Captain Homan, it is imperative that you dispossess the Zulu of the golden bull's head amulet he carries in a small pouch. It is of the utmost urgency that you do whatever you must to get it, but be forewarned, this might require his death.
>
> You are charged not to harm Mr. Arendt, if it can be avoided.
>
> Once you have the amulet, you will proceed forthwith from Port Natal, directly to Cape Town and the

> Colonial Office. There you will ask for Mr. Gregory and show him this letter. Hand over the amulet to him, and he will see to it that you are generously recompensed for your loyal service. You will then return to Port Natal to await my arrival.
>
> Understand well, Mr. Homan, that should you not promptly turn the amulet over to Mr. Gregory, you will be a ruined man. You well know our power. Do not betray us. Keep all secret.
>
> Yours, Thomas Lovell

Dirk knelt there, head on his knee, dismayed that Lovell would have done this. He was startled by another splash and turned to see Mazibe throwing a dead sailor over the railing, Homan's body already having dropped.

Staring down at the water, the Zulu said, "They wanted to feed sharks."

With a shock, Dirk remembered the amulet and grabbed Mazibe's arm. "Where is it?"

Mazibe held up the amulet so that it dangled, sparkling, in the yellow light of the ship's lanterns. Then it was returned to the leather bag and tied with a thong around the induna's waist.

The two did not speak as they moved to the stern of the ship, where the frenzy of the sharks could not be heard. There, the only light was the silver of the moon, now fully risen. Dirk leaned on the railing, gazing at the twinkling red firelight of Port Natal, knowing he would have to deal with Lovell when next they met. But how? If Mazibe knew why this had happened, Lovell was a dead man. What was so important about this bit of old jewelry that it could turn a soft-living gentleman like Lovell into an adventurer willing to murder?

Mazibe recovered his spear and knobkerrie and sat down near the wheel, well back from the railing, as if he did not want to be close to the side of the ship again.

"These sea birds are not safe, with their snaring nets and greedy sharks," he said. "I like it better in lion country."

Dirk decided not to tell Mazibe that Homan had been acting under Lovell's orders. That matter would have to be finally resolved back in Zululand. Although Mazibe did not ask, Dirk offered that these seamen had been some common thieves who fancied his amulet.

"Perhaps," Mazibe said, touching the pouch at his waist. "But how did they know it was there? And they did know, though we did not tell them."

"Thieves, that's all," Dirk muttered, feeling the knocks he had taken on his head and face. He went off to find the bottles of Macassar oil, which were below in Lovell's packs, and put them in two satchels, three bottles in each.

Coming back on deck, he said, "We'll cut the anchor cable and let the ship drift out to sea on the night wind; no one will know what happened here." He gave Mazibe a satchel of bottles. "Let's return to the country of the boy with the beard, where it's safer."

☾ ☾ ☾

They sailed the smallboat back into the bay, followed by moonlight, guided by the fires and lanterns of Port Natal. They did not talk until Dirk was about to spring into the water and haul the boat ashore.

It was then that Mazibe grasped his arm and said, "Thank you, Dirk." They shook hands. "It is our custom that when one man saves another's life, the man who is saved shows his gratitude by begging for a gift."

"Begging?"

"It shows respect and deference. My life belongs to you, and you are responsible for me now."

Dirk would have laughed had Mazibe not been so serious. "I don't want to be responsible for you, induna."

"Then I beg you for a gift; give it, and you will no longer be responsible for my life."

"What gift?"

Mazibe hesitated, and the boat bobbed in the gentle surf as he chose his words. "I smell rain coming."

Dirk sniffed. He smelled no rain.

Mazibe said, "If it should rain before we return to kwaBulawayo, I want you to take the amulet."

"What?" The very thought of possessing the amulet thrilled Dirk, and the strength of that emotion startled him. "You said I'm supposed to give you the gift, man! Anyway, what would I do with it?"

"Accept it only as its temporary protector, not as its possessor, lest it possess you."

Mazibe might have said more, but Dirk leaped into the water and pulled the boat toward the sand.

"I don't like this talk, and I don't smell any rain; come on, help me beach this thing and let's get out of this place. We have a Zulu king to honor, and I don't want any excuses from you when I beat you—you complaining that you were afraid of rain . . ."

He chattered on, confused at the powerful feelings stirring up within him. Mazibe said nothing more until the boat was landed. Then he faced Dirk and spoke firmly.

"My life is yours. The bull's head is no longer for me to bear, and yet it must be protected. If not you, then who? The white thing, Thomas Lovell?"

With that, Mazibe strode away, leaving Dirk standing in the sand.

Dirk shuffled back to the edge of the water and soaked his hands, washing them over and over, as if they were bloody. He was tormented by the thought of carrying that wonderful, incomprehensible golden amulet. Whatever its powers for good or for evil, it had been the reason for four men dying that night. Not even the clean, cold seawater could cleanse his hands just then, but how many more would die because of the amulet? And if he carried it, how many more would he have to kill? Or would they kill him first?

And why? In God's name, why?

HARD ADVICE

Rachel rode around the outskirts of the moonlit farmyard, letting Tempest cool off and trying not to feel so sad. She was already late for dinner, but could not go in yet, wanting to talk to someone about Gerrit's proposal. Who would understand her refusal?

Sannie was too weak to hear such startling news, and Johannes would not be sympathetic. He would just say, "Marry Gerrit, the best possible husband!" It would have to be Tante Emmy, just waking from a nap in her trekwagon.

"Ach, child, it's good to see you," Emmy said from the dimness of the tenting; she wrapped her massive belly with a blanket against the evening chill and beckoned for Rachel to come up the short ladder and sit. "It's good to see you, even if you look like you want a shoulder to weep on."

Emmy called sharply to a serving girl for some tea, listened to Rachel hurriedly tell about Gerrit's proposal, then embraced her as if she really were a child. It felt good. The wagon was dark except for the moonlight and one candle, and Rachel was grateful, for her tear-streaked face would not be so visible.

"There, there," Emmy said, "you're not the first maid to weep at a proposal of marriage. But mercy me, usually they're tears of joy, or maybe tears of sorrow if the suitor's old and ugly in a made match. Who would have imagined a pretty girl bawling because an upright, wealthy jonge like Gerrit Schuman wanted to make her his bride?"

Dismayed, Rachel sat back. "But, Tante Emmy, I don't love him, and I can't marry a man I don't love, but I'm sorry about causing him such pain."

The girl brought the tea, approaching slowly, trying to eavesdrop until Emmy told her to mind her own business. The aroma of dinner at the cooking fires was in the air, but Rachel had lost her appetite. Over at the farmyard lanterns were twinkling, and at Gerrit's wagons the campfire was bright in the darkness.

After gulping half a cup of tea, Emmy wiped her mouth and wagged a finger at Rachel. "Now listen, girl. I have to be straight about this, and no romantical notions. You came for advice, and you'll get it." She leaned forward, face close to Rachel's, and said, "My advice is—marry him."

"What? Tante Emmy, I don't love him!"

Emmy waved that off with her fat hands and leaned back, shaking her head. "Romantical love and trekking into the wilderness don't go together. Survival and trekking do go together. What young man's better for a husband than Gerrit? Tell me that!"

Rachel had no ready answer. "Tante Emmy, you've been married three times. Surely you understand what love is."

"Ach, yes, I understand love, indeed, child." She adjusted the blanket robe as if she were some giant bird nesting in the shadowy wagon box. "I loved my first husband passionately, and we had three of the happiest years in anyone's life. But he died young, whether I loved him or not, and what good did love do me then?

"I married my second because he was rich, a widower with good servants who would take care of me and my children. A decent man, a man I liked well enough, though he had his shortcomings. We'd be back in Graaf Reinet now, making more babies, if he hadn't gone off drunk to argue with the English army and got himself shot down in the road as a rebel."

In the half-light, Rachel saw Emmy's lower lip quiver at that. Emmy stopped to catch a breath and clear her throat. She had borne eight children from those two marriages, four of them dying, and four by now already married themselves, two of those off on the Arendt trek. Her third husband, André, she had married about six years ago, and they had produced no offspring, nor did they expect to, for Emmy was almost sixty.

"I married André because he made me laugh—and of course he had a good purse that made him highly respected and an even better catch." She giggled. "Now I delight in the old blind rascal, and he still can tell me new stories of his adventures. He's the wisest creature I've ever met, and he knows just what I'm thinking before I do."

She giggled again and drank tea.

"You love him?" Rachel so wanted Emmy to say she did love André, with all her heart.

"Love him? He's an old man, I'm an old woman, and the binding of our many years is stronger than any romantical notions young folk worship so much!" The good cheer in her voice turned hard. "In the wilderness there's no room for such notions, Rachel. Love in your situation is a delusion. Suicide!"

There was a pause as Emmy caught her breath. The dinner bell rang at the farmhouse. They had organized it without Rachel, and she felt irresponsible, further adding to her disappointment at hearing Tante Emmy's cynicism.

Bravely, she said, "Thank you, Tante; I admire your wisdom and respect your honesty, but we'll never agree on this. There has to be romantical love out in the new homeland! Has to be!" Putting down the teacup, she rose to leave. "Or why would we go there?"

"You wanted my advice, child, well there it is." Emmy's voice was cold, and it rose in pitch as she looked away and went on. "Gerrit will protect you and provide for you better than any man I've ever known, and I've known some strong ones, believe me!"

Not wanting to feel sad anymore, Rachel climbed down the ladder, saying lightly, "I won't forget what you've said, Tante. But don't think too badly of me if I end up an old maid."

She had meant this mostly in jest, but Emmy growled from in the dimness of the wagon, and her hand slapped the side wall.

"Try to stay an old maid in the north, and you're a damned fool!"

How that stung coming from beloved Tante Emmy, who never before had spoken a sharp word to her. Head down, Rachel left the wagon, slowly leading Tempest through the darkness and into the farmyard, where a few tallow lamps hung. She saw her colored serving girl, Millie, stealing a moment from chores to walk arm in arm with Jacob, Emmy's blacksmith. In the shadows, they kissed and laughed, then strolled toward the kitchen door.

How lucky they are, Rachel thought, and wondered what it was like to love someone that way. Perhaps Tante Emmy was right, though. Perhaps Rachel's heart was plainly wrong, or it might be that she simply was foolish, asking too much of life at a time like this. *Oh, how the world's turned so completely around!* Prosperous farmers tearing up the roots of two hundred years and journeying into a wilderness where romantical love could not thrive!

She did not want to believe that.

Young people would always fall in love, even in times of great danger, even before the promised land was safely won. Surely, Tante Emmy did not really mean that a woman who wanted love was a damned fool. Rachel's sadness at refusing Gerrit had passed. Now, she just felt angry with it all.

THE BEARDED ONE

Dirk and Mazibe started their race well before dawn, running out of Port Natal while it was silent except for a barking dog or two. They trotted up the long slope to the ridge overlooking the bay and proceeded side by side for an hour, neither saying much. At break of dawn, Dirk saw no sign of the *Red Witch.* She had drifted out to sea. If found, she would not be the first derelict floating without a crew. Before long, she would be swept ashore to founder on the rocks.

Each man carried three wrapped bottles of Macassar oil snugly fitted into the satchels, Dirk's under his rifle, Mazibe's next to his spear and knobkerrie. After a few hours, Mazibe began to pull ahead. It was just a matter of yards, but he always kept in front, not permitting Dirk to take the lead. Several times Dirk sprinted, but the Zulu did not let him pass. By the end of four hours, neither had rested or eaten, drinking only splashes of water snatched from a canteen or a Zulu gourd as they ran. Mazibe was showing no signs of stress, but Dirk was feeling the strain. Still, he stayed close and would not allow himself to lose ground on the first day.

It was in shady jungle that they met the escort of boys coming wearily down the trail toward Port Natal. Mazibe and Dirk passed them, giving a friendly wave and calling out that they should follow, leaving them standing there with jaws dropping. The dismayed boys no doubt had been hoping to visit the settlement, rest, and see the ocean. Now they had to turn around immediately, though they were completely spent, their faces sunken, eyes empty. Dirk glanced back and had to smile to see them gamely reforming to change direction. Mazibe's resolute son, the good-looking Senzana, was once again at their head, urging them on.

The day stayed cool, their running now mostly under mangrove trees. Mazibe was setting the pace, testing Dirk, who was up to it but, by late in the day, felt strained. They did not stop for food, and Dirk did not complain. He often sang to himself to relieve the monotony in his mind and the stiffness in his legs, but there was no idle chatter from him. From time to time he chewed biltong, which gave him strength.

As the sky lost brightness, Dirk wondered how far they had come. The trail was familiar at times, and he guessed it was at least thirty miles from the settlement. As they approached a fork in the path, Mazibe pointed to the left.

"That way there is a boatman who can take us across the River Tugela. He is an old friend, and he has a daughter I want to marry."

Dirk agreed to turn off, glad to hear the induna say the way was short, and they could sleep in a hut that night. Had they followed the trail they used coming down, there would be only treetops for beds, and crossing the river would have required swimming and wading through mud flats, for the kraal with dugouts was on the opposite bank. The rainy season had not begun yet, and the river was low, a mile or more wide. At least there were no crocodiles there.

Mazibe may truly have wanted to see his old friend with the eligible daughter, and even to sleep in a hut, but Dirk soon thought this detour had another purpose: The track went steeply upwards, a slippery trail in the shadow of the hills, and Mazibe did not slow the pace as he took it. Dirk felt the hurt in his lungs and thighs now, but he held his position a few paces behind.

It was a relief half an hour later when the trail mercifully turned downward, toward the river flats, and the fresh sweetness of moist air wafted up to meet them. Just as evening closed in, they arrived at a clutter of grass huts on the bank of the Tugela, where Mazibe was received with near ecstasy by the boatman and his large family.

Through a haze of exhaustion and sweat, Dirk greeted them all, and found himself being introduced painstakingly, one person at a time by a chuckling and talkative Mazibe. Dirk met the old wives, the young wives, the married daughters, their husbands and sons, the unmarried sons who soon would be warriors, and the married sons with their young families, the shy children who had never seen a white thing before—and even the babies were brought to meet the reeling Dirk, who was told their names, one by one by one. . . .

"Mazibe," he said afterwards, as he finally slumped down on his blanket and guzzled water, "You're a damned rascal, but I'll greet the whole Zulu nation if you want me to, and stay on my feet, too."

The induna chuckled, drinking water, then pouring it over his head, and the laugh became a high-pitched giggle, for Mazibe was himself a little giddy from weariness. The laughing made Dirk laugh, too, though it sounded weak.

For all that the people here wanted Mazibe to win the race,

Dirk was welcomed and comforted, given a comfortable bed, and fed the headman's own amaSi. It could have been worse. And better. Mazibe was up half the night playing his thumb piano for the beautiful youngest daughter, who was destined to become his fourth wife. As Dirk struggled in a pained and restless sleep, he thought he heard Mazibe wander outside with her.

"How could he really have the strength?" someone was saying in Dirk's dream, but he was not certain who.

☾ ☾ ☾

The next day it was more of the same after the runners crossed the broad, muddy Tugela in the dugout. They ran at a steady pace, and for the first few hours Dirk stayed with Mazibe, but it hurt. Mazibe drew steadily ahead, and by the fourth hour was a hundred yards in front, always around the next bend.

Dirk was running without thought by now. He was sure Mazibe was suffering, too, but it would have helped to see the Zulu's face and be certain. The morning wore on, and Dirk knew he had better find a rhythm before it was too late. He could not run at Mazibe's pace. He had to find a strategy before his legs or heart gave out. It was then that he remembered what he had said to Shaka—that to beat Mazibe he would run until his heart burst. Well, before that happened, he would run according to his own ability and would find a way to win.

Before the fifth hour was up, Dirk was forced by leg cramps to slow to a walk. Mazibe was nowhere in sight, and probably a thousand yards ahead. Dirk munched on some dry strips of biltong, knowing there would be no more kraals where he could stop for food and drink along this stretch of trail. He was leaving the coastal forest and entering lion country, a high plateau of scattered thornbush trees and deep grasses. Somewhat back from the trail, prides of well-fed lions lay in the shade under large trees, but Dirk did not mind them. He worried about hungry lions, the ones that hid in tall grass, waiting.

As long as there was activity all around him—monkeys and baboons chattering angrily down from trees and climbing rock ledges; graceful elands with their long horns bounding across the trail; an occasional ostrich calmly gliding through the grass—he knew no lions were on the prowl nearby. As the day drew to a close, however, the noises of the jungle and grassy meadows began to change, from sudden raucous excitement as he passed, to hushed, ominous sounds, and then there descended an eerie stillness all around.

Dirk ran on, knowing it was becoming ever more dangerous. By the failing light of sunset, he could still see Mazibe's tracks and could tell the induna had passed here less than an hour before. That meant several miles to Mazibe's advantage. If Dirk could run an extra hour or two after dark, he would stay very close to the Zulu, perhaps even pass him in the night. With the full moon beginning to light the sky beyond the treetops to his right, there would be plenty of light to see by.

As he ran, he unslung the rifle, which was kept loaded and frequently checked. He held it sloping downward in the crook of one elbow or the other. He was utterly weary by now, but would not stop yet. Mazibe probably had found a safe place to sleep by this hour, and with every stride Dirk was gaining on him. The chances were good that no lion would find Dirk, but if one did, he was sure to sense it stalking him and could shoot before it leaped.

Yes, the chances were good that he would be all right, he kept telling himself over and over, whispering the words, listening for every crackling sound, every rustle of grass. If he continued to feel sure of himself, he would run all night in the moonlight, and Mazibe would be hard-pressed to recover the lost ground. That thought in itself gave Dirk a rush of inspiration as he ran on.

Stars were faint in the pale wash of moonlight across the heavens. Dirk was feeling better now, sure he was soon to pass Mazibe, who might be fast asleep while he swept by. Then a low growl sounded frighteningly close. He gave a start and sprinted forward, looking from side to side. That was unmistakably a hunting lioness.

She was somewhere behind. Dirk's rifle was primed and ready. All he needed was an instant's warning to aim and fire. As long as the powder was dry, the load not shaken loose by constant running. . . .

The growl came again. Movement in the bushes to his left rear. He dare not stop. He dashed forward even faster. The trail was clear in the moonlight. If the lioness sprang, he would be ready.

Suddenly branches overhead shook, and something dropped lightly to the ground in front of him. Dirk skidded to a stop. A leopard? He brought up his rifle. Now there were two beasts, but he had only one shot! Take the leopard—

"It is I, down from the trees." Mazibe stood before him, eyes and teeth gleaming in the dimness.

Dirk put up the rifle, panting for breath.

"Induna, firesticks don't know the difference between Zulus and leopards."

"What are you doing now, umuntu? Offering yourself as a feast for the bearded one? Listen to me when I say you must find a safe place for the night or—"

A roar!

They ran. The lioness bounded from cover. They could not get away on foot. Dirk was about to turn and fire when Mazibe yelled and sprang up onto a branch. Dirk jumped, too, but the lioness was there and slashed at him as he yanked himself up, thrusting feet-first onto a limb, and in the same movement grabbing another and keeping on climbing. Mazibe was already up, shouting at the snarling lioness and pointing with his spear. Dirk was high enough now, and he turned to aim his rifle at the beast, which was on hind legs, growling and pawing at them.

"No," said Mazibe, touching the rifle barrel. "Kill her, and others will come to trouble us—packs of hyenas will smell her blood and will linger all tomorrow, and leopards, who well know how to climb trees; let her go."

For a moment, Dirk held the hungry lioness in his sights as she mauled and clawed the bark. Soon, she dropped to all fours and walked around and around the tree, growling. Dirk calmed down, letting the rifle rest on his knees, taking a deep breath, which felt like the first since the lioness attacked.

"You want to run on tonight?" Mazibe asked. "She will keep you company. But if you stay up here she will go back home and let you sleep."

Dirk was glad to be with Mazibe again. It was also good that the induna was not ahead of him anymore. They sat on the branch, and Dirk opened the flask of peach brandy, sharing it with Mazibe. After a while, the Zulu leaned back against the tree trunk and sighed with weariness.

"My white friend, you cannot beat me in this race in daylight, but if you try to beat me in darkness you will be eaten by the bearded ones."

Dirk did not answer at first, for he did not want to sound too hasty. "I will run in darkness if I must to beat you; I won't lose because of a bad-tempered tao."

The lioness roared and leaped, pawing furiously, as if she had heard Dirk use her name. Mazibe made a sound of exasperation and put a finger to his mouth. Then he spoke almost kindly and with much respect to the beast, telling her they would never come down. She circled the tree, growling, as Mazibe spoke to Dirk.

"I will not be happy to win this race if it is because the bearded one invited you back to her lair to meet her young. I know you cannot beat me; even the bearded one knows you cannot beat me."

"The bearded one knows? Why do you say that?"

"Listen, when she chased us, she knew who was slower, and went for you."

"She didn't catch me."

"Look at your clothing."

Claw marks slashed through the seat of Dirk's pants, as if cut by knives, yet there was not a scratch on his body. He did not know whether to be startled or relieved, but his skin crawled. He looked down at the lioness, but all was quiet below, as if she had departed.

"She knows you now," Mazibe said, "and she will recognize you tomorrow night by her personal mark on your behind . . . if you run after dark."

Dirk gave his own sound of exasperation. "By dark tomorrow, induna, we'll see whether you are as strong as you are today, and whether you or I will be easier prey for her. I'll make you push hard all day tomorrow; you might even have to run at night yourself."

"At night I will be wrapped around a high tree branch, safe

from bearded ones." Mazibe smiled. "You had better do the same."

Dirk lashed the rope around his body and tied himself to the tree, then secured the rifle so that it was suspended by the stock, ready in case any lions or leopards tried to climb. It was safe up here, but uncomfortable. Oh, how his body ached, legs throbbing, lungs and throat raw. He was sure Mazibe felt the same, though the Zulu did not show any pain.

No matter that Dirk hurt so much, he fell asleep almost immediately, and did not dream.

☾ ☾ ☾

Dirk was roused by a shout from Mazibe.

Shaking himself awake, almost falling off the branch, he tried to clear his mind. He was sore from head to foot, but refused to think about it, believing he would run off his aches in an hour or so. Mazibe's voice came again, from somewhere on the ground. It was dawn, the night sky beginning to empty into soft morning tones of clear blue. In the dimness, Mazibe could be seen kneeling at a spring, surrounded by the wavering shadows of dry rushes. He was drinking, on all fours, lapping the water as an animal would. Nearby was his pouch of hair tonic.

Dirk still had bread and biltong, and he jumped down to offer some to Mazibe, who was grateful, but said little as they prepared to start the third day of what would be a four-day race.

When they had eaten, Dirk said, "It will be more fine weather, no clouds, no rain."

Resting with his back against a tree, Mazibe nodded and let his hand dangle in the water, soaking a strip of biltong to soften it. Dirk voiced a worry that had haunted him for some time.

"Induna, will you be in danger of punishment from Shaka when I win this race?"

"Lord Shaka is king, and life and death belong to him, his to give or take away."

Dirk thought about that before continuing.

"He might execute you on a whim, yet you serve him, and you carry the amulet for him?" Dirk could not understand this loyalty to a king who had murdered so many Zulus.

"The will of the king is never a whim," Mazibe replied, getting to his feet. "The will of the king is the will of the mighty amaZulu, whom Lord Shaka forged into the greatest fighting force of all, and for that he is revered forever, and for that we bow to his radiance!"

Mazibe's eyes were wide.

"I do not anticipate death, umuntu, but when it comes to meet me, I will accept it and pray that my life had been lived for the amaZulu."

Dirk reflected that no self-respecting Boer would ever worship any other human being as the Zulus worshipped Shaka—no king, no religious leader, not even a war hero. Boers knew no master but themselves, guided by the will of Jehovah, as they personally interpreted that will. On the frontier and on the farm they were loners, their rigid self-discipline and faith sustaining them through crisis and hardship. They united in large numbers for only two occasions: One was the seasonal Nachmaal celebrations, to worship en masse and to marry off their children; the other was war. How different his people were from the close-knit Zulus, yet similar in their fierce pride and willingness to fight ruthlessly for their nations.

"I serve my people," Mazibe went on, "and King Shaka is the Bull of the People. We are his."

After a respectful silence, Dirk asked, "If Shaka is so powerful, why can he not wear the amulet?"

It was an insolent question, but after all that had happened, he felt Mazibe would answer it. Mazibe thought a moment before replying.

"I do not understand this bull's head or all its powers, and I believe its power is different for each one who faces it; but I do know the amulet can reveal one's deepest desires, just as it reveals one's true nature."

Mazibe paused, and Dirk waited until he continued.

"In Lord Shaka's fury, he has slain many, even those he loves." Mazibe's breathing was shaky. "A man's deeds—even a king's—confront him if he carries the Amulet of White Fire, so that he cannot escape from them . . . and some amulet bearers must relinquish the bull's head or go mad."

"Did this happen to Shaka?" Dirk asked this more abruptly than he had intended.

Mazibe stiffened.

"That is not for me to judge. I simply accept it that Lord Shaka asked me to bear the sacred amulet until those moments when, in his wisdom, he wishes to consult it."

Dirk considered that. "What good can the amulet do? What good is it for Shaka, for you, or the Zulus?"

"Let it be understood that the White Fire reveals truth," Mazibe said. "And the amulet is as strong for good or evil as the bearer is strong for good or evil."

"And you?"

"Until now, I have been able to carry it because no demon torments my dreams." He sighed. "But now I fear—fear I am weakening, fear my mind is leaving me, for I see visions I do not understand, visions I do not wish to see! I know it is time for the

Amulet of Truth to leave me, for it has told me so." He looked into Dirk's eyes. "Perhaps it has already told you something."

Dirk had no reply.

Mazibe picked up his weapons and stepped onto the trail. Dirk followed, slinging the loaded rifle over his shoulder, the satchel of hair tonic across his back. Both men shook off their ominous discussion and flexed their legs. Dirk tried to ignore the induna's last remark, though it stayed with him. He glanced sidelong at the pouch bound by a thong around Mazibe's waist. What did an ancient talisman have to do with a Boer scout, anyway? And why did he want so much to touch it, if only just once?

He was eager to run. They shared a last drink of peach brandy.

"Enough talk." Dirk offered Mazibe his hand, and the induna grasped it. "There will be a moon again tonight, and it will light my way past your sleeping place."

The Zulu shook his head.

"May your gods protect you, umuntu."

"And yours protect you." Dirk could not help but grin, and so did the induna.

Abruptly, right hands still clasped, they sprang with a yell onto the narrow trail, shouldering each other as they surged forward, each man trying to get the lead, until they wrenched apart and crashed between dense, overhanging bushes. If lions were watching, they surely slunk off, startled by these wild creatures, white and black, who sprinted through the forest like raging beasts of prey.

THE HAND OF GOD

At Sweetfountain, as often she did early in the morning, Rachel walked with her Boerhound to the graveyard on the hill. She enjoyed this time most of all, at first light, before the heat began. As she strolled, she carried a bunch of flowers loosely behind her back. The cool blush of dawn was at her right, the eastern sky turning pale blue as stars in the west faded. The dew hung, shimmering, on the long grass, and Jaeger bounded through it, stopping now and again as if to listen and smell the breeze.

Making her way up the path toward the hilltop, Rachel thought she heard music, but could not tell from where. There was activity down at the farmyard and around the Toulouse and Schuman wagons. Johannes had said they could leave in a few days, for Sannie was much better than expected. They might even catch up with the Arendt trek in a month.

When that music came to her once more, Rachel recognized it as the concertina of André Toulouse, from just over the hill. She hurried forward to find him alone, sitting on the bench outside the white pickets that surrounded the graves. Brought here by his mixed-blood servant, Freddie—who was dozing in the grass down the slope—André faced the approaching dawn, playing his concertina, head back, swaying with the music.

Rachel called to him, and he kept playing as he replied, "Come here, chérie, and listen to the music of dancing girls in Cape Town and of wise old Swazi chiefs. Come sit by me."

She went to his side, enjoying that familiar tune of his, "Believe Me, If All Those Endearing Young Charms." Its melody was beautiful, making Rachel think England must not be all bad (as some Boers insisted) if it had brought forth such music.

After a moment, still playing, André asked, "You want to get married yet?"

That took her by surprise, but she understood his teasing humor.

"Don't tell me you're proposing, too, Uncle André! You already have a wife."

He cackled. "Would that I could propose, chérie! I'd have one beautiful wife and one wise wife."

"And who would be who? Tante Emmy is very beautiful."

"Ah, yes, very beautiful, even more beautiful than when she was young and thin like you. I know, for I used to admire her from afar for many years, and when I returned from the jungle, a blind man, she decided to marry me because I told her she looked more beautiful than ever!"

He played on, softly and with much sentimentality.

"And what could a blind gentleman see of her beauty, may I ask?"

"Ah, child, you are too young to understand the beauty that I feel and hear, and in my own way see, for I remember sight, and when Emmy speaks, I see the most beautiful woman in creation! More beautiful than any woman ever seen with these eyes."

Rachel liked that and wanted him to know she was smiling, so she laughed a little to let him hear.

"You've admired Tante Emmy for so long, then?"

"Yes, with an aching heart, from afar, just as your beau, Gerrit Schuman, has admired you for so long."

She wanted to change the subject to anything else, and began to talk of the weather, and how Sannie was stronger, and that someone was coming, driving up on the road from Graaf Reinet in a Cape cart, followed by two riders.

André did not let her change the subject. "My wife said you are not in love with young Schuman."

"He is not my beau." She got up and went to lay the flowers on the graves, kneeling for a moment beside her father's mound of stones.

André went on. "Emmy said you ought to marry him anyway." With a flourish of the concertina, he stopped playing.

Rachel sighed. "I feel so uplifted by your music, Uncle André. If you would only play and not talk of marriages."

"You are right to wait for love."

"What?"

"You are right to wait, chérie, for you will never be happy unless you marry for love."

She caressed a yellow mimosa flower growing at her feet. Why was it that even when André said just what she wanted to hear, she still did not know what to think?

"Love, Uncle André? Tante Emmy says there is no place for that sort of love in the wilderness. How many people truly marry for love?"

"Not enough," he said with a broad gesture, then turned to face her, as if seeing. "You are different, and you must not deny your heart."

He smiled, and Rachel thought he looked even older than his years, older, and so very wise, as Tante Emmy had said.

"Believe it, Rachel," he continued, his expression becoming serious. "There are some who must wait for love, but if they do not have the courage to wait until it stands before them, they will never be happy, will never find peace."

"Oh, Uncle André, you just want to make me feel better." She did not feel better, though.

He was staring at her with those blind eyes that were so kind.

"Love such as yours is like the fire of electricity, for nothing can stop it once it is released, and nothing can withstand it. Have a care how you release it, lest it burn one who is not meant to touch it."

He played. The sun was about to burst over the horizon, the sky a radiant blue. The Cape cart and riders were coming closer. Rachel wanted to hear more about the fires of love and electricity. It distracted her, and for now that was enough.

She mused: "Romantical love, electric fire . . . are they just the same, then?"

"Yes! And nothing quite like them!" Then he caught himself and hastened to add: "Well, wait; I have to say there is another fire like them."

He rocked a little faster, back and forth, the English song louder, as if his thoughts excited him.

"What fire?" Rachel came to sit beside him.

"The white fire of the amulet!" he whispered, and she had to lean over to hear him. "A fire I'll never forget as long as I live."

"Tell me."

André became more agitated and spoke rapidly.

"The Swazi chief said it made one see the truth, and by heaven, ever since the day I felt its fire I've seen a glimmer of truth more often than I like, sometimes!"

He set down the concertina. The sun was bright in their

faces. Rachel wanted to know more about this amulet and was about to ask him to go on when he took her by surprise, declaring, "There was one other mighty fire, and that was the bolt of lightning that struck me in the jungle and took my sight away. Yes, now that was electric fire, too! Did you know that? Well, it's true, the scientists have found out that lighting is the same as electricity—"

She wanted him to go back to love's electric fire, and touched his arm. "Uncle André, you were saying that I should marry only for love?"

"What? Yes, yes, that's right." He picked up his instrument and began to play again. "Do something with your fire of love, do what most are too afraid to do, or are not wise enough to do—yes, for beautiful as you are, you . . . would be the wise wife, chérie."

He cackled, and Rachel laughed, too, thinking him full of charming flattery. As she went to kneel on the soft grass next to her mother's grave, she wanted André to speak on, and he did.

"The fire of love will reveal itself, and you will come to know what romance is, but also what it is not, and that it is no guarantor of happiness in this life."

That she did not understand.

"You must follow your heart if it is romantic love you seek," he said, "but remember, there are other kinds of love, and Gerrit is indeed a very good man."

The spell was broken, but she was grateful for André's kindness and counsel. In some ways, though, she was more mixed up than ever.

"Thank you, Uncle André." She went to kiss his cheek. "Shall we go down and see who these visitors from Graaf Reinet are?" The cart and riders were close to the farmyard now. "The horsemen are Redcoats!" she said, feeling a chill, for the Boers hereabouts despised British soldiers.

André rose and took her arm, saying, "They've heard about the trek and have come to stop us, the government being against it."

☾ ☾ ☾

Followed by a sleepy Freddie, they went down to the farmyard, where the others had gathered around the cart and soldiers. Everyone was there except for Gerrit, who was out riding amongst his herds. Tante Emmy was overflowing in a large chair, where her servants had seated her, waiting to hear what the visitors had to say. The Redcoats were officers from the small military post at Graaf Reinet, and in the cart was the Reverend Albert Roos, dominee of the Dutch Reformed congregation, whose church was in that village.

The portly Reverend Roos, in his black frock coat and wide-brimmed hat, was given a warm welcome as he was helped down from his horse cart. The soldiers were all but ignored until one of them asked loudly to have all the people gathered at once, to hear an official proclamation.

Johannes, who was standing beside Rachel, answered.

"They are all gathered. What do you want?"

The officers, a mustached captain and a baby-faced lieutenant, looked at each other. They were hot, their short stovepipe hats and red tunics covered with the dust of the long ride. Rachel thought they must be put out that no one offered them the same hospitality given the dominee.

The captain addressed Johannes: "We understood there were forty or fifty families gathered here, all about to migrate out of the colony. Is that so? Where are they?"

Johannes laughed and indicated the grasslands. "Soldier, look with your eyes and see how the grass is flattened for a mile across, and then follow that track if you are able to keep sight of it. By the time you find our folk, they'll be out of the colony, beyond your authority, and we will join them, as will thousands more in years to come."

The captain ignored Johannes's rude tone and drew a paper from his saddlebag, shaking it open, clearing his throat.

"I read from a proclamation of the lieutenant-governor, which warns you people against causing trouble if you are so misguided as to leave Cape Colony."

In spite of loud grumbles, he began to read in a clipped monotone.

"Whereas certain farmers are migrating out of Cape Colony, beyond the protection of the crown and into unsettled lands not administered by crown courts of justice, therefore it is officially declared that any disturbance beyond the borders between those aforesaid emigrants and the many peaceful native tribes will be considered an act of inciting to riot and disturbing the peace, if not wholesale instigation of foreign war. . . ."

The proclamation went on in this way, declaring that while there was no specific British law preventing inhabitants from leaving the colony, the emigrants were forbidden to take firearms or ammunition over the borders, and any such attempt would be prevented by force. Obviously, it was already too late to gather enough troops from the meager British garrisons to stop the trekkers and disarm them. No one replied to the proclamation, though the officer glanced around, as if expecting an argument.

Reverend Roos clambered back onto the cart and removed his hat, revealing thin gray hair and a pate that gleamed in the sunlight. He spoke in a ringing voice:

"Dear friends, it is my duty to tell you that the church is opposed to her congregants departing en masse for unknown lands, weakening our already small congregations and causing dissension amongst those who stay behind—for many would follow if they were able, and our churches would be left empty!"

"Let them come, too, then!" Johannes yelled. "And you come with them and protect our souls!"

The dominee turned red and began to explain that no minister would ever be permitted by the Dutch Reformed Church to leave the Cape Colony against the will of the government, not even to "shepherd God's flock in the wilderness."

"What kind of life will there be out there without the church, without God?" Reverend Roos implored.

"God is everywhere," Emmy said.

Roos looked frustrated. "How would you conduct baptisms, burials, Sabbath worship, weddings? Would you have your children grow up to take spouses and live in sin?"

"The hand of God! I knew it!" Gerrit was galloping in, waving his hat and shouting. "The dominee has come! Right on time! It's the hand of God!"

With a jolt, Rachel realized what he meant.

Emmy was watching it all closely, hands folded on her belly. Rachel quickly recovered, and now was more angry at Gerrit than sorry for him. He was jubilantly riding around the minister's cart and the startled officers, calling out:

"It's the summons of God! The dominee is here, and now we can be—"

"Reverend Roos!" Rachel almost shrieked, shutting Gerrit up. He drew his horse to a halt beside her, a light in his eyes as she quickly said, "Reverend Roos, may I ask you a question?"

A bit befuddled, the minister leaned down and smiled kindly. "Yes, my dear?"

"Reverend Roos . . . was it the hand of God that sent you out here today?"

"What?" He chuckled, became quite jolly, and looked about him. "Well, my dear, I am God's servant, and all that I do is in his work, but—"

"There!" Gerrit asserted, pointing at him.

Rachel folded her arms. "But. You said, 'But.'"

Roos went on: "—but in fact I came out here today because Captain Bailey asked me to join him, and to convey to you the concerns of the church with regard to your intention to migrate from the colony."

"So, it was not some divine inspiration you had while praying last night that sent you to Sweetfountain?" Rachel stared hard at him.

"What?" He laughed. "Well, not exactly—"

"Not a direct act of God."

"Direct?"

Gerrit's expression was murky.

"You're not here to bury anyone, are you?" Rachel pressed.

"I hope not, but of course if necessary—"

"Or to baptize any child?"

"I could. That would be wonder—"

"Or to marry anyone?"

"Well, not that I know of. No, I didn't come out to perform any of my usual duties. Why do you ask, my dear?"

Before answering, Rachel glanced sidelong at Gerrit, whose

eyes were half-closed as he cogitated hard.

"I didn't think it was the hand of God that sent you, because there's no need for burials or baptisms or even weddings in the neighborhood today." She smiled brightly. "Of course that's because almost everyone's already gone trekking, obeying God's summons, unlike yourself, who came out here only because Captain Bailey asked you to come."

From the back of the crowd, André cackled and declared, "Indeed, child, you'd be the wise wife!"

There came another giggle, this time from Tante Emmy.

Gerrit was gaping at Rachel, who resolutely did not look back, her arms still folded. In the next moment, he sprang aboard his horse and galloped away.

Johannes and Sannie could not help grinning, though they seemed sympathetic as they watched Gerrit return to his herds. At Sannie's urging, Johannes invited the minister and officers to come into the house for refreshment on the condition that they not discuss the trek or politics. The company of the dominee would be more than welcome, for there was always news and gossip to be heard.

The servants were pleased to have had a little excitement, and they chattered happily while getting back to work. Even the Englishmen were cheerful now, their formality let down a bit, for they appreciated the offer of hospitality. Though out here most Boers wanted nothing to do with soldiers, there was a code of honor on the frontier that required a householder to accommodate travelers, even British officers.

André, guided by Freddie, intercepted Rachel before she went to the house, and he asked where Gerrit was now.

"He's gone off, unhappy," she answered, "and I'm very sorry, but it's his own fault."

André grinned, "He's thinking that you've either intentionally embarrassed him or intentionally contradicted the will of God, and he's not sure which." He cackled again.

It was a comfort to Rachel that André was on her side, and she watched as Freddie took him back to his wagon. Rachel went to the farmhouse to help receive the visitors. Out on the veldt, there would be no more trouble from British officers, and the trekkers would be able to get along well enough without meddling dominees who cared more about the numbers of their congregants than about the happiness and liberty of the folk.

DIRK'S HEART

Dirk and Mazibe ran side by side, the ground rough, the trail broken. They ran through many small streams flowing from the hills to their left, streams that swallowed the track and dragged the runners down to slide into slippery, stony gutters that resisted letting them go again.

They ran without stopping.

Dirk had never suffered such agony, but he battled to stay with Mazibe. The Zulu had to show signs of tiring soon. It was a terrible pace. Four hours passed and then five. Now Mazibe was always three strides ahead. Whenever Dirk made a move to close up, Mazibe increased his speed just enough, just maddeningly enough to prevent his passing.

Six hours passed. The sun was bright, the breeze strong in their faces by early afternoon. The country climbed steeply, then plunged into numerous dongas, deep and slashing gullies of loose stone and scrubby bushes. The trail no sooner led up and out of a donga than it shot down again to suddenly rise up once more. Each upward climb seemed steeper to Dirk, for the gullies were endless.

Mazibe claimed a lead of thirty yards.

Northward, ever northward, all that day they ran without

pause. They passed two small kraals on the way, where the Zulus rushed to the gate and waved, cheering Mazibe on, falling silent and staring as Dirk ran by. Laughing little boys dashed alongside them for a while and then fell back, shouting goodbye. Neither man stopped to eat or rest at these kraals, though Dirk was famished and exhausted. Occasionally, he took a bite of hard bread and a drink from his canteen, but he did not stop.

Seven hours and then eight.

By now Dirk did not know or care whether the surroundings were open and grassy or if he were in thick forest overhung with mangrove trees. Everything was more of the same, a blurring rush of green and yellow under a blue sky. He instinctively knew enough to watch out for snakes lying in the road, or for crocodiles in the sun beside streams. Twice he startled crocodiles that hissed, splashing away into the water as he nimbly sprang aside.

Dirk ran and ran, stride after stride, closing the distance between them, pushing hard until he saw only the track ahead and the flashing white soles of Mazibe's feet. Step for step they ran, and Dirk found strength he did not know he had. He managed to keep close, driving Mazibe on. The Zulu glanced back whenever they took a twist in the trail down into a donga or thrust themselves up the slope of a sharp turn.

Nine hours.

Sometimes, when Mazibe looked back, Dirk grimaced a smile, dry lips sticking to his teeth, like a death's head. The Zulu was impassive. More than once Dirk heard himself groan in pain, though it was as if the voice belonged to someone else, that the pain was hurting someone else. His legs were numb by now, muscles stiff as iron. Air did not seem to enter or leave his lungs. He could not feel his throat. That nagging ache at his side, the one that usually went away after some running, kept stabbing at him, dogging him, just as he dogged Mazibe.

Yes, he was like a dog, a determined, tireless dog, and he ran that way, putting one foot in front of the other, in front of the other, in front of the other, not thinking about anything except for the path and Mazibe's white soles rising and falling. Ten. Eleven. Twelve hours. The sun sank at his left shoulder. The jungle had returned around him, darkening with shadows, shadows that lengthened, as if they, too, were tired and had to lie down, to stretch out, to rest, to rest. . . . Thirteen hours had passed; day was almost night. Mazibe was much farther ahead now. When did that happen?

Why was Dirk doing this, anyway? To bring hair dye to a vainglorious, murdering Zulu chieftain? He laughed, but it was a rasping, pathetic sound. To beat Mazibe, the greatest runner he had ever encountered? Yes. To prove himself to someone? To whom? To Lovell? That snake! To Benjamin David? Benjamin was in danger if Dirk did not return with the Macassar oil. To himself? Because he was an arrogant Cape Dutchman who had never been beaten in a race and never would be beaten, not by some long-legged Zulu who damned well wouldn't admit pain, wouldn't admit that he was in agony, too, suffering just like Dirk, but was too damned proud, too damned Zulu to yield? He laughed again and tried to spit out dust, but nothing came.

On they ran.

The moon appeared.

They ran.

On and on, up stony terraces above dry watercourses, down slopes, slipping on rocks and earth that scattered underfoot. It was too dry! Too dry! A bit of rain would do the world good now, would do Dirk good. Cold, fresh, wet rain! He felt water splash his face, and it was a surprise that it was from his own canteen, thrown by his own hands, stale water that dripped down his cheeks, into his mouth, and was not fresh, God-sent rain at all.

There would be no rain. Shaka had doctored the clouds. The king's medicine would keep it dry from Port Natal to kwaBulawayo. Dutchmen knew how to run in rain, but Zulus liked it dry. Veldschoenen felt good on slimy ground slicked with rain. Zulu feet, those white soles, white soles beating the ground, white soles lifting and falling, lifting and falling, endlessly—they would slide on muddy ground, would slip on wet logs. Mazibe would lose if it rained. If it rained soon. If it did not rain soon, Mazibe would defeat Dirk Arendt. Never defeated before.

What had Sebe said? A fighting man who has not tasted defeat has not learned wisdom? Wisdom? Was defeat a lesson in wisdom? Ah, but Dirk ached! *Are we all doomed to learn wisdom by defeat, Sebe? Sebe-mamba! Sebe-changeling! Sebe-diviner! Sebe-rainmaker! Ah, Sebe, make rain now!* But rain would mean Shaka's medicine had failed, that the king was dead. . . .

Dirk growled, suddenly making for those flashing white soles with all his might, darting down into a donga on a twisting trail. He leaped over a bend in the path, gaining a few yards. He closed fast. He sprinted hard, feet flying, throwing up loose stones. Mazibe was not ready for him. Dirk cut another corner, and was there at Mazibe's shoulder. The Zulu winced to see Dirk with him.

Then Dirk's feet went out from under.

His knees scraped and banged against the hard earth and rocks. He slid, slid and slid, unable to stop himself, and began to roll in an avalanche of stones and dirt. He tumbled, fought to catch himself, bounced to his feet, staggering. He was twenty yards off the trail, which turned upwards, rising out of the donga, up to the sky, up to where the tall, black figure of Mazibe stood, pausing to look back before he disappeared into the lilac twilight.

Cursing, his mouth too dry to articulate, Dirk scrambled back up, hands and feet working, clawing fingers, scraping toes, his knees cut and bleeding. He was dizzy and had lost a shoe. He turned angrily to look for it. He was no Zulu. He could not run barefoot. He had not been trained by ruthless Shaka to run on thorns, though he could have done it if he had to, if it was for the welfare of the Boers. He was no Zulu, but a proud and free Boer of southern Africa, the proudest and most free white men in the world.

Where was that shoe?

No man would force him as Shaka forced his warriors to be more than human, to be madmen, to be miraculous runners. No man could force him to do anything, no man, not even the King of England could force Dirk Arendt to do anything he did not want to do, even on pain of death. Shoving the torn shoe back on his foot, he wished he could go barefoot like a Zulu, could run like that tall, black, mythical figure who had vanished over the crest of the ridge and into the lilac sky . . . one whose white soles rose and fell, rose and fell as if there were no end to it. No end to it.

Darkness.

The trail led into deeper forest. The moon left the eastern horizon, rising over the roof of the jungle, the mangroves, the baobab trees, the palms and the scrub oak. There were no white soles of feet to follow, and how far ahead those feet were Dirk did not try to guess. Where was the moon? Blocked by the treetops. It was too dark here. The moon could not light the way soon enough. Not enough light. *Too much pain!*

Dirk was walking.

The lioness would be abroad, already on his scent, stalking him. He was so very, very tired, his heart beating too fast. And yet, if he made it through the night, he would pass the resting Zulu. Could Mazibe be any more than a mile ahead? A mile of darkness, of somber forest, of trees sheltering the trail from faint starlight.

Oh, that the moon would break through and show the way! He could not see in the dark like the big cats. *Shine, moon, before it's too late!*

Dirk would not climb a tree and lose the race tomorrow. He would fight the cats if he must. He would go on all night. He would not lose to a hungry lion. He would not lose to Mazibe. He would push on all night. No white man could run like a Zulu, but a white man would run at night, run in moonlight, elude the lioness, and win the race.

What was that?

Moonlight, coming through the branches, dappling the track, showing the way. His spirits lifted. Stride and stride and stride along the trail, he was beginning to run again, as if his legs had a will of their own. It was level here, deep jungle, soft earth, no more damned gullies and stream beds and sliding rocky slopes. He ran on, unslinging his rifle, ready for whatever might be around the next bend. His heart thudded. His head began to spin. Again he became dizzy. Still he ran on, though feeling he might be sick, might vomit.

His heart pounded furiously, as with a will of its own, sore and heavy, as if it might . . . *I would run until my heart burst, if only I could defeat the induna.* Ah, but his chest ached.

"Halt!"

Dirk reeled to a stop. Mazibe was there, a cloudy figure at the base of a great baobab, that tree which an angry spirit once tore out of the ground and thrust back upside down so that its roots became branches. So said old Joop. Dirk wavered, almost falling. Dazed, he tried to focus on the Zulu. Heart thundering in his chest as he had never felt it before, never felt it—Dirk grinned.

"Induna!" he croaked, trying to shout. "Come on, Zulu, let's run while the moon is up." He turned to go, but Mazibe grabbed his arm. "Let go, you bastard!" Dirk whipped the rifle butt around, narrowly missing Mazibe's face, then lurched away along the path, reeling drunkenly.

Mazibe followed close behind. "You're a dead man if you do not sleep in the trees tonight!"

Dirk could hardly think straight. He might be dreaming, or imagining it all, perhaps back in Leyden on some carouse, having drunk himself into a stupor. But why was his rifle here, so heavy and smooth and hard? And why did his racing heart, always so strong, now hurt so terribly? His heart pounded.

"Tao!" Mazibe shouted, and in the same instant came a blood-chilling roar. Dirk's rifle found the cat's glowing eyes and fired. The lioness landed, paws twitching, at Dirk's feet. He dropped to one knee, panting for breath, chest tight and aching.

"Another!" Mazibe bellowed and dashed past Dirk, who tried to reload, jerking a cartridge from his shirt pocket, biting the wax paper from the charge, pouring the powder down the hot barrel, dropping in the lead ball, yanking out the ramrod, driving down the ball, replacing the ramrod, priming the firing pan with black powder from the cartridge casing, bringing up the rifle—

And there was Mazibe, howling as he took a huge black-maned lion's charge full force, ducking under it, driving his spear up into the chest of the leaping beast and hurling it over his shoulder. The lion shrieked, impaled on the spear, then spun, roaring, charging Mazibe, now unarmed.

Bang! The rifle kicked. Dirk staggered from the impact on his shoulder, dropping once more to his knees. Smoke burned his eyes as he struggled for another cartridge in his pocket, bit off the end, poured powder into the barrel. . . . How his heart ached! He was screaming Mazibe's name over and over. Pulled out the ramrod—

"I am here, Dirk."

Silence.

"I am here!"

Acrid gunsmoke mingled with the scent of the lioness. Dirk looked up. The Zulu's black face was wreathed in smoke, streaked with moonlight and spinning stars, and Dirk passed out.

☾ ☾ ☾

It was raining.

Dirk felt it on his face, eyes blinking as he opened them. He sat up, his head whirling. Rain pattered, gentle and wet, dripping through the leafy boughs, everything green, even the sky, grayish green, cool and soothing.

"How are you, my friend?" Mazibe appeared, and Dirk realized the Zulu had not left him behind.

Dirk's throat was parched; he was almost unable to speak. Mazibe let him drink from a gourd.

"How long have I been out?"

"Since you smote the bearded ones with your firestick and saved me—again."

The water was soothing, better than the taste of the tin canteen. He began to remember: Mazibe shouting, the lioness charging, falling dead, and Mazibe springing over him with only a spear to fight the black-maned lion. Why was there such an ache in his chest, tight as a new-made barrel?

"You stayed, induna?"

"I have been busy," Mazibe said with a grin. "I spent the night chasing away hyenas and guarding against leopards and more bearded ones."

"You saved me from the blackbeard," Dirk said.

Both beasts lay on the track. The male was enormous. He had a bullet hole between his eyes. *Lucky shot,* Dirk thought. A real Hawkeye shot. But then Hawkeye didn't have lions in his forests. Mazibe had removed his spear from the male lion's belly and had cut the ends of their tails off. He handed the brushes to Dirk, saying they were trophies for a lion-killer.

Giving one back, Dirk said, "Something to remember our race by."

Mazibe seemed as if he wanted to smile, but did not, and Dirk sensed he was troubled.

Suddenly, Dirk remembered: "It's raining!"

Mazibe dropped his gaze.

"Shaka! His rain medicine! You said if it rained, he might be—"

Methodically tucking the lion tail into the satchel with the Macassar oil, Mazibe said, "Something has happened. I must press on."

"Rain is just rain, that's all." Dirk tried to ease his friend's heart, but did no good.

"I must go," Mazibe said, ready to leave.

Dirk was woozy as he tried to get up, and fell back again before forcing himself to rise, leaning his rifle butt on the ground and heaving himself to his feet. Could he run? His legs were trembling. Mazibe grasped his shoulder to steady him. Dirk felt as though it was all so ridiculous, for the sake of hair tonic.

Trying to grin, he said, "I'll need a cane to race you, or perhaps you can carry me on your back!"

Swaying to keep his balance, he looked at Mazibe and said what he did not want to say, but could not deny: "I cannot outrun you, induna."

Mazibe looked closely at him.

Dirk said, "You have won."

Strange, but he felt no regret in defeat, his first and only defeat as a runner. He had never imagined feeling this way, losing the race of his life, almost dying. Yet, he had no regrets. It was worth it. He was grateful to have run.

"In God's name! What a race, induna!"

The Zulu was speaking: ". . . because you fell—"

"No!" Dirk held out his right hand. "Falls and lions were part of the bargain; you could have left me to be devoured, and even now would be entering kwaBulawayo."

Mazibe regarded him a moment, then gripped his hand and said, "You are a man, umuntu."

Dirk clasped his other hand onto Mazibe's arm. "You are a champion, induna."

They proceeded a little way down the trail. Mazibe said it was only a short distance to the first kraal of central Zululand, where they could eat before resuming the final twenty miles to kwaBulawayo.

They walked through a steady downpour, the track turning to slick mud. Dirk's legs were agony, and he limped. Indeed, he needed a stick for support and could not have run at all. Mazibe showed a limp of his own, but clearly was still able to run. Dirk urged him to go on, but the Zulu refused to leave him.

After two hours they came to the edge of a cliff that looked down on the heart of Zululand. Here, on this glorious height, they stopped to rest. The rain felt good to Dirk as they sat on rocks, gazing through mist at the small kraal far below on level land, and surrounded by grazing cattle. Though his chest felt better, Dirk hurt all over and was inexpressibly weary. This was a beautiful place from which to look upon the world. Dirk knew the world would never be the same, but did not know why he was so certain. Mazibe seemed lost in thought.

After a few moments, the Zulu rose.

"And now, it must be done," he said solemnly.

With effort, and wondering what the induna meant, Dirk made himself stand up and waited for Mazibe to speak. Were those raindrops or were they tears in the Zulu's eyes? To Dirk's amazement, he realized Mazibe was holding out the leather pouch containing the bull's-head amulet. The induna's hands quaked almost imperceptibly.

Dirk felt a profound calm come over him, and he shook his head.

"Induna, Shaka would not permit you to do this."

Mazibe did not hesitate: "Shaka is no more."

Dirk sensed it was true, but the rational part of him forced the question, "How in God's name can you be sure?"

"I am." Mazibe gestured again with the pouch, offering, and his hands trembled a little more.

Dirk made no move. *It is not mine. I am not worthy.*

"No one is worthy," he heard Mazibe say. "Yet it must be protected on its journey."

Mazibe had drawn out the amulet itself, holding it as Shaka

once had, so that it dangled and gleamed before Dirk's eyes, fascinating, enthralling. The golden bull's head was so very beautiful, glowing white, as if rays of the sun reflected from the stone. Yet there was no sun, only gray clouds and rain. Dirk's heart raced, but this time without hurt. Instead, he experienced a poignancy, a thrill coursing through him, a thrill that might even be called joy. Mazibe made another movement, offering the amulet a third time, and now his hands were rock-steady.

"If you can see the white fire, my brother, then accept the bull's head as its temporary protector."

Dirk's eyes held to the image of the shining crystal stone. That clear white light! The amulet was in his hands, still shining, and he heard these words:

"The bearer of white fire sees what is truth, and what is falsehood. The bearer cannot possess the amulet, and when the time comes, must send it further on its journey."

"Its journey?" Dirk looked at Mazibe in question.

Mazibe's lips were pale, his eyes closed. "It will journey with you, and for that I am grateful."

Dirk saw that the amulet now looked quite ordinary—pretty, but ordinary, the play of light having changed, perhaps.

"So be it," he said, carefully replacing it in the pouch Mazibe gave him; then, with a resolve that seemed to have a voice of its own, he said, "I will protect it."

Mazibe trembled all over.

Dirk wanted to grasp his shoulders, but the induna raised a hand to hold him off until the trembling passed. When he had recovered, Mazibe smiled, gripping Dirk's hands.

"I wish you strength, my brother. Should it ever be in my power to aid you, I will be there." Taking a deep breath, he asked, "Can you run?"

Dirk shook his head.

"Then I must go alone to this kraal and learn what I can of Shaka." He looked Dirk over. "Follow, but with care. Your companions must be found and join you."

Mazibe ran off.

Dirk tied the pouch with the amulet around his waist, then limped down the long slope toward the kraal. He would gladly stay and rest here. If Mazibe wanted to run on triumphantly to kwaBulawayo with the Macassar oil, he deserved it. Once more the rational in Dirk asked what Shaka would say about his having the amulet. If Dirk went on to kwaBulawayo, how would he get out alive? He could not prevent Shaka from taking back the amulet, and that troubled him. Still, intuition told him that Shaka was, indeed, no more.

And the rain had stopped.

SONG OF THE WILD

On the day Rachel Drente left Sweetfountain, rain would have suited her more than this blue sky with the scattered clouds that sailed up from the south on a chill wind.

She sat cross-legged on a bed in the back of Johannes's trek-wagon, Sannie lying under a quilt. The bed covered the whole inside except for a few boxed shelves and some drawers Johannes had made. The women were gazing through an opening in the tented canvas of the wagon, watching their farmhouse slowly sink into the grasslands. All that could be seen now was the thatched roof and the graveyard hill. The hill stood out, especially when the sun broke through, illuminating its patches of dark green grass. From here, Rachel could see the white path to the top of the hill, the path she had walked so often, the path leading to poignant, thoughtful silence beside the graves, and then back to the lifelong comfort of the house.

As Sweetfountain diminished in the distance, Rachel was no longer sobbing, but could not stop the tears she kept wiping away. Sannie seemed cried-out by now. In Rachel's hands was the small brown book of Vondel's poetry. It gave her comfort. She did not open the Bible, but she did need the old wisdom of her forebears, who had said so many goodbyes to home and traveled to the ends of the earth, never to return.

The trekwagon swayed and jolted, moving along at two or three miles an hour on level ground. This would be their home for many months, perhaps years. No one knew. The journey would be much the same from day to day: They would trek for three or four hours in the morning, rest two hours at midday, outspanning the oxen, then inspan and travel through the afternoon until making camp well before dark.

Like the others, this trekwagon was long and narrow, eighteen feet by six feet, yoked with four pair of magnificent oxen. This team was Johannes's best "short" breed, the red and white ones that could pull for eight hours steady if need be. Other oxen, called the "tall" breed, were extremely powerful and would be used for difficult pulls over short distances, such as crossing rivers or ascending hills.

This wagon was the last in a line of eight, with Klaas driving, and a servant boy as *voorloper,* or forerunner, at the head of the lead team. Up ahead, driven by Jacob, the blacksmith, in company with Millie, was Rachel's own wagon, with its single bunk. Gerrit's wagons were in the lead, followed by Toulouse.

There were too few wagons to lock up and form a strong circular laager for defense, but they would not have to worry about that until they crossed the Orange River, a hundred miles ahead. Beyond that country were bands of outlaws and roving parties of black raiders. When Rachel's party reached it, they would have to build a wall of crates and thornbush to seal the laager at night. In these first hours of the first day of the trek, the promised land seemed so very far away.

"Read me something, Sis," asked Sannie, turning over so that she lay on her side.

Rachel opened the book of Vondel's poetry. Yes, better to

read than to weep. Sannie asked for the poem about Amsterdam in 1631, "the capital city of Europe," as Vondel's verse said. It was a poem of Amsterdam's glory in Holland's "Golden Age," when bold merchant seamen made the Lowlands the center of western commerce: "What waters are not shadowed by her sails?" Amstelredam, Vondel called the city back then.

Rachel read aloud, the words rising rhythmically above the grinding of the wagon wheels and the plodding of cloven hoofs. Ahead, distant hills were coming in view, a pretty range with gaps, through one of which they would pass. Rachel would rather recite "About Amstelredam" than watch her native country drift away.

The rivers Ij and Amstel embrace the capital city of Europe,
Crowned as Empress; its neighbors' support and hope;
Amstelredam, who unto heaven's axis lifts her head,
And shoots, at Pluto's breast, her roots right through the swamp.
What waters are not shadowed by her sails?
Upon which markets does she not sell her wares?
What folk under the light of the moon has she not seen?
She, who makes the laws over all the Ocean?
She, who spreads her wings by the waxing of many souls,
And hauls her way into the world with overloaded holds.

Sannie said, "My people came here from Amsterdam, and so did your father's grandfather."

"They wanted to see the world," Rachel replied, "though they never got back home again, did they?" She sniffed, trying to wipe a tear without Sannie's noticing.

Gazing up at the white canvas tenting, where a colorful cloth doll hung, looking back at her, Sannie said, "Our Amsterdammer's blood has been to almost every corner of the earth, and now it journeys once more into unknown lands."

Rachel gazed at the dark green hill with the graveyard, where her parents and Sannie's children lay, and she sighed, "But some of our blood always stays behind . . ."

Sannie finished: "And forever."

The green hill was smaller now. Soon, they would not see it anymore. That thought made Rachel restless, and she did not like the feeling. She did not want to be sad. She could not stand it. She would not be sad! Another Joost van den Vondel poem—one that would inspire her and Sannie!

Thumbing through the book, and there: "Song of the Wild," about the cheerful little birds of the orchard, where the sunlight is wonderful, "of richness and of treasure."

We birds fly, warmly feathered,
In peace, from branch to branch.
The heavens give us drink and nourishment,
The heavens are our roof.
We neither sow nor mow

The poet's land provides the wild birds with food.

Whoever would become a bird,
Puts on feathers,
Avoids the city and noises of the street
And chooses a wider space.

Fair Sannie smiled, so beautiful in her weakness and her radiant goodness.

"We trekker birds are choosing a wider space, in the far-off promised land, though no one seems to know where it is or what awaits us there or in our future."

"You know, Sis-birdie," Rachel said, smiling through her tears and reaching over to pat Sannie's pregnant tummy. "You bear our folk's future inside you, our child of hope."

THE AMULET BEARER

With sunlight bursting through the clouds, Dirk entered an open gate in the thornbush wall of the kraal, finding to his surprise that the place was empty, utterly silent, as if everyone had run off, letting food burn in kettles and even leaving the gate of the central cattle pen wide open.

It was in the center of this pen that Dirk saw Mazibe. His head was hanging as he stood alone near a large chair. Dirk called out and hobbled as fast as he could through the gate, then pulled up short to see Mazibe standing over a massive corpse. It was King Shaka himself.

A dismal sight. The noble Zulu induna, shoulders sagging, wept over the grotesque, twisted body of his king. Blood was spattered on the wet ground, puddles of rainwater mingled red with it. Nearby was the toppled chair in which Shaka had been holding court before he had been slain, stabbed many times with spears, one of which still lay beside him. His leopard-skin kaross and the white oxtail fringes on his legs and arms were stained red. His mouth was open, eyes wide. To kill such a giant had required many cruel, deep wounds, and Shaka had suffered them.

At Mazibe's feet was the satchel of Macassar oil. Laying his own bag of oil on the ground, Dirk touched Mazibe's shoulder, and the induna shuddered, just as he had after giving the amulet. Mazibe knelt to examine the bloody spear, then spoke hoarsely:

"Dingaane and his assassins have destroyed the Bull of the amaZulu." He shook his head. "Lord Shaka believed the oil of youth would keep him king forever. It has come too late."

The long, blue feather of the lory bird was broken from Shaka's cap, and Mazibe knelt to touch it lightly, though he did not pick it up. He became calmer.

"See how the hyenas and jackals have not disturbed Shaka's body, though it has lain exposed here through the night. His body is protected by magic, waiting for me to bury it. But who else of the amaZulu will be here to honor the glorious memory of Shaka?"

Black Africa's greatest empire-builder lay dead, alone, in a muddy cattle kraal. The army was yet far away, and now, after all Shaka had achieved, the people he had made into a mighty nation were too frightened to attend him, lest the rebel conspirators come to slay them also. Dirk had no love for the Zulu king, but this was a foul end. He was sorry for the storm of slaughter, the civil war, that surely was about to break upon Zululand.

Mazibe hefted the two sacks of Macassar oil, staring at them. "Ah, such sorrow will begin for the people now. The nation Shaka created, the amaZulu as I have known them, are no more."

He rose up, and with a roar dashed the satchels against the king's chair, then hurled them to the ground. The bottles were smashed, black hair tonic flowing into the mud, a trickle making its way to Shaka's outstretched hand to stain his stiff forefinger.

Almost in a whisper, Mazibe said, "Farewell, Lord Shaka, Bull of the Nation."

There came a yell from the forest edge. They spun around. It was Benjamin David and the expedition, with their horses and packs, hurrying into the kraal.

"Thank heaven you're alive!" Benjamin declared, running up and hugging Dirk, then looking him over, startled. "But just barely alive! What in God's name happened to you?"

Dirk said he would tell about that later; then he greeted Sebe, who showed concern for Dirk. Then Sebe bowed in greeting to the downcast Mazibe. Dirk paid no attention to Thomas Lovell, who was staring at Mazibe.

"There'll be hell to pay in Zululand," Benjamin said, adding that he and the others had been hiding in the forest, afraid of what would happen next. "Shaka came out here yesterday on a ruse, lured by Dingaane and the witch doctor Dayega; they and the traitorous bodyguard cut him down, then ran off to rally their followers, to raise an army against loyal forces who will avenge Shaka."

Sebe said, "We waited here for you, Baas Dirk, to warn you. The impis have not yet returned from the northern campaign, but when they do, Dingaane will declare himself king and call them to him. He will wipe out anyone who opposes the assassination of Shaka."

Mazibe spoke up, "Dingaane has much power now." He stepped back from Shaka's body, saying, "I must rejoin my impi for the coming war against Dingaane. You must flee across the mountains immediately, for Dayega will hunt for you at Port Natal, believing you will go there." He said quietly to Dirk, "He covets what you carry."

Lovell's gaze was still fixed on Mazibe. Dirk could guess why.

He would deal with Lovell later, but first they must make a plan of escape.

Sebe said, "My old bones tell me we must depart quickly—"

A fierce war shout erupted, and the kraal gate filled with Zulu warriors, who rushed in and surrounded them with a ring of spears. Two Zulus went for Mazibe and pinned his arms back, a third holding a spear point at his throat. Dirk's arms, too, were pinioned by two warriors. There were about twenty of them, recognizable by their red oxhide shields as followers of Dingaane.

Mazibe demanded, "What is the meaning of this, you fools?"

"Who is the fool, induna?" That voice, that mocking, croaking voice was unmistakably Dayega's, and he appeared from behind his men, sidling up to Mazibe with that half-crouching gait. "It is you who have been outwitted, induna, you and your white sorcerers, outwitted like fools! Like fools! Now you will pay the price! But first, hold the induna still!" Dayega tore back Mazibe's blanket robe and clawed at his chest.

Recoiling, Dayega gave a shriek. "The amulet! The bull's head! Where is it?" He frantically searched Mazibe's garments, then screamed, "Hand it over! It is mine! Mine!"

Mazibe laughed. "It is not yours."

"Where is it? Speak, if you would die quickly!"

Mazibe was cool, smiling scornfully as he said, "I do not have it."

Dayega screeched and clawed at his own face.

Lovell, himself caught by a man at each arm, begged of Dirk, "What does he want?"

"The amulet," Dirk answered. "But Mazibe no longer has it."

A high-pitched howl rose from Lovell, and he shrilled like a madman: "He got it! Bless Captain Homan! He got it!"

Dayega beckoned, and Ineto appeared, having been lurking

behind the warriors. The executioner drew out a knife and stepped toward Lovell, who began singing a hymn, head thrown back, eyes rolling, almost delirious.

A mighty fortress is our God

Ineto yanked Lovell's head back by the hair, exposing the man's throat, knife point aimed. Benjamin yelled Lovell's name in warning, but the Englishman ignored him, apparently no longer caring what happened to himself.

A bulwark never failing

The two Zulus holding Dirk were distracted by Ineto, who seemed to hesitate. Dirk's blood was up, though his body was weakened. He caught Mazibe's eye. Lovell sang. Ineto paused.

"Slay the white thing," Dayega commanded.

Ineto tensed, but his knife hand dropped slightly.

"Strike!" Dayega shrieked, hopping about and waving his arms. "Slay the white thing!"

Dirk yanked at the Zulu on his right, butting him savagely in the face. The man went down. The other thrust his assegai, and Dirk felt the terrible blow in his belly, but he ripped the spear from the Zulu and struck him on the head with the end of the shaft, then drove the point home. Now everyone was fighting, yelling, screaming, iron spear blades ringing against the steel of clubbed rifles. Ineto still had not thrust.

Lovell was looking heavenward, singing.

Dirk brought his pistol up at Ineto, who vanished into the melee.

Lovell kept singing.

Our helper He, amid the flood
Of mortal ills prevailing

Mazibe wielded a spear ferociously. Benjamin was protecting his back, swinging a knobkerrie and yelling in fear and fury. Dirk saw Dayega. The pistol banged, but a Zulu got in the way and fell. The witch doctor, too, disappeared in the milling, fighting throng. Sinking to his knees, gasping for air, Dirk reloaded. Sebe and two bearers appeared at his side, firing rifles.

Suddenly, a shower of spears fell among Dayega's warriors—well-aimed spears, for several men fell dead, and two staggered, wounded, across the kraal, stuck with assegais. Another group of warriors rushed through the gate: It was the escort of boys, led by Senzana, charging into the kraal and yelling like fighting men. It was they who had thrown the spears. Dayega's warriors scattered, and he ran for the thornbush wall of the kraal, but it was too full of sharp thorns to get over. He cast about, trapped.

Sebe and the bearers fired a volley, and more of the enemy went down, one slumping dead on top of the wall. Seeing his chance, Dayega used the body to scamper up and over the thorns, Dirk's quick pistol shot missing him. Dirk dragged himself to the wall, but Dayega had escaped into the forest, and as suddenly as it had begun, the fight was over.

Dirk slumped down, heart throbbing. Sebe came to his side. Dirk looked at his stomach, expecting blood to be pouring out. It ached, but there was no blood, though his shirt was torn from the spear thrust. Too spent to comprehend what had just happened, he knew he had not been stabbed after all. His heart fluttered, and now he admitted to himself that it had been damaged in the race with Mazibe. His days as a runner were done. Sebe put a blanket over his shoulders and brought boyala to drink. Dirk stared at the ground, willing his heart to rest, his breath to return.

Two bearers were dead, two wounded; none of the Zulu boys was hurt. Mazibe proudly embraced them, especially Senzana, then sent scouts out to make sure no other attackers were around. Benjamin was calming Lovell, who had stopped singing but seemed bewildered, dazed. Himself cut and bruised, Benjamin sat Lovell down to recover near the horses and packs, which were at the main gate of the kraal.

Mazibe proceeded to finish off the wounded Zulus in the warrior's tradition: a killing knobkerrie blow to the head, then a slash across the belly to allow the man's spirit to escape. Later, there would be a cleansing ritual for Mazibe and the boys to make sure the ghosts of those they had slain would not haunt them. Sebe and the bearers proceeded to bury their two dead companions outside the kraal.

As the burials and ritual killing were carried out, Dirk went to the horses to think over what he would do. There was no time to hunt down Dayega, for the survivors of the expedition must get away before more of Dingaane's followers came after them. He limped to Blueboy, soothing him. Dirk noticed then that the leather pouch had been slashed. The hard leather had deflected the spear thrust, which otherwise would have killed him.

He took out the amulet, relieved to see it was undamaged. Feeling faint, he leaned against Blueboy to keep from falling. He sensed someone watching him, and turned to see Lovell, seated in the shadows just a few yards away. The Englishman was gaping, mouth open. Lovell began to rise, pointing in amazement at the amulet. Shock and anger overtook Dirk, and he quickly enclosed the amulet in his fist, regretting his momentary lapse. Lovell should have known nothing about the amulet.

Now it was too late.

Eyes wide, Lovell was muttering, "You have it . . . the Stone of White Fire . . . you . . ."

Dirk stepped forward to confront him, keeping the amulet concealed in his hand, "Homan and his men died because of your greed."

Lovell gulped, as if brought back to sanity. "I tell you, Arendt . . . it does not belong to you!"

Dirk moved closer, boiling. "Say no more, or I'll leave you here for Dayega and his vultures." The amulet felt warm.

Lovell paled, but composed himself. "You do not comprehend your peril."

"Comprehend your own peril!" Dirk shouted, the effort bringing him to the brink of exhaustion. "It's like this: We escape over the mountains, you go back to England."

Lovell stared hard. "And the amulet?"

"It will vanish! Say nothing more about it! Do you understand?"

If pushed, Dirk might very well leave Lovell here to fend for himself. How warm the amulet seemed, but Dirk did not want to open his hand.

Lovell was steady as he replied, "I well understand, Mister Arendt, but it does not matter whether I live or die. It is for your own good that I warn you—this is not your affair. If you take the amulet, you will regret it the rest of your days."

"Perhaps I already regret it." Dirk wanted to lie down, to sleep.

"You need not regret it!" Lovell was on his knees now, eager. "This amulet can serve you, Mister Arendt, can make you rich as a king! We can show you how it can lead you to gold, to diamonds! With our help, you have the power to discover the ancient mines of Ophir, the lost riches of Solomon himself!"

The amulet was almost burning his hand. The image of Lovell was wavering in front of him, was hard to see clearly.

"Let us show you how it can be used," Lovell pressed. "Then, when you are done with it, we will unburden you." He was almost begging, but his voice was strong. "Mister Arendt, we know you to be an honorable man, and trust your word, if you will only strike a bargain with us—"

"No!" Dirk heard his own voice, as from a distance.

Through his grogginess, he saw, as in a flash, a raw power of evil surging inside Lovell, a power controlling his very will.

"You must listen to me!" Lovell implored.

"Enough!" Dirk commanded, speaking to the evil, not to Lovell. "Silence!"

In the next moment, Dirk's anger was overwhelmed by pity for the wretched Lovell, who had eased back, eyes hooded. Oh, but Dirk wanted to rest. The amulet had cooled, as had his emotions. How strange that burning had been!

A voice said in Bantu, "Leave him and his demon behind."

It was Mazibe, peering at Lovell, who had to look away. Mazibe could not understand the Dutch spoken by Dirk and Lovell, but apparently comprehended enough.

"Leave him for Dayega."

Benjamin hurried over, exclaiming, in Dutch and then Bantu, "What are you saying? Leave Tom behind? What's the meaning of this, Mazibe? Dirk? Have you both gone mad?"

Lovell snapped, petulantly, "Arendt has our amulet! I saw him conceal it. He meant to keep it secret for himself. Have a care, Benjamin, that after me you will not be his next victim!"

Benjamin looked at Dirk, as if about to protest, then seemed to think better of it.

"There is no time for squabbling now," Benjamin said. "We must be gone. Of course Tom goes with us!"

Mazibe turned away.

"We go," Dirk said to Benjamin, "after they bury Shaka."

☾ ☾ ☾

At first, the Zulu boys were excited about the battle, feeling like grown warriors, but when Mazibe brought them to stand over Shaka, they huddled close to the induna, sobbing like children.

It was a burial without formality. There was no time for anything more. They dug a hole in the center of the kraal and buried him there. Village cattle were driven back and forth over the grave, so that it could not be found and despoiled. In this way, parts of mighty Shaka's body would never be stolen for use by Dayega or anyone else in making black magic. Dirk watched it all from a distance, wrapped in a blanket, sipping broth Sebe had heated in an abandoned kettle. Dirk had recovered a little strength, but felt like a babe in swaddling, with Sebe the nurse.

It was decided that the remaining bearers, who were on foot, would have the best chance if they fled northeast to the Portuguese colony of Lorenco Marques, guided through the jungle by a few of the Zulu boys. The whites and Sebe would immediately go northwest, crossing through a pass in the Dragon Mountains that led to the high veldt, where their horses would allow them to travel fast.

Dirk had bound up the leather pouch with the amulet and tied it securely around his body, concealed inside his shirt. Nearby, Sebe was filling their packs with food from the village. As Sebe worked on the packs, lashing them to the backs of the horses, Dirk made a decision.

"I bear the amulet now," he said, looking at Sebe, who made no reply, not even acknowledging that he heard; he silently finished his work.

"You must be thirsty, then," Sebe said at last, and fetched them cups of boyala. They drank, Sebe sitting on his haunches beside Dirk, neither speaking until Sebe began. "Where it goes, dangerous enemies will follow."

Dirk well knew that. "Would you rather I had kept the amulet a secret from you?"

"I must admit that my medicine had already told me you possessed it." He glanced at Dirk, a smile breaking on his lined face. "I am glad to have your trust, Baas."

Dirk did not believe Sebe had known about the amulet, but it did not matter that the rascal boasted as usual.

"I have to trust someone," Dirk said.

"Yes, that you do, Baas, that you do. Bearers of such things need trustworthy friends—friends who know better than to carry such things, if one has a choice in the matter!"

Whether or not Dirk had a choice was not brought up in this brief conversation. He sensed, however, that it could become a rich subject for debate with a Xhosa witch doctor who claimed to know everything about everything, even about ancient amulets. Dirk wanted to release Sebe of his sense of obligation.

"You need not go any further."

"Where you go, I go," Sebe said.

They finished their boyala, nothing more to say.

Shortly, all of them gathered outside the kraal gate, standing in the warm midday sun. The dismal spectacle of death was left inside the cattle pen. Already, *aasvogels,* as Boers called vultures, were flapping in to perch on the thornbush wall and wait.

By now, Tom Lovell sat on horseback, dull-eyed and in

silence, ready to leave. Dirk decided this was not the time to say anything to Benjamin about the conspiracy with Captain Homan. There was enough else to think about for the time being. They would be traveling for weeks across the mountains, eventually to approach Cape Colony and safety from the northern frontier. If Dingaane discovered their route and sent an impi after them, they would be hard-pressed to escape.

The Zulu boys sat on their haunches, bone-weary despite the exhilaration of "washing" their spears for the first time in an opponent's blood. Preparing to mount Blueboy, Dirk observed Mazibe standing with Senzana and felt a rush of friendship for them. He grinned at Mazibe, then called out to Senzana.

"Tell me, young warrior, how it was that you caught up to us so soon?"

"We marched all night, umuntu," the youth beamed.

"All night?" Mazibe touched his son's arm. "You are as mad as a Boer! And did the tao not find you?"

"It was so, my father," Senzana replied, then shouted at a pair of smaller boys, who dashed away to the nearby tree line, one returning immediately, staggering under the weight of two fresh lion skins. The rest of the boys were aglow with pride, but Mazibe became grave.

"This is the blackbeard and his mate," he said. "You did not slay them."

"No, my father," Senzana replied. "We thought you would like to have them." He pointed at the tree line, saying, "These are ours."

At that moment the second boy came lumbering up, covered completely with three more lion skins, so that only his skinny legs showed. Mazibe held his head in mock disbelief, and the boys all grinned.

Dirk politely refused the offer of the skins of the black-maned lion and mate, saying they were for the boys, in thanks for their rescue. That earned many warm expressions of gratitude.

"We must depart," Mazibe said, and Senzana stirred the boys to readiness. "I go to find my impi before Dayega assembles more warriors and tries to catch me again, and perhaps you, too. You must all leave Zululand. It may be that you can never return."

He bid farewell to Sebe and Benjamin, pausing briefly to stare at Lovell, who did not lift his eyes. Then Mazibe turned to Dirk.

Offering his hand, Dirk said, "Goodbye, my friend. I will not forget you."

"We are as one," Mazibe said, placing both hands inside Dirk's in a gesture of homage.

"We are as one." Dirk placed his own hands inside Mazibe's. He was trying not to think of the worst that soon might come upon the induna in the conflict with Dingaane and Dayega. "I pray we meet again."

"May your god protect you," Mazibe said, "and may the judgment of the Stone of White Fire always find you pure of heart."

☾ ☾ ☾

The westering sun's shadow darkened the flanks of the Dragon Mountains as Dirk's party rode slowly upland on a steep and rocky trail. Exhausted, feverish, he was barely able to stay on his horse. Benjamin rode close behind to keep him from falling off.

Dirk sensed Benjamin's worry for him, and felt also his friend's confusion about the amulet. How could Benjamin understand its importance? How could anyone who had never seen that white fire understand? Dirk had been changed, but did not know how. He had left something behind, something of himself, of his life, something that would never be again. And he had taken something up. Was it the amulet that had changed him? His thoughts drifted to the witch doctor, Dayega, who was so obsessed with it. Would he come after them? Dingaane, too, wanted the bull's head as a token of Shaka's power, with which to rule the Zulus. And what about Tom Lovell, now turning to peer back at him? What would Lovell do next? Whatever happened on this long journey home, Dirk knew he would protect the golden amulet with his life—but he did not know why.

It took effort to shake all this from his mind, and he touched the pouch that held the amulet, soon drifting away, again seeing the face of the woman from his dream. He wanted to call to her, and perhaps he did, or was it she calling to him? He could hear their words, over and over and over.

"I am with you. I am with you! . . ."

SMOKE

People coming!"

The shout went up at the campsite a hundred yards away from where Rachel sat on a little kopje under a clump of scraggly trees. She rose and peered northward, over the waving grass, to see dust rising, but it was too far off to tell who was riding this way—and coming fast, by the looks of the moving cloud behind them. She shaded her eyes with the broad brim of the felt hat she wore.

Perhaps it was Gerrit, who had ridden out yesterday to catch up with the Arendt trek. Johannes thought the others were no more than thirty miles ahead by now. Lord, but it had been ages since Rachel's trek had seen other people. They had journeyed for forty lonely days, each day pushing one or two miles more than the six or seven that was usual for trekwagons. Forty days had been enough for the Israelites to make their way through the wilderness, but it seemed not enough for the trekkers to find their promised land.

The Arendt trek had flattened a two-hundred mile long, half-mile wide corridor for them to follow through the grasslands, a swath beaten down by hooves, rutted by trekwagon wheels, and grazed low by the stock. There were graves, too, three of them so far: an old woman who had died of homesickness, a child of fever, and one of the young colored outriders, killed during a mishap while the wagons were crossing a drift, as fords were termed. Such news was left for Rachel's party in letters placed under piles of stones at the Arendt trek's abandoned campsites, where Rachel's folk often stayed the night.

The Arendt trekkers, too, were growing weary, and some were talking about stopping and making a home for themselves. Rachel did not want that. This place was fine, but it was not Sweetfountain. She hoped that somewhere ahead, in that land of milk and honey the elders spoke about, there would be country equal to that of her lifelong home. The oxen teams were as exhausted as the people, that was sure, but the ground was not so difficult now that they were on the open grasslands and there were fewer dry rivers and deep gullies to cross. Grass was plentiful, too, and the supplies of food were holding up well enough.

This was a vast and distant land.

To the east, at Rachel's right, the purplish blue of mountains lay on the horizon, maybe eighty miles off. The trekkers would not go that way, for there were wild nations there, with thousands of warriors, who surely would attack them. This country to the west of the mountains was empty of native peoples, with only the eerie remains of burned-out kraals, where wind and dust blew through. Death at the hands of Shaka's rampaging warriors had struck these folk without mercy. Zululand itself was beyond those purple eastern mountains, but if the Boers could make homes here, strengthen themselves, and be on the alert for raiding parties, then the Zulus would not so readily come back again.

The cloud of dust was closer.

Rachel saw Johannes had mounted up and was riding out to

meet whoever it was. She called to Tempest, grazing close at hand, and caught him. As she trotted off, the Boerhound, Jaeger, sprang out of a hole where he was digging and joined her. Away they went, Rachel leaning low in the saddle, Tempest at full stretch. Rachel's hat blew back, held by a chin strap around her neck, and her brown hair was loose in the wind. She would wear no vrouw-like kappie while riding on the veldt.

Beside her leg, in a leather case fixed to the saddle, was a rifle, and she well knew how to use it. Johannes and her father had taught her to fire and reload while mounted, like a Boer fighting man on kommando. These days, her brother often reminded Rachel to carry the rifle when riding any distance from the wagons, which she liked to do. Native raiders or outlaws or lions—there was ever the need for a firearm out here.

Soon she came alongside Johannes, who said, "Looks like Gerrit coming back, and he's got two others with him."

"Really? Hoorah!"

They urged their mounts into a canter.

Rachel was thrilled, and Tempest sensed it, champing and eager to run again. Gerrit had found the Arendt trek, which could not be so far away, now. The sight of other faces would be welcome—or so Rachel thought, until she realized that riding with Gerrit was Anneke Graven, the annoying hussy who was the youngest daughter of blacksmith Ton Graven. Ton, too, was with them, sitting his stallion like a stump on the saddle, while the tall and graceful Anneke rode beautifully, her chestnut mare every bit as good-looking as she was.

Johannes remarked on Anneke's coming back to see them, saying Rachel and Sannie would be glad for the female company.

"You can catch up on all the gossip you've missed, Sis," he said with a grin. "That is if you can pry her away from Gerrit."

He laughed at that, and Rachel shrugged.

"Let Gerrit do the prying for himself, though I think he won't try too hard."

"Anneke fancies him, but he wants you."

"No," Rachel said, jamming the hat back on her head and giving a toss of the long hair hanging down her back. "Just wants what he can't get."

"Maybe. But I'll wager he'll get what he wants from Anneke if you don't put a stop to it, quick-like."

She had no reply.

Rachel actually was not sure how she felt about Anneke Graven being with Gerrit. Nor did she know what to think about him, for all that they had been together in camp after camp, day in and day out. Nothing about Gerrit made her heart leap, although he was sweet most of the time, and she was getting used to his coarse manners and kind-hearted blundering. She had a certain affection for him.

"Listen, I don't care that Anneke's after Gerrit," she told Johannes as they came swiftly closer to the other riders. "It's the way she does it that plagues me—how she always laughs so daintily and spouts all those 'oh, la's' and 'oh, reallys,' and 'oh, how wonderfuls,' as if she's some royal lady and I'm a lowly handmaiden there to wait on her."

Johannes laughed heartily, and she stuck her tongue out at him.

Rachel wondered how the blond Anneke always seemed to look so perfect—as she did now in her neat riding kappie, hair properly tucked away, and a lambskin half-mask protecting her pure and unblemished skin from forehead to just above the mouth. How did so delicate a meisje get to be such a fine rider when her cheeks had seldom felt a rush of wind or the sting of dust? Well, Rachel would never wear one of those masks. She could take the sun and wind and dust, and did not mind if she got a blemish or two or a sunburn. There was nothing to be done about it, anyway. Too late to try to look like Anneke, who even from here could be seen laughing gorgeously at something Gerrit had said. Anneke should take care at showing her pretty teeth, for the evening breeze was kicking up, the dust coming with it, and if she kept laughing she would get a mouthful of grit.

"Serve her right, the hussy," Rachel muttered, though Johannes did not hear, for he was up ahead, cheerfully greeting Gerrit and the others.

Gerrit was riding a pack horse, leading his own stallion, which had come up slightly lame. Rachel could not help but ask innocently who that person was behind the mask.

"Come, now," Gerrit scoffed. "You know Anneke Graven, don't you, meisje?"

Anneke smiled at Gerrit, then said, "You're such a handsome vrouw, Rachel, why don't you get a mask, too, and take care of yourself, the way you deserve."

Vrouw! Who's a mature woman?

Rachel did not voice what was raging inside her then, but, indeed, Anneke was only seventeen. She was three years younger than Rachel, who expected to be called meisje, or even *Juffrouw*—"Miss"—but no one had ever called her a vrouw before! She tried hard to ignore it and asked Gerrit about the Arendt trek, especially about Marta and Willem and their boys. The questions cheered her up and excited her again.

The party turned to ride back to Rachel's trek, and she made sure not to get stuck next to Anneke, nor to ride between her and Gerrit. Rachel did not want to seem to be jealously forcing herself between those two. Ton Graven was happy to ride beside

Rachel, perhaps only to give his daughter a chance to chat with Gerrit. Ton said there were plans to send five wagons back to meet Rachel's trek.

"Uncertain country here," he said in his remarkably deep voice, "and your trek don't have enough wagons to circle up for a proper laager at night."

Gerrit added that fifteen men would be coming back with the wagons to help protect Johannes's party. Rachel felt immense relief to hear that.

"Scouts from the Arendt trek've seen sign of kaffir bands roving over toward the mountains," Ton continued, gesturing eastward. "Now be the time to git all of us together in one group."

Gerrit added, "The Arendt trek'll wait where they be till yours catches up."

There had been no trouble all these days on the trek, but always the undercurrent of danger lurked in the unknown. Rachel's little trek with a dozen or so rifles needed to be supported in this land where the Zulu had raided and destroyed or driven out every human being in their path. The Arendt trek had more than two hundred fighting men, and if past Boer history was any indication, they could hold their own defending a laager against thousands of native attackers. Of course, the Boers had never yet fought Zulus.

At the expectation of the treks' finally coming together, Rachel felt a weight had been lifted, a weight she had not been fully aware of all this time. Then Anneke's dainty laugh and her "la-ing" made Rachel glance back to see Gerrit and Johannes glowing with admiration for the hussy, who rode between them. Anneke Graven was like that. She had this effect on men, even normally level-headed men like Johannes, who could love no one but Sannie, and would die for her. Yet Anneke could make the most sober man a little giddy, and Rachel had to admit it was quite a power for a woman to possess.

Anneke was talking to Johannes. "We'll be ever so glad to have you all back with us again! We so miss your violin and your singing, Johannes. Why, dear Gerrit was welcomed into our company last night like the prodigal son! La! Gerrit, I don't think you've ever in your life been kissed so much! Or have you?"

Ton rumbled a hoarse laugh, saying, "The kerel vanished for an hour after dinner, and every meisje in the laager was asking after him!" He lisped an imitation of girlish voices: "'Oh, my! Where did Gerritje go?' 'What happened to Gerritje?' 'Has the dear left us so soon?' Then there was them girls who wasn't so nice, and they said real angry-like, 'Who did he go off with?' 'Who got her clutches into him?'"

Rachel stood in the stirrups and looked back. "Who did you go off with, then?"

Ton rumbled a laugh again, and Gerrit blushed a little. Anneke smiled and looked away, as if to suggest she had been with him.

"Ach, Rachel," Gerrit replied with a shrug, "don't tell me you be jealous?"

Rachel took off her hat and tossed her beautiful hair, knowing even Anneke had to envy it. She was considering a reply when she saw smoke rising about half a mile to the east, beyond a low line of kopjes. She pointed at it, and her party reined in. Johannes had a spyglass that he opened full length and observed for a moment.

"Campfire, I'll wager. Just started up, so we chanced to see the smoke." He passed the glass to Ton, and then it went to Gerrit and Rachel. Anneke, whose mask would be in the way, waited to hear what they thought.

"Have to go look into this," Johannes said, and Gerrit agreed.

Ton said he would stay with the women and wait for Johannes and Gerrit to return with word of who was there. The two of them turned their horses' heads in that direction.

"I should go," Rachel said.

Gerrit shook his head. "If there be trouble, then someone's got to ride to the treks and warn 'em."

"You won't get far on that pack horse if some kaffir mob comes after you," Rachel insisted, yanking out her rifle and checking the priming.

Johannes agreed, taking up his own rifle. "Rachel can come halfway with me, and if I signal with my hat, then she signals to you, and all come on; but if I start to run, then she will, too, and you split up and warn the treks."

It was agreed. Ton would make for the Arendts, and Gerrit and Anneke would go to Rachel's trek. Rachel and Johannes cantered off, leaving the others to dismount and look to their saddles and cinches in case they had to ride hard. In this country, a campfire was unlikely to be friendly whites, although some daring giraffe hunters did come out here from the Cape Colony to get that hide, which could be turned into the finest bull whips. More than likely it was native hunters, or maybe even Griquas, outcast borderers who too often were bandits and raiders.

Already, the smoke had dissipated as the wood or dried dung took hold and burned. If Rachel and the others had passed by here a minute or two earlier or later, the smoke would not have been visible at all. Then they would have ridden past with no idea who else was out there in the grasslands, whether friend or foe.

SPELLBOUND

For all his weariness, the footsore, saddlesore journeying day after day, and the tangible presence of the bull's-head amulet—now hanging in its pouch around his neck—for all these burdens, what Dirk Arendt wanted most of all was a good cup of strong coffee.

"Boer's comfort," they called it, and he needed that kind of comfort more than ever. His clothes were tattered, his beard left to grow, and he had not washed much in all these days from Zululand. Benjamin and Lovell looked as trailworn as he did, but Sebe seemed as fresh as ever. Lovell had changed considerably in these weeks on the run. He had lost his paunchiness and now looked almost lean. His eyes were darker, sunken, and in them was a hunger that had not been there before. A hunger for the amulet, no doubt, although he had not troubled Dirk about it again.

Still, Dirk had often felt Lovell's eyes boring into him, and Sebe, too, seemed concerned, for he was ever watchful. At night, Sebe lay close to Dirk or else stayed awake at the campfire. Dirk had not seen the Xhosa sleeping soundly during their flight from Zululand.

Pulling off Blueboy's saddle while Sebe blew sparks through

the dung fire to get it started, Dirk thought of his mother's coffee and smiled to remember those early mornings at home after the first chores with the livestock were done. They all would come in, his father and brothers and the colored stockmen, and they would crowd around the kitchen table for coffee and *koekjes.* So long ago, it seemed. Now that his little party of fugitives had finally escaped the mountains, home in the Cape Colony was within reach for the first time in years.

It was still a couple of hundred miles to the northern borders of the colony, and that was a long way, since there were only two horses left. Benjamin's had broken down, and the three whites were taking turns walking and riding. They did not move as fast as Dirk wanted, yet home was within reach. Soon they would have to double up on the horses, Sebe hanging onto a stirrup, so they could put distance between them and the shadow of those mountains.

Dirk laid the saddle down, saw to Blueboy's hobbles, and began to make a bed for himself. It would be dusk soon. He was grateful for the rest, though he had recovered much strength during this month-long journey. Hunting had been good, and Sebe always found edible plants where it seemed only stones could grow. There were other things, too, that the old Xhosa brought in and cooked up, making a rich stew that Dirk preferred not to investigate too closely. It had kept them alive.

Benjamin and Lovell paid little attention when Sebe cooked. They were usually too busy debating philosophy and world politics, whether they were on the trail or around the campfire. Those two were designated to fetch water, if there was any, and to gather the night's firewood or dried dung, while Dirk did the hunting and Sebe scoured for other food along water courses, in brushwood, and sometimes under rocks.

This was fine country, open and grassy and well-watered with plenty of springs. It was dotted with clumps of tall yellowwood trees and shaggy sweet-thorns. These groves offered shady campsites like this one and told of water to be found far beneath the surface. A well could be dug here, a farmhouse built. Yes, it was good country. Dirk could not help but think that his parents might come this way if, indeed, they had trekked. Perhaps that was why he had just thought of his mother's coffee—a frivolous thought, perhaps, but he could almost smell that brew in the air, and he grinned to himself as he savored it.

"Is the baas listening to a good story from the bull's head?" Sebe asked, piling more chips on the smoky fire.

Dirk wondered what Sebe meant. Then he realized his hand was on the bulge of the amulet under his shirt. He had not taken the amulet out since leaving Zululand, but he was conscious of its being there—always conscious, always.

"Ach, ancient one, I'm just dreaming of your dinner-magic, and wondering what dainties you'll conjure up for us tonight."

Pity, Dirk thought again, that they had no coffee. He sat down to rest a moment before setting out on foot to scout the surrounding countryside from the top of a kopje. He did not know what to expect here, whether there might be inhabited kraals or Xhosa herdsmen grazing their cattle, or even wild outlaw bands. Of one thing he was certain: Zulu impis were on the move near the mountains. He knew it in his bones. But more than that, during those weeks trying to find a way across the Dragon Mountains, his party had met Zulu families fleeing the civil war, Dingaane's followers against Shaka's loyalists. They had told that Mazibe was beaten, Dingaane firmly enthroned as successor to Shaka.

The witch doctor, Dayega, was leading a force of Dingaane's warriors in pursuit of Mazibe's outnumbered force, intending to wipe it out. Or so the refugees had put it. Dirk knew there was more to it than that. Dayega was first of all seeking the amulet—seeking Dirk.

"When do we turn south?" Benjamin asked wearily, tossing his saddle and blankets beside the fire. "Aren't we already far enough west from the mountains to keep us clear of Zulu war parties?"

"Tomorrow," Dirk replied. "But we'll have to move faster, for if they find our trail, they'll come on at the run over this country; we'll have to push hard for the next few days."

It was likely that Mazibe had put up a fight now and again, risking himself and his warriors to slow or divert Dayega's pursuit of Dirk. What else could explain why Dirk's party had not been caught yet? Time for their escape must have been bought with blood. Dirk prepared to go on his scout, and as he slapped the dust from his hat, he thought of bold Senzana, Mazibe's son, imagining him in battle, a boy up against mature warriors. Dirk sighed and pulled the rifle from its case, hearing Lovell and Benjamin continue their ongoing debate.

"Your perfect world," Benjamin was saying, "will be a world ruled by one government, one religion, one race. Well, I'm not of your race or religion, so it doesn't appeal to me."

"The Judeo-Christian law, man, don't you see?" Lovell was standing over Benjamin, who sat wearily on his saddle blanket, sketch pad out and drawing Blueboy, who was grazing near a sweet-thorn tree. "We all have our place in the order, man. It's for everyone's benefit, for everyone's salvation." He gestured at Sebe. "Even for this benighted knave and his kind. They and all darkest Africa will be doomed to eternal misery and conflict if they're not taught by us wrong from right, if they're not taught that obedience to the one law is liberating, ennobling! For everyone! Heathens and Christians, alike. You Hebrews, too."

Dirk had heard this argument one way or the other for weeks, with Lovell spouting the belief that his fraternal masters held out the only hope for the creation of a peaceful world. Lovell condemned the Russians and Germans and French as rulers of evil dominions that would tyrannize humanity, while his own masters would "illuminate it with one pure faith, one order."

This ongoing debate often brought in the German philosophers who had such influence these days—Schopenhauer and Hegel, both of whom Dirk had read at Leyden. Lovell paraphrased Hegel: *Reason is the candle of the Lord.* Benjamin countered with Schopenhauer: *Our world is the mind's creation, and our understanding of it is limited by our intellects.*

Benjamin believed that human intellect had created the concepts of space and time, and that reality is beyond our understanding.

Lovell declared, on the contrary, that mankind can make a "perfect world" with a "world soul" if the veil that conceals Truth *is torn aside by the "right philosophy." Then will arise a social order in which man's inner convictions become one with his voluntary obedience to the law.*

"We're beginning here, in Africa, with our international mission for mankind," Lovell was saying with mounting passion. "We're international pilgrims, indeed, we of the brotherhood." He stretched out his arms. "One day, the map of Africa will be painted red! Yes, the red of empire, from the Cape to Cairo!"

Dirk saw a sharp light in his left eye.

"And you, my Boer baas—it has been given to you to carry a mighty power, one that is not yours to possess, but which must be yielded up freely, sacrificed by you, returned to those to whom it rightfully belongs."

Dirk's restrained his anger, saying nothing as Lovell continued in a voice that seemed to come from deep within.

"The bull's head is the eternal symbol of sacrifice—self-sacrifice, do you not see?" He leaned toward Dirk, almost whispering, "Do you not see?"

Dirk spoke more calmly than he felt. "One day, Lovell, you must tell me the full story of this amulet, so I can judge whether you speak the truth about it."

"The truth about the amulet?"

"Yes, you will tell me the truth about the amulet."

"The truth about the amulet."

Lovell took a deep breath, and the light in his eye went out. "That is a long, long story, indeed." He recovered composure, straightening up. "A long story, beginning before the floods of Atlantis, even before the Lemurian epoch—a story that has no beginning that I know of, a story which will not end with you, be assured, it will not end with you, whether you cooperate with us or defy us."

"Is that a threat?"

This sounded harsh, but Dirk meant it as a genuine question, not as a challenge, and Lovell seemed willing to take it the right way.

"My good Afrikaner," he said with a supercilious smile. "The power of the amulet's rightful owners is only a threat if one defies it."

"I defy what threatens me." Dirk's blood was beginning to heat up. "Am I threatened?"

Lovell paused. Benjamin and Sebe looked and listened.

"Is he threatened?" Lovell asked himself, and that light was again in his left eye. "My associates much prefer alliances to conflict, and mutual profit to victory for one, defeat for the other."

His glinting eye absorbed Dirk, almost spellbinding him, but there was a moment in which he was not sure who was spellbound, he or Lovell.

"Bearer of the Stone of White Fire," the Englishman said, "if you truly love your Boer folk and would have them enjoy that peaceful life they value so, then ally yourself with us."

"If?" Dirk demanded. "What do the Boers have to do with any of this? Speak."

"The Lost Mines of Ophir." Lovell was indeed enthralled.

Dirk's will held him. Even that light in the man's eye did not go out, as if it could not escape, as if Lovell was compelled to answer.

"The wealth of the earth . . . the treasury of past ages . . . a power of wealth, yes, scattered upon the ground—wealth that you and your dirt-bound kind would only scorn, misuse, plough under if they could for the sake of forage, corn, fat babies, cattle, sheep, and horses!"

Lovell was trembling so that Dirk thought he might collapse. It was not right to hold him like this. The amulet was warm, heavy.

"The Stone of White Fire," Lovell said, as from a distance. "Created in that epoch of the first corruption of kings, of those who betrayed their divine mandate." He stared, unseeing, at Dirk. "In our epoch, man's higher will must be redeemed, must reign again, must rule over the earth and all the lower creatures, rule over all who must obey, or be destroyed and cast forever into outer darkness!"

Dirk wrenched himself away from Lovell, who groaned and sat down clumsily. Dirk's hand was again on the amulet. Benjamin was looking to Lovell. Sweat trickled down Dirk's face and back. Sebe's bony hand on his arm steadied him. The heaviness and heat of the amulet passed, and Dirk felt better.

"May I say, Baas," Sebe remarked quietly, "that for my people, the bull is the symbol of immortality, and if the amulet bearer has faith, he will learn to see . . . to see with the eyes of the soul."

Where did Sebe find that one? When Dirk looked at him, he saw not a grizzled old Xhosa guide, but an ageless visage, at once familiar and beautiful. In the next moment, in a blink, the familiar old Sebe was there again, turning away to tend his fire and his cooking, singing to himself in that clicking tongue of his. It was a song Dirk recognized as a Xhosa lullaby.

Benjamin, kneeling beside Lovell, tried to soothe everyone's feelings.

"Friends, we are on the last part of our journey, so for heaven's sake let us remain steadfast." He gave the feverish Lovell a little brandy. "Dirk, I beg you, have a care with Tom; he's still suffering from all he's been through. Please spare him your resentment."

Dirk was sorry Benjamin thought him at fault, but he respected his friend's kind heart and his worry for a sickly man. Dirk had not yet told Benjamin about the plot to steal the amulet from Mazibe. He prepared to go on his scout, but then heard something in the distance and turned to the others.

"Hark!"

Sebe set an ear to the ground and exclaimed, "Horses!"

"Get ready!" Dirk told them and ran up the slope to take a position at the top.

He tossed aside his hat and peered over the undulating grassland. He could actually feel someone there, beyond the nearest rise, but could not see them. Sebe came to his side, spear and club at the ready.

"Tell me, Baas!"

"I don't know." Dirk listened, the throb of hoofbeats louder in his mind. "Riders, approaching slowly."

"There!" Sebe pointed off to the left. "Two of them, one stopping on high ground, the other coming on." He eyed Dirk before saying, "You have something now, Baas, something even this rainmaker does not have."

Dirk tapped the muzzle of his rifle.

"Yes, this."

"And more."

Sebe went to get the others. They would have to make a stand if these riders were from a band of Griqua outlaws known to range through here, where there was no law to restrain them. Dirk did not think this was an enemy, however, though he did not know why. Perhaps they were hunters or even the scouts from a trek. His heart leaped at this last thought. Had his family set out after all?

The first rider drew nearer. Benjamin and Lovell, with rifles, joined Dirk, lying in the grass. Sebe took cover in his own way, lurking in bushes, where he could not be seen. Lovell's frenzy seemed to have left him, although he sweated, wiping it away with his ever-present handkerchief.

"We must fight to the death rather than yield up the amulet."

Dirk made no reply. He fully intended to fight to the death.

"Hear me!" Lovell pressed: "We must bury it—immediately!" When Dirk did not answer, Lovell insisted: "Under that big tree, bury it there, now, before it's too late!"

Dirk stared coldly at him, and Lovell abruptly looked away. His trembling returned.

"We must protect it," he whispered, rifle aimed at the rider, finger on the trigger, tightening—

"Not yet!" Dirk growled, blocking the hammer with his hand, preventing the rifle from firing.

"You must protect it!" Lovell implored, scrambling back down the hill, leaving Dirk with the rifle. "You have the duty to protect it!"

Sebe was there, as if ready with the spear. Lovell dropped to his knees, praying, sobbing. No demon of a light was in his eye now, just tears. Benjamin had seen all this, but did not leave his position. His own rifle was at the ready.

Dirk peered at the rider, saying, "No point starting a war if there's no—" He gasped. "Before God!" He leaped up, waving his hat and shouting. "Johannes! Johannes Drente! Over here, jonge! Over here!"

DIRK AND RACHEL

Rachel saw Johannes waving his hat to come. She waved to Gerrit and the Gravens, then kneed Tempest forward, wondering who, out here, would be a friend. Jaeger loped along beside her.

When about fifty yards from where Johannes had dropped out of sight beyond a rise, Rachel was startled to see something moving in the long grass, off to her right. She pulled up, and in the same moment Jaeger barked and went after it. Rachel whistled to him, and he skidded to a stop, close to whatever was in the grass, a dark something. The Boerhound stood, stiff-legged, growling as Rachel rode slowly forward, the hair on her neck prickling. She cocked her rifle, letting the butt rest on her thigh, and peered into the grass, her heart skipping. She would have called to Johannes, but he was nowhere in sight. Were other somethings elsewhere in the grass, perhaps all around her? If so, she could not see them.

She stopped Tempest beside Jaeger and called out in Afrikaans. "Hey, there! Hey, you!"

There was movement. The flutter of red cloth caught the wind. Tempest recoiled, nostrils flaring. Jaeger wanted to lunge.

"Stay, Jaeger."

Rachel quaked a little, mastered it, and brought the rifle to bear, calling out again in her gruffest voice, "Hey! Come out!" Then in broken Bantu. "Come, you! Firestick speak!"

That did it.

The grass parted, and a slender young native in a red hooded cape stood up, large eyes fixed on the Boerhound. He was very black, his skin shining under the hood, arms held out so she could see he carried no weapons. He would have been good-looking, almost pretty, had those eyes not been so strangely protruding, so intense. They flickered at Rachel, then back at Jaeger, as he brought his hands together in a sign of friendship.

"Keep this beast from me," he said softly in Bantu; he did not appear to be Xhosa.

"Who are you? What are you doing hiding in the grass?"

"I am Ineto, outcast of the Zulus, and I mean only to find a new home where I can dwell in peace." He half bowed. "I was concealed because your people there may want to slay me."

Those eyes were larger than ever. Rachel caught herself, realizing she had been distracted by them. She had to bring this man to her brother. In a few moments, Gerrit and the others would appear over the rise, but she did not want to wait.

"Go before me," she said, gesturing with the rifle, though she did not want to use it. "No one slay you. You make no trouble."

"My life is yours."

"Get belongings. Go."

He half-bowed again, watching Jaeger sidelong as he cautiously picked up a bundle and reached for a knobkerrie and a stabbing spear. Rachel ordered him to leave his weapons where they lay, and he did so. Without speaking, Jaeger close behind, he made his way through the grass toward the high ground where Johannes had gone. Before they reached it, Gerrit came thundering up, Ton and Anneke close behind.

"What have you here, meisje, a robber?"

Gerrit looked proud of her, but barely listened when she started to explain what had happened. He rode alongside Ineto and roughly began to question him. When Ineto did not readily reply, Gerrit slapped his head, demanding answers. Ineto stopped walking.

"Leave him be, Gerrit!" Rachel demanded. "He's mine. I found him."

"Where you taking him?"

Just then, Johannes and four others appeared, standing at the top of the rise, and Gerrit rode to them. Ineto bowed his head. Rachel observed the men with Johannes as they and Gerrit shook hands. There was a big, fair-haired ragged one who looked like an impoverished Bush Boer. This one, like his companions, seemed not to have bathed in an eternity. The tall, dark one had a gracious bearing, but his clothes were also in tatters and dirty. The short one did not meet Gerrit's eyes as they shook hands, but the grinning elderly black man looked so full of good humor that he made Rachel smile.

Who were they? And why would they want to kill this boyish Zulu fugitive meekly standing with head bowed, hands clasped?

"Good work, jonge! Good work!" the big, bearded fellow was shouting as he jogged down to the Zulu to stand before him, hands on hips. "You caught a treacherous snake, here, jonge!"

Rachel wondered what jonge this worn-out Bush Boer was talking to. Then she realized with a start that he was talking to her.

"But you're lucky, young fellow!" he said, pulling out a long knife that had been concealed under the red cape. "Next time dig well through your prisoner's drawers or else—"

"What!" Tempest reared.

The man waved the ugly blade at Rachel.

"—or else he'll shove this up your arse when you're not looking!"

Rachel exploded: "You! Why, you!" Tempest whirled, and Rachel would have liked her stallion to give this oaf a taste of his hooves. "How dare you talk to me like that!"

Johannes was laughing aloud, and Gerrit trying not to. Anneke hid behind her mask, but not her pretty smile, and her father was red with embarrassment. The Bush Boer oaf stood slack-jawed.

"What?" he asked stupidly.

"Did you say 'What'?" Rachel shouted, both Tempest and Jaeger as agitated as she. "Did you say 'What'? You rude . . . rude . . . Bush Boer!" She spun Tempest and rode away, leaving him with his mouth open. No man had ever talked to her like that. No man! Who was he? That oaf! Dolt—

Rachel did not know how far she galloped through the grass, embarrassed and angry and insulted. Then someone was riding at her side. It was he! Galloping his stallion bareback. Right next to her.

Rachel reined in and turned her mount's head. Her own head—her nose—was held high.

"Ach, meisje, please forgive my . . . my—"

"Stupidity!"

"Ja, if you wish. I am sorry, I thought you were a jonge, and you can't blame me for that, after all . . ."

Exasperated, Rachel kneed Tempest and cantered back to where they had started. The Bush Boer was at her side, but a little behind, as if trying to think of some way to atone. His stallion and hers shook their heads from time to time, one trying to bite the other, both restless, wanting to kick. As they approached the rest of the party, the fellow spoke again.

"I truly am sorry, young lady, for . . ." He sighed. "I just meant to warn you never to underestimate a man you've placed under your gun."

Tempest was pulled to a stop, stamping.

He hurriedly went on. "I meant no disrespect by that unfortunate remark about the blade—just thought you were a guy, not a girl . . . I mean, your clothes—"

"Drop it!" Rachel was breathing quickly, her breasts rising and falling as she turned to confront the fellow, meaning to say some hard things, but she was surprised by the eyes behind his unkempt hair, eyes that disarmed her, eyes that were—actually beautiful.

She shook that off. Her hat fell back on her shoulders.

"Fine," she said, looking away. "I accept your apology."

"It's just that I never expected a girl to be able to capture so formidable a character as this! He's a Zulu executioner, meisje. Yes. A bad one. How did he yield so easily?"

That she did not know.

"Looking into my rifle muzzle, I suppose."

The fellow chuckled, and Rachel almost smiled, though she preferred to stay annoyed. His hat was off now, too, and in the best of courtesy, he said, "Permit me to introduce myself—"

The stallions went for each other, and the riders fought them down. The fellow laughed, and it sounded good to Rachel, who found herself laughing, too. The Boer custom was to let stallions fight it out on the grass, without riders, until one triumphed and reigned as leader. Until then, they would nip and kick and go for each other.

"Dirk Arendt."

"What?"

"My name is Arendt."

"Who?" His messy hair and ragged clothes were the image of a border outlaw, a vagabond. Not— "Dirkie? You?"

"Huh? What did you say?"

"I know you." She was dismayed, limp. Unbelieving. "Or, I used to."

"You! Not Rachel! Johannes's sister! Not that little brat—"

Tempest almost reared.

"I am. That brat! And you are that miserable teaser!"

Dirk chuckled and shook his head. He regarded her closely, up and down, in a way no stranger would have been permitted to look at her, but Rachel was not angry anymore.

"You're like a jonge only from a distance. But you've become a very nice meisje. Or should I say vrouw? Are you married to some fortunate fellow by now?"

It seemed that nothing Dirk Arendt could say would be right just then. Rachel shook her head. Instead of talking, she held out her hand for him to clasp it in proper greeting. He wiped his hand on his shirt before taking hers, and all she could think of to say was:

"I adore . . . your parents."

"You know where they are?" Dirk's eyes were alight.

"I do," Rachel laughed, drawing her hand away. "Less than a day's ride."

Now it was for Blueboy to rear, and Dirk howled with joy.

"All of them," Rachel declared. "Your brothers, too. All four: Piet, Henk, Paul, and Artemus, trekking with Marta and Willem, and they're laagered just to the north." She asked Blueboy's name. "What a handsome fellow he is, though you've used him hard, I'd say."

She looked closely at Dirk Arendt and saw past his weariness, his foul clothes and hair, and that scruffy beard. He was still handsome, too. She could see that.

"Ach, ja," Dirk answered, patting his stallion's neck. "Used Blueboy hard of late, Rachel Drente; we both need a good rest, he a bag of oats, and this kerel some Boer comfort, if you can spare some."

"Of course," she said, smiling.

Side by side, they cantered back to the others, not saying another word. All the way, Rachel found herself smiling, though she did not really know why. Nor did it matter.

☾ ☾ ☾

Dirk could not help stealing a glance at Johannes's sister as they rode. How pretty she had become, although he scarcely could remember what she had looked like as a girl. She seemed familiar somehow, as if he already had met her as a woman. That, of course, was impossible, unless she had come to Europe while he was there.

Why had no one caught her yet? Was she such a hard one to tie down? One thing was certain, she was a marvellous rider. Probably one of those meisjes who likes horses better than jonges. No doubt that was it. No doubt that was why no one had managed to get Rachel Drente to marry him.

COFFEE

It worried Dirk that Ineto had caught up with them. Why had he come? Was he a scout for Dayega, or a spy sent to observe all he could before slipping away to alert his master? Ineto was walking in their midst, a rope halter around his neck, hands tied in front, Sebe next to him. Dirk would interrogate the Zulu later tonight.

As the party approached the laager of Johannes's little trek, Rachel and Anneke were riding together in front, and now that blond Anneke had removed her mask, Dirk was struck by her prettiness. He was behind the women and could not help observing how different they were. As boyish and lively as Rachel was, so was Anneke feminine and delicate. Anneke assumed the bearing of a fine lady; indeed, Dirk had seen plenty of her kind in Europe and Capetown. Rachel, by contrast, was not at all mannered, yet she had a natural grace and beauty that far surpassed Anneke.

There came a shout from the campsite—a semicircle of wagons with the opening blocked by crates and trunks and a thornbush fence that was hauled open to let the party enter. Everyone was excited to hear that the main trek was so close. Rachel's maidservant, Millie, did a little jig with Jacob when they heard the good news. Sannie appeared and embraced Johannes, who told them they would be in safe hands soon.

"Five trekwagons are coming back to join us, along with a reinforcement of fifteen rifles," he said, patting her belly. "You'll have plenty of company when your time comes, dearest."

Dirk wanted Ineto bound hand and foot, and Jacob saw to it. Benjamin and Lovell went with Gerrit's servants to wash up and change into clean clothes. Tante Emmy, in her over-large chair, looked Dirk up and down as he was introduced by Rachel as the Arendts' long-gone son. Emmy was dismayed.

"What happened to you, Dirkie? Where in heaven's name have you been? Is that what Europe does to our jonges? Before God, you look like an outlaw on the run . . . living in a den with wild dogs!"

Dirk grinned and bowed, not intending to take her hand in greeting until after he washed up, but Emmy reached out to him and gripped his hands, her eyes softening.

"By the grace of God, you have come back to us, Dirkie!" She wiped away a tear and caught her breath, then scolded: "Away with you and clean up! What would your mother say if she knew you presented yourself to me like that?" She yelled over her shoulder, "André! Freddie! Get Dirk Arendt some good clothes—but have him cleaned up good first!"

Emmy clapped her fat hands, and a bevy of servants appeared. With them was André, whose blind eyes sparkled with joy.

"Dirk? Dirk? Is that really you?" He made his way with the help of Freddie. "Oh, let's have a look!"

André's hands felt Dirk's face and beard and chest, his fingers touching the bulge of the amulet, so that Dirk instinctively pulled a little away.

"What's this?" André said, reaching toward the amulet.

"Good luck charm," Dirk said, firmly holding André's hands. "Just don't take a whiff of me, old uncle. I've been on the run from Zululand."

"Zululand!" André gasped and dragged Dirk to him. "Miracle you escaped, *mon ami!* You must tell me all about it!" He held Dirk at arm's length and said, "Freddie, this puppy's been rolling again. Wash him up, and give him my best shirt."

André again felt for the amulet, and Dirk again gently removed the hand and squeezed it affectionately.

"Your best shirt, Master?" Freddie asked, with a twinkle in his bloodshot eyes.

"You heard me. Get moving! Clean this young baas up. And if one drop of this stink gets into that shirt, I'll tan your hide!"

Freddie smiled good-humoredly at Dirk. "Methinks the young baas is somewhat too broad in the shoulder to fit into any of your shirts, Master."

André thought a moment, then drew a long breath, and with effort raised his bent body to its full height. It was a surprise to Dirk that he was almost as tall. Though hunched and bony these days, André had once possessed a strong frame.

"If you say that, you knave, you don't know what shirt I mean, and you're a worthless servant. I don't need a worthless servant."

"Indeed, you do not, Master, you need the most worthy of servants to await your every whim!" Freddie was used to this banter, and appeared to be enjoying it as much as André. "Say the word, Master, and I will go back to Cape Town in search of a better servant for you so I can live out my old age at the fireside."

"Just do your duty!" André feigned resignation as he declared, "I'm so used to incompetence that I wouldn't know what to do with a worthy servant."

Emmy's belly laugh rolled across the campsite. "The wedding shirt, Freddie! It'll look dandy on the young baas. But clean him up first. Soap him like a piglet going to market."

Dirk tried to protest that André's wedding shirt was too much to ask, but André grasped his elbow and, with Freddie helping, began to haul him away. Just then there came another laugh, this one high-pitched and full of good humor. It was Sebe, pointing at André, and singing out in Bantu:

"I knew it! I knew it! I knew it! My medicine told me I would find you again, you hard-bargaining smous from Toulouse!"

Struck with astonishment, André whirled, as if he could see.

"You! I knew my tonic would preserve your miserable life longer than you deserve, you Xhosa charlatan! Hah!" He held out a hand, palm open. "So pay me! You never paid me for the tonic! Where's the *geld?*"

In the next moment, blind French trader and wiry Xhosa rainmaker were embracing and laughing, to the amazement and curiosity of the onlookers.

"This, Emmy, is the misbegotten son of a dust storm I told you about!" André howled. "The tongue-clicking, insect-eating witch doctor I found out on the high veldt, dying of snake bite, malaria, crocodile bite, suffering from thirst and exposure, and stuck with Bushmen spears tipped with fatal poison from the deadly mamba!" He slapped Sebe's shoulders. "I saved his life with my most potent elixir—and a waste of good medicine, it was!"

Sebe chuckled, clasped his hands in greeting to Tante Emmy, and said in halting Afrikaans, "This sightless smous and one no-good guide be lost and getting loster when I find them, and it my honor to lead them safely home."

"Took three long weeks!" André creaked.

Emmy slapped her knee. "Old one, you don't owe him anything for the tonic." Sebe bowed graciously. "We'll find a shirt for you, too."

André had Sebe sit down at a campfire where there was a steaming pot of stew, and as the Xhosa ate, they began to talk of where they had been these past few years. Dirk went with Freddie for a bath and clean clothes, thinking how good it was to be with his own kind at last. He smelled the aroma of brewing coffee. Then Rachel was there, with a beaker full, and Dirk gratefully accepted it.

"You're very thoughtful, meisje."

"You're still one of us," she replied, smiling. "Even if you have been sailing the great water like a foreigner on the very edge of the earth."

Dirk sipped the coffee, soothing after all these weeks on the run. Looking at Rachel over the rim, he noticed her contemplating his ragged clothes and dirty face and hands.

"Maybe you'll recognize me after Freddie cleans me up."

"What? Oh, well, I already do," she said, smiling and patting Jaeger's big head, for the Boerhound had jealously pushed his way between them. "I already do."

☾ ☾ ☾

A little later, as the sun began to go down, and fires and torches sprang into flame, Rachel and Millie brought coffee to the other men who were journeying with Dirk. Benjamin and Lovell had washed and been given clean clothes, which they tried to pay for but were refused. Rachel could not help smiling to see these two uitlanders dressed like Boers in old flannel shirts, with baggy corduroy trousers tucked into their high, English-style boots.

Benjamin bowed elegantly as she gave him the beaker. He

had not shaved off his dark beard, and Rachel thought it suited him, complimenting his brown eyes and patrician demeanor. He wore the clothes well, making them look better than they would on just anyone. As she watched him stroll away with his coffee to join Sebe and André and some others fooling with the friction machine, Rachel thought Benjamin must be the very image of a young European lord.

Lovell, on the other hand, apparently did not care how he looked, for he was rumpled, disheveled, though clean enough now. The Englishman seemed distracted as he accepted the coffee from Millie, who curtsied to him. Wiping his brow with a handkerchief, he asked the girl whether she could speak Bantu to the prisoner. The serving girl glanced nervously at Rachel and then Lovell and back to Rachel.

"Mistress, I be too scared of that there Zulu to go near him." She gave Lovell a shy, apologetic look as he shook his head in exasperation.

Rachel wondered why Lovell was so impatient to interrogate the Zulu when there were others here, including Benjamin and Dirk, who could speak Bantu. She was about to ask that when a howl of delight and excitement went up near the Toulouse tent, where Sebe—in a new yellow shirt—was working away at the friction machine's crank. Benjamin was there, shaking out one hand, apparently having just been shocked. When Rachel turned back, Lovell had gone to the end of the trekwagon, where the prisoner, tethered to the wagon by ropes around his legs, was sitting on the ground. Rachel was holding a cup of coffee for the Zulu. After all, he had done nothing to harm her. Once they found out why he was here, they might just let him go. She did not know. It was not her business.

As she approached the end of the long wagon, she was surprised to hear voices, Lovell and Ineto conversing. Further, they were speaking Afrikaans, something about a "red brotherhood." She hesitated. So the Zulu had his secrets.

"Is this familiar to you?" Ineto was saying, his bound hands brought up so that the right hand was touching his chin.

They were in profile against torches set up around the laager to scare off wild animals, and for a moment Rachel thought they exchanged some sort of hand signal, as Lovell's hand went to his chin also. She proceeded toward them, hearing Lovell giggle, somewhat hysterically.

"Yes, I should have known, should have known . . . of course, the brotherhood wouldn't leave me out here alone."

Ineto gasped to see Rachel. She was puzzled, but came forward as if she were unafraid of this Zulu who had been Shaka's executioner. Ineto kept his eyes lowered. Lovell glared at her.

"For you," she said in Afrikaans to Ineto, wanting to leave, but trying to mask her uneasiness. "Food's coming soon."

Ineto accepted, nodding. Rachel turned to Lovell, who blinked and looked away.

"Kind of you," he said absently.

Rachel forced a smile and withdrew, relieved when André's concertina began to play and Johannes's fiddle joined in. To her delight, she even heard Sannie singing, the first time her sister-in-law had sounded so cheerful since leaving Sweetfountain. Rachel went toward them, then caught sight of Dirk approaching from André's wagon, Freddie walking behind, glowing with pride. No wonder.

Rachel caught her breath. Dirk had shaven, his hair trimmed and combed, and that white silk shirt made him look . . . look . . . like nothing and no one she had ever seen before. Rachel stood gazing as he approached, walking fast, deep in thought, not noticing her as he hurried past. Awkwardly she asked him to come for dinner and hear the music.

"Can't." He scarcely looked at her. "Got to find out what this Zulu came here for; I've already wasted too much time."

"Well," Rachel muttered, "it's not a waste of time for a decent man to wash himself once in a while."

Dirk gave a laugh and was turning to answer her, but she would not give him the satisfaction, not if he was in such an all-fired rush. She had the urge to look back over her shoulder for a quick glance, but forced herself not to. She strutted away to join the fun, making sure she gave a careless toss of her long hair as she went, just in case he was watching.

☾ ☾ ☾

Why are you here, King's Knife?" Dirk demanded of Ineto a few moments later.

Still bound hand and foot, the sullen Ineto sat on a low stool. Dirk spoke Bantu. He was uneasy, worried, and hungry, for he had not yet eaten or drunk, save for Rachel's coffee. More important than the meal most of the others were enjoying just then, Dirk had to know what Ineto was after.

It was fully dark by now, the sides of the wagons and the canvas tents illuminated by firelight and the ring of torches. The white trekkers and most of the servants were at the dinner tables, save for two boys riding guard around the campsite. André and Johannes had laid instruments aside and taken their places at the table, but Johannes's servant, Klaas, was still playing the clarinet, sweet music that lifted into the night sky, full of stars mingling with wood smoke.

As Dirk interrogated Ineto, Tom Lovell paced back and forth

nearby. Benjamin David was seated on a camp stool, looking pensive, and he translated for Lovell.

Ineto told them he had fled Zululand to escape enemies out for vengeance. He had only chanced to encounter Dirk's party, finding their trail a few days ago, and hoping to beg for some food until he discovered it was they. His large eyes avoided Dirk as he spoke.

"When I saw, too late, who I had been following, I attempted to flee, but then the female white thing with the lion dog found me." He spoke carefully, choosing his words. "I have done you no harm; I ask only to be allowed to remain with you a few days, then to continue my journey toward the setting sun, where—"

Dirk had a hand to the amulet inside his shirt. Ineto's eyes flickered. He appeared unable or unwilling to go on, his breathing louder now. Whatever was the truth, the executioner was skirting it. Dirk sensed that the truth was a threat to the trekkers. If Dayega and an impi found the treks, there would be bloodshed. His heart quickened. He pointed at Ineto, who winced.

"Why have you followed us, King's Knife? Speak!"

"Because . . ." Ineto almost whispered. "I must."

"Why must you? Why? When you know we would kill you and leave you to rot like a beast, without slitting open your belly to liberate your Zulu soul, and even your own people, who curse you, would thank us for it."

Ineto was inscrutable, rock-steady.

"If you slay me, then you will never know why I am here."

Dirk had to know. "Is it for this?"

Ineto gasped. The bull's-head amulet dangled in front of him. He was unable to look away.

"Speak the truth, King's Knife, by the power of the Stone of White Fire."

Dirk felt the amulet's light rather than saw it, felt himself one with it, and his heart slowed its beating, as if suffused with power and crystal-clear insight. Ineto's countenance reflected the white fire, his mouth working, forming words.

"I am commanded . . . commanded to find you, commanded . . ." He hesitated, struggling willfully.

"By whom? To do what?"

". . . by the brotherhood to . . . to join you!" He wavered, short of breath. "I have obeyed the command . . . I have come . . ."

"Why?"

"I know not!" he blurted. "I know not yet what is my final task, my duty!" He was gasping, in pain.

"Who will tell you?"

"He . . . will tell me!"

"Who will? Who?"

"The . . . brother!" Ineto was enthralled by the amulet, the white fire in his eyes.

"Speak?"

"Him! Him!"

The Zulu was looking past Dirk, who turned, but saw no one, just the circle of torches and darkness. That distraction gave Ineto release, and he keeled over, the stool falling with him. He lay still. Benjamin knelt to examine him, saying he had passed out.

"Best wait until morning to continue," Benjamin said to Dirk, who had put the amulet back in its place under his shirt. "Whatever you just did with that bauble, my friend, it got the best of him."

Dirk sighed, immensely weary. Ineto had made no sense. What was the "brotherhood" he spoke of? Danger was near, perhaps just beyond the torchlight. It troubled Dirk that he might be imperiling these farmers, who wanted only to build new homes.

Benjamin laid Ineto on a blanket and covered him over as Dirk began to pace. Lovell had left during the interrogation, perhaps too exhausted. Or had he seen the light of the amulet and been frightened by it? Dirk needed to know what was really happening.

"Did you see the amulet glow, Benjamin?" he asked.

Benjamin rose from attending to Ineto and shook his head before asking in turn, "Did this Zulu?"

Dirk nodded.

"Be grateful, Benjamin, that it is not for you to see the white fire." Recovering, Dirk said they would have to take turns guarding Ineto. "If he escapes, he'll likely go to his kind and will come back with a fighting force."

To think this made him heartsore.

"I fear I have brought trouble to my folk, Benjamin. The sooner I go away from them, the better, though first I must see my family."

"Then we go to the Cape Colony?" Benjamin asked.

"I suppose." Dirk sighed again. "Though I'd rather join my own kind and trek away from all of this."

"You cannot!" a voice said; Lovell reappeared from out of the darkness, mouth turned downward. "You must go to Cape Town, amulet-bearer. You well know you must."

Dirk gazed at the trekkers laughing and enjoying their meal, Sebe amongst them. Would that Dirk had only to journey with his folk into the unknown and begin a new life. Would that it could be so simple. No, he was not meant to trek, not yet, although he did not say this to Lovell, who was standing over Ineto, as if to see whether he still lived.

Singing could be heard, or rather the sound of the folk humming to André's accordion. Dirk recognized the favorite English public house tune, and it sounded good. The folk hummed because they did not know the words. Dirk did.

Benjamin patted him on the shoulder and said, "I'll stand guard for a spell. Go and eat now, and charm the lovely maidens!" He grinned. "I see they've got some fair women out here wandering the wilderness, true beauties that might be described as Boer mermaids . . . in a sea of grass."

Dirk went to join the others and soon was singing with them. He found himself leading, singing about one lover assuring the other that even old age will never diminish their love.

Believe me, if all those endearing young charms
Which I gaze on so fondly today,
Were to change by tomorrow and fleet in my arms
Like fairy gifts fading away

Thou wouldst still be adored, as this moment thou art,
Let thy loveliness fade as it will,
And around the dear ruin each wish of my heart
Would entwine itself verdantly still.

Dirk's voice carried over the humming of the Boers and their servants. It was a heart-warming sound, and he was moved. Rachel Drente's lovely soprano joined with him, and when he looked at her, she smiled. Then another voice was there, a practiced, wavering tenor that carried over the rest and sang confidently in English.

It was Tom Lovell, standing at the edge of the firelight, singing his heart out, and it seemed he was crying.

TALKING DRUMS

It was as good a celebration that night as any Boer could ask, good food, good drink, and good company. Yet, through an evening of song and laughter, Dirk could not shake the dread that had come over him since Ineto appeared. He sat with André Toulouse much of the time, telling about Zululand and Shaka, but saying nothing about the amulet, though there were moments when he found himself touching it—moments when André was intently questioning him, probing about something, not being specific.

After the singing, the old Frenchman gripped Dirk's arm.

"My Boer adventurer, you have been at the heart of danger, and have escaped by a hair's breadth," André wheezed, "but it comes to me that you're not telling all—not that it's my affair, of course, but I discern you have some deep secret, Dirk Arendt."

That made Dirk restless, but he had a soft spot for André, who was unusually serious right now.

"We all have our secrets, my friend, including you, I'll wager." Dirk noticed Rachel Drente across the campfire, observing him.

"Sometimes secrets are best kept secret, for everyone's sake," André rasped, pushing back his straggling white hair. "And then there are some secrets that are too great a burden for one to bear, and these are meant to be shared with others who can help."

"Well said," Dirk replied.

"In truth, I would rather not hear about Zulus after nightfall." André's visage darkened, though the firelight played upon it. "Such talk brings back evil memories, and will keep me awake."

Dirk knew something about André's adventures in Swaziland years ago, and of his own narrow escape from Zulu marauders. He had wandered alone in the jungle, lost and near death. Dirk also knew André had a special intuition, an uncanny sense of the future. Even now the old fellow appeared to be busy in his mind trying to divine Dirk's thoughts. Dirk's skin tingled.

"Yes, yes, mon ami," André was saying, his empty eyes seeming to have sight in another realm. "And yet, my friend, there is something in your secret that has to do . . . to do with me, no?"

Dirk felt the tingling even stronger, and his hand found its way to the amulet. If not for the faint flurry of a distant talking drum, he might have told all about the bull's head right then. Instead, he sat up, listening. *Yes!* A drum was beating out a message. He asked André whether he heard it, but the Frenchman shook his head.

Dirk turned back to ask Freddie, half asleep, seated behind his master. He did not hear it. Dirk looked to Sebe, who was at the edge of firelight, near Gerrit's trekwagon, throwing the divining bones and litter from his medicine bag. Dirk excused himself and went to the Xhosa, all the while listening for that drum, which had fallen silent, but could mean an enemy was on the move, within striking distance. When Dirk asked if he had heard the drum, Sebe looked up from his witchery, eyes a bit glazed, and said he had not.

"There!" Dirk cupped a hand to his ear. The drumming seemed just beyond the next rise. "We must hurry to arms!"

Sebe stood in Dirk's way.

"The talking drum is for you, not us."

"You can't hear it?" Dirk's gripped the amulet.

"No," Sebe said, gesturing toward the mountains. "But there are drums there, and they are coming closer."

Johannes's violin began to play. Dirk wanted it to drown out the drum beat, but it did not.

☾ ☾ ☾

Rachel was sitting next to Gerrit Schuman, with Anneke and Ton on his other side.

Johannes played them a sentimental old song, and Rachel remembered her parents and Johannes's beautiful children. Oh, so long ago! Her thoughts unexpectedly wandered to that uncomfortable moment in the presence of Tom Lovell and the Zulu prisoner, and to what they had said about a brotherhood, a "red brotherhood." She had asked Johannes about it earlier, but he had no idea. He told her to question Lovell himself, but that gave her a chill. She also had asked Tante Emmy, who suggested she put the question to André, for he knew so many things about the world.

Rachel thought perhaps Dirk Arendt would know, but he might make fun of her for minding a stranger's business, for eavesdropping like some nosy gossip. Now Gerrit was speaking to her, leaning over, hat on his knee.

"It's not polite to stare, meisje."

"What?" She stirred from her reverie.

"You're staring like a lovesick puppy at Arendt over there."

"What do you mean?" Rachel shook herself, seeing Dirk deep in conversation with Sebe. "How do you know who I'm looking at?"

Gerrit was serious. "I want to walk with you tomorrow and talk—"

"Impossible. I go to the main trek tomorrow, with Mister Arendt and Mister David."

"You can't do that!" Gerrit said sharply. "It's not right, going off with a man, and you a single girl!"

"I can if I want to!" Rachel would not let him dictate to her.

"I won't stand for it!"

"Gerrit, Mister David will be there to chaperone, if you're so afraid for me."

"What? He's not one of us! How do you know he can be trusted?"

"Trust me, then. Can you do that?"

Gerrit let his long legs stretch out in front of him, fingers thrumming on his hat. Johannes's violin was so beautiful, and Rachel did not want to spoil it by having to tell Gerrit off. She tried to listen, and closed her eyes a moment. Gerrit thought something through, pulled in his legs, then leaned toward her and spoke quietly.

"You reconsider my proposal, meisje?"

Rachel was wrenched from the music.

"Your brother'll gladly give you to me." Gerrit was squeezing his hat hard.

"Don't ask this, not now, not when there's so much uncertainty, when, when—"

"When Arendt be coming among us like some foreigner to turn your little head?"

She looked right at him, not caring that Anneke was watching them, wondering what they were saying. The emotional old song and the rush of memories mingled with the heat of the wine and with her surprise at Gerrit's bluntness.

She looked into his pale blue eyes, took a deep breath, then abruptly leaned over to get Anneke's attention, and smiling brightly, said, "Say, girl, has Gerritje ever shown you his beautiful window?"

"Window?" Anneke's eyes widened as she looked at Gerrit, then back at Rachel. "What do you mean?"

Anneke was really a charming girl, and was interested now in the most genuine way.

"What window, Gerritje? You brought a window, all the way out here?" She let her fingers brush his hat brim, then said almost sadly to Rachel, "No, no, I suppose it's not for me to see such a wonderful thing as his precious window."

"Ach!" Gerrit's legs stretched out again. "It's not that I don't want to show you the window, Anneke."

"That's all right, Gerritje." She was delightfully appealing, this Anneke, as she stood up, smiled pertly at Rachel, and walked away.

Gerrit was harrumphing and slapping his hat on his knee, trying to find the words. Rachel touched his arm.

"Show the meisje the window, dear. She deserves it."

The song ended to a flurry of clapping and calls to Johannes in compliment. Gerrit clumsily stood up, whacked his leg with the hat, and stalked after Anneke. Rachel smiled, and in that moment saw Dirk Arendt staring back. That excited her, and she looked away, then back, glad his eyes were still on her.

Perhaps to keep Rachel from following Anneke and Gerrit, Ton Graven poured her some brandy, and as she drank a burning sip it occurred to her that she had that important question for André, who was rising, Freddie guiding him to bed. She hurried over.

"Uncle André," she said, pressing the cup of brandy into his hands. "This will help you sleep."

He chortled and drank it in two swigs, then displayed his usual intuition: "What is it you want of me, ma chérie? Go on, ask, before the brandy fuddles my mind, and weariness undermines my judgment."

"Uncle, have you ever heard of such a thing as a . . . a red brotherhood?"

André gave a start, clutching Rachel's forearm, unsteady on his feet. Freddie fetched a nearby camp stool, and André sat down, one hand still gripping Rachel's arm.

"Oui, I have heard that name before, but it was in a dark time, an evil time, a time to forget, and I never expected to hear it again . . . certainly not from your lips, my child."

More curious than ever, she hurriedly explained.

"When I was bringing them coffee I heard the Zulu and the Englishman speaking about it, but I didn't understand any of it."

André's hands were on his knees, his head bowed, and if he could see, it might be said his eyes were fixed upon the ground.

"It is not a pleasant memory—oh, no. It is a memory of the deaths of good friends and of the bedeviling jungle and the bolt of lightning that took my sight."

"Oh, Uncle, I am so sorry, I shouldn't have—"

"Rachel, I have little strength for this." He found her hand and squeezed it. "It is all too much for me—Dirk telling his story of Shaka, and now you, asking about the Red Brotherhood." His upper body moved forward and back, forward and back. "The Swazi chief told me so, he told me so."

Rachel did not press him, for he seemed near to collapse. Freddie, concerned, rested a hand lightly on his shoulder. After a moment, André stood up.

"Give me until tomorrow, dearest, and I will tell Dirk Arendt what I know, and then he can tell you what you need to know of it, though the less the better. Will you ask him to meet me before breakfast? There, near that torch outside the laager."

Rachel agreed and left André with his faithful Freddie, who led him away, the servant humming that sentimental English tune, perhaps to soothe André and quiet him.

Rachel returned to the campfire, but folk were departing for bed. Lovell and Benjamin shared a tent close to Ineto, who slept under the trekwagon where he was tethered. Sebe would sleep in the spare Drente tent with Dirk—an arrangement that would have been objectionable to most trekboers, who required blacks and whites to eat and sleep apart. These were unusual times, however, and it seemed Sebe was something of a bodyguard to Dirk.

Then Dirk himself was standing in front of Rachel. There was André's message to pass on, and more, for she had to tell just what she had in mind.

"You're going to your parents tomorrow?" she asked, rubbing Jaeger's ear, for the hound had appeared at her side.

"I am."

"Before you go, André Toulouse wishes to speak with you . . . it's important." She told him where and when.

"Of course," Dirk replied. "But I have to be off early, so I can reach the other trek before dark."

"Yes. And I will go with you . . . and Mister David, of course."

"No," Dirk said, shaking his head. "You stay here. Who knows what we'll meet on the way."

Rachel did not want to hear this.

"Mister Arendt, I can ride and I can shoot, so tomorrow I intend to go to your parents' trek, with you or on my own."

"Why?" Dirk appraised her. "What would Johannes say?"

"I have my reasons, and Johannes is not my father." Rachel wavered momentarily. "If you must know, I want to visit your parents, for they've been kind to me, more than kind—" She found a giggle rising, probably from the brandy, and was unable to stifle it. "After hearing your mother read so many of your letters aloud, I want to be there at the moment she sees her prodigal son returning, after all these years as a European dandy!"

Dirk laughed and turned to face the dying fire. "Yes, meisje, I long for that moment myself."

To her own surprise, Rachel touched his sleeve, and more to her surprise was his hand lightly on hers as she said, "Better find a good Boer shirt, then, Mister Arendt, not a French wedding blouse, or your parents will think you really are a European dandy."

Jaeger whined. Dirk took a bit of meat from the table and tossed it to the hound.

"Yes," he said, "André and I have much to discuss, much in common."

Rachel drew her hand away and thought it would be good if he would repeat that last, but mean her, not André. He did not, of course, and they politely said good night.

☾ ☾ ☾

An hour or so later, unable to sleep, Rachel strolled in the dimness just outside the laager, as she liked to do, enjoying the stars and the evening breeze. Jaeger was with her, somewhere ahead in the darkness, snuffling through the grass.

So much was happening, so much Rachel could not comprehend. She still felt that light touch of Dirk's hand, almost nothing, and yet she still felt it. Did he remember it now, as he lay in the tent? Everyone seemed to be asleep by now, save for sentries posted here and there. The campfires were low, but kept going by the guards, who tossed fuel on them from time to time. It was a lovely night, and for all her confusion, Rachel had not felt so good since before her parents died.

The Boerhound let out a playful bark that was followed by Gerrit's voice.

"Hey! Get off me, hound."

"Oh, la! You scared me!" Anneke's giggle was joined by Gerrit's deep laugh; they were lying out there in the darkness.

"Slobbered all over me," Gerrit chuckled.

"You thought it was me? Oh, la!"

They laughed again, and Rachel backed away so they would not notice her. She smiled to think of Gerrit and Anneke together. They were a fine match. She could not help herself giggling when she thought of Jaeger licking their faces. The dog was now by her side, and Rachel was almost back to the wagons when she heard Anneke call out.

"Sleep well, Rachel."

Rachel paused, then said, "Watch out for Zulus."

"Oh, la!"

More laughter.

Rachel thought it a perfect end to a very interesting day.

☾ ☾ ☾

We are coming.

In the chill darkness before dawn, Dirk heard the talking drum. He sat bolt upright in his bed of straw and blankets. Sebe was fast asleep, though the drum was louder than before.

We are coming.

Dirk threw back the blanket and pushed open the tent flap to go out and stand in the cold, listening, sweat starting from every pore. He heard the talking drum no better out here than in the tent. When he covered his ears, it was still there. At least the drum was only in his mind, not yonder on the veldt, not the drumbeat of an impi on the march, of the witch doctor, Dayega.

Or was it?

We are coming.

The message was intended for him.

REUNION

As first dawn and fading stars lit the eastern sky, Dirk met with André just outside the campsite, where Freddie had built a small fire and brought them stools, a pot of coffee, and beakers. While Dirk and André talked, Freddie kept at a discreet distance, drinking his own coffee and leaning against a wagon wheel.

André told of his time in Swaziland six years back, and how it had been brought to a brutal end by the Zulu attack that wiped out the kraal, killing the chief. That same story could have been told about hundreds of native kraals in southern Africa, destroyed in these years at the command of Shaka. The inhabitants were enslaved or slaughtered, as it suited him, their possessions and livestock taken back to Zululand as pillage, enriching that nation. The Zulus had grown ever stronger under Shaka, ever more feared.

As Dirk listened, the first glimmer of sun turned the cloudless sky from dark to radiant blue. When André told about the bull's-head amulet and the "white fire of the sacred crystal," as the doomed Swazi chief had termed it, Dirk hardly breathed. He was astounded. André mustered his strength to complete the story of that night in Swaziland, the Zulu attack, and closed with a description of the witch doctor, Dayega, stealing the amulet.

"The Amulet of Truth it is sometimes named," said André, "because whoever sees its white fire must speak the truth, just as he who carries it cannot lie."

Dirk kept his hand from touching the amulet under his shirt. He knew every word was true.

André went on: "But he who is unworthy of bearing it, he who lusts after its powers, will be destroyed by the fire of his own desires."

"Yes," Dirk said distantly. "Dayega gave it up to Shaka, but Shaka could not wear it, for too much blood was on his hands . . . so it was carried for him by a valiant induna—a man who became a friend of mine."

André appeared to be staring, but not at Dirk's face. It was as if he were staring at Dirk's hand, which had moved, without Dirk's realizing it, to the bulge of the amulet. Dirk felt a kinship with André, and in the next moment the amulet was between them, dangling from his hand. André was overwhelmed, his eyes opening and closing as if he could see. He did see something.

"The white fire," he whispered.

"You have seen it before."

"As have you."

André did not turn away until Dirk put the amulet back in its pouch. Resting his head in his hands, André continued, speaking with much feeling as he recalled how helpless he had been when the Swazi chief placed him in the glare of the stone's light.

"My Swazi friend told me—" He lifted his head and breathed deeply. "—he said to me: 'The bull's head must never return to those who would enslave us.'" Sitting up straight, André said, with all his strength, "Dirk Arendt, it is the Red Brotherhood that would enslave us. And we wanderers here in the wilderness are in great danger."

"It is my fault," Dirk almost groaned.

"No," André replied. "It is destiny. Destiny."

With that, he slumped down, just as the Swazi chief had slumped on that terrible night of massacre years ago. Dirk caught him. Freddie hurried over and lifted André in his arms as if carrying a child and took him back to his trekwagon. Dirk watched them go, worrying about the old man, wondering whether it was wrong to have placed the amulet before him. Even now, Dirk had endangered someone without intending to.

Then came an angry shout: *"Sacre bleu!* What in blazes are you up to now, you scoundrel? Put me down! Put me down! I haven't had my breakfast yet!"

Freddie was saying he would get breakfast in his bed, just like a French nobleman.

Dirk smiled, relieved. He stayed on that stool a while longer as morning broke. There was so much to think about.

☾ ☾ ☾

Later that day, on the ride over the rolling, endless grasslands toward the Arendt trek, Dirk finally told Benjamin about Lovell's attempt to have Captain Homan murder Mazibe and steal the amulet. Rachel had ridden a little ahead with Jaeger to see whether the reinforcement wagons were in sight yet.

At Dirk's tale of Lovell's duplicity, Benjamin was struck dumb. Head hanging, he rode in silence. Dirk continued.

"I didn't tell you sooner, my friend, because you didn't need to carry the burden, too."

Dirk scrutinized him, wondering what he was thinking. Benjamin was grim, pale, and when at last he spoke, his jaw was set, eyes troubled.

"Lovell warned me that you would say such a thing."

Dirk was not surprised to hear this, but it did trouble him, for he was not sure how Benjamin felt, or whom he trusted more, Lovell or him.

Benjamin was obviously struggling against turbulent emotions and doubts when he said, "Lovell said you would lie to me because you are in thrall to the desire to possess the bull's-head amulet, although you know—he says—it is not yours to possess."

Dirk was glad Sebe had stayed behind to guard not only Ineto, but to keep watch on Lovell, for there was no telling what the man would do next. When Dirk made no reply, Benjamin went on, gamely trying to lift the gloom that hung over them.

"I want no part of this magic amulet, my friend, nor do I want part of any feud between you and Tom; I simply want to get out of this alive, and save poor Lovell, too, for all this has affected his mind."

Up ahead, Rachel was standing in her stirrups, waving excitedly.

"Look, Benjamin! Wagons must be there! Maybe my brothers with them! Let's ride!"

They heeled their horses into a gallop as Rachel disappeared over a crest. At the top of that rise, Dirk took in the welcome sight of five big trekwagons, each hauled by four magnificent spans of oxen. Rachel was already with them, and three riders were racing toward Dirk and Benjamin. Dirk whooped, lay low on Blueboy and urged more speed, for those were his brothers, Piet, Henk, and Paul. In a moment, they were all dismounted, embracing, slapping each other on the back, and Dirk was yanking at their frizzy beards. Piet, the youngest at fifteen, had little to yank. Paul Arendt was the eldest, at eighteen, and Henk was seventeen.

Benjamin trotted up, Rachel joining him, enjoying the boisterous fun. In Henk's saddle bag was a puppy a few months old, and he proudly showed him off to Rachel. How the boys had grown, Dirk thought. How fine they looked. They all rode back to the wagons, which ground to a halt for the midday laager necessary for resting the teams. To the crack of riems and the whistles and shouts of drivers, the oxen were outspanned and led to a pool beside some trees. The carts were too few to make a proper circular laager of their own, but added to those of Johannes's trek they would form a strong defensive wall whenever the company stopped for the night, or if danger were at hand.

Dirk renewed several friendships to rough laughter and exchanges of insults that recalled days and childhoods of ten or even fifteen years earlier. These were all young, unmarried men, although Paul was just engaged—as his brothers both shouted, saying he would soon marry, with a dominee present or not. Henk declared that Paul's prospective wife, of German stock, had not wanted to trek out of the colony with her own family until she had heard Paul was going, too. Now Gretel Schmidt was the most enthusiastic trekboer the promised land would ever see. Indeed, this very country might be the promised land for Paul, who wanted to stop here and build a home.

That gave Dirk pause.

"This country's not safe yet, jonges," he said to the gathered young men as he unsaddled Blueboy. "Not yet. Zulus are on the loose, maybe coming this way, so no one can break off from the trek until the situation's clear."

Dirk told them to send out scouts to avoid surprise. Paul

asked whether there would be a fight. Dirk hoped not, but added that this group must get their rifles to Johannes Drente's trek as fast as possible. He said it would be best if these young men left the wagons, let the oxen graze, and rode immediately to join the smaller trek.

"I'll be coming back through here tomorrow, and with my father's permission, we'll hasten to Johannes and pick up these wagons and teams later."

If all goes well, he thought, for the drumbeat had returned, flurrying, sporadic, yet louder, just like his heartbeat.

☾ ☾ ☾

The welcome at the Arendt trek was even more joyous than Rachel had imagined. Marta Arendt was in tears, embracing her Dirkie. Willem, too, had a moist eye, and the youngest boy, Artemus—who was twelve—was trying to show how grown up he was until Dirk picked him off the ground and tossed him into the air, catching the yelping boy and then complaining that the lad was much too big for that anymore.

Marta, Willem, and Artemus were embracing Dirk, when, to Rachel's surprise, she found herself dragged by Marta into the happy clutch. The family's eldest servant, the Hottentot Joop, was hovering nearby, grinning, and when Dirk saw him, he hugged the old fellow, saying he had lately put to very good use what Joop had taught him about native tongues and bush lore. Hundreds of others in the trek dropped what they were doing and hurried over to the excitement, delighted to see Dirk and Rachel, and intensely curious about this distinguished European stranger, Benjamin David.

It did not take long for a feast to be planned. First, however,

Dirk took his father aside and said preparations must be made to repel an attack by Zulus. Word was passed for weapons, ammunition, and horses to be looked to. At the same time, a festive dinner was being cooked at a score of fires, and tables were spread with bright cloths and delicate veldt flowers. The laager was reinforced by men and boys, with help from whatever girls were not busy preparing the meal and setting tables. Dirk got his father's permission to hurry the small reinforcement of young men down to Johannes's trek tomorrow, leaving their five wagons where they were for the time being.

In an hour, just before sunset, the trekwagons had been shoved closer, end to end in a tight circle, each *disselboom*—wagon tree—run under the wagon bed in front. This arrangement afforded stout protection for riflemen standing behind or in wagons, and also gave shelter for those lying and kneeling underneath. Had there been four hundred more people and double the eighty-five or so trekwagons, an outer ring would have been formed as a firing line, with another, inner circle of wagons to hold the best livestock. For now, one wall of trekwagons was all they could form, but it was almost impenetrable. Thrown spears were the first concern, and most of these would be stopped by the sides of the wagons. The most potent threat would come from ranks of determined warriors trying to crash against the wagons, turn them over, and clamber across. Before any attackers reached the wagons, however, they would meet a wall of lead from well-aimed volleys. The Boers would keep up an impassable, constant fusillade for as long as the ammunition lasted.

As he and his father worked with extra branches and strong rope to strengthen the laager's gate of thornbush, Dirk told of his travels and of the expedition to Zululand with Benjamin

David. He left out the amulet for now. There was plenty else to tell, some of it terrible. Later that night at dinner, Dirk would hold forth for his mother, too, relating the more entertaining tales, those that would not horrify her.

☾ ☾ ☾

In a kitchen area, Rachel helped with preparation of the meal and enjoyed her own reunion with Marta Arendt, catching up on all she had missed these past six weeks. When asked, Rachel affirmed she had not committed to Gerrit, and that she had no intention of doing so. This pleased Marta, though she did not mention it again.

When the feast was ready, tables laden with precious bottles of wine and brandy, jars of confits and sweetmeats, and everything lit with standing torches that grew brighter as night settled down—Marta hustled Rachel away, saying she had something important to show her.

☾ ☾ ☾

The bell rang for prayers before the meal.

Dirk removed his hat and stood beside his little brother and Benjamin as all the folk gathered close, heads bowed. This felt good, comfortable and familiar, for all that they were so far from his childhood home. The ever-present Boer fiddler was there to play a hymn as everyone listened in pensive silence. Even the uitlander, Benjamin David, seemed quite reverent just then.

When the hymn was done, the folk looked around, happy and hungry and soon chattering, most utterly oblivious of the danger that might come upon them. For tonight, Dirk thought, that was all right. His own silence during the hymn had throbbed with that single, persistent drum. He shook off his dread, though it did not leave him completely. He would be in good spirits, if only for tonight, for the sake of his family and his friends. Tomorrow would have worries enough unto itself.

With this thought, Dirk looked up and saw Rachel Drente about to take a seat across the table from him. He was startled, for she was radiant. Marta had dressed her in a gown from her own youth, a simple but elegant pale blue satin frock over petticoats, with a neckline that revealed a Delft blue pendant at Rachel's throat. Dirk recognized it as his mother's favorite, brought over from the old country. Rachel wore no kappie, her hair held behind in a knot, revealing her womanly beauty all the more. It seemed everyone noticed her at the same instant, and a buzz of admiration passed through the folk as she sat down. Rachel lowered her eyes and smiled self-consciously, and many a man in that laager surely wished that smile was meant for him.

Dirk had never seen anything like her.

☾ ☾ ☾

Benjamin David was seated beside Rachel, and for the first time she had a good talk with him, learning about his past in Amsterdam, his diamond-merchant family, and also how Dirk Arendt had been thrown out of the university for fighting with some official's rude scion. It was all fascinating to Rachel, who did her best not to look too often at Dirk. Anyway, he was busy with his family, as a prodigal son ought to be.

For all that she wanted to talk with Dirk, Rachel really enjoyed Benjamin's company. They became friends that evening, and by the end of the meal she could not resist asking how far he had traveled in his life in a straight line.

"A straight line?" He was quizzical. "You mean in one direction of the compass?"

"Yes, that's what I mean."

"Well, it's thousands of miles from Holland to here, if that's what you mean."

"Well, yes, sort of, but what I mean is, have you ever been in danger of coming too close to ah . . . ah, the edge?"

"Of the earth?"

"Yes."

"Where would that be?" There was a hint of humor in Benjamin's eyes. "The edge of the earth."

"All around, no?" She wanted to be serious. "If you go far enough."

"Well, you never know, they say, when you're close to the edge. . . ." He sat back and took a sip of peach brandy. "It either gets you, or it doesn't."

"Just like that?" This was so intriguing.

"Tell the truth, Benjamin." That was Dirk, leaning forward, hands folded at his chin.

"The truth, Dirk?"

"Yes, about the time your ship got caught in one of those edge-of-the-earth waterfalls, and it was dragged faster and faster to the brink, and everybody was praying—"

"And I jumped out?"

"Jumped out?" Rachel gasped. "Into the water?"

Dirk said, "Had no choice. The ship was done for."

Everyone around the table was quiet, Dirk's father puffing hard on his long-stem pipe, eyes twinkling. Rachel's eyes were on Benjamin, who seemed lost in this fearful memory.

"How did you survive?" she asked. "Weren't you being dragged over, too?"

Benjamin looked across at Dirk, whose folded hands were now pressed against his lips.

"How did I get out of that one, Dirk?"

To Rachel's surprise, Dirk seemed troubled, as if struggling with something, as if in pain. In the next moment, he opened and closed his eyes several times, sat back and found his breath before speaking to Benjamin with a curt laugh and a shake of his head.

"Remember, friend, I told you that telling fibs wasn't possible anymore? Well, I'm learning the hard way, and you'll have to get out of this one yourself."

Rachel thought Dirk seemed ill, and his mother remarked with concern on his pallor.

"Just a passing effect . . . maybe too much good food, Mam." He reached to squeeze her hand and, with some tightness, said to his friend, "All right, Benjamin, enough suspense, finish your story."

Willem spoke up then, smoke puffing from his mouth as he said slowly, "Me, I grabbed an albatross."

All eyes turned to him as he leaned forward. "I knew enough to feed the critter real well all those months I was a sailor, so when the ship went over the edge, that albatross swooped down and plucked me out of the drink, nobody else." He eyed Benjamin. "And you?"

Dirk coughed, or was he laughing?

"I?" Benjamin pointed at himself. "Oh, no albatross did I feed, more's the pity. I went right over the edge, grabbed a piece of wood that was handy, and floated on it down, down, down the waterfall . . . right down till I landed in Africa." He smiled gaily at Rachel. "And here I am today."

Some were laughing, others puzzled, but Rachel was just plain suspicious.

☾ ☾ ☾

When the dinner was over, the children bundled off to bed, and the last of the music left in one's thoughts, Rachel made her way from the kitchen area, where she had been helping to clean up. She was feeling sleepy and content as she strolled barefoot, the way she liked to, through grass cool with evening dew. Her thoughts drifted to tomorrow's journey back to the other trek. Tonight was special. Tonight, she had been with Dirk Arendt, if only across the dinner table in company with the entire trek.

She would never forget it.

There was Dirk now. He stood at the edge of the laager, his back to a flaring torch, peering into the darkness, one foot on a keg. He wore no hat, but had riding shoes on, and a bandoleer of cartridges slung over his shoulder, as if he wanted to be ready to ride out at a moment's notice. His rifle was beside him, butt-down on the ground, leaning on the keg. Rachel walked past, on her way to a bed in one of the Arendt trekwagons. She was dispossessing young Artemus, who would have to sleep under a wagon.

With Jaeger beside her, Rachel walked slowly, wishing Dirk would turn and notice. She did not want to call out to him, like some cheap flirt. When he did not turn, she felt selfish to be disappointed, to expect more, for it ought to have been enough just to have been with him on the ride all that day, and tonight, along with his family. Tomorrow, there would be another horseback journey together. . . .

"Have a good sleep."

She looked around. It was Dirk, calling over his shoulder. He smiled. Rachel's heart skipped. Her hand came up to her face, inadvertently bringing the shoes against her cheek, and she felt clumsy, especially when she almost tripped over Jaeger, who had stopped in front of her.

"Yes . . . thanks, Mister Arendt. And good night to you."

They were about thirty feet apart. She was standing there, not wanting to go.

☾ ☾ ☾

Dirk did not want her to go, either.

"I was just looking at the Southern Cross," he said.

"Oh? Yes, it's lovely tonight . . . I mean I'm sure it is, but I can't see it for the torchlight." She put a hand to her eyes, as if blocking out the glare, and peered upward. Again it was the hand with the shoes, which bumped her face.

"You can see the stars from over here," Dirk said.

In the next moment, she was beside him, gazing up, hands and shoes at her side. He was looking at her, not at the stars. How fine she was, this Rachel Drente. How fine. It was almost too much to bear, she so close, and he not touching her. He saw dirt streaking her face where her shoes had touched, and he laughed.

"Now you look like the Rachel I remember."

"Huh?"

He gestured. "Grimy face."

"What, really?" She rubbed her cheeks. "There? Is it gone?"

"Almost." He was closer, his hand near a cheek. "There's a little more."

She gazed at him, and he at her. He brushed her cheek with the back of his fingers. She blinked. Jaeger whined, almost growling.

"How glad I am, Rachel, to have come back in time to see you."

Her hand was trembling when she reached for his, holding it ever so briefly at her cheek.

"And I . . . Dirkie—I mean Dirk, I mean Mister—"

They both laughed. Jaeger forced himself between them, panting and whining.

"Well, good night, Dirk," Rachel said, stepping away, their hands lingering until the last.

The hound barked then, excited, and spun around twice, happy to have Rachel's attention once more. She looked back at Dirk, eyes alight. At that moment, Dirk knew—against all that was logical and practical—knew he was in love with her. Though this might be the worst possible time and place to fall in love, it was so, and his heart would not let him deny it.

THE WEALTH OF THE EARTH

The Arendts wanted Rachel to stay with them when Dirk and Benjamin returned to her trek, but she declined. For one thing, she worried about Sannie, whose time was not far off. For another—which she did not mention to Marta or Willem—she wanted to be with Dirk, who was agreeable to her coming along.

They rode away at first light, before the sun was up, making good time at a steady lope, the tireless Jaeger keeping just ahead. Dirk's fears of a Zulu attack hung over them in those first hours, and they spoke little as they rode mile after mile across the grasslands. After two hours, the riders stopped to rest in the shade of a yellowwood and let the horses graze, unsaddled, nearby. Dirk broke out some of his mother's bread, and passed it around. The subject of the flat earth came up when Rachel said, with good humor, that she knew they had been making fun of her last night, but admitted she still did not understand exactly why. Rachel's hat hung down her back as she wiped her face with a cloth dampened from a canteen.

"I had a chat with your father, Dirk, and he told me the earth really is a ball," she said. "However that could be possible, I don't know."

Benjamin was lying back, hands behind his head, hat over his eyes. He was the first to answer Rachel.

"Sorry, meisje, if I took it too far, but where I come from, anyone who says the earth is flat is in for a lot of teasing." He rose to his elbows and smiled winningly, so Rachel could not help smiling, too. "But who really knows?"

He waved a hand at the sea of grass surrounding them, undulating in rises and broken by clumps of trees, seemingly endless.

"Maybe it *is* flat!" Benjamin said. "If I'm out in this country much longer, I'll side with you, Rachel, and say the earth is flat."

She tossed the wet cloth at his face and laughed.

"Dutch Jews can be teasing *skelms,* just like Boer jonges, I've learned that much!"

She finished the bread, put her hat on, and got up to saddle Tempest. Dirk and Benjamin went for their own mounts. Dirk was near her, Benjamin a little ways off.

"You're all the same, all rascals," Rachel said, just to make him talk to her, which he had done very little so far.

"Now, meisje, I know you don't think all Boer jonges are skelms." Dirk cinched the leathers tighter on Blueboy. "That Gerrit Schuman, for one, now he's an admirable fellow."

Rachel mounted, glanced down at Dirk, and shrugged, looking away.

Dirk asked, "Doesn't he want to marry you?"

"I don't love him." She steadied Tempest, who was ready to go.

"You love someone else, then?" He got up on Blueboy.

"I don't know." She walked Tempest back to the trail, Dirk following, Jaeger trotting ahead. "Maybe I do."

"Anybody I know?"

Rachel thought Benjamin was intentionally leaving the two of them alone. He was a dear. Unexpectedly, she felt nervous. Perhaps Dirk was about to test her, to see what she was made of.

She tried to ignore her uneasiness, but could not.

"Who do you know?"

Benjamin began singing André's song to himself, or maybe to them.

Thou wouldst still be adored, as this moment thou art,
Let thy loveliness fade as it will . . .

☾ ☾ ☾

Dirk had a powerful urge to touch the amulet and ask Rachel about her loves and what she thought about him, but he absolutely would not permit himself to do that. He had to press her a little, though, for he did want to know:

"You need a strong man like Gerrit out on the veldt," he found himself saying, but Rachel did not answer as the stallions moved into an easy lope, Tempest a few lengths in front. "No man better than Gerrit for trekking." He closed the gap between them a bit when she did not reply. "Or that's what I'm told."

"That's what I'm told, too."

"Rachel, you surely don't mean to trek into the wilderness without a man, do you? That would be impossible for—"

"You sound like Tante Emmy," she said with a quick glance. "Uncle André, at least, agrees that I should marry only for love."

"For love?" Dirk felt a surge of that love and smiled.

"Yes, for love! Is that so funny to you?"

"What? Oh, no! That's admirable . . . I agree with you."

"You do?"

Ruefully, he said, "I have to speak the truth."

"Well, I would hope so." She looked at him over her shoulder.

"Really, I do."

"Really? Then why did you say the earth was flat last night?"

"Ach, meisje, just a joke." It was remarkable how the discomfort that had come over him with one small lie had been too much to bear. "I couldn't keep it up, though, as you saw."

"Why not?"

"Maybe I'll tell you someday."

He was grinning until the drumbeat was there, louder than ever. Closer than ever.

"Is it such a big secret?"

We are coming.

"For now." He was distracted by the drum; he knew better than ask whether she heard it, too.

"You can't lie," she said coyly, "but you can have secrets—"

"Ach, I shouldn't be talking about this with you."

We are coming.

"No? All right. Fine."

Rachel seemed annoyed, but Dirk did not know what to say to smooth over his unintended curtness. They fell silent, and Benjamin stopped singing, as if Dirk's troubled mind had overspread all of them and spoiled the moment. Yet he needed that moment for something other than pleasure, needed to think, to feel, to understand something—something working in his heart. Something other than drums was calling to him.

Off to the right was a broad, dry watercourse, a river in the rainy season. He wanted to go to it. The drumbeat diminished.

"What's the matter?" Benjamin asked, riding up to join Dirk, who had drawn Blueboy to a halt while Rachel was going on ahead.

"I don't know, but I have to go over there for a look; go on, both of you. I'll catch up."

Dirk's mind whirled, but his thinking was clear as he cantered off toward the river bed. Then Rachel was there, saying Benjamin suggested she accompany Dirk.

"I'm not such good company right now," Dirk said, looking down, listening to the clop of hooves on the dry wash.

"That's all right; I am with you."

Heart leaping, he drew up his mount and turned to her. The vision in his dream appeared, the woman. But it was not a dream.

"What did you say?"

She answered, as in the dream.

"You," he said, as Rachel gazed at him. "You . . . you've been in my dreams for so long!"

"What?" Rachel looked confused, but was smiling. "Me? Really? You haven't seen me for years. Me?"

Dirk wanted to say the right thing, but his heart was pounding, and perhaps this was no time for such talk. He had a duty.

"Forgive me for saying that, Rachel."

She was so beautiful. But she was in danger—all of them in danger—because of him.

"Forgive you, Dirk? Why?"

"Because I mustn't do this now, not to you." He felt an overwhelming, excruciating rush of love.

"You say you can't lie." Rachel said sharply, kneeing Tempest alongside Blueboy, the two stallions head-to-tail, much too near to each other, becoming worked up. "Is the earth flat?"

"Ah, no."

"Do you like me?"

"I do."

"Better than European girls."

He had to grin. "Much."

Tempest and Blueboy nipped and stamped but stayed put.

"How much?"

Dirk and Rachel were holding hands now.

"Maybe too much . . . at a time like this." He looked around, uneasily, restlessly, then back at her. "We have to move on."

"Do you love me as I love you?"

Surprised, pleased, Dirk said, "I do love you."

They kissed hard, desperately. The mounts wanted no part of it, snorting and pawing, and stepping aside, so that Rachel and Dirk slid slowly to the ground, still kissing. That kiss was perfect, but in the next moment the lovers found themselves lying on pebbles and stones that bruised. They laughed and yelped in discomfort. Jaeger barked and barked until Dirk tossed him some biltong, which quieted him. Trying to find a position for an even better kiss, Dirk picked up a sharp stone to toss it away, but Rachel snatched it from him.

"How wonderful!" she declared, and Dirk saw it was clear, as if of glass. "Look, there are others. What are they?"

Dirk examined one, about the size of a small bird's egg. It was heavy, feeling so smooth that it was almost greasy. It seemed like— *Could it be?* Lovell's words came back to him. *The Lost Mines of Ophir. The wealth of the earth!*

"Is this a diamond?" he whispered.

Rachel caught a breath, hand to her mouth. Dirk knew it was, indeed, a diamond. Miraculous! All around, diamonds mingled with the river wash, mixed in the pebbles and sand. Rachel was on her feet, picking them up, diamonds large and small, and she put them into the hem of her shirt, laughing with delight each time she found one. It was amazing. How far did this river bed extend? How many diamonds could there be?

Then something came over Dirk: If word got out, this country would be invaded by thousands of treasure-seekers. The Boers wanted land and water, room for their herds and their children's herds, for the good life, for the lekker leven. They had no use for diamonds, but if they settled here, they would one day be driven out. This country would attract the worst of men, and with them the armies of avaricious governments.

Rachel came to kneel beside Dirk, one hand holding the hem with the diamonds, the other touching his hand, which was on the amulet at his chest. His mind was elsewhere, the drumbeat again hard and insistent.

☾ ☾ ☾

Rachel let the hem of her shirt drop, the diamonds tumbling to the ground. She did not care. They were nothing more than pretty stones. She was worried, for he looked pale.

"Kiss me again, Dirk Arendt."

That brought him out of his thoughts, and his arms went around her, and they kissed passionately as if nothing else mattered. But something did.

Dirk held her back and looked with eyes loving and troubled.

"I want to tell everything, Rachel, yet I fear involving you in the business that brought me here, and which you had best keep out of."

"So Uncle André said." She kissed him lightly, trying to reassure him that he could tell her what was in his heart.

"I wish to be rid of the burden I carry," He touched her hair. "I want to be with only you from now on."

That thrilled her, and she kissed his hand. "Tell me or not, whatever you think best, dearest."

She did want to know. She did.

And there, in the next moment, held dangling between them, was a golden amulet, set with a clear stone. Rachel observed it, thought it quite pretty, and asked if she could touch it. Dirk hesitated, but let her take it.

"What is this thing?" She turned it over in her hand, holding the stone up to the sunlight. "Is it a Zulu charm?"

Dirk looked closely at her, then took it back and let it dangle.

"Rachel, tell me, do you see . . . a light when you look at this?"

"Light? No . . . just the reflection of the sun. That's all." She had no idea what he was talking about. "But, Dirk, dearest, you were telling me about this burden you carry, the burden you want to be rid of. . . ."

Dirk sighed. "What if I told you this trinket is the burden?" He looked at her so intently that she felt uncomfortable. "Told you that it has a mighty power, a power we cannot comprehend, and that it is being sought, even as we speak, by men who will never give up until they possess it or are destroyed in their quest."

"This thing?"

Rachel sat down, puzzled, feeling a chill, although the sun was warm. Then Dirk told her about Dayega and Shaka, Lovell and Mazibe and Ineto. He even told her that André Toulouse knew something about the power of this bull's-head amulet, and he told her about the white fire that some could see when they looked at the amulet.

When Dirk was done, Rachel shrugged. "Why such a lot of fuss about an old talisman?"

"You're sitting in the reason for that fuss," Dirk replied. "The amulet led me here, to this diamond field, and it can do the same for others."

"Led you here?"

"Believe me, my love."

"My love!" Rachel got to her knees, impatient, excited, and kissed him. "'My love!' Oh just say that again to me, Dirk, and don't trouble your heart with talk of diamonds and amulets, not now. Oh, my love!"

She kissed him, but his hands were on her arms and gently pushed her back.

"Oh, would that it was so simple," he said sadly. "But those who want the amulet will kill whoever gets in their way."

He was searching her, and she did her best to appear resolute, though she was frightened.

"Then let them have the amulet and these stones!" She threw a handful of diamonds away. "If they want it all so badly, let them have it, Dirk."

"I can't tell you why, Rachel—I don't really know why myself—but it's my duty to protect this amulet, to keep it from them as long as I can, and that's why I must go away from here, lest I place you and our folk in danger."

She kissed him impetuously, and this time he did not stop her. She forced him back to the stony river bed, and his arms went around her.

"I am with you," she said, taking a breath, and as he drew her to him, she said again, "I am with you, Dirk Arendt! With you, come what may."

☾ ☾ ☾

They did not stay long at the river of diamonds, riding off with a batch of precious stones in their saddlebags. They wondered whether to tell Benjamin, who would be waiting for them a mile or so ahead, dismounted, and probably sketching a view of the landscape. Dirk's hand was on the amulet as he contemplated what he would tell his friend, the son of Amsterdam diamond merchants and cutters. Benjamin could help them, would know what they had found, could be trusted implicitly—if first he would swear not to reveal where the diamonds came from. Secrecy would be in his interest, too. Anyway, maybe these were not diamonds at all, just some quartz stones, worthless.

Maybe it was all madness, illusion.

Dirk agonized about this, and at the same time overflowed with love for Rachel Drente. As they rode, he knew she was watching him. Could she sense the drumbeat? It seemed everyone had to be able to hear it. In time, he willed it away, or at least quieted it. He needed a plan, needed to think. The Boers could settle this vast, depopulated land, and it might be generations before anyone found out about the diamonds. By then, the folk could put down roots, become strong and independent; Dirk and Rachel could establish themselves in the diamond business with Benjamin and use some of the funds to help their people.

"Benjamin!" Rachel said, pointing ahead. "He's coming back fast."

Something was wrong. Dirk and Rachel galloped to meet him, and in a moment heard his terrified shout.

"Zulus! Zulus! They're here!"

FIRST BLOOD

"The boys!" Dirk shouted, meaning his brothers and the other young men with the wagons. "We must warn them!"

They galloped at full speed as Benjamin beckoned them to follow, then turned back the way he had come. Catching up with him, they kept on riding as he blurted out what he had seen.

"Beyond the rise! Hundreds of Zulus, heading south, moving fast!"

Aiming right at the young men with the wagons. The three riders drove their mounts on, heading for the rise, where they stopped, awestruck by the sight of a full impi, trotting away to the right, not singing, as if bent on a surprise attack.

Dirk told Rachel and Benjamin to race back to the Arendt trek and warn them. He would go to the young men, and hurry them on to the smaller trek.

Rachel grabbed Blueboy's bridle. "I'm with you, Dirk!" she exclaimed. "Live or die, I'm with you!"

Benjamin shook Dirk's hand, kissed Rachel's, and was off, his dust rising as he rushed northward to the Arendt trek. Dirk and Rachel galloped on, keeping the crest of the hill between them and the Zulus, taking a parallel path toward the young men. There was not a moment to spare, for they soon came out of a shallow, mile-long donga and crested a rise to see the five wagons, moving slowly, right below. To the left, just a thousand yards off, came the Zulus, running faster now, as if they had seen Dirk and Rachel. Dirk yanked out his pistol and fired, alerting the boys.

Dirk could see them drawing out rifles, leaping from wagon bed to horseback, jumping onto their mounts, which were already saddled and tethered alongside the trekwagons. Dirk and Rachel galloped down the slope, and in the distance rose the thunder of a Zulu war shout. The impi was running full speed now, their chants an ominous rumble.

"Ride!" Dirk shouted, as the young men mounted their excited horses, some of the boys trying to save personal possessions from the wagons. "Leave it all! Ride!"

Henk Arendt was the last, clambering out of a trekwagon, slinging a mandolin over his back, the squirming puppy clutched in one arm.

"Go!" Dirk shouted at him.

A swarm of warriors came over a nearby crest that had concealed their advance. There were fifty of them, almost upon the Boers. Spears flew, missing everything but one horse, which was grazed, and it bolted while its rider was trying to mount. The man fell. Henk. A Zulu dashed in, assegai raised. Dirk cut between them, firing his rifle from close in. The warrior went down, but Henk took the spear in his shoulder and fell back with a scream of pain.

Dirk sprang down for his wounded brother. Another Zulu was charging. Dirk turned to meet him. A rifle fired, and the Zulu was blown off his feet. It was Rachel, face smeared with black powder, eyes alight with fear and courage. Dirk heaved Henk over Blueboy's saddle and leaped up beside him. Then all the Boer rifles fired at once, dropping a dozen of the first attackers. The startled Zulus wavered. They had never faced gunfire before. Quickly reloading, the Boers fired a second volley, just as lethal, giving Dirk time to join them. Then the riders took off, escaping another hail of spears that fell short. They soon outdistanced the impi, and slowed their foaming horses. Dirk anxiously looked to Henk, whose blood smeared them both. The wound was ugly.

"Hold on, jonge!" Dirk cried out as his brother's eyes began to glaze. "Stay with us, Henk!"

At that, Henk fought for consciousness, licked his dry lips, and tried to grin. In the next moment, Rachel was alongside, and she called to him.

"Look, Henk! Look who's here!"

The puppy was in her arms, twisting and yelping to get free, but she did not let it jump on the lad, for Dirk had enough to contend with. Henk smiled faintly, tried to speak to the pup, then passed out. They had to stop soon to stanch the bleeding, to bandage the wound. Dirk calculated the ride to Johannes's trek would take two hours at this rate. Since Blueboy and Tempest were weary after the morning's travel, they would only slow the others. It was better that most of the men dash ahead and prepare the defenses as best they could. Rachel, Paul, and Piet would stay with Dirk and Henk, making a calculated, measured escape, staying a mile or so ahead of the Zulu impi, and trying to keep Henk from bleeding to death.

When the others had gone, Dirk's party stopped briefly to tend to Henk. Dirk flooded the wound with brandy, then forced some into his half-conscious brother's mouth. Rachel took a blouse from her saddlebags and tore it up to bind the wound, managing to slow the bleeding. Henk was hoisted up in front of

Piet, with the pup slung in a knapsack beside him, and the riders went on, wary of being surprised again by another Zulu flanking party rushing down from high ground to the right or left.

Then Dirk realized something, and he jerked around to Rachel, asking with amazement, "The pup! How did you get him?"

☾ ☾ ☾

It had happened so fast, and now seemed a blur to Rachel, who recalled leaping to the ground and snatching up the puppy after firing her rifle at the warrior. Now she felt the terror she had not had time for then. The blood drained from her face.

"Just happened," she said, feeling faint, swaying a little.

His hand was at the small of her back.

"Want to rest?" he asked.

She shook her head, leaning against his shoulder as he put an arm around her. The dizzy spell passed. For now, the two stallions did not resist being side by side, perhaps too weary to object. Dirk kissed Rachel's hair, and she heard him say something about being proud of her.

Just then, Piet, riding at the rear, called out, "They come."

Rachel looked back to see a dense mass of warriors advancing down a long slope, about half a mile off.

"They can run," Piet said.

Dirk agreed that they could. The riders picked up speed, but were unable to travel fast enough to put a comfortable distance between them and the Zulu host. Then the riders crested a ridge that gave a good view over the veldt, where the little laager of Johannes's trek looked pathetically small, standing in the open grassland. The riders arrived to see everyone at work piling crates and barrels and even furniture in a barricade at the side without wagons. The gate of thornbush was opened, and they rode in to shouts of greeting. All hands were bent on the grim task of preparing to defend against an enemy that could never be held off.

Henk was carried to a bed near a central campfire, where Tante Emmy took charge of him, André on hand for moral support. Their horses were tethered with the others at the center of the laager. Dirk announced that everyone should have a horse at the ready, and after the first assaults had been repelled and the Zulus had lost their eagerness for the next one, the Boers would charge the weakest place in the enemy ranks and break through. Orders were given to prepare a light, two-wheel Cape Cart for Tante Emmy, André, Henk, and any who could not ride.

First, the Zulus had to be repelled at least once.

The work on the defenses went on, almost in silence, and Dirk met with Johannes at the barricaded side of the laager, the direction from which the Zulus would appear. He hoped the Arendt trek would dispatch a strong kommando to save them.

Seeing the first plumed warriors come into view across the grasslands, Johannes said quietly, "Can a kommando get here in time?" He pursed his lips. "We'll have to do this ourselves."

Johannes did not look at Dirk, as if trying to mask his inner doubts. Dirk did not reply, nor when Johannes muttered that they had come such a long way for it all to end like this.

"Gentlemen? I have something to say."

They turned to see Tom Lovell standing there, and beside him was Ineto, the halter taken from his neck, feet untied. Lovell looked dazed, but determined. Ineto was expressionless, eyes fixed on the ground. Lovell spoke haltingly, short of breath.

"It's Dayega leading that force." He eyed Ineto. "Our prisoner here told me so; and he has something important to explain to us."

Ineto's eyes were raised, but remained blank.

"Speak," Johannes ordered.

"Dayega wants only one thing," Ineto said in excellent Afrikaans, facing Dirk. "He wants the bull's-head amulet."

Johannes began to demand an explanation, but Dirk waved him off, saying he would clarify that shortly. Dirk had no doubt Ineto was right, and that Ineto and Lovell shared some secret, a secret that would have to wait.

"Does he know the consequences of taking it by force?" Dirk asked Ineto, who nodded. "And he will still attempt it?"

Ineto's gaze was clear now. "If it were willingly given up to him by the bearer, he would be eternally grateful, for then it would be his by right of being a gift, and it would belong to him—for the time being."

Zulu singing, deep and rhythmic, came to them, growing louder with every minute, with each step the impi took toward them. Johannes was impatient. He shouted for everyone to take their positions. There were more than thirty rifles, and the women and children and old ones were placed behind the men, prepared to reload. They would take fired rifles and pass on loaded ones. Rachel was standing near Dirk and Johannes, protected by a crate, her rifle at the ready.

The singing grew louder now, the shout *"uSuthu!"* clearly heard. The feathered headdresses of the first warriors could be seen clearly as they advanced in perfect regimentation, shields and spears held before them, an astonishing, terrifying sight.

Dirk stared at Ineto.

"Will Dayega strike a bargain?" he asked.

"It is possible."

"The lives of this trek in exchange for the amulet, willingly given up to him?"

Ineto and Lovell looked at each other before the Zulu replied, thoughtfully, slowly: "If Dayega would swear to such a bargain and then betray you, the power of the amulet would torment him all his days, unto death—and this he well knows." After considering for a moment, Ineto went on. "Unbind me, and I will go to him and speak for you before the impi eats you up."

"Can I trust you?" Dirk demanded, sensing Lovell stir uneasily.

Ineto stared. The amulet was there, dangling between them. The Zulu trembled, swallowing over and over. Lovell was breathing hard. Dirk could feel the anxiety.

"Answer, by the power of the white fire," Dirk said, as the amulet's light flickered in Ineto's eyes. "And if you lie, you will be the first to die, for I will slay you, here and now."

Ineto began to speak, but the next voice was Tom Lovell's, quavering and rasping, but decisive.

"This man must obey the bearer of the Stone of White Fire."

Dirk held up the glowing amulet, his eyes fixed on Ineto, his ear harking to Lovell. The rumbling Zulu chant was close, the warriors deploying to face the laager. Lovell was speaking.

". . . he is one of us, one of the Red Brotherhood."

Dirk looked closely at Ineto. "Is it so?"

"It is so," the Zulu whispered. "I must obey the bearer of the Stone of White Fire . . . I will do what you command."

"Then go to Dayega, and tell him the amulet is his, given

freely, if he will spare everyone . . . yes, including you."

"It will be done."

The amulet was put away.

The light in Ineto's eyes went out, and he shivered. Dirk, too, was trembling. Lovell moaned and leaned against a wagon wheel. Dirk felt other eyes on him, and he looked up to see that Rachel had observed it all. She seemed to tremble before turning away to look at the warriors.

☾ ☾ ☾

The Zulu war song was at once terrifying and hauntingly beautiful. Rachel would never forget this moment, if she lived. Nearby, Gerrit stood at the ready in the small space between two trekwagons, and beside him was Anneke, who would load for him. Three extra rifles leaned on a wagon wheel, and slung from it were boxes of cartridges.

How good Gerrit and Anneke looked together in this bleak moment. Rachel wanted Dirk at her side just then. She wanted to fight and die beside him, if they must. If he did not come soon to her, she would go and find him when the end was near, and would meet death while touching him. She still felt his kiss.

"uSuthu!" the Zulus roared. "uSuthu!"

Formed in a semicircle a few hundred yards from the barricaded side of the laager, the impi swayed and chanted, indunas one after the other springing out in front of the ranks to dance and jump in a giya, plumes shaking, spears and shields held high. Rachel heard someone calculate nine hundred and eight warriors. That was Sebe counting, so cool and calm.

Then began the rattling of knobkerries on shields, faster and faster, and the chief induna of the impi came to the fore to leap higher and dance more wildly than any other. Then, Dirk was with Rachel, a hand in hers. At the end of the giya, this induna gave a mighty shout, springing high, and came down with his spear stabbing the ground. The attack must soon begin.

The singing diminished, then abruptly stopped. Even the Zulu induna stood still, staring, as if surprised, at a lone black figure making his way to them through the waist-high grass, hand raised in greeting, and in supplication. It was Ineto. Rachel could feel the hostility rise from the impi as this slender executioner moved toward them.

"Do not be afraid," Dirk said. "Do not be afraid for me."

She gripped his hand tighter in question.

"I must go out there, Rachel."

She thought she would scream to hear this, but somehow she did not, though her knees nearly buckled, and tears came of their own. Dirk spoke again.

"It is our only hope, my love." He kissed her forehead, a lingering kiss, and in the next moment was over the barricade and following Ineto.

"Dirk!" she murmured, and he looked at her, the force of his love filling her as she said so only he could hear, "I am with you."

☾ ☾ ☾

Dirk caught a breath, touched fingers to his lips, and turned to follow Ineto's track through the grass. By now, Ineto was approaching the Zulus, a seething mass of anger and battle excitement, their singing beginning again. The lead induna met Ineto and hustled him toward the front ranks, which parted to let them through, then closed again.

Dirk kept walking until halfway between the laager and the

impi. There he stopped, legs apart, arms folded, waiting. The amulet hung around his neck instead of being in the pouch. For the first time, this amulet-bearer was actually wearing the Stone of White Fire, though it was concealed by his shirt. Likely this would be the last time he would wear it. That thought brought a twinge of pain, and for a moment he was short of breath.

The Zulu singing and swaying went on, from one end of the impi to the other, a hundred yards wide of black warriors, heads plumed with brown feathers, oxhide shields matching in patterns of reddish brown and white.

"They sing well, Baas Dirk."

It was Sebe, smiling as he gazed serenely at the Zulus. He was unarmed, wearing a black cloak that Dirk had never seen before, and looking wise and wrinkled and ageless, the lion's claw suspended above his eyes by a thong. Dirk could not help but grin, looking at the rumbling Zulu host as he addressed his friend.

"I didn't think a self-respecting Xhosa rainmaker would want to die trapped inside a Boer laager."

The Zulu ranks parted, and Ineto appeared, walking in front of a litter carried by four warriors.

"Where and when I die, Baas, depends on the wisdom of the amulet-bearer."

On the litter was a ragged pile of withered humanity. Dayega, scowling, as ugly as ever.

DAYEGA'S DESIRE

"Permit me, Baas," Sebe said quietly, "to speak for you, as is appropriate, until the proper time comes."

Dirk gave a nod and touched the amulet inside his shirt.

Sebe said, "Let us yawn."

Dirk glanced sidelong to see the Xhosa languidly yawning, as if utterly unconcerned. Not intending to, Dirk did the same, though not so wide as Sebe. It felt good.

The litter with Dayega approached.

Out in front were Ineto and the chief Zulu induna, with spear and shield. They stopped ten yards from Dirk and Sebe, Dayega squinting from one eye. The impi chanted, stamping in place as they looked on. A single drum was beating, this one real. Dayega squawked for the bearers to put him down, and he half crawled, half slithered from his place, moving hesitantly toward Dirk, giving a hiss when he recognized the Xhosa. Ineto was back a step at the witch doctor's left, the induna at the other side. Dayega skittered nervously from side to side, wheezing and hissing as he alternately eyed Dirk and Sebe.

Ineto spoke.

"Lord Dingaane's loyal inyanga demands to see the Stone of White Fire to be sure it is truly the self-same that belongs to him."

Dirk yawned, this time as widely as had Sebe.

Dayega glared, chafing his forearms with claws of fingers.

After a moment, Sebe nonchalantly replied: "No such stone belongs to a crocodile fraud!"

Dayega stopped scurrying and hissed again.

Sebe went on: "The Stone of White Fire remains with its rightful protector, and no crocodile will touch it until such time as the amulet-bearer chooses to part with it."

Dayega crouched, a bundle of dirty rags and feathers, eyes glinting. Ineto spoke once more, but was hesitant, as if not expecting Sebe's defiance.

"The inyanga will . . . have the amulet, but he wishes that it be given freely, willingly, in exchange for. . . . What does the present unrightful bearer ask in return?"

"Unrightful?" Sebe's arms began moving, elbows resembling wings, and he made as if he were about to swoop down on Dayega, who took a step backward and squeaked. "You dare insult the bearer of the Stone of White Fire?"

The startled induna gripped his spear shaft tighter, and the litter bearers were confused. Sebe was soaring.

"This eagle soul sees all, what has been and what is to be, and as he flies overhead, sees the crocodile in grave peril, grave peril, if the crocodile would bring down upon himself the wrath of the Stone of White Fire, the wrath that dooms the unworthy to a death most hideous, a liar's grave, to be pecked apart by vultures, devoured by hyenas."

Dayega tried not to cringe, but his beady eyes showed fear.

Sebe spoke: "Look upon the Stone of White Fire and tremble, you who are unworthy."

Sebe gravely bowed to Dirk, who raised the amulet before them. Dayega whined, one clawed hand coming up for it. Force rushed into the amulet, white light reflecting in Dayega's eyes, and he cringed, shaking uncontrollably, then shrank back, terrified. In that moment, Dirk knew this would be the last time he would hold the golden bull's head.

A burning suddenly coursed through him, a fire in every nerve and fiber, almost intolerable, yet outwardly he was rock-steady.

"It," Dayega whimpered, "is mine. Is mine."

Sebe spoke slowly to Dirk. "It is this eagle's counsel, amulet-bearer, that the bull's head be withheld forever from this crocodile."

"Mine!" Dayega wailed, fury and fear and desire in his ugly face. "Give it to me! Or I will take it! Will take it!"

Dirk's heart thundered.

"He is no amulet-bearer, Baas," Sebe declared. "Just a fraud! Let us turn our horses and firesticks loose on these assassins and rub them out to the last man!"

The induna recoiled, indignant, though he controlled his anger. Dayega was snarling, showing his pointed teeth, but he could not tear his eyes from the amulet.

Sebe clucked casually. "No, no, Baas, if this dog gets the amulet, he'll probably lose it down some shit hole."

"Mine! Mine!" Dayega wailed, both hands working.

Sebe's head was bowed. He was finished.

Dirk drew in a long breath and then spoke:

"Your oath, Dayega, your sacred oath to withdraw these warriors and harm none of my folk, not even this executioner."

Dayega grimaced. "Done!" he blurted and wheezed. "Your liberty in return for the Stone of White Fire—"

"Truth!" Dirk demanded, summoning all his strength, all his force of will. "By the power of Nzambi Ya Mpungu, Ancient of the Ancients, lord of all amulets, speak the truth and be bound by it!"

Dayega whimpered, rasping, unable to look away from the bull's head.

Dayega wailed, "Truth. . . ."

"Swear by the Stone of White Fire!" Dirk ached from the scorching of it. "Swear, or we ride against you and the amulet will disappear forever!"

"I so swear!" Dayega screamed, eyes wide. "I swear you and yours will not be harmed!"

The witch doctor shuddered, grasping to possess the amulet, and at the same instant shrinking from it. He had an inner reserve of strength, however, and recovered enough to make his own demand: "Swear you will not turn your firesticks and horses upon us!"

Dirk nodded."I so swear. Now, give your oath!"

Dayega spoke in a weak voice as the white light held him.

"The impi will withdraw and do you and yours no harm after you freely give Dayega—" He whispered. "—give freely, willingly, the Stone of White Fire."

A profound calm came over Dirk.

It was right to give up the amulet. It was no longer for him to carry. The burning vanished, although his heart still pounded.

"It shall be as you desire."

Dirk stepped toward Dayega, the amulet held out, dangling on its thong. The witch doctor cowered, shivering.

"Your oath is accepted, Dayega, and mine is given, as is the bull's-head amulet, freely given, for you to bear as long as you can do so."

Dirk's heart had slowed its beating, but something gripped it, held it, squeezed it tight.

"No one is worthy," he said, remembering how Mazibe had given him the amulet, passing it on, hand to hand, to an equal and saying what Dirk now said to Dayega: "The bearer of the Stone of White Fire sees what is truth, and what is false."

Dirk bent to place the thong over the witch doctor's head, as if laying a sacred duty upon him, and Dayega whimpered as Dirk went on.

"The bearer does not possess the Stone of White Fire, and when the time comes, must freely send it further on its journey."

The amulet was no longer Dirk's to carry.

"So be it," he said, and a weight lifted from him.

Dayega groaned, sagging.

Dirk stepped back.

Around them was an expanse of stillness. The Zulu host stood watching silently, plumes flickering in the breeze. The Boers in the laager waited, also silent, rifles at the ready.

Dayega barely had the strength to raise his arm for the litter bearers to help him back onto his seat. Already, the amulet had vanished out of sight within his stinking, wretched rags. The Zulu induna seemed shaken, and Dirk wondered what he had seen of the white light, what he understood of Dayega's quest or why the witch doctor had led his impi here beyond the mountains to pick a fight with Boers. Sebe was drenched in sweat, eyes half closed.

Only Ineto seemed unfazed by all that had transpired, a smirk on his face as he deftly helped Dayega onto the litter.

"Koom!"

Startled, Dirk looked up.

"Koom!"

The Zulu salute before battle carried over the veldt.

"Koom!"

Many voices joined in that shout, but it did not come from Dayega's host, who themselves seemed startled to hear it. Suddenly, a mass of Zulus in tight formation came over high ground to Dirk's left. Their plumes were white, as were their shields, about four hundred of them.

"Mazibe," Sebe gasped, eyes ablaze.

"Koom!"

Dayega squealed and bounced up and down where he sat on his litter, rejuvenated by the thirst for revenge.

"Induna!" he shrieked at the commander of his impi and pointed at Mazibe's approaching regiment, all that was left of the once-powerful uFazimba. "Your warriors will eat after all!" Dayega shook a gnarled fist at Dirk. "Already the bearer of the amulet profits from his good fortune!"

Mazibe's force trotted down the slope and drew up in perfect precision a hundred yards from Dirk and three hundred from Dayega's impi, which began to sing a war song. Mazibe did not threaten a charge, but awaited the next move of Dayega's force. Dirk could see his friend standing formidably in front of the uFazimba. Mazibe had come to rescue Dirk, who thought about his trek's horses and rifles, and how the Boers could join with the uFazimba, who were outnumbered by more than two to one.

As if reading Dirk's thoughts, Dayega screamed at him.

"Keep out of this! Or the bargain is renounced, and you, too, will be devoured!"

Dayega howled with glee, urging the bearers to hasten him to rejoin his warriors, who were stirring excitedly, clattering their clubs on shields. Their chief induna strode toward them and shouted a command, invoking a mighty roar as they prepared to advance against Mazibe. Ineto and Dayega disappeared into the midst of the impi as their induna executed a hurried giya that

Dirk thought was without conviction. No wonder, for this man would be personally taking on Mazibe of the uFazimba.

As Dirk and Sebe returned to the laager, Rachel rushed to embrace Dirk. She was shaking, tears streaming, and he held her close, wishing he could tell her everything was all right, that they were safe, but this nightmare was not yet done with.

☾ ☾ ☾

Since childhood, Rachel had heard stories of the frontier wars, of warrior hosts descending by the thousands upon Boer farms and communities, or battling on the open veldt against her father and uncles and grandfathers, attacking the fortified laagers of those first trekkers who had pulled out of the Cape Colony years and generations ago. Those great armies of Xhosa and Tembu and Fingo—themselves a people not long in southern Africa, having migrated there from the east and north—had been utterly defeated by the Boers. The stories were blood-chilling to hear, yet no fireside legend, no wild imagination, could have prepared Rachel for this sight.

Though these were small armies compared to the sweeping engagements of full-scale war in southern African, it was astounding to see them so organized and warlike, drawn up face to face, just two hundred yards from where she stood behind the barricade. Dirk was beside her, pale and weary. How she loved him. They would come through this together, or not, but she would never leave him again, that she knew.

The Boers and their servants crowded together at the barricade or stood in wagon beds, holding each other, some praying, all of them riveted to what was unfolding. No one could be sure what would happen if Dayega's impi were victorious over

Mazibe and their warrior's blood was up. Dayega's oath might mean nothing after Mazibe was destroyed, and the Boers could well be next. Rachel noticed Tom Lovell at the back of the crowd, standing on a crate, rocking on his heels, hands in his pockets, and whistling nervously. Lovell seemed to be elsewhere with his mind, his watery eyes staring but unseeing.

The low rumble of the Zulu forces—Mazibe's to the left and Dayega's to the right—turned into shout after shout, shields rising and falling in unison, spears shaking rhythmically. In other times, these men had been comrades, relatives, counting even brothers, uncles, and nephews in the opposing force, but there was civil war in Zululand. This impi, loyal to Dingaane and under the command of Dayega, would win praise from their new king if they could crush Mazibe and his rebellious uFazimba, "The Haze."

The impi moved first to join the battle.

Their induna in the lead, they advanced at a walk, soon breaking into a trot, assegais held behind shields. Mazibe's regiment stood waiting, their own shields before them. To Rachel, it seemed the defenders were simply too few to withstand so many. She took hold of Dirk's hand.

"Bullala!" the attackers shouted and broke into a run. "Bullala! Kill! Kill!"

From out of Mazibe's force stepped a rank of warriors, advancing a few paces to accept the assault, which was picking up momentum. Dirk told Rachel those were the youngest, the junior warriors, who would take the first weight of the attack and slow it. Not yet full-fledged members of the uFazimba, these youths wore no head ring, the mark of a mature, married warrior. Behind their thin rank was the next age group of warriors, and behind those were the oldest, most battle-tested men, who would enter the fray when it counted most. Those junior warriors who survived the crash of the enemy's front ranks would be worthy to become full warriors if they still lived at the end of the day.

"I know some of those boys," Dirk said distantly.

In front of the youngest warriors stood Mazibe, shield at the ready, spear held high. Dayega's impi charged. Out in front of the attackers was their chief induna. Mazibe ran forward and took him on.

Their shields collided, full force, a crash that could be heard in the laager, and Dayega's induna reeled backward. In the next instant Mazibe was on him, hooking his own shield behind the opponent's to rip it aside, following instantly with the spear thrust.

"Ngadla!" Mazibe roared, yanking out his bloody assegai as the induna fell. "I have eaten!"

The boy warriors stepped up to join Mazibe, the full might of the enemy impi smashing against them, shield against shield, assegais stabbing, warriors groaning, others exulting, "I have eaten!" Iron spear blades clanged, blood spurted, bodies fell, battle cries and death cries rose above the tumult. Mazibe was a rock. The junior warriors stood and fought and many died until the second rank of older men barged in from behind with a shout, their momentum driving Dayega's outfought impi back in retreat.

"It be over!" Gerrit yelled. "God be praised! Arendt's man has triumphed!"

Dirk leaned forward on the crate where he stood, his heart aching. Rachel's hand touched his shoulder.

"They have won," she said to him. "In God's name, they have won."

Dirk looked up and saw Dayega's impi reforming, rallied by other leaders who took the place of their fallen induna. Dirk felt his heart pounding the way he had felt it on the race with Mazibe, but he tried to shake off the pain.

"They're all Zulus," Dirk said. "It's not over yet."

Mazibe's depleted ranks closed up, then stepped forward to put the dead and wounded behind them. A roar erupted from Dayega's force as it came on again. Mazibe lifted his shield and spear, his men close behind. When the attackers were almost upon him, he gave a shout, and his force leaped forward at full speed, their own momentum exploding against the enemy's mass of shields and spears and bodies rushing at them. The two forces bounced off each other, recoiling, a writhing mass of fallen bodies between them. They roared as one and crashed in again, stabbing and driving. The fury of battle raged, the uFazimba not yielding an inch.

Then Dayega's warriors made their move in Zulu fashion. While the middle ranks, the "chest" of the impi, engaged Mazibe's front, two wings, or "horns," swept around the right and left of his force, intending to surround the dwindling uFazimba and wipe it out.

Dirk was desperate to rally his own men, to have them leap on their horses and race to Mazibe's side. Oath be damned! He had to save his friend! No, he could not break his oath.

Now a wing of Mazibe's force drove toward the tip of one horn. In this counterattack were the veteran elder warriors, who struck with ferocity, driving over the shattered enemy, forcing the survivors to turn and run. The veterans of "The Haze" raised their bloody assegais and let out a shout of victory. Seeing this, the other horn of the attack faltered and retreated, as did the enemy chest.

The next thing Dirk knew, he was on his knees, his heart thundering, thundering, louder than the battle roars of the Zulu regiments, and aching, as if an assegai had struck him. He felt very cold.

"BAYETE" AND AMASI

"Dirk!" Rachel grabbed for him, his head bowed, sweat pouring off his face.

Johannes and Sebe were there, and they carried Dirk to a cot near the wounded Henk. Tante Emmy was beside him, agile and decisive as she called for herbs and poultices, massaged his arms and legs, got Sebe and Johannes to work doing the same. Dirk lay there, conscious, but short of breath.

"My heart isn't what it used to be," he murmured to Rachel, who was unable to speak as she gripped his hand, then kissed it.

A shout of triumph came from Boers watching the battle.

"The enemy be on the run!" Gerrit yelled. "Whacked but good this time!"

Rachel cared only about Dirk, sweating and hurting on that cot as Tante Emmy anxiously ministered to him.

"Fetch Sannie," Emmy ordered.

Rachel would not leave and, instead, sent Millie. Rachel's sister-in-law was wise in the healing arts, and Emmy wanted her near.

"Ach, Emmy," Dirk gasped, trying to laugh, "just give me one of your big sloppy kisses and I'll be fine."

"Warm water! Bring a pot here!" Emmy called out, and a servant rushed to the cook fire. "Sit him up, pillows at his back." Freddie was there, propping Dirk up with folded blankets.

"I'll be all right, dearest," Dirk said as Rachel knelt at his side. "What's happening out there?"

"You heard him!" Emmy gripped Rachel by the shoulder. "Go watch the fight! Go!"

Rachel could not go. Would not go. But she got out of the way when Sannie appeared with a box of herbs—thyme and St. John's wort, she told Emmy. Warm water was poured into a large bowl placed on Dirk's lap. Tante Emmy laid his forearms in the water and told him to leave them there.

"You're out of it now, Dirk Arendt, so sit still and stop worrying." She bussed him on the cheek. "There! You're finally clean enough to kiss, and the way things are going, only Rachel Drente'll get at you in future, so I best take my chance to smooch you now."

"Dayega's not beaten yet!" Ton Graven shouted.

"They're coming back!" called Johannes.

At Dirk's insistence, Rachel tore herself away and climbed into a trekwagon to look over the stricken field, where so many black bodies lay dead and dying. Mazibe's regiment was decimated, but readied for the next attack. By comparison, Dayega's force seemed larger than ever, though it had lost twice as many men. It had regrouped, ranks closed, shields turned to its foe. Another induna was in front, haranguing the warriors, no doubt calling upon them to give their all for this, the decisive attack. And it appeared one more attack would overwhelm Mazibe's little regiment. The Zulus of Dayega's impi began their war song, and in reply Mazibe's sang theirs. It would be over soon.

What would happen to the trekkers then? Afraid, Rachel turned to look at Dirk, who was watching her from the cot in the center of the laager. He raised a hand to her. How could she tell him of his Zulu friend's hopeless situation?

Dayega's impi abruptly stopped singing.

Rachel turned to see the warriors were looking right, left, and behind, as if confused about something. The successor induna rushed into their mass and disappeared from sight. What had happened? Uncertainty, indecision, swept over those Zulus, their shields lowered, assegai blades touching the ground. Mazibe's uFazimba stood watching, alert, but it was apparent something had delayed the next attack.

Sebe sprang up on the wagon beside Rachel.

"What's going on?" she wondered.

"They are leaderless," Sebe said, although Rachel could not grasp how he knew.

Both forces were now silent.

Rachel turned to look at Dirk, who was sitting up, staring at her, longing to know.

"Aiee, there is a man!" Sebe declared.

Rachel whirled around and saw that Mazibe was walking toward the impi of Dayega. Mazibe was unarmed, with not even his shield. Every Zulu was staring at him, as were the trekkers. Just thirty yards from the impi, Mazibe came to a stop and raised his arms, calling out to them in a booming voice.

Sebe clucked, and slowly shook his head, giving a sound of admiration and delight.

"I am blessed to have such a tale to tell my grandchildren's children!"

Then Dirk was being helped by Freddie and Johannes onto the wagon.

"I have to see this," he said, and Rachel held him against her side with both arms.

A shout went up from the enemy impi, and another. They advanced on Mazibe, a great crescent of warriors beginning to encompass him. Their surviving induna appeared at the fore and strode toward Mazibe, who lowered his arms and stood stock still, as if accepting what was coming upon him. His own regiment was absolutely silent, too far away to be of support.

When the crescent was halfway around Mazibe, Dayega's host stopped. Their induna approached him until just a few feet away. Then the man laid down his shield and spear, put his hands together, and placed them between Mazibe's in a gesture of obeisance. In the next moment, the man fell to his knees, and Dayega's entire force laid down their spears and shields and also knelt before Mazibe.

"Bayete!" they sang out, in a chant both beautiful and haunting. "Bayete! Bayete! Bayete!"

Relief and joy flooded Rachel in that astonishing moment, and she held Dirk close, wanting never to let go. Until Millie hurried up, tugged at her sleeve, and whispered anxiously: "Come quick, come quick, Mistress Sannie's time is upon her."

☾ ☾ ☾

Dayega is no more," Sebe declared, and Dirk knew he was right.

Rachel had hurried off to Sannie, and Dirk leaned against the old Xhosa, who cackled about telling this story to his children. Sebe helped Dirk down from the wagon as Johannes and Gerrit asked exactly what had occurred.

"Dingaane's Zulus despise Dayega," Dirk said, "but now they're somehow liberated, and they've had enough, so they offer homage and peace to Mazibe."

Sebe strolled through the laager to announce this in his halting Afrikaans, and the trekkers watched the Zulus come together, mingle, embrace, and weep.

Dirk wanted to go to Mazibe. Though weak, Dirk could walk well enough, for Tante Emmy's tonics and massages had been invigorating. Then Sebe returned, looking troubled.

"The Englishman is gone, Baas, and with horses."

"Gone?" Why would Lovell dare ride away on his own? "He'll never survive out there, never make it to Cape Town alone."

"Baas," Sebe said, "my medicine tells me he is not alone."

Ineto. The amulet. Dirk's heart started up again, but he forced himself to calm down. After all, this amulet business was over and done with.

"Ach, Sebe, Englishmen and amulets are not my bag anymore."

☾ ☾ ☾

A little later, they found Dayega, sprawled on his litter in the rear of his impi's battle lines. His throat had been slit.

Dirk stood looking down at the body, along with Mazibe, Sebe, and Senzana, who like his father was cut and bruised, but otherwise unhurt. Mazibe explained that Dayega's litter bearers had been pressed into the battle, leaving the witch doctor alone with Ineto. Three litter bearers had fallen in an attack, and the fourth had returned to find Dayega dead, Ineto gone.

"When the impi heard of Dayega's murder, they had no more reason to fight me." Mazibe looked sad. "Would that it had happened sooner, before our fratricide."

Both he and Dirk knelt at the body and carefully searched for the amulet. Certainly the Zulus would have been too superstitious, too frightened of black magic, to dare rob the witch doctor's body. Dirk found only the amulet's thong, sliced by the slash that had killed Dayega. Ineto had done this, without question, had done it to steal the amulet.

Dirk told Mazibe about Lovell's flight on horseback—likely to join Ineto in accord with some prearranged plan. With horses, they could go many miles without stopping, outrunning even Zulu pursuit. Dirk did not speak of his heart troubles, not revealing that he had no strength to ride after them as yet. Nor would he ask any Boers to chase down the fugitives, who were no doubt fleeing to Cape Colony. Trekkers should not be involved with the amulet anyway.

"It's gone," Dirk said to Mazibe. "Likely forever from this country."

The induna considered that before replying. "You, too, have carried it. Do you truly believe the Amulet of White Fire is gone from this country forever?"

Dirk looked away. "That is my hope."

"And yet, for you and for me," Mazibe said, "it will always be there, never in this life to be forgotten."

☾ ☾ ☾

Later that day, when the doleful work of burial of their own dead was finished, Dingaane's impi assembled for the return to Zululand in the East. Mazibe and his men would move into lands far in the West. The uFazimba could never return to Dingaane's realm, whose impi could claim to have driven them off today, if not wiping them out.

Dingaane's returning warriors trotted away, chanting rhythmically, spears and shields proudly held in place, though they all were dead-tired and carried many wounded on sling litters or shields. The impi meant to show these Boers just how strong they were, even after such a battle. The Boers, standing quietly outside the laager, took note.

A few moments later, as if on signal, a hushed mass of Zulu women and children and old men flooded over the high ground where Mazibe had first appeared. Moving hesitantly, slowly, these were the families of Mazibe's regiment coming to join their men, coming to embrace the heroes, tend the wounded, weep, and bury the dead. The warriors met them, but there was little elation, just relief that the battle was over. Wailing went up each time someone heard of the death of a loved one. First there would be the burying, and then Mazibe's people, too, would depart.

☾ ☾ ☾

The Boers kept their distance as the ritual and singing went on for hours a few hundred yards from the laager. Listening to the laments, Rachel stood outside her brother's trekwagon, bedraggled and exhausted. Yet she was relieved, for Sannie had delivered twins, a girl and a boy, now howling from their mother's bed in the wagon. Sannie and the babies were fine, and midwife Tante Emmy had never looked more proud of herself.

When the Zulu burial ceremonies were finished late that afternoon, Mazibe and Senzana approached the laager and were invited inside. As a gesture of peace, they laid down shields and weapons before passing through the thornbush gate. Few black warriors would ever have such a gate voluntarily opened to them. In the confines of the laager, Mazibe and his son were majestic figures in full headdress and plumes. Dirk announced them to the company gathered around.

The Boers were polite, though uneasy for the most part. Gerrit, especially, did not like any native chieftain entering a laager, where the man could take note of the trekwagon defenses, perhaps to discover a weakness that would be remembered one day. Yet Gerrit said nothing as he stood there with Anneke on his arm, closely observing Mazibe and Senzana, who were brought to a table. There, they took interest in how to sit on some fancy chairs that had been set out for them.

Dirk, Sebe, and Johannes sat down at the table and ceremoniously shared sour cream and milk curds—the Boers' own amaSi, offered in honor of Mazibe's triumph. This was followed by strong coffee that Rachel had brewed and was served in her best cups and saucers. Before long, Sebe invited young Senzana to come have a look at André's friction machine, and André, with Wortelkop on his shoulder, went along to help demonstrate.

Seated at the table, Mazibe remarked to Dirk that the laager was an imposing fortress, stronger than any kraal's thornbush wall he had ever seen.

"It is my cherished hope that I never have cause to attack such a place."

"And ours," Dirk replied, not translating any of this for Johannes, who was looking over at Sebe cranking away at the friction machine while André showed Senzana something of interest.

Then came a shriek and a simultaneous flash of electricity, and Wortelkop gave his own screech as he flew up onto a tree branch. This was not just horseplay, however, for André had taken the force of the shock and now lay, crumpled, beside the friction machine. Folk rushed to him, the despairing Emmy pushing her way through the crowd, calling out her husband's name, while the parrot squawked and hopped in fright and fury high above. Sebe and Emmy knelt at André's sides, vigorously rubbing his arms, both mumbling away, as if dealing out their most potent medicine, but he did not stir, not even breathing.

"Poor old André," Ton Graven groaned. "Struck down by his own lightning."

"After going through all this," Dirk muttered sadly to himself as he stood over André.

There seemed to be no hope, for the old man was ashen, eyes shut tight. Rachel gripped Dirk's arm, and he held her close. It was a sorry tragedy to occur at what should have been a happy moment of celebration, of—

"He lives!" Emmy gasped.

Sebe cackled in that high-pitched way of his, and the astonished folk all babbled at once as André sat up, dazed, but apparently all right. He, too, began to laugh.

"Ma chérie!" he said to Emmy, touching her face and grinning.

"You—" She gasped, taking hold of his hands. "You mean? Can you?"

"Oui! Mon amour! Oui. And I see you are more beautiful now than ever!"

Emmy howled for joy, drowning out even Wortelkop.

Lightning had stolen André's sight, and lightning restored it.

☾ ☾ ☾

Mazibe and Senzana did not stay much longer, for their people were assembled, ready to depart.

Outside the circle of trekwagons, Dirk and Mazibe

exchanged farewells. The uFazimba stood in marching ranks, their huddled families seated nearby, waiting. The trekkers came outside the laager to watch, men quietly smoking pipes, women in kappies standing behind them. Dirk and Mazibe brought their hands together and bowed, and then shook hands.

"It is done, my brother," Mazibe said, sober but able to smile. "Though my wandering has just begun."

"Until we meet again, my brother," Dirk said.

With that, Mazibe turned away, his regiment saluting him with raised spears, then breaking into a song of journey. They faced westward, away from their homeland, marching off, followed by their wives and children. Wearing a bright orange, slightly singed, parrot feather in his headdress, Senzana was at the head of the junior warriors. Not many were left, but like their elders they were resolute, prepared to roam the high country until they found a place to settle down. These Zulus had something in common with these voortrekkers who were watching them depart.

"Nomads all," Sebe said to Dirk, who thought he meant both Zulu and Boer. "Wanderers until they wrest a home from someone else and send them in their turn to wandering . . . as ever it has been in southern Africa, as ever will be until the time comes when men love peace more than victories."

THE SOUTHERN CROSS

As soon as Mazibe's Zulus were gone, Rachel saw to it that Dirk rested. He was grateful for it.

Before nightfall, with the laager's fires and torches blazing, and André's concertina playing softly, Rachel sat at a fire beside Dirk, watching for any relapse. He ate her soup and Millie's bread and seemed much better. Rachel was grateful he felt no urgency to mount up and pursue Lovell and the amulet. She never wanted to hear about that thing again, though she could not deny that she would like to travel with Dirk to Cape Town one day.

It all seemed a bizarre dream.

Rachel thought of the diamonds concealed in her wagon, but she forced aside any concern for them. They frightened her. She just wanted Dirk to recover and for everyone to get to the Arendt trek, safe and sound. Henk was doing well, lying on a cot with the puppy asleep on his chest. His conversation with Dirk was welcome and cheering, and as she leaned against her man Rachel felt an inner peace come over her, and knew it was because of the love she shared with Dirk.

"Listen!" he abruptly said, grasping her arm.

There was a rumble, a shaking of the ground.

Someone shouted a warning, and men rushed to arms, but Dirk called out, "Boer horses," and laughed. "Put on the coffee, vrouwen! Company coming."

The place exploded with joy as out of the twilight galloped a hundred Boer riflemen, springing down from their mounts and swarming through the gate to much laughter, greetings, and hugging. With them was Benjamin David, drawn and exhausted but elated to see everyone unharmed. He was pleased with himself that he had achieved the remarkable feat of riding nonstop to bring back the rescue force. Dirk and Rachel welcomed Benjamin warmly and invited him to eat with them. The newcomers scattered throughout the laager, sharing food and drink, some teasing Henk about his "scratch," others saying that at least he would not be able to pester them with his mandolin for a while—which was not so, for he soon struck up a tune.

Henk's friends carried him away, and he kept on playing, Johannes joining in with his fiddle, Joop his clarinet, so that dancing and singing began, and peach brandy flowed with the plum. Someone even broke out bottles of *jenever,* that favorite old Holland drink now just becoming popular among the Boers: gin was the English name.

It was a merry time, although Benjamin was troubled to hear about Lovell and Ineto fleeing with the amulet. He did not voice his feelings, but Rachel realized that he, too, must be thinking how to get back to Cape Town if Dirk could not take him. That issue remained with Rachel as they sat at the campfire, savoring their happiness. Then André Toulouse appeared, accompanied by Freddie, who showed concern, since he was still weak. André took a chair and Freddie sat down nearby.

"Not playing your squeeze box, Uncle André?" Rachel asked cheerily, then saw how serious he looked.

"No, dearest, not tonight, not tonight." Hands on his knees, he contemplated the firelight. "I've come to speak to you, Dirk Arendt, but if there's anyone here who has no business with the Stone of White Fire, then I ask that he or she withdraw."

Benjamin stirred, about to go. Dirk asked him to stay, saying he had every right to hear about the amulet.

André wasted no time. "Are you going after it, my boy?"

Rachel felt a chill down her spine, and she resisted the urge to answer *No!* for Dirk, who took a moment to reply.

"Why should I?" he asked. "I have no desire to go after it."

"Good," André replied, tapping his fingers on one knee. "It is good you have no desire to do so."

He drew a breath and looked more troubled than Rachel had ever seen him before. There was silence around their fire, although the others in the laager were enjoying themselves heartily. In that silence, Benjamin looked from André to Dirk.

"The late Swazi customer of mine warned that the Stone of White Fire must not go back to the Red Brotherhood."

Rachel almost got up and left. She never wanted to hear about that damnable amulet again. Yet, she had to stay, had to hear what Dirk would say.

"Can I prevent that happening now, Uncle?"

André rocked a little, chewing his lower lip as he thought about the answer.

"Maybe not," he said. "Maybe not. But it occurs to me that it would be good for your folk's sake, for their future, if you knew just who had the bull's-head amulet, so that with your help, they might be prepared in case something comes of it in the future."

Rachel could not help but interrupt. "What do you mean, 'comes of it'?"

"Ah, my dear child." André reached for her hand. "You're

part of this now, hearing these questions, which have answers that lie far in the future for our people . . . and yet the questions are here now, long before the answers ever come clear."

His other hand reached back for Freddie, who helped him get up.

"Rachel, stand by Dirk, for one day he will need your wisdom and strength as never before, though it may be many, many years to come."

After a pause, Dirk said, "I will think on what to do next, Uncle André, that I promise."

"Good," the Frenchman said, smiling as if everything were fine. "That is all we can ask of you, my boy."

Then he went off, and before long, his accordion struck up a tune, though his playing was less carefree than usual. Listening, Dirk, Rachel, and Benjamin sat quietly for some time until Dirk rose and went to the back of the trekwagon, where he reached in to pull out the satchel with the diamonds. He returned, sat down, and took out a pouch full of stones. Benjamin nearly fainted.

"Where did you get this?" he gasped.

"I will ask you never to put that question to us again, my friend," Dirk replied. "But there are more, many more, as much as we could ever want, and I have a business proposition for you."

It was then that Rachel knew Dirk was going to Cape Town with Benjamin and the diamonds, and she was resolved that she would go with them, whether Dirk liked it or not.

☾ ☾ ☾

He did like it.

Later that night, with most of the folk sleeping soundly in

and under wagons, in tents, and beneath the stars, Rachel and Dirk strolled outside the laager, hand in hand in the gloaming beyond the torchlight. Near the horizon, in that glorious African night sky, hung the five bright stars of the Southern Cross.

"In Cape Town," Dirk began, turning Rachel to face him and drawing her close, "in Cape Town we can marry, if you think my heart will stand it."

Rachel pressed against him, head on his shoulder.

"Is that a Boer's proposal?"

"With all my heart, Rachel Drente."

She drew back to look at him, joy and tears mingling.

"Then I accept, Dirk Arendt, with all my heart."

They kissed, never to let go. Jaeger, lying close by, contentedly chewing on some biltong, did not object.

☾ ☾ ☾

On a rainy day six weeks later, with fog drifting in off the Atlantic Ocean and cloaking Cape Town, Dirk and Rachel Arendt bade a warm farewell to Benjamin David as he boarded a steamship bound for London. They would miss him, and of course they hoped he would get home safely with their diamonds.

By now they knew Thomas Lovell had left the colony, also sailing to England. With the help of some influential friends of Benjamin's, they had found Ineto, a condemned prisoner in a government jail. He had been accused of murdering one Mr. Gregory, a functionary in the Colonial Office. Dirk recalled that name from Lovell's letter to Captain Homan, in which this Gregory had been described as an associate of Lovell's.

Resigned to his fate, Ineto had scoffed when confronted with this name and the letter.

"Yes, Mister Gregory was to receive the bull's-head amulet on behalf of the Red Brotherhood," Ineto had sneered. "But Lovell could not give it up—the fool! No, he will never give it up, for it has driven him mad, it obsesses him so that he betrayed even me, who brought him out of the wilderness." He scoffed again. "So, Mister Gregory had to die—but not by my hand, gentlemen, no, not this time, not by my hand."

Leaving Ineto to face the executioner—a fate that neither Dirk nor Benjamin would try to change—Thomas Lovell had fled with the bull's-head amulet, fled Africa, and apparently was fleeing from the Red Brotherhood as well.

EPILOGUE

Benjamin David arranged to have the diamonds cut and sold in Amsterdam. The source remained a secret, and over the years Dirk shipped more stones in annual consignments to Benjamin, who never returned to Cape Colony or southern Africa. He became an artist of some note, and the sketches from his African travels, rendered in color, made a sensation when shown in several European capitals.

The money from the diamonds not only made Benjamin and the Arendts extremely wealthy, but it was used to further the political and economic interests of the Boer trekkers, who in the next three decades were joined by thousands more families. The Boers eventually went to war with the Zulus, and there was much loss on both sides, but the trekkers held their ground, made peace, and sent down deep roots. In time, they created two republics that declared independence from the British Empire, which at first did not trouble itself with them and their apparently worthless, grassy wilderness.

Almost forty years passed since Dirk's expedition to Zululand. He and Rachel stayed in Cape Town, journeying regularly to the north for more diamonds and to visit family members, who never learned the precise foundation of their wealth. The Arendts became leading figures in the colony, and raised a large, happy family, though there were more adventures and dangers for them. Dirk's weakened heart stabilized and gave him very little trouble, even in his later years. Of course, he often wondered about the bull's-head amulet and whether it would turn up again. Somehow, he expected it would.

Although Dirk and Benjamin tried to determine what had happened to Thomas Lovell, nothing more was heard of him in all these years. Then the Arendts received a letter from Benjamin, with an enclosed clipping from the *Times* of London. It was a brief obituary of the "recluse" Thomas Lovell, "formerly a highly regarded" official in the British colonial office who had left government service "precipitously at the height of a fruitful career." Lovell had been living on a remote island off western Scotland all these years, in a cottage close by a small fishing village. The clipping said he had been a devoted congregant of the local kirk, "and for many years took the greatest pleasure in serving as its choirmaster."

Since Lovell had no will and no known heirs, said the article, his few possessions were to be sold at auction to benefit that kirk:

> The meager personal estate of this monklike, ascetic man, who was devoted in his early and middle years to furthering the goals of the British Empire, includes only a few books, some Chinese silk handkerchiefs, and a golden cow trinket said to have been brought home from his travels, long ago, in darkest Africa.

Scribbled in the margin of the *Times* article was a note from Benjamin, who had circled the auction date: "I was too late! Sold, and I don't know to whom."

☾ ☾ ☾

Epilogue

Not long after this, diamonds and gold were discovered in the two republics that had been established by the Boers.

To the dismay of the elderly Dirk and Rachel Arendt, a massive, uncontrollable rush of treasure-mad prospectors inundated the Boer republics and their diamond fields. The cherished liberty of the promised land of the voortrekkers was threatened, even doomed, by the wealth of their earth. The British Empire claimed the rich diamond and gold country, fully intending to annex the republics, even if it meant war with the descendants of the voortrekkers. The incomparable mineral wealth of voortrekker country, funneled to Great Britain, would make her empire the most powerful in the world.

The more ambitious British imperialists were determined to control as much of Africa as they could—or as they liked to express it in public, "to paint the map red, from the Cape to Cairo."

The End

GLOSSARY

Afrikaner Words

Aasvogel—vulture, buzzard
Afrikaner—a white resident of southern Africa, usually of mixed Dutch, German, and French blood, speaking Afrikaans, which is mainly Dutch, but also includes English expressions.
Baas—master, boss
Biltong—dried antelope meat
Dominee—a minister of the Dutch Reformed Church
Inspan, inspannen—to harness draft animals
Outspan, uitspannen—to unharness draft animals
Jenever—gin
Jonge—young man, boy
Juffrouw—miss
Kaffir—In 1828 this term, which comes from the Arabic word for "infidel," generally meant blacks of southern Africa and was not intended as an epithet, although late in the 19th century it became comparable to the term "nigger."
Kappie—a woman's bonnet
Kerel—knave, guy, fellow
Koekjes—cookies
Kopje—a small hillock or rise
Kraal—a circular enclosure (corral); name for stockaded native villages
Laager— ring of wagons
Lekker leven—the good life
"Machtig!"—"Almighty!"
Meisje, meisie—miss, girl
Mevrouw, mevrou—Mrs.
Morgen—about two acres
Myneer, Mijnheer—Mister
Nachmaal, nagmaal—periodic gathering of the Boers for worship and feasting
Riem—a length of rawhide
Skelm—rascal
Smous—a traveling merchant, peddler
Tante—aunt
Totties—Hottentots
"Tot ziens!"—"Until we see each other again."
Trek—to haul or pull, or to travel by ox cart.
Trekkers—those who travel, in migration, by ox cart
Trekpad—the route of a trek
Uitlanders—foreigners
Veldschoenen or Veldskoen—soft leather shoes
Verdommte—damn, "Damn it!"
Voorloper—forerunner, one who goes ahead of the trek-wagons
Voortrekkers—pioneers
Vrouw—woman, lady

Bantu Words

amaZulu—People of the Heavens
amaSi—milk curds, food only for Zulus or their honored guests
Assegai—a short spear with a wooden shaft and an iron blade
Bayete!—"Hail!"
Boyala—native beer
Bullala!—"Kill!"
Dagga—hemp for smoking
Donga—ravine, a hollow
Giya—pre-battle dance of individual warriors
Impi—Zulu regiment
Induna—captain or leader of an impi
Inyanga—doctor
isiCoco—a Zulu warrior's head ring, worn by married fighting men.
isiGodlo—Shaka's harem
Knobkerrie—a Zulu war club
kwaBulawayo—At the Place of He who Kills
Mfecane—"The Crushing," Shaka's ten-year campaign to destroy all who would not obey his rule; as many as two million died.
Ngadla!—"I have eaten!"
Nzambi Ya Mpungu—Ancient of the Ancients, lord of all amulets
Tao—lion
Umlungu—white thing
Umuntu—white person
uSuthu—battle cry of the Zulus
Xhosa—a Bantu-speaking people of southern Africa

IMAGES FROM THE PAST

Publishing history in ways that help people see it for themselves

WASHINGTON'S FAREWELL TO HIS OFFICERS: AFTER VICTORY IN THE REVOLUTION

By Stuart Murray

In the sunlit Long Room of Fraunces Tavern, on a winter's day in New York City, 1783, George Washington's few remaining officers anxiously await his arrival. He has called them here to say goodbye-likely never to see them again. The British redcoats have sailed away, defeated in the Revolution. This moving incident, one almost forgotten in American history, was among the most telling and symbolic events of the War for Independence.

As they anticipate their beloved general's arrival, the officers recall how their struggle for the sacred cause flickered, almost went out, then flared into final victory. In the story of Washington's Farewell are the memories of long-struggling patriots—the famous and the little-known—men committed heart and soul to the cause of American liberty: Knox, McDougall, Lamb, Hamilton, Steuben, Shaw, Humphreys, Varick, Burnett, Hull, Fish, Tallmadge, the Clintons, Van Cortlandt, Fraunces...Heroes all. Index. Bibliography. 42 prints and maps.

5" x 7", 240 pages ISBN 10884592-20-1 Cloth $21.00

AMERICA'S SONG: THE STORY OF YANKEE DOODLE

By Stuart Murray

During the first uncertain hours of the Revolution, British redcoats sang "Yankee Doodle" as an insult to Americans - but when the rebels won astounding victories this song of insult was transformed to a song of triumph, eventually becoming "America's Song."

This is the first complete chronicle of the story of "Yankee Doodle," perhaps the best-known tune in all the world. From its early days an ancient air for dancing, through the era of Dutch and Puritan colonial settlement, "Yankee Doodle" evolved during the French and Indian Wars and the American Revolution to become our most stirring anthem of liberty. Index. Bibliography. Illustrated with 37 prints and maps.

5" x 7", 248 pages ISBN 1-884592-18-X Cloth $21.00

RUDYARD KIPLING IN VERMONT:
BIRTHPLACE OF THE JUNGLE BOOKS

By Stuart Murray

This book fills a gap in the biographical coverage of the important British author who is generally described as having lived only in India and England. It provides the missing links in the bitter-sweet story that haunts the portals of Naulakha, the distinctive shingle style home built by Kipling and his American wife near Brattleboro, Vermont. Here the Kiplings lived for four years and the first two of their three children were born.

All but one of Kipling's major works stem from these years of rising success, happiness and productivity; but because of a feud with his American brother-in-law, Beatty, which was seized on by newspaper reporters eager to put a British celebrity in his place, the author and his family left their home in America forever in 1896.

6"x9"; 208 pages; Extensive index. Excerpts from Kipling poems, 21 historical photos; 6 book illustrations; and 7 sketches convey the mood of the times, character of the people, and style of Kipling's work.

6"x9" ISBN 1-884592-04-X Cloth $29.00

6"x9" ISBN 1-884592-05-8 Paperback $18.95

THE HONOR OF COMMAND:
GEN. BURGOYNE'S SARATOGA CAMPAIGN

By Stuart Murray

Leaving Quebec in June, Burgoyne was confident in his ability to strike a decisive blow against the rebellion in the colonies. Instead, the stubborn rebels fought back, slowed his advance and inflicted irreplaceable losses, leading to his defeat and surrender at Saratoga on October 17, 1777—an important turning point in the American Revolution. Burgoyne's point of view as the campaign progresses is expressed from his dispatches, addresses to his army, and exchanges with friends and fellow officers.; 33 prints and engravings, 8 maps, 10 sketches. Index

7"x10", 128 pages ISBN 1-884-592-03-1 Paperback $14.95

NORMAN ROCKWELL AT HOME IN VERMONT:
THE ARLINGTON YEARS, 1939-1953

By Stuart Murray

Norman Rockwell painted some of his greatest works, including "The Four Freedoms" during the 15 years he and his family lived in

Arlington, Vermont. Compared to his former home in the suburbs of New York City, it was "like living in another world," and completely transformed his already successful career as America's leading illustrator. For the first time he began to paint pictures that "grew out of the every day life of my neighbors."
32 historical photographs, 13 Rockwell paintings and sketches, and personal recollections. Index. Regional map, selected bibliography, and listing of area museums and exhibitions.
7"x10", 96 pages ISBN 1-884592-02-3 Paperback $14.95

THE ESSENTIAL GEORGE WASHINGTON: Two Hundred Years of Observations on the Man, Myth and Patriot
By Peter Hannaford

Why did Thomas Paine turn against him? Why did Elizabeth Powel call him "impudent"? What is the truth about the cherry tree story? What was his single most important quality? These and many more questions about the man called "the father of his country" are answered in this collection. The reader meets Washington's contemporaries, followed by famous Americans from the many decades between then and now and, finally, well-known modern-day Americans. Included are Benjamin Franklin, Thomas Jefferson, Abigail Adams, Parson Weems, Abraham Lincoln, Walt Whitman, Woodrow Wilson, Bob Dole, George McGovern, Eugene McCarthy, Letitia Baldrige, Newt Gingrich, Ronald Reagan—and many more. Read in small doses or straight through...either way, the book gives a full portrait of the man who—more than any other—made the United States of America possible. Over 60 prints and photographs.
5" x 7", 190 pages ISBN 1-884592-23-6 Cloth $19.50

LETTERS TO VERMONT Volumes I and II: From Her Civil War Soldier Correspondents to the Home Press
Donald Wickman, Editor/Compiler

In their letters "To the Editor" of the Rutland Herald, young Vermont soldiers tell of fighting for the Union, galloping around Lee's army in Virginia, garrisoning the beleaguered defenses of Washington, D.C., and blunting Pickett's desperate charge at Gettysburg. One writer is captured, another serves as a prison camp guard, others are wounded—and one dies fighting in the horrific conflict in the

Wilderness of Virginia. Biographical information for each writer (except one who remains an enigma) and supporting commentary on military affairs. 54 engravings and prints, 32 contemporary maps, 45 historical photographs. Extensive index.
Vol. 1, 6"x9", 251 pages ISBN 1-884592-10-4 Cloth $30.00
ISBN 1-884592-11-2 Paper $19.95
Vol. 2, 6"x9", 265 pages ISBN 1-884592-16-3 Cloth $30.00
ISBN 1-884592-17-1 Paper $19.95

ALLIGATORS ALWAYS DRESS FOR DINNER:
AN ALPHABET BOOK OF VINTAGE PHOTOGRAPHS

By Linda Donigan and Michael Horwitz

A collection of late 19th- and early 20th-century images from around the world reproduced in rich duo tone for children and all who love historical pictures. Each two-page spread offers a surprising visual treat: Beholding Beauty—a beautifully dressed and adorned Kikuyu couple; Fluted Fingers—a wandering Japanese Zen monk playing a bamboo recorder; and Working the Bandwagon—the Cole Brothers Band on an elaborate 1879 circus wagon. A-Z information pages with image details.
9 1/4"x9 3/4", 64 pages ISBN 1-884592-08-2 Cloth $25.00

REMEMBERING GRANDMA MOSES

By Beth Moses Hickok

Grandma Moses, a crusty, feisty, upstate New York farm wife and grandmother, as remembered in affectionate detail by Beth Moses Hickok, who married into the family at 22, and raised two of Grandma's granddaughters. Set in 1934, before the artist was "discovered", the book includes family snapshots, and photographs that evoke the landscape of Eagle Bridge, home for most of her century-plus life. Two portraits of Grandma Moses—a 1947 painting and a 1949 photograph, and nine historical photographs. On the cover is a rare colorful yarn painting given to the author as a wedding present.
6" x 9", 64 pages ISBN 1-884592-01-5 Paperback $12.95

REMAINS UNKNOWN

By Michael J. Caduto with 16 pencil sketches by Adelaide Murphy Tyrol

He somehow found his way to Vermont soon after the Mexican War. It was a long journey, the beginning of a private purgatory that lasted over 150 years. At last, with the help of friends he'd never met, he took

the final steps in a quiet cemetery by the river on a sultry afternoon. In this strange and haunting tale, based on a true story, the reader enters a world suspended between our earthly existence and the realm of the human spirit. A small community of people embarks on an adventure that compels them to bring the mysterious, mummified remains of one long dead to a resting place of peace and grace. With help from two distinct spiritual traditions, and a dose of healing humor in the face of grief, the journey unfolds with a sense of dignity and compassion.
5"x7", 80 pages ISBN 1-884592-24-4 Cloth $15.00